BARBARIANS
ON THE
DANUBE

BARBARIANS
ON THE
DANUBE

MARK RICHARDS

ISBN Paperback: 9798322905462

Printed in the United States of America

Book Cover and Interior Design: Creative Publishing Book Design

ACKNOWLEDGEMENT

Special thanks to my daughter, Mary Brady, and her son, Owen, for their assistance in completing this novel.

PROLOGUE

Oppidum Ubiorum Legionary Fortress, Germania
March AD 31

Valerius Maximus, the imperial governor of Germania Inferior and Superior, scowled as he read the latest dispatch from Rome. While he was not ill-tempered by nature, he slammed the offending document upon the tabletop in disgust. Outside, mirroring his mood, freezing rain pelted down on the roof of his private residence, the Praetorium. The hypocaust floor-heating system and the strategically placed charcoal braziers were fighting a losing battle against the cold. His home was by far the most elaborate and lavish in the legionary fortress, which was not saying much, as most of the buildings in the citadel were grim barracks, grain storage facilities, and military supply shops. If he had his druthers, he would be in his private home outside the fortress. While comparatively smaller, it was more tranquil. But as the appointed imperial governor of Germania, protocol dictated that he reside in the fortress.

He looked up as his wife, Hereca, entered his office, her auburn hair shining despite the drabness of the day. She shook the rain off her cloak and hung it on a wooden peg. Almost as tall as her husband, with an

1

attractive figure even after bearing four children, she moved toward him. "Foul weather out there. But it will pass as it always does, and brighter skies will ensue. Spring is almost upon us. Warmer days approach."

Valerius gazed at her, smiling. Hereca's statement about the cold and rain reflected her true essence. Neither the weather, the evildoers—who were many here in Germania—nor the hefty responsibilities of governing a volatile territory seemed to faze her. Together, they had survived some precarious situations over the years, emerging stronger than before. He was fortunate to have a woman such as her by his side.

Hereca was a German princess of the Dolgubni clan. The unlikely pair had joined forces under extremely perilous circumstances many years ago. Despite their vastly different upbringings—he was from a rich Roman family of the equestrian class and she was the daughter of a Dolgubni chieftain—they had rescued each other. While Hereca had become Romanized, she maintained her fiercely independent and indomitable German spirit. She was kind to the poor and disadvantaged but also a lady of iron, capable of dressing down even the fiercest German chieftains.

"Don't forget we have a meeting this afternoon with the Bructeri leaders," she reminded. "I know they're anxious to meet with us. They're concerned that other tribes may replace them as trading partners. You know how protective they can get of their turf and their share of Roman commerce."

Valerius was about to reply when his best friend and right-hand man, Marcellus, a retired centurion, appeared in the doorway. Although twenty years older than Valerius, he still retained the muscle mass of a serving centurion, and woe be to the man who underestimated him.

"Colder than a well-digger's arse out there," Marcellus groused. "Weather fit for neither man nor beast. As my old centurion used to

2

say, 'this is good training weather.' Good thing I'm not in the legions anymore. I thought it was supposed to be spring."

"I have other things to worry about than the miserable weather and meeting with the Bructeri!" Valerius exclaimed. He picked up the rolled dispatch he had been reading. "Just got this from Rome earlier this morning, and it undeniably takes precedence over other matters. It seems Tiberius wants to see me in person. Doesn't that dour old bastard realize how long and arduous a journey to Rome is, especially at this time of year? The winter storms have yet to subside on the open seas."

"You're referring to our beloved imperator as that *dour old bastard?*" Marcellus inquired with a snort.

"I could throw in a few other choice words as well."

"I'm sure you could. But take heart, we're coming with you," Marcellus replied. "Right, Hereca?

"Yes, dear. We will both join you."

"But of course you will. I should not be deserving of all of the joys of life."

"Stop being so morose," Hereca chided. "We have to go, so let's make the best of it. Although I must say, I'm not looking forward to traveling by sea at this time of year. What does he want to see you about?"

"That's the problem—I don't know. This dispatch is rather cryptic. It just states that I must come to Rome to discuss urgent matters. We were just there a little over two years ago when he appointed me as imperial governor. And we've made spectacular progress here since then. The northern border of the empire is secure, and commerce is booming. What could he possibly want? Have I displeased him in some way?"

"I think not," said Hereca. "But I would venture to guess it's something important."

"I don't look forward to the journey either," Marcellus said. "It will be tedious and perilous. But then again, I will get to see the magnificent chariot races at the Circus Maximus once more. Echoing Hereca, stop being so glum. You'll enjoy yourself once we are there. You'll see."

"Then so be it. I will arrange for our transport," Valerius said with finality. "I'd like to leave within a week. Let's conclude any urgent business and then set off to Rome."

CHAPTER I
NEW ORDERS

Rome
Spring AD 31 (Six Weeks Later)

Valerius absently gazed out of the third-floor window of the luxurious imperial apartments, where most of the emperor's dignitaries and guests were lodged. The dwelling was spacious, with tiled floors, colorful frescoes, ornate tapestries, intricate statuaries, and flowing fountains. Rome spared no expense in housing foreign luminaries, ambassadors, and high officials. In the streets below, there was the usual raucous din. The boisterous cries of vendors and the voices of the tightly packed masses drifted upward.

Peering down from his lofty perch along the length of the Sacra Via, he could see the magnificent temples, their marble edifices gleaming in the afternoon sunlight. At the far end of the main avenue stood the Roman Curia, the senate building, the crown jewel of the forum. Here, he—Valerius Maximus, Procurator of Germania—was at the heart of the Roman dynasty. The vast empire was governed by the imperial palace, the senate, and the various government offices in this small but resplendent section of the city. For any outsider, the gleaming buildings would be both imposing and awe-inspiring, made deliberately so. The city was built to impress, and it did. No other metropolis in the Roman world could compare to the majesty and opulence of this seat of power.

Valerius coughed as dust and noxious fumes rose to the third floor. He disliked this city. No, *dislike* was not a strong enough word to describe his feelings. *Loathe* was more like it. And it was not merely due to its crowded, dirty conditions. Yes, Rome truly was the seat of imperial power, where many flocked from the four corners of the empire to seek their fortune and to fulfill their destiny. The Roman Empire encompassed all of the nations and territories adjacent to the Mediterranean and stretched north to the provinces of Gallia and the territories of Germania Inferior and Superior. To the east, the Roman domain covered the countries south of the Danubius, all the way to the Black Sea. But with power comes political intrigue and treachery. One wrong word or deed could put you out of favor with the reigning elite and ultimately get you killed. Valerius had done his best to eschew the politics of Rome, but being the appointed governor of Germania—one of the most prestigious posts in the empire—here he was, like it or not, right in the thick of it.

Valerius's disdain for Rome was not a recent sentiment. He had grown up and been schooled in the city. A son of wealthy parents, he had enjoyed a life of privilege, but he had recognized at an early age that he was not of the senatorial class, the highest in the food chain, and thus would not have the career of the ultra-wealthy but would be forced to feed off the crumbs. However, he was not bitter about it and had decided as a young man that his destiny would be fulfilled elsewhere in the empire. Despite his parents' objections, he was strong-willed and prevailed. Subsequent cataclysmic events had rocked the empire, beginning with the Varus disaster in the Teutoburg Forest over twenty years earlier, which he had, as a young tribune, been a part of but miraculously survived. In the subsequent retaliatory campaign, he had distinguished himself but had been captured by the Germans. Again, he persevered. Upon escaping captivity deep in the heart of Germania, he reached the Roman side of the Rhenus, marrying a German princess and settling there, far away from the streets of Rome, the heart of power and political intrigue.

He was anxious about his scheduled meeting with Tiberius the next day. He could not comprehend why he had been summoned from the far reaches of the empire all the way to Rome. A request to appear before the emperor was not necessarily a good thing, as many unsuspecting individuals had discovered, much to their mortification.

A gentle breeze fanned through the window, warming him. He had to admit the climate here was more temperate than the harsh winters of Germania, but he missed the cleaner and fresher air up north. Rome, with its multitude of people, was squalid despite the aqueducts and sewer systems.

Suddenly, Hereca approached him from behind and hooked her arm in his. "Come, darling, don't look so miserable. We will soon have our audience with Emperor Tiberius, and then, we can be on our way back to our family. 'Tis a mere inconvenience."

Valerius, visibly fretting, separated himself from Hereca and began pacing back and forth—a habit when agitated. "Why did he summon us all the way from Germania? Could he have not just sent us a dispatch if he wanted something done? Have I displeased him in some way?"

"Don't be silly, dear," Hereca scoffed. "You've executed your strategy magnificently. The German tribes are at peace, there are no wars, and trade is expanding. We have even built roads and wharves on the opposite side of the Rhenus to facilitate markets. Goods are flowing all through Germania and Gallia, and many, including the Germans, are prospering. Has Tiberius even hinted that he is dissatisfied with you?"

Answering herself, she continued, "No, he has not. He should be parading you before the senate for all you have done to successfully implement Rome's foreign policy. The Rhenus border is secure, and the German tribes on the other side of the river are content, or at least placated."

Valerius continued to worry. "I still don't understand why he couldn't have just sent me my marching orders. We receive dispatches from Rome every week—mountains of them. What could be so important that he wants me here?"

Hereca shrugged. "I don't know why. But it is this woman's intuition that it is significant—something he needs to discuss with you in person. Look, you are the most powerful procurator in the empire. You control, what, eight legions? He appointed you governor two years ago because he likes and trusts you. You are his man. It was you who sniffed out the coup by General Mellitus two years ago and saved old Tiberius's arse. He is indebted to you. Not many fall into that category. More significantly, the most volatile and dangerous border of the empire is secure and peaceful now, thanks to you. Perhaps he wants to give you a triumph," she ended with a chuckle.

Valerius threw her a reproachful look, clearly not appreciating the humor. He was about to respond when a heavy knock was heard at their door. Hereca waved away a servant, saying, "I'll open it." Swinging the heavy wooden door open, she revealed Marcellus, his heavily muscled frame filling the doorway.

"Anyone know where I could get some decent wine?" he asked, sauntering in.

Hereca grinned. "Perfect timing, Marcellus. I was just telling Valerius not to worry about his audience with Tiberius. Everything is fine, don't you agree?"

Marcellus contemplated the question for a moment. "I must admit, I never thought I'd see the day when Germania was at such peace. I've been personally fighting those arseholes—present company excluded, Hereca—for a long time, over thirty years. So, if Tiberius is not satisfied with the state of affairs, he is out of his fucking mind. Pardon the language, Hereca, but that's the truth of the matter."

Hereca beamed triumphantly. "See, even Marcellus agrees. You're not in trouble with Tiberius."

Valerius sighed. "Stop ganging up on me. I just cannot understand why he couldn't have communicated by dispatch. Why drag me all the way to Rome?"

Marcellus snorted. "No idea. Never been an emperor, and I have no desire to be one. We'll find out tomorrow. In the meantime, why don't we all relax and get some good food and wine?"

Valerius offered a slight smile. "After all this time, you still think like a common legionary: 'How far do we have to go, when do we stop for the night, and when do we eat?'"

"Hey, Tribune, those are good words to live by. That intonation served me well for many years."

"I imagine so. Let's go see if we can get some wine ordered for our room. I'm sure it comes with the accommodations, and if it's from the imperial cellars, I'm sure it will be exceptional."

* * *

The next morning, Valerius, Hereca, and Marcellus ventured upward to the imperial palace on Palatine Hill, just a short distance away. At the entrance, they were escorted by several stern-faced

Praetorian guards through a beautiful flowering garden with fountains. Entering a long corridor, they walked about halfway down when the centurion commander escorting them halted and rapped politely on a large wooden door to the right. It was promptly opened by another guard in an impeccable uniform.

"Wait here," the centurion instructed them before entering the room. A muffled conversation was heard from within. The centurion then returned, gesturing with his arm. "The Emperor awaits you."

Valerius entered first, followed by Hereca and then Marcellus. The room was of moderate size, with a tiled floor and several murals decorating the walls. In the center stood a rectangular, polished, wooden table. At the head sat Emperor Tiberius, flanked by two men—one in a military uniform and the other in a cream-colored toga. Standing off to the side was a third man in a military pose, whom Valerius immediately recognized as the prefect of the Praetorian Guard, Lucius Aelius Sejanus. He made brief eye contact with Sejanus before approaching the table, maintaining a neutral expression. He hoped he did not betray his true feelings for Sejanus, a malevolent man who had ingratiated himself with Tiberius to the extent that many believed he ran the empire.

Unsure of the seating arrangements and protocol, Valerius positioned himself at the end of the table, facing Tiberius. The emperor had aged significantly since their last encounter several years ago. His hair was thin and gray, and the lines on his face had deepened. Glancing at the four men in attendance, Valerius tried to read their expressions, which he was fairly adept at due to his experience with the German chieftains, who could be conniving and churlish. Were their expressions grim, a telltale sign that they were to discuss an unpleasant subject? It did not appear that way, but they were not smiling either. He would just have to wait and find out.

"Procurator of Germania, Valerius Maximus, welcome to Rome once again. I see you have brought your usual retinue with you," Tiberius greeted.

Offering a tight smile, Valerius replied, "Yes, I did. Both Hereca and Marcellus are my right and left hands, instrumental in governing Germania. They need to hear what you have to say today. I hope you don't mind."

"Not at all, Governor Maximus. I am well aware of the substantial roles they have played in Germania. Let me introduce you to my small advisory council. This is Senator Marcus Hordeonius Flaccus, and on my other side is General Sextus Paulius Tuscus. And, of course, you know my Praetorian prefect, Sejanus."

The prefect nodded stiffly at Valerius without a trace of a smile. Valerius turned his attention to the two figures seated alongside Tiberius. Flaccus, middle-aged with a thick mop of hair now turning silver, had a smile plastered upon his face, no doubt from years of practice in the senate. As for General Tuscus, Valerius vaguely recalled encountering him many years before as a young tribune on the campaign in Germania. He was the senior of the two men, but despite his age, he maintained an erect posture and continued to wear the armor and trappings of the legion.

"A pleasure meeting both of you," Valerius greeted.

"Now we can get down to business," Tiberius declared. "I have been most pleased with the progress you've noted in your dispatches. The northern border of the empire is at peace." The emperor paused for Valerius to respond.

Feeling Hereca nudge his foot under the table, Valerius caught her I-told-you-so look. "Yes, sire, all is well. I am pleasantly surprised at the state of affairs in Germania. Even the most belligerent tribes, including the Cherusci and Suebi, appear to have accepted our presence. You fought there, sir. You know how ingrained their hatred is for anything Roman."

'Yes, indeed, I do," Tiberius acknowledged. "I never would have believed the Cherusci would come to heel."

"Ah, sire, I would not use that term," Valerius cautioned. "Perhaps they have ceased their bellicose ways for the time being, but they are not subjugated."

"To what do you attribute your success?" Senator Flaccus inquired.

Valerius paused, carefully forming a response. "As you are no doubt aware, Senator, I made my living trading with the Germans. My wife Hereca is German by birth and has a keen understanding of how people think. The answer is quite simple: The Germans enjoy trade and the benefits it brings. Most of the tribes have developed a taste for Roman goods. Wine, jewelry, mirrors, iron tools, dishes, oil, mirrors, and a host of other things are in demand. You name it, they want it. In return, we receive hides and lumber. As a result of the trade, many of the German chieftains are becoming filthy rich. Furthermore, while the German tribes remain wary, they no longer believe that the legions on our side of the Rhenus are poised to invade their lands."

"And this has curbed their hostile actions against the Roman world?" General Tuscus inquired.

"It has thus far. We, especially Hereca," Valerius said, nodding to his wife, "are in constant communication with the leaders of the tribes." While I am fluent in German, she is well-versed in the nuances of the language and understands their thinking. She knows when to press them and when to withdraw.

Hereca took over seamlessly, smiling brightly. "We talk a lot and listen to their concerns and complaints. We have established roads into the interior of the German tribal lands, built by the legions to facilitate commerce. We have deliberately avoided establishing any military presence across the Rhenus—only civilian outposts, docks, and trading stations. I fear we would return to open conflict if we established any permanent legionary outposts on their side of the river."

"Rome has taken notice of your accomplishments on the German border," said Tiberius. "In fact, I am parading you before the senate to boast of your accomplishments. However, things are not going so well with our provinces along the Danubius. The barbarian tribes on the other side of the river are constantly raiding and pillaging our provinces. They are not major invasions—at least, not yet—but the barbarians continue to sporadically loot and kill Roman subjects. This will not do. The inhabitants of our provinces deserve our protection as client states of Rome. I believe it is only a matter of time before we face a significant incursion. In addition, I am convinced that we need a coordinated approach to governance. Each of the four provinces along the Danubius has its own way of doing things, not all to my liking. This is where you enter the picture. Governor Maximus, I would like you to replicate your success in Germania on the Danubius. Stop the incessant raiding of our provinces, and bring Roman commerce to the Danubius. I have been informed that these barbarian tribes have much in the way of gold and silver. Rome's treasury could benefit mightily from this infusion of precious metals."

At first, Valerius was too stunned to respond. Never in his wildest imagination had he envisioned this scenario. Masking his trepidation, he attempted to respond in an even tone. "Sir… that would put me in charge of two theatres of operation. And they have an additional, what, five, six legions along the Danubius?"

"There are six legions, and yes, I'm aware that this responsibility would include two theatres with separate legionary and naval forces," Tiberius said sharply, clearly displeased with Valerius's impertinent response.

"It's just that I would be spreading myself over two vast geographical areas, and I have little knowledge of the Danubian tribes, our legions posted there, or our naval fleet."

"Nonsense," Tiberius dismissed. "Have General Labenius, your military commander in Germania, run things while you are away so you can concentrate on the Danubius. Labenius is quite capable, is he not? And while you will face initial obstacles, I am confident you will adapt as needed, just as you did in Germania."

Valerius quickly realized that refusal was not an option. "Yes, Labenius is very capable. Pardon my lack of enthusiasm, sir. Your edict caught me by surprise. It was totally unexpected."

"Listen," Tiberius began, "you showed the same hesitancy when I appointed you as governor of Germania. I know you will face challenges, but I cannot think of a better person for the task at hand. Rome has been butting heads with the tribes along the Danubius for many years. It's time we got the upper hand. As I said, I am particularly interested in their mineral wealth. I remember fighting them early in my career—a tough bunch. My nephew Germanicus and I waged a hard campaign there for over three years. I need someone on the ground that I can trust, and that someone is you."

Valerius silently sighed. He had no choice but to accept the assignment. "Very well, sir. When would you like me to begin this new posting?"

A smile creased Tiberius's craggy face. "Immediately, but before you go, as I mentioned, I am going to have you presented to the senate. Selecting governors for imperial provinces such as Germania and the Danubius is my responsibility and prerogative, not the senate's. However, I want the senate to know what a good job you have done in Germania and that you will take over responsibilities on the Danubius frontier. Senator Flaccus here will do the honors and introduce you. Also, it's an event you will have to attend alone—just you, not your wife or Centurion Marcellus.

Valerius offered a tremulous smile. "I understand, sir. And when is this going to happen?"

Flaccus smiled. "First thing tomorrow morning. You are already on the docket."

* * *

The next morning, Valerius and Senator Flaccus, surrounded by several bodyguards, walked through the forum and toward the *curia*. He was wearing his best toga—also his only toga—which was faded and slightly tattered at the hem. In Germania, he did not require a toga, as such formality was unnecessary. So, if anyone was expecting him to impress the senate leaders with his attire, that was not going to happen. He looked up as they rounded a corner and approached the venerable building. From the outside, it was a plain structure—rectangular and featuring brick-faced concrete with huge buttresses at each angle. The lower part of the front wall was decorated with slabs of marble. A single flight of steps led up to two huge bronze doors that yawned wide open. Four beefy guards stood at the entrance, ensuring no outsiders disturbed the proceedings. Valerius gulped nervously. He had never stood inside the senate building.

Flaccus noticed Valerius's trepidation. "What's the matter, never been here before?

He proffered a sheepish smile. "As a matter of fact, no."

Flaccus chuckled. "Don't let it bother you. You will do fine. Another good thing, we are first on the agenda, so no waiting around.

Trailing Flaccus, he entered the hallowed building, surprised at how austere the walls were, veneered in marble about two-thirds of the way up. The floor was slightly more lavish. Beautiful cut stones and colored glass were embedded in the floor, creating colorful swirls of geometric designs. The gallery for the senators, flanking both sides of the long rectangular building, comprised three broad steps where benches were set in rows, capable of seating several hundred. A murmur of conversation and muted laughter among the milling senators filled the hall as they waited for the session to begin.

Flaccus led him by the arm toward the rostrum facing the crowd of senators. Valerius peered down the length of the hall and noted an altar with a statue of winged victory. He had only heard about the symbolic statue before.

Noticing Valerius and Senator Flaccus, the head of the senate, a rather rotund figure, strode to the front. Valerius could not recall his name, although he thought it might be Strabo. The figure pounded the gavel on a wooden stand, signaling the senators to take their seats. After everyone was settled, the man with the gavel spoke in a clear and loud tone. "The first item on the agenda is Senator Flaccus, who will speak of the current state of affairs of our northern border and introduce us to the current procurator of Germania." With that, he nodded at Flaccus.

"Stay here to the side until I call you forth," Flaccus instructed quietly, patting Valerius's arm reassuringly before turning around to confidently approach the rostrum.

"Esteemed senators, I bring forth to you today a true hero of Rome. Valerius Maximus, son of Sentius Maximus, served as a tribune in the German campaign under Germanicus. He subsequently settled into civilian life as a trader of goods in Germania. As many of you will recall, at the behest of the emperor, he almost single-handedly put down the rebellion of the Frisii tribes. After that, on his initiative, he disrupted an attempted coup by the former governor of Germania. He was rewarded for his brave deeds by Tiberius and appointed procurator of Germania. In the few short years he has governed in Germania, there have been no rebellions, and markets are flourishing. The northern frontier of the empire is secure. There is a Roman peace. We all owe a great debt to this man. As I said, he is a true hero of Rome. Please welcome Governor Valerius Maximus."

Flaccus motioned for Valerius to come forward. As he approached, he was startled to see the entire senate rise and give a booming applause. Caught off guard, he offered a nervous smile, nodding to his audience. The applause continued, and some shouted out, "Speech, speech!"

Valerius turned about and looked in bewilderment at Flaccus, who smiled back at him. "Well, give them a speech, Maximus."

Startled, Valerius silently reprimanded himself for coming unprepared. He should have known better, but he was so preoccupied with his new appointment by Tiberius that it had escaped his muddled mind. However, he was used to thinking quickly on his feet, especially with the Germans, who could be untrustworthy and vulpine in their dealings.

Valerius raised his hands for quiet, all the while contemplating what to say. Eventually, the clamor diminished. He looked to his left and right and then to the center of his audience, scanning the faces staring back at him. "Honored senators, please excuse me for not having any prepared remarks. I find myself a bit nervous, as I have never been in this revered chamber before. So, I will just speak extemporaneously. At the request of Tiberius, I arrived in Rome from Germania several days ago. I've brought with me twenty barbarians, fierce German warriors. They are poised outside the doors of this building as I speak."

Many senators looked toward the doors, fear evident on their faces.

Valerius laughed lightly, and many of the senators joined in the mirth, realizing his words were meant in jest. "Please excuse my rather feeble attempt at humor, but there is a purpose to it. I wish to stress a particular point. Make no mistake: the German tribes are fiercely independent and do not care for our presence. They are not conquered. To think otherwise is to do so at one's peril. I hope you all understand this. However, saying all that, they appreciate Roman goods such as wine, fabrics, cookware, olive oil, iron plows, and even jewelry. They desire what we have. Many of them have become wealthy through their trade with us. Greed is a strong motivator. The Germans seek our commerce, but the tolerance stops there. We have built roads and shipping facilities on German land. Thus far, they have not objected, but we dare not establish any permanent military bases on their side of the Rhenus."

Valerius paused, glancing around the gallery once more. "Senators, the eight legions stationed along the Rhenus will stay on our side of the river. No military campaigns have been planned. Not to give you a history lesson, but the great Augustus dictated years ago, after the Teutoburg disaster, that Rome would not extend her borders beyond the Rhenus. The legions posted there ensured there were no German incursions into Roman territory. So, the next logical step is to appease these tribes with gifts and trade while firmly holding the line. The troops stationed along the Rhenus are bored, but I will make that trade any day—bored legionaries over angry Germans. I hope the peace and prosperity that currently exist on the northern frontier continue. Thank you."

The senators rose again and applauded. Flaccus moved forward, slapping Valerius on the back. "Well done, Maximus," he exclaimed, taking over the rostrum once more. He faced the senators. "There is one more thing. Emperor Tiberius appointed Governor Maximus to oversee the Danubius frontier, aiming to replicate the success he achieved in Germania."

The senators applauded once more as Valerius exited.

CHAPTER II
DISCUSSIONS ON THE PALATINE

The next day, they gathered at Tiberius's palace once again. Valerius, Marcellus, and Hereca huddled around a square wooden table with a large map spread on it. Tiberius, Senator Flaccus, and General Tuscus stood with them, gazing at the map of the Danubian territory.

Tiberius looked up with a smirk. "I heard you took the senate by storm yesterday. That is just what I wanted from my future governor of the Danubius. Now, let's discuss what you will be facing." He nodded at Senator Flaccus to begin.

With a wooden pointer, the senator indicated specific places on the map. "Here is the Danubius, flowing west to east. Note that its origins are close to the source of the Rhenus, which flows in the opposite direction, northeast to northwest. Now, on the southern side of the river going from west to east are the Roman client states of Raetia, Noricum, Pannonia, and Moesia." He tapped each province with the pointer.

"Just so there is no confusion about your authority," Tiberius interjected, "the governors of these provinces will report directly to you and me. You will ask them to do as you see fit. If they choose to whine and complain to me, they do so at their peril. Your first and foremost mission is to keep these client states at peace and commerce flowing. We don't want any rebellions within the provinces. Things have been relatively stable there for the past twenty years or so, and we want to keep it that way. I will have you briefed about the governors later in the day."

Valerius nodded in affirmation.

"Now comes the difficult part," Flaccus continued. Using the pointer, he traced an arc on the map from west to east on the north side of the Danubius. "These territories are occupied by tribes who are not overly fond of Rome. Again, going from west to east are the Marcomanni, Quadi, Iazyges, and the Dacians. There are some smaller tribes as well. If you ask me, they're all a giant pain in Rome's arse. Your second mission, and the more problematic one, is to encourage these belligerent tribes to become friendlier and align with Rome's initiatives, just as you did in Germania. We will ensure you have the allotted funds to ease this transition. General Tuscus, over to you."

"Thank you, Senator," said General Tuscus before addressing Valerius. "There have been sporadic infiltrations across the Danubius by these tribes. Nothing major, but you never know what might come next. The good news is that the legions stationed along the Danubius function as a reaction force and can quickly reach any trouble spot in a reasonable amount of time. Our naval fleet along the Danubius is first-rate. We have chased any intrusions back across the river. The troops are well-trained and know how to handle themselves. The six legions posted along the river include the First, Second, Third, Seventh, Tenth, and Fourteenth. We have watch towers, fortresses, and outposts along the length of the river. The road system and naval fleet ensure quick movement to any area of disturbance. It might not be as good as the Rhenus, but it is more than adequate."

Valerius paused briefly, contemplating what he had heard. "That is a vast territory, stretching from eastern Germania to the Black Sea. I don't know the distance, but it's hundreds upon hundreds of miles."

"Yes, it is," affirmed Tiberius. "I know it's a considerable undertaking, but if you make even half the progress you have achieved with the German tribes, it will be well worth it. Our goal is not to pacify these tribes but to curb their belligerence and have them become friendlier toward Rome."

"I know some of their language. It's a different dialect than that spoken by the Germans along the Rhenus and sometimes difficult to understand," Hereca said.

Tiberius beamed. "See, you already have an advantage. Your wife, Hereca, is once again going to play an essential role."

"Sir, pardon the interruption from an aged centurion," Marcellus said. "I served under you, your brother, Drusus, and your nephew, Germanicus. I have dealt with the Marcomanni before, both on and off the battlefield. Their territory stretches along the Rhenus and east to the Danubius. They are difficult to get a read on. Just when you think firm relations have been established, they come back at you. I sincerely hope the other tribes, whom I am unfamiliar with, are not as duplicitous."

Tiberius chuckled slightly. "Oh, it will be a tough undertaking, no doubt about that. I don't expect instant results, but we need to start somewhere. We have to convince them that there is a better way. I view this as an extended process that will be years in the making. As I mentioned yesterday, I have issued strict instructions to the governors that they are to fully cooperate with you. Any disobedience will be viewed as a defiance of my mandate."

"How long do you anticipate I will be in this new role?" Valerius asked.

"Not sure," Tiberius replied. "But as a minimum, I need you to get this initiative underway. Once progress has been achieved, I will look for a permanent governor."

Valerius turned to General Tuscus. "Sir, what of the legates that are commanding the various legions? I ask this question because of the unfortunate troubles we experienced over the last several years in Germania." Before the general could respond, Valerius turned and faced Tiberius. "I know it is a delicate subject, but given the past events, I had to ask the question."

The emperor scowled. "If I were you, I would probably have put forth the same question. To answer your inquiry, the legates have all been carefully vetted. Like the governors, any disobedience toward you will be viewed as insubordination. You will have full control of the legions. If someone displeases you, let me know, and I will appoint another."

The discussion continued long into the morning, covering troop strengths, river depths, weather patterns, the availability of commercial vessels, and patterns of hostile intrusions into the Roman provinces.

* * *

That afternoon, Hereca, Marcellus, and Valerius relaxed in their apartment, savoring wine from the imperial cellars. Marcellus smacked his lips in appreciation. "Now, this is good wine. Whoever selects these vintages in the imperial palace, bless his bones, has a good palate."

Marcellus was about to continue when one of the appointed servants appeared and stood before Valerius. "Please excuse the interruption, but Senator Quintus Salvius is here to see you."

Valerius recognized the name right away. Quintus had been in Valerius's training class for their appointments as tribunes in the legions many years ago. Quintus was an amiable sort, and Valerius considered him a friend. He recalled Quintus was of the patrician class, a purple striper, and the son of a senator. Valerius had not seen him since his posting to Germania over twenty years ago and had lost track of him over the years.

"Please bring the senator into our quarters," Valerius instructed the servant.

A few moments later, the servant appeared, followed by Quintus Salvius. He had aged but not too much. His frame was still trim and fit. He had a handsome face framed by short brown hair and a patrician nose and was dressed in a formal toga. An expansive grin creased Quintus's face.

"Maximus, we meet again. Look at you, appointed governor of the Rhenus and Danubian territories. I have followed your career closely here in Rome. You've done well for yourself. Who would've thought this was possible so many years ago?"

Valerius beamed in return. "And what about you? The esteemed Senator Quintus Salvius, I hope all is well."

"It is, it is."

"And you have a family?" Valerius inquired.

"Yes, I have three children—two sons and a daughter. I am raising them to be proper Romans."

Valerius turned and introduced Hereca and Marcellus. "Hereca and I have four children back in Germania. My parents, Sentius and Vispania, are watching them while we are away."

"And how are your noble parents?" I trust they are well."

"They are fine. Thank you for asking. They seem to love their new home in Germania, as do I. Come, have some wine with us. We can catch up on old times."

"Don't mind if I do. I tried to chat with you in the curia, but you were swept away as soon as you finished your impromptu speech." He chuckled lightly. "It was quite good, by the way. I enjoyed your jibe about the twenty barbarian warriors at the entrance. I thought some of our esteemed senators would shit their togas."

"Thank you, Quintus. It was a spontaneous thing. I had no idea I was to address the senate."

"You did well, but I must admit you looked a little frazzled. I would have been too. Listen, I would love to reminisce about old times, but I need to talk to you about some urgent matters."

"Sounds serious," Valerius said.

Yes, as a matter of fact, it is." Quintus glanced around to ensure they were alone.

Valerius took the hint, rose, and dismissed the servants. After they departed, he faced Quintus. "You can speak freely in front of Hereca and Marcellus."

Quintus adopted a solemn expression. "Of course, let me get right to it. You must be extremely careful. Some in the senate are envious of your appointment. Those postings are usually reserved for members of the imperial family or high-ranking senators. They would like nothing better than for you to fail. I have heard some of them talking. Apparently, you are not considered worthy because you were not born of the senatorial class. They view you as inferior. Bunch of snooty, patrician pricks if you ask me."

"Quintus, I did not seek an appointment to my current position. Tiberius bestowed it upon me, and *bestowed* is a kind word. He essentially declared this as my new posting and made it clear dissent was not an option. Now, if any of these senators have experience in German affairs, I'd hand this job over to him in a heartbeat. This evening, I have been invited by Senator Flaccus to a dinner party at his residence. Most of the guests are his senatorial colleagues, some of whom, I assume, do not particularly care for my well-being."

Quintus chuckled. "Yes, and you will get to meet them up close and personal. Lucky you. I will be there as well."

There was a brief pause as Marcellus handed wine goblets to everyone. All four politely sipped their wine.

"Any advice?" Valerius asked.

"As a matter of fact, yes. They are a pretentious bunch. Be polite, but don't take any guff from them. You may not be of the senatorial class but don't feel inferior. You have much more power than they will ever hold and are twice the man they could ever become. At the first sign of a German rebellion, even the most experienced among them would probably wet themselves. They are a feckless lot. You are the right man for this position. No one else even comes close."

"Thank you for those kind words, Salvius. You know I just wanted to run my trading company in Germania, but it seems Tiberius has other plans for me. I keep getting sucked into events I have no control over."

"Tiberius has great faith in your abilities and views you favorably, but beware of some in the imperial circle who do not. Of course, I'm speaking of Sejanus."

"Oh him," Valerius murmured in disdain.

"Yes, him, and do not underestimate the man. He has significant influence and is a diabolical figure with much sway over the emperor."

"No need to warn me. I have, in the past, had several terse exchanges with him. I do not believe he views me favorably. My only saving grace is that I am eight hundred miles away from Rome on the Rhenus.

Marcellus joined the conversation. "I have served Rome all my life, and I know a thing or two about people. That man is an arsehole, pure and simple."

Quintus muffled a snicker. "Yes, but a dangerous arsehole. I believe that's an appropriate way of describing him. But listen, he's ambitious and not to be trusted. Tread lightly around him. Many who have displeased him are no longer around. Innocent men have been condemned with false claims of conspiracies against Tiberius. He reads and filters all of Tiberius's correspondence. If you wish to convey something politically sensitive to Tiberius, use me. Send your dispatches to my attention, and I will ensure that Tiberius gets it, unread by others. I have my sources and contacts in the Imperial Palace."

"Thank you for the offer, Quintus. I may, at some point, need your services. At one time, I used Lady Agrippina, Germanicus's widow, as an intermediary, but sadly, she is no longer with us."

"Yes, Agrippina was a breath of fresh air in the imperial palace. I miss her." Quintus sipped deeply of his wine, finishing it. "Take care, Valerius. You have done well for yourself and served Rome. I am proud to call you a friend. I'm sure your visitors are being monitored by you know who. So I must not linger. This must appear as nothing more than a quick, social, courtesy visit."

* * *

Early that evening, Valerius, Hereca, and Marcellus were escorted by a trio of bodyguards to Senator Flaccus's residence, just a few blocks from the forum area. As usual, Marcellus groused about wearing a toga, saying that his garment might slip off his shoulder, exposing his arse for the world to see. He received no sympathy from Valerius or Hereca. Valerius was wearing the same toga he had worn to the senate.

Hereca, on the other hand, was wearing a magnificent pale green *stola* she had purchased the previous day. Her burnished hair and blue eyes contrasted beautifully with the garment, which accentuated her womanly shape. She looked radiant. Upon reaching their destination, Valerius gazed at the residence, surrounded by a high brick wall. They were admitted through an iron gate and led up marble stairs to the main entrance, featuring a pair of massive wooden doors that yawned wide open. The large atrium welcomed them, where people mingled about. The atrium featured a pond with an ornate fountain, spouting water from the mouth of a sculptured dolphin. Off the atrium were open rooms to accommodate the crowd. A servant approached with a polished tray of silver goblets filled with wine. The place resonated with light laughter and idle chatter as the rich and powerful elite of Rome mingled.

As the trio sipped the scarlet nectar, agreeing it was good stuff, Valerius turned to Hereca and Marcellus. "Time to separate. Remember what Quintus said. Be polite but don't let them lord over you. We must be careful what we do and say here."

Hereca threw a scornful look, letting him know she could handle herself and did not appreciate the lecture. Valerius recognized the look and realized his blunder.

"Sorry, I did not mean to patronize."

"Well, you did," Hereca said before giving him a sly smile. "I eat people like these for breakfast."

Valerius smiled. "I know, my dear. I've seen you do it countless times. Try not to be too harsh on these esteemed guests."

With that, two senators, unknown to him, appeared and guided Valerius into a secluded corner for a private conversation.

In a matter of moments, two hawkish-looking women—their faces heavily made up—no doubt senator's wives descended upon Hereca. They introduced themselves as Silvia and Pulchia. Silvia spoke in a condescending tone, "Your husband is a famous man. I hear you are a German princess. Can you speak Latin?"

Hereca adopted a neutral expression and replied in guttural German.

The two women blanched, staring at her like she had two heads.

After a pause, Hereca replied in near-perfect Latin with just a trace of an accent. "Most certainly I speak Latin. I also speak four dialects of German and passable Gallic. I need to be fluent in many languages to assist my husband in governing his territory. Many of those whom we deal with cannot speak Latin." She then tilted her head and innocently added, "Can either of you speak any foreign languages?"

Both ladies shook their heads.

Hereca offered a thin smile. "A pity. You should try it sometime. It will expand your horizons." With that, she made a graceful exit, casting a triumphant backward glance over her shoulder.

She did not get far before she encountered another woman. Hereca appraised the lady. She had shiny dark hair accented by a pale blue stola of fine weave that appeared to be similar to Hereca's. She wore a magnificent golden brooch, not a gaudy piece, but obviously worth a small fortune. *Oh no, here's another one ready to offer snide remarks to the German barbarian from the frontier.*

To Hereca's surprise, the woman proffered a warm smile. "You must be Hereca. My name is Claudia. I'm the wife of Quintus Salvius. You and your husband are the talk of Rome. Quintus told me of your meeting. He gushed on and on about the two of you. I'm so glad we finally have the opportunity to meet." She linked arms with Hereca and guided her to a quiet corner where they would not be interrupted. "You must tell me all about your life in Germania."

At first, Hereca was speechless. This woman was so different from the others, sincere not condescending. Hereca returned her warm smile. "What would you like to know? Life is much unlike what you experience in Rome."

Claudia laughed lightly. "I'm sure it is. My husband says that you have a major role in the governance of the territory and you negotiate with men on matters of commerce. Not something you would find a Roman woman doing here in the city."

"Sometimes, being a woman has its advantages. The men think they are superior to me and will prevail in any negotiation. I let them think that way, but in the end, I am the one who gets the upper hand, and they don't even realize it."

Claudia clapped her hands in delight. "I would love to witness that! I must hear more of this. Would you visit me before you leave? We can chat in a more private setting and speak at length. Please?"

Hereca beamed. "Claudia, I would love to visit you. Quintus said you have three children. I would really like to meet them."

"Excellent! How about we gather at my house in two days at around the sixth hour? I will give you the address."

"I believe I'm available. Yes, that should be fine. I look forward to our next meeting."

* * *

Senators Petrus and Theodius had deftly maneuvered Valerius into a secluded corner. "You know, Maximus, we have a trading company that functions mainly in the east, but we are considering expanding into Gallia and Germania. If you could grant us exclusive shipping rights to certain trade goods from the Germanic ports, we could make you very rich."

Valerius eyed the two men. They had unabashedly cut right into the heart of the matter. No skirting around the edges. He decided to let them off politely. "Thank you for your consideration. What a lucrative opportunity, but I'm afraid I must decline. I have divested myself of my trading company as the appointed governor, and besides, I have no need for additional wealth. I am quite comfortable with my financial circumstances, but thank you again for the offer." He nodded at both men and abruptly stepped away.

As he turned away, he spied Hereca engaged with two senator's wives. He grinned. Hereca would handle them. She could outmaneuver even the most belligerent German chieftains, so these two matrons would pose no problem.

Out of the corner of his eye, he observed Marcellus engaged with two dowagers. He watched as Marcellus deftly grabbed another goblet off a serving tray and replaced it with an empty one. His deep voice resonated above the idle chatter in the room, regaling the ladies with tales of the legions, though probably only half were true and perhaps a quarter had any veracity at all. Valerius could hear the ladies tittering at something Marcellus had said. The centurion had certainly embraced the spirit of the gathering in a hurry though he, ironically, was the one who did not want to come.

Moving through the crowd, Valerius spotted the host. Flaccus greeted him with a wide grin. "Maximus, so glad you make it! This is a more informal setting than the imperial palace."

Valerius returned the smile. There was no way he could have possibly turned down this invitation. He was sure both the emperor and Flaccus expected him to be there. "I must say, this is an impressive dwelling you have. What beautiful accommodations. This atrium is quite lovely. I don't believe I have seen one as charming—so peaceful yet richly decorated. And what a striking collection of plants and flowers surrounding the reflecting pool. My compliments to you."

Flaccus beamed. "Yes, I have the best that Rome has to offer. I am indeed fortunate. Now, listen, before we get too far into the evening, beware that you may be approached by some of my colleagues for business ventures. Stay clear of them."

"Thank you for the warning, Senator, but I've already had a few pedaling some corrupt scheme or other."

"What did you say to them?" Flaccus asked.

"Oh, I just told them that I have divested myself of all trade ventures while I am governor. I also mentioned that I have been successful and have no need for additional wealth on the northern frontier."

Flaccus beamed and slapped him on the shoulder. "Good thinking. You will do well in your new posting. Come, let me introduce you to some of my friends. You know, you're the talk of the senate but many have never met you. They have heard of your exploits and are eager to learn more about you."

Flaccus guided him to a quiet corner, where two middle-aged men were chatting quietly and in confidence. "Valerius, let me introduce you to an old pair of friends in the senate. This is Magnus Decebalus," he said, indicating the taller of the two, "and this is Cornelius Egnatius. It's men like these who hold the empire together. They work tirelessly on behalf of Rome to ensure its prosperity. You know, many of our senators are a pompous lot; their sole purpose in life is to enrich themselves. They don't give a fig about Rome. In fact, far too many engage in this behavior, as far as I am concerned. It's a sad state of affairs that such men are responsible for organizing and administering the Roman world."

I appreciate all you have done for Rome," Cornelius said. "Bringing peace and prosperity to the Rhenus. Truly a remarkable feat. As I'm sure you are aware, there is a great deal of jealousy and envy among some of our senators regarding your appointment."

"Indeed, I am. Senator Flaccus, perhaps you could mandate that our esteemed senators embark on a journey to the German territories one day," Valerius suggested. "They will quickly realize how different these barbarians are in their customs and the lives they lead. It would be an enlightening experience for these senators."

"Maybe we could put your suggestion up for a vote in the senate," Magnus chimed in facetiously.

Flaccus grinned. "I would support that, but I do not believe it would pass, not even close. But seriously, Valerius, I want you to know that there are men in the senate dedicated to the service of Rome, who are not looking to augment their wealth at every opportunity. You can count on the support of men like these two. If you face difficulty managing your new assignment, do not hesitate to get us involved. We do not hold power, but we can exert influence. Please remember that. It's good to have friends in the senate."

"Thank you. Tiberius has given me a free hand to accomplish my mission, but there are those who do not have Rome's best interest at heart and might impede what I do." Glancing around to ensure no one could overhear their conversation, Valerius continued. "I think you all know to whom I am referring."

The three men nodded sagely. "We hope things go smoothly for you," Magnus said. "The task is difficult enough without interference from Rome."

Before you leave for your new assignment," Flaccus said, "I will inform you how you can communicate with us without arousing the suspicions of certain individuals. We are all being watched and monitored."

"Thank you," said Valerius. "I appreciate the offer. We should all meet again before I leave."

"I agree," Flaccus affirmed. "Again, we will support you in any way we can."

After that conversation, Valerius wandered around, greeting other senators, who politely congratulated him and inquired about the state of affairs in Germania. He chatted briefly with his friend Quintus Salvius, before moving on to the others gathered to the festivity. Valerius noted that some of the senators appeared wary of him. He could see it in their eyes and the way they regarded him as someone who should not be displeased. Then, it struck him like a lightning bolt. Their trepidation was due to the high regard Tiberius had for him, and the senators were collectively frightened of Tiberius and the quiet reign of terror unleashed by Sejanus. The emperor ruled with an iron hand and brooked no dissent. Senators who had opposed Tiberius's plans were no longer around. Valerius congratulated himself once again for pursuing a career on the northern frontier and not in Rome.

A young senator with a foppish look, including stylized curled hair and an immaculate toga of finely woven silk, appeared in front of him, slurring his words. "Maximus, I declare, you have awed the senate. Good job up there in Germania. My name is Marcus Lucianus. I come from a long line of senators in my family. What is your father's name? I do not recall it."

Valerius eyed the elitist, knowing full well that the man was aware of his family background. This snob was just trumpeting his aristocratic lineage in a poor attempt to put Valerius in his place. He knew the type. Their pedigree often made them believe the sun rose in the east out of their noble arse. But two could play this game. "My father is named Sentius. For years, he was a magistrate in Rome, but he and my mother have joined us in Germania. They absolutely love it there. By the way, have you ever had any foreign postings out in the provinces, perhaps during your military service?

The young senator frowned. "No, I have spent my entire career here in Rome."

Valerius patted the man on the shoulder in a condescending manner. "You know, you should get out and see the empire. It might help with your career in the senate. There are many peoples and places that are very different from Rome. Nice chatting with you. What did you say your name was again?"

"Marcus Lucianus."

"Well, it was nice meeting you, Marcus. I hope you heed my advice and travel to some of the provinces. It will open your eyes." With that, Valerius turned away and moved on.

After much feasting on delicacies, featuring fresh oysters and stuffed partridges served on silver trays, Valerius caught the eyes of Hereca and Marcellus. They moved toward the door, paid their respects to their host, and exited the dwelling. Finding their bodyguard escorts, they began making their way back to their apartment. After a respectable distance, Marcellus said, "I have only been in Rome a few times, and I'm not sure I will ever get used to it. I enjoyed myself and told some of my stories, you know what I mean. You've heard them before. This one senator's wife kept rubbing her ass against me. I tried moving away, and she moved with me. Said we should meet someplace private sometime. Maybe in my younger days, but now, I am a happily married man."

"No such thing in Rome," Valerius opined. "That goes for women too. Rome can be a bit of a cesspit, especially among the aristocracy. Perhaps you were encouraging those women with your legionary tales, seducing them."

Picking up on Valerius's implication, Hereca spoke. "I promise not to tell your wife, Brida, when we return. At least I think I won't."

"But I didn't do anything," Marcellus said in a plaintive tone.

"So you say," said Valerius, sounding skeptical. "I heard you embellishing your stories and making them laugh. Of all things, my former centurion seducing wives of senators."

Marcellus suddenly halted, causing Hereca and Valerius to stop. "Both of you cease this jibing. I know when you are attempting to put one over on me."

"Would we do that to you?" Hereca asked innocently.

"Yes, and I know when you do it. So stop it."

Valerius and Hereca threw mocking grins at Marcellus. The former centurion spluttered with laughter. "You really had me going there."

CHAPTER III

SEJANUS

Early the next day, a polite knock was heard on the door to their imperial quarters. A servant promptly attended to the call but returned looking pale as he ushered in Sejanus, who strode in boldly, carrying his helmet in the crook of his right arm. He was followed closely by two severe-faced Praetorians in spotless uniforms. Valerius, who had been sitting in the adjacent main living room, rose to greet his guest. He remembered the warning from his friend, Senator Quintus Salvius, about how dangerous Sejanus could be and that he should not underestimate his duplicity. *I wonder what he wants. I will try to be polite. No sense in irritating this extremely powerful man.*

"Sejanus, you grace us with your presence. What brings you about this day?"

Sejanus offered a disingenuous grin. "Oh, nothing much. Like everyone, I enjoyed your speech in the senate yesterday. You certainly have a daunting task ahead of you on the Danubius."

"Oh, I did not know you were there in the senate."

"I make it my business to observe events of importance in Rome." He looked around, and on noticing Hereca enter the room and several of the servants standing about, he added, "I wonder if I could have a few words with you in private?"

"Certainly. There is a meeting room off to our left. Follow me."

The two men entered an alcove. Once they were seated at a polished wooden table across from each other, Sejanus began. "I wish you well in your endeavors along the Danube. I hope you mirror the success that you worked so hard to achieve in Germania." He paused briefly, considering his next words. "You know, the two of us have a lot in common."

Valerius raised his eyebrows. "How so?"

"We are both former military officers of the legions and fought in the same campaign against the Germans so many years ago. But more importantly, the Emperor has great faith in both of us. You as a statesman, military governor, and diplomat for Rome, and me for my assistance in managing his affairs of everyday governance and protecting the realm. You know, as sure as the sun rises, there will be those who seek to depose Tiberius and become the next emperor."

Valerius remained noncommittal. "I am far from Rome and do not stay in touch with the political events. Is there some nefarious plot I should be aware of?"

"No, not at the moment, but we must always be vigilant." Sejanus fidgeted. "I guess what I am trying to say is this: What would happen to either of us if Tiberius should be ousted or die of natural consequences? He is getting quite old, you know. Have you given any thought to that?"

Valerius paused. He did not care for the tone of the question and needed to be obtuse. "I concentrate on the issues that directly confront me on a daily basis out on the German frontier, and soon the Danubius, and not on things that I cannot control in Rome. But as to your question, I would assume that the new emperor, whoever that might be, would probably select someone else to assume my role and perform my duties. Replace me with his own man. I have some understanding of how the system works. If that is to be, then I will return to being a trader and merchant."

Sejanus wore a sour expression. "I assume you've heard the rumor that Tiberius has selected his great-nephew Gaius, Germanicus's son, to succeed him. They call him by his childhood nickname, Caligula." He offered a scornful laugh. "He is only a boy and has no understanding of the intrigues and workings of the empire."

"Then so be it," replied Valerius. "It is, after all, Tiberius's choice."

Pretending to ponder Valerius's response, Sejanus spoke in a conciliatory tone. "I guess what I'm attempting to communicate to you is that men in our position should look out for each other as well as Rome. I would hate to see a civil war break out upon Tiberius's death. Some might choose to take advantage of a young, inexperienced boy thrust into the role of emperor."

Valerius contemplated his guest's words. "Again, Sejanus, I will be hundreds of miles away. I am far removed from the politics of Rome. You are much more familiar with the ebb and flow of Rome's affairs."

Sejanus continued to press on. "But what would you do if someone seized the throne against the wishes of the senate?"

"Then I would vote no," Valerius responded flatly.

Sejanus chafed. "Vote no. I don't understand. What is that supposed to mean?"

"Just what I said. I would vote no…along with the fourteen legions under my control stationed along the Rhenus and Danubius. I am a patriot and wish only what is best for Rome. Another civil war is the last thing we need."

Sejanus visibly paled. "I see. Thank you for taking the time to chat with me." He abruptly did an about-face and exited the room.

Valerius watched Sejanus's retreating form. What was he really saying? Was Sejanus seeking his endorsement to seize power upon Tiberius's death? Was his ambition so high that he aimed to be the next emperor? To Valerius, the answer was obvious: yes.

* * *

The next day, Valerius returned to his guest quarters after yet another exhausting morning of never-ending meetings concerning the state of affairs along the Danubius. He had attended the conferences alone, sparing Hereca and Marcellus from the drudgery. Frankly, he had had enough of these discussions and was eager to return to Germania and see his children. After that, he would begin his new quest along the Danubius.

Valerius changed out of his formal toga and into a more comfortable tunic. Upon emerging from his bedroom, one of the servants appeared. "Sir, there is a messenger for you at the door. He insists he must deliver the document directly to you. I tried to explain that I would hand the dispatch to you, but he would not be dissuaded. He said he had strict orders to deliver the parcel only to you."

Valerius sighed. "All right, so be it. Please send him in."

Moments later, a large, bulky figure—certainly not like any messenger he had ever seen—approached with a cylindrical case.

Tired from his morning of meetings, Valerius was not as attentive as he should have been. As the figure approached, he suddenly realized something was amiss. "You have documents for me? May I ask who they are from?"

Instead of stopping at a reasonable distance out of politeness and replying, the figure continued to advance. At the last moment,

Valerius noticed a shift in the courier's eyes and his right arm reaching behind his back. A frisson of dread tingled down his spine. Valerius instinctively extended his left arm and thrust it forward.

In a flash, the figure drew a long dagger from behind him, but Valerius countered the man's downward thrust with his left arm. Grabbing hold of the assassin's wrist, Valerius held on for dear life. He then used his right arm to pin the figure's left arm, forcing him backward. The two men grappled back and forth across the room with neither gaining the upper hand. Valerius shouted for help.

The attacker was as strong as an ox but so was Valerius. His sinewy arm muscles, used to draw his large war bow, which he practiced constantly with Marcellus, countered the bulky power of his assailant. Even so, Valerius could feel his strength waning against the much larger opponent. The two men shifted back and forth, grunting, each grappling for dominance. He stared at the cutthroat's face, noting a dispassionate expression. No doubt about it, this man was a hired assassin, a stone-cold killer. Gasping, Valerius exerted the last of his fading strength as the dagger slowly edged down toward his exposed throat.

Valerius briefly considered head-butting the man but discarded that notion. That action would bring his throat closer to the dagger. In desperation, he kicked his adversary's knee, hoping to topple him over, but the man, versed in street fighting, quickly shifted his legs away.

Hearing the commotion, Hereca hurried into the room and gaped at the sight of the two struggling figures. She found one of the servants cowering in the corner, paralyzed with fear. Scanning the room for a means to assist her husband, she found no weapons in sight. Then, to her right, she spied what she needed. Rushing to a pedestal, she grabbed a ceramic vase on display, a heavy piece with raised figures of Mars and Jupiter against a blue background. She swung it with all her might at the assailant's head, causing it to shatter against his skull.

The assassin collapsed and sprawled on the floor, his scalp bleeding profusely. A scarlet rivulet formed around his now motionless head, tracing its way across the tiled floor.

Uncertain of how badly the man was injured, Valerius quickly snatched the dagger from his hand. Bent over at the waist, huffing from his exertions, he looked at his wife with amazement. "Thank you. I was nearly at the end of my endurance."

Before he could continue, a group of Praetorians rushed through the door, led by one of the servants. The officer halted in front of Valerius, gauging the scene before him. He glanced at the insensible figure on the floor and the thin, pointed dagger in Valerius's hand. "Any idea who this miscreant is?" The officer asked gruffly.

"No idea. Never seen him before. He came here under the guise of delivering a message to me. I caught on to his deception at the last moment and thwarted his scheme. My wife hit him over the head with a rather expensive-looking decorative urn."

The officer nodded. "Very well. He appears to be breathing still. We will take him away for questioning and discover who was behind this." He gestured at two of his accompanying guards. "Take this piece of shit to the dungeon. I will deal with him there."

He then turned to Valerius. "I will report this to the Praetorian prefect, Sejanus. This has never happened in the imperial apartments. Don't worry, we will uncover who was responsible for this murderous act."

Hearing the tumult, Marcellus entered from his adjoining apartment. Valerius threw him a warning glance not to speak. Once the Praetorians left the room, he motioned Hereca and Marcellus to follow him into a small vestibule, out of the servants' hearing range.

Assured they were alone, he spoke in a sotto voice. "That was a planned assassination, pure and simple. I do not believe it was a coincidence that I had a rather terse conversation with Sejanus yesterday. I briefly mentioned to you what we had discussed. As I noted, he intimated that the two of us should stick together in the event of Tiberius's death to protect Rome. He stated that it was rumored that Gaius, also known as Caligula, was the heir apparent. Furthermore, he asserted that Gaius was only a boy who knew nothing of the workings of the empire. Sejanus alleged that others might attempt to seize the throne from Gaius, leading to civil war. I don't believe I shared my response with you."

"And how did you answer?" Marcellus asked.

"I played it coyly, stating that I would serve the wishes of the senate and support whoever they confirmed as heir. I said that was how I would cast my vote. Sejanus sneered at my statement, saying that my individual vote would mean nothing. I somewhat agreed with him but then stated that my vote would be supported by fourteen standing legions and could not be ignored."

Marcellus laughed deeply. "Good retort. You've come a long way from that gangly tribune of so many years ago. You know, this attempted murder makes sense. Sejanus cannot have you arrested on some contrived charge. You're too powerful for that, and Tiberius holds you in high esteem. The only avenue available to him was to have you assassinated."

"We need to leave Rome," Hereca stated. "We are far safer in Germania, although not completely out of his reach. How much longer do we need to stay here?"

"I will attempt to finalize discussions with Tiberius tomorrow," Valerius said. "I'm anxious to leave, and it serves no purpose to linger here."

* * *

The next morning, Valerius appeared before Tiberius as scheduled. It was a private meeting in a small room with just the emperor's inner circle—General Tuscus, Senator Flaccus, and Sejanus. Although Valerius reached before the appointed time, he was the last to arrive.

Tiberius greeted Valerius. "I heard about yesterday's incident. Sejanus briefed me about it. I am glad to see you are all right. What happened?"

"A man posing as a messenger claimed he had a dispatch that he would only deliver to me. At the last moment, I recognized something was amiss and thwarted his attempt to skewer me. While I was grappling with him, Hereca bashed him in the head with a rather expensive-looking vase and flattened the man. The guards then hauled him away."

Tiberius chortled. "Your wife is an amazing woman." He then turned to Sejanus and gave him a laconic glance. "How could this happen in the imperial apartments? Is no place in Rome safe from evildoers? What did the rogue reveal to us?"

"Unfortunately, sire, the man died under questioning before we could discover who was responsible."

Valerius seethed. *In the pig's arse. Of course the man died, probably minutes after the Praetorians hauled him away.* He had to give Sejanus credit. The man was unflappable and a good liar.

Tiberius frowned. "That's unfortunate. Oh well, let's get on with the business of the day. To recapitulate, Valerius, you, as the procurator of the provinces on the Danubius, have free reign to encourage peaceful trade with the barbarian tribes on the opposite side of the river. As for the how's, who's, and when's, I will leave that to your discretion. The senate and the people of Rome agree that the empire should not expand beyond the borders of the Rhenus and the Danubius. Instead, we will cultivate relationships with the barbarian tribes. Under no circumstances will Roman legions cross the rivers for military conquest. However, if you deem a retaliatory strike against one of the tribes is warranted, you have the power to carry out such an operation. Are my directives clear?"

"Yes, sire, they are. Thank you for granting me the latitude to deal with these people. I will keep you apprised of our progress as we begin our undertakings. I may seek your advice if we encounter any stiff opposition."

"Very well, Valerius. You have my confidence. Just so you know, Rome will be watching you from afar. I intend for the updates on your progress to be presented in the senate. Now, I believe we are just about finished here. I tire of Rome and the heat. I desire to retreat to my residence on Capri before the weather gets too hot. You are dismissed."

"Sire, am I free to return to Germania?" Valerius asked.

"Not just yet; perhaps another day or so. I may have a few more matters to discuss with you."

* * *

Later that day, Hereca was warmly greeted by Claudia in her home, not far from the palace. The two embraced like long-lost friends.

Claudia led the way to their atrium, featuring a rectangular pool with flowering plants and shrubs. It was a grand home, equal to, if not more spectacular than, Senator Flaccus's dwelling. Water tinkled from the sculpted mouth of a large fish, creating a peaceful setting. As they sat at a small table by the reflecting pool, two servants appeared, bringing a small chalice of wine and a plate of various fruits and cheeses.

"You have a beautiful home. It's pleasing to the eye and exudes comfort," Hereca said. "Tiberius's palace, on the other hand, is a bit ostentatious if you know what I mean."

"I know exactly what you mean. I consider myself so fortunate to live in such luxury. Tell me about your home in Germania."

"My husband designed our home to mirror his boyhood residence in Rome. It shares some features of your home, like the open courtyard and garden pool, but it is not nearly as elaborate. Germania is much colder than Rome. I hope to return to our home when we finish his term as governor. I miss it a great deal," she said wistfully. "For now, we live in the praetorium of the fortress. We've decorated it nicely, but it's not the same."

Claudia sipped at her wine. "I can imagine. You are surrounded by thousands of legionaries."

They chatted for several hours on many topics—the German people, the various clans, imperial politics, and other regions in the empire. Then, Hereca was introduced to Claudia's three children. At no point did Claudia attempt to lord over or belittle Hereca's humble background. For Hereca, it felt as if they had been lifelong friends. The conversation flowed effortlessly as if they had known each other for years.

"Before you go, I want to offer my support to you and your husband. Quintus discusses everything with me and often seeks my advice, so I understand the political situation you are facing. My husband and I must tread carefully as well, as there is danger lurking here in Rome and on the frontier. Please do not hesitate to call me for help. Count me as a friend. I do wish you lived in Rome," she said wistfully. "You are such a strong and resilient woman, and I wish I could see you more often. But such are our circumstances. Again, please do not hesitate to call on me for help. We are allies against a common foe."

"Thank you, Claudia. I may indeed take you up on that offer, for who knows what fate awaits us. I will keep in touch with you. Perhaps, someday, you could visit us in Germania."

"My husband and I would love that."

CHAPTER IV
SETBACK

As twilight descended upon the city, Tiberius and Sejanus sat at a small table in the emperor's palace. Sejanus was almost done summarizing the important dispatches received over the last few days. "On a positive note, the grain ships are arriving every day. Our warehouses are almost full of the needed grain. It was a bountiful harvest in Egypt this year."

"Excellent," Tiberius exclaimed. "My predecessor, Augustus had to face two grain shortages. That is not a problem we want to deal with on top of all of the others that we face. What other dispatches do you have?"

Tiberius glanced at the last of the documents. "This report indicates continued unrest in Judaea. Despite being such a small province, these people continue to challenge Roman authority, with so-called prophets and messiahs urging rebellion against Rome."

Tiberius waved his hand dismissively. "I am more concerned with events on the Rhenus and the Danubius frontiers. That is where the danger lies. Judea is insignificant in the grand scheme of things." He heaved a sigh. "Send a strongly worded dispatch to Governor Pilatus granting him free reign to execute any troublemakers or dissidents." Tiberius, weariness etched on his face, looked at Sejanus. "Is there anything else? I am fatigued and wish to rest."

"As a matter of fact, I do have one other item requiring your attention. You know my chief responsibility is to ensure your survival and root out any conspiracies against your reign. As you are aware, I have managed to uncover several plots and have had the conspirators executed."

"Is there another conspiracy I should know about?"

"No, sire. Not at this time. All is quiet at the present, but I would like to propose a precautionary measure, if I may." Sejanus hurried on before Tiberius could interrupt. "I know you have great faith in Maximus, and he has served you well in Germania. Of this, there is no doubt. My concern is that he has been given even greater power with his assumption of duties on the Danubius. Between the Rhenus and Danubius theatres, he will have fourteen legions under his command. That is half of Rome's twenty-eight standing legions. I would like to propose appointing a senior commander to oversee the Danubius legions. He will report to Governor Maximus but owes his loyalty to us. This is only a defensive measure but one I believe to be prudent."

Tiberius narrowed his gaze. "And what do you think of Maximus? Is he a threat?"

Sejanus knew he was being challenged since Tiberius did not appreciate his decision being second-guessed. "I have no opinion, sire, only that we are concentrating too much power on one man. Remember the recent actions of General Mellitus, who used the legions of the Rhenus to seize control of the empire? Who would have thought that? I had always viewed him favorably, and look what he attempted to do. Some might persuade Maximus to grab power. I do not believe Maximus to be disloyal, but some may seek his backing to overthrow your reign. Again, this is only a precaution and will not undermine his authority along the Danubius."

Tiberius scowled. "If I recall correctly, you had suggested appointing Mellitus as procurator in Germania."

"Yes, sire, and I was mistaken. I freely admit it. But that just proves my point. Can we trust anyone when the stakes are so high? We need to have checks and balances in place."

Tiberius paused in thought. "Very well. So be it. I assume you have a name for me to assume this command."

Sejanus offered a triumphant grin. "I do, sire. His name is General Didus Voculus. He has just returned from a command in Hispania and is awaiting a new assignment. Better yet, he previously served on the Danubius as commander of the Seventh Legion, so he is not only an experienced commander but knows the territory as well. He comes from a good family and is an excellent legate—a perfect fit for this posting. In fact, Rome needs more men like him. I will meet with him later this evening and arrange a brief audience with you tomorrow."

* * *

That evening, Sejanus welcomed General Voculus into his private chambers. Voculus entered attired in his military uniform, carrying his helmet in the crook of his right arm. Sejanus grinned. "Welcome, Didus, or should I say General Voculus, commander of the forces of the Danubius."

"So your meeting went well with Tiberius?" Voculus inquired eagerly.

"Yes, it did. Any proposal I make regarding the emperor's security and the safety of the realm is usually accepted with complete faith.

The emperor relies heavily upon me in this respect. All I had to do was hint that one man controlling half of the standing legions of the empire posed an extremely dangerous precedent, no matter how trustworthy the individual."

"That is good news," Voculus replied. "I am keen to begin this assignment."

Sejanus proffered a sly smile. "Maximus is a problem. He and I do not get along and have different views of the empire and how it should be governed in the future. I cannot dispose of him, unlike many others who have displeased me, since Tiberius thinks highly of him. Maximus must not be allowed to succeed in his new posting as governor of the Danubian provinces and territory. You must impede him as much as possible without it being traced back to you and, ultimately, me."

Voculus grinned wolfishly. "Perhaps the newly appointed governor will meet an unfortunate accident."

"Even better, but you must be extremely careful how you tread. He will be well guarded, and above all, nothing must be redirected back to you. Beware of his wife and his constant companion, Marcellus, his former centurion. They are a formidable trio. Tiberius has accepted my recommendation to have you as the commanding legate. Anything you do will reflect upon me.

"I hear your words of caution loud and clear. I will take care of this Maximus. Consider it done."

Sejanus glowered and spoke in a laconic tone. "Voculus, perhaps you were not listening well. Maximus is extremely resourceful and cunning. He has bested several ambitious people in the past. He was no more than a merchant and trader yet managed to insert himself and his colleagues into turbulent situations that would have defeated most men. He is not to be underestimated—do so at your peril. You must be extremely wary; I cannot stress this enough."

Chastised, Voculus bowed his head. "Understood, sir. When do I begin my quest?"

"I will arrange for you to meet Tiberius tomorrow and ensure you meet Maximus before he departs back to Germania. The sooner you get to the Danubius region, the better. You will be in place long before Maximus arrives. I sense he will spend some time in Germania getting his affairs in order before beginning his new assignment along the Danubius."

* * *

The next day, Valerius was summoned to the imperial palace on the Palatine for yet another meeting. While being escorted by several Praetorians to one of the many meeting rooms, he hoped this meeting would be the last one. Upon entering, Valerius observed Tiberius sitting in a curule chair at an ornate table, flanked by Sejanus and a stranger—a military man attired in the uniform of a legate. His silver breastplate, engraved with various martial gods, gleamed. Of medium height and around Valerius's age, the veteran's face had that weathered look of the legions.

"Welcome back to the palace," Tiberius greeted. "I know you must be tired of these endless meetings and conferences. I believe this will be the final order of business to be concluded, and then, you can be on your way. Have you decided when you will begin your governance of the Danubian provinces? I need you there as soon as possible. I am eager to pacify the Danubian tribes."

"Sir, my first order of business will be to ensure stability in the Germanic territories and a sound chain of command before I depart. To this end, I intend to appoint General Labenius as acting procurator in my absence. I know you share my confidence in him. Although I will be far removed, geographically speaking, I intend to have my finger on the pulse of Germania. The last thing we need is an uprising while I am away. Thus, while I'm eager to begin my new responsibilities, I will proceed with caution. Once I get the lay of the land along the Danubius and meet with the legates and governors, I will develop appropriate strategies to bring peace and prosperity to that territory."

Tiberius frowned. "Understood, but again, I cannot stress enough that I am anxious for you to take command of the Danubian territory." Gesturing at the legate, Tiberius continued, "I want you to meet Didus Voculus, who will assist you in your endeavors. At the recommendation of Prefect Sejanus, I am appointing Voculus as the commanding general of the Danubian legions. He will report directly to you. He previously served as legate of the Seventh Legion on the Danubius, so he knows the region and is familiar with the hostile tribes. More recently, he commanded two legions in Hispania. He has the experience and knowledge to assist you in your governance.

Valerius steadied himself, masking his emotions behind a benign smile. "A pleasure to meet you, General Voculus. Have our paths ever crossed before in the legions? Perhaps you were stationed in Germania at one time?"

Voculus smiled thinly. "Sadly, no, I was not, but I have heard much of your exploits. It will be a pleasure to serve under you. I know the barbarian tribes of the region will pose a challenge to you and Rome, and I look forward to assisting you in your governance."

Valerius shifted his gaze to the left, noting the smug grin plastered on Sejanus's face. He then returned his focus to Voculus. The man looked professional and said all the right things. No doubt he had an impeccable record beyond reproach. However, Valerius's intuition told him that this legate was not here to *help* him. So even before he assumed the mantle of responsibility, he had a formidable obstacle to overcome.

"General Voculus, I can certainly use your knowledge and experience in dealing with the hostile tribes," Valerius responded.

Tiberius beamed. "Good! I hope the two of you can get the Danubian tribes under Roman control. General Voculus is leaving soon for the regional headquarters at Vindobona in Pannonia. He should be there in three or four weeks. Governor Maximus, I need you to get back to Germania as soon as possible and then proceed to your new posting."

"I plan to depart immediately," Voculus said. "Since I will be arriving before you on the Danubius, do you have any orders for me?"

Valerius paused in thought. "As a matter of fact, I do. I want you to evaluate the readiness of the legions and naval fleet stationed there as well as any imminent threats we might be facing. I am keen to understand the competency of friendly forces and what we are up against. I look forward to meeting with you when I arrive in Pannonia."

The discussions continued for nearly half an hour. All the while, Valerius maintained a veneer of politeness, but underneath it all, his thoughts were troubled. He should have anticipated Voculus's appointment. This man would report every setback and misadventure back to Rome, casting Valerius in a bad light. He resolved to consult with Hereca and Marcellus about this development when he returned to their quarters.

Valerius made the short walk from the palace to his apartment, where he found Hereca and Marcellus waiting for him. Nodding to the two servants, Valerius said, "You are excused. Come back in about an hour." After they departed, Valerius sat down, facing his wife and Marcellus. "It was not a good meeting. Tiberius has appointed a military commander for the legions of the Danubius."

Marcellus darkened in anger. "That imperious shit! How could he do this? What is the rogue's name?"

Valerius gestured placatingly with his arms. "Marcellus, we should have foreseen this. Shame on us. Actually, I don't blame Tiberius. I would have done the same thing in his place. He needs some form of checks and balances, given the authority I will have over two theaters of operation. That is just too much power to delegate to one individual. But to answer your question, the man's name is Didus Voculus. He is a former legate of the Seventh on the Danubius and was recently responsible for the two legions in Hispania. The real problem is that our friend Sejanus was responsible for the selection. I have no doubt that this man will be both a spy and an obstructionist to our mission. Behind the scenes, he will be working against us."

Hereca scowled. "You are correct, my husband. We should have expected this appointment. Even as much as Tiberius trusts you, as an emperor, he cannot afford to trust anybody completely. But the fact that this man was hand-picked by Sejanus is more concerning. However, we have dealt with scoundrels of worse ilk than this Voculus and thwarted their intentions."

A broad grin creased Marcellus's face. "You are spot on, Hereca. We have overcome other malefactors in our times together." Marcellus looked around to ensure that no servants had lingered. Seeing no one, he continued. "If this Voculus becomes too much of an obstacle, perhaps he will have an unfortunate accident. I hear the Danubius can be a dangerous place."

Valerius frowned. "Let's not get ahead of ourselves. Now, I believe we have no other business to transact in Rome, and I, for one, have no desire to remain any longer than necessary. Tiberius stated that this was the last of our meetings, so we need to procure our transport back to Germania. I do have one more meeting scheduled with Senator Flaccus and two of his senatorial colleagues. But I will take care of that tonight, and we can depart tomorrow.

That evening, Valerius visited Senator Flaccus's home once again. He had been looking forward to the meeting. During his short stay in Rome, he had garnered the support of two strong allies, Senators Flaccus and Salvius. Upon his arrival, he found Senators Cornelius Egnatius and Magnus Decebalus sitting in a small library along with Flaccus. Flaccus moved to the doorway and looked around to ensure they were alone. Then, he firmly shut the door. "Welcome, once again," Flaccus greeted.

"Just so you know, I have my final marching orders, and I will be departing imminently, but not before I got a good kick in the arse from Tiberius. He has appointed General Voculus as the commander of my Danubian legions. He reports to me, but I believe he has a different master."

"I wonder who could have suggested this appointment," said Cornelius derisively. "I have vaguely heard of this Voculus. I did not know he was in league with Sejanus.

"Once again, our omnipotent Prefect Sejanus has his hands in this," Flaccus said.

"I told Marcellus and Hereca that I should have anticipated this," Valerius said. "It appears we have been outmaneuvered again. But it is just something I will have to deal with in my new posting."

"I have already taken the liberty of informing Cornelius and Magnus about the attempted assassination in your quarters," Flaccus said. "We all agree that Sejanus was behind it. He is brash. Someday, this will be his undoing. The man is a rogue."

"A powerful rogue," Magnus ventured.

"Yes, and the purpose behind this meeting," Flaccus began. "As you know, any dispatches you send by Rome's courier service will be intercepted and vetted by Sejanus. He scrutinizes everything, allowing Tiberius to see only what he wants him to see. So, if you have politically sensitive correspondence—information you wouldn't want Sejanus to get his hands on—you might want to employ a private courier. Sejanus has his thumb on the military couriers. You could use your mercantile contacts to get messages to us. It will be much slower, but only our eyes will get to see it. Before you leave, I will give you the street addresses in Rome to be used for each of us. I have a contact within the palace who will ensure any messages delivered to me reach Tiberius."

Senator Magnus clasped Valerius's shoulder. "I'm sure you know this, but you must be very careful and discrete. I have witnessed firsthand what Sejanus is capable of doing, and he has a long reach to all corners of the empire. Members of the senate, some of them close friends, were tried and convicted of conspiracy on trumped-up charges for merely opposing Sejanus or being critical of him. The man is vile. There is no doubt he has designs on the realm. At some point, he will attempt to usurp power."

"Yes, and for the time being, we must keep our opposition to him quiet, lest we end up like the others," Flaccus added.

"All my life, I have attempted to avoid Rome and the political machinations of the empire, but as you can see, I have not been successful," Valerius responded ruefully. "I will do what I can to establish terms with the tribes of the Danubius while avoiding Sejanus and his plots. I informed Sejanus rather bluntly that I would back the wishes of the senate for a peaceful transfer of power upon Tiberius's death and that I would support that wish through the fourteen legions under my jurisdiction. Sejanus knows that I am not his ally and that he cannot seize power as long as I am in command of Germania and the Danubian territory."

Flaccus chuckled lightly. "I wish I could have witnessed that conversation. It surely knocked him down a peg or two."

"I do not envy you," Cornelius said. "You are in a precarious situation. Please know that the three of us are your allies, and we will support you. Since Flaccus is on the advisory council, he can be particularly useful to you."

"May Jupiter and Mars watch over you," Flaccus wished as Valerius departed Flaccus's residence a short while later.

A sinister figure, clad in a dirty tunic and in desperate need of a good barber, stood in the shadows of a nearby tavern. Little did Valerius know that he and the others who had gathered that night were being watched. The report would be on Sejanus's desk by early the next morning.

CHAPTER V
BACK HOME

**Roman Territory of Germania Inferior
Fortress of Oppidum Ubiorum (Present Day Cologne)
Weeks Later**

Valerius huddled in his headquarters with Marcellus, Hereca, and General Labenius, his military commander of the eight legions stationed along the Rhenus. He and Labenius had been boyhood friends, and together, they had attended their military training in preparation for being commissioned as tribunes in the Roman Imperial Army. That seemed like a lifetime ago—over twenty years—and much had transpired since then. Labenius, along with Valerius, Marcellus, and Hereca, had been instrumental in foiling a plot by a mutinous legate named Mellitus, who had previously commanded the eight legions of the Rhenus as the military governor, to overthrow Tiberius.

Valerius had just returned the day before after a lengthy sea voyage of over six weeks. It had taken longer than expected because of a lack of prevailing winds. He desperately wanted some time with his wife, children, and parents, but duty called. He needed to begin the process of transitioning from being the procurator in Germania to overseeing his new territory along the Danubius. Perhaps once he got the whirlwind process started, he could find time to reunite with his family. *Probably not,* he thought.

Bright sunlight beamed through the spacious windows in his richly appointed office, adorned with tapestries and statuaries along the walls and beautifully woven rugs from the east on the polished wooden floors. Being a simple man with simple tastes, Valerius had not demanded the luxuries and extravagances for his own pleasure but heeded Hereca's suggestion to transform the austere offices into a space embodying beauty and form. The purpose was to impress the German leaders and show them the luxury that Romans enjoyed, and they succeeded.

Valerius glanced across the table at Labenius, noting that his friend had a few more gray hairs and deeper lines on his face. Smirking silently, he thought, *if he looks haggard now, wait till I tell him the news.* "Labenius," Valerius began, "thank you for holding the fort while we were away. I know I can always count on you. As you have heard through my dispatches, I am to take over the Danubius territories as well."

Labenius proffered a tremulous smile. "Yes, we received your post informing us of the change. I have not communicated this to the officers and legions under my command. I wanted to wait for you to return."

"No matter," Valerius said. "Word is bound to leak out soon. We have much to do, but first let me get to the heart of the matter. General Labenius, I am appointing you as acting procurator while I am away. You functioned as the governor while I was in Rome, so you are a natural choice. In fact, you are not only my choice but Tiberius's as well. He suggested you take over command while I am gone. Like me, he has a high opinion of you, so congratulations on your appointment."

Marcellus rose and clapped Labenius on the back. "You're the man! You will do well."

Hereca joined in, giving him a warm hug. "We have faith and trust in you."

Labenius beamed. "Thank you. I accept the position."

"This is what I envision happening," Valerius said, laying out the plan. "Marcellus, Hereca, and I will head to the Danubian territories. We will not leave until I'm assured everything here is stable and secure. In this respect, we need to call a meeting with all the legates and senior staff to make this transition appear seamless. I don't want any of these Germans thinking that now would be a good time to take advantage of us. You know how disingenuous and truculent some of them can be. Tiberius wants us there now, but the German lands must be at peace before we depart."

Labenius nodded. "I understand. I will begin to make arrangements for the grand meeting right away."

"Good," Valerius said. "Now, another thing. As I'm sure you are aware, Tiberius has his spies here in Germania, courtesy of Sejanus. You must ensure that the legions continue to venerate Tiberius and swear allegiance to him."

"I wholeheartedly agree," he affirmed. "We had ceremonies and parades dedicated to the emperor while you were away." Labenius suddenly paused and fidgeted in his chair uncomfortably. "There is one thing. I hope you don't mind me bringing it up."

"Please, be candid. We're all friends here."

"I fear we may have difficulty placating these Germans without your wife around to help mollify them when they get their tunics in a knot. She understands them so well."

Marcellus laughed. "Now we know who the real procurator is in Germania."

Hereca grinned at Labenius. "Why, thank you, General, for the promotion. I wanted to tell Tiberius that he could appoint me to govern the Danubian territories. I would show them how to handle these barbarians. Are you listening to this, my husband?"

"That's not what I meant," interjected Labenius sheepishly.

Valerius laughed. "I understand. Hereca, you know you are indispensable in dealing with these Germans, unlike some former centurions I know." He shot Marcellus a wry grin.

"I resent that," Marcellus retorted. "After all the loyalty I've shown you over the years."

"If you want, you can stay here with me, Marcellus," Labenius quipped.

"So there. See how you get along without me by your side," Marcellus jabbed at Valerius.

"Perhaps we have gotten off course here," Valerius said. "As to your original question, Labenius, yes, Hereca has been instrumental in keeping the Germans on their side of the Rhenus and soothing their injured feelings. She will be coming with me to negotiate with the hostile peoples along the Danubius. However, if you believe things are beginning to spiral out of control and you need Hereca, we can arrange for her to return to Germania. That goes for Marcellus and me as well. Above all, we must ensure the security of the lands along the Rhenus. If we make progress in the Danubian lands, it cannot be at the expense of the German territory. The worst-case scenario would be losing control of both territories. There is a risk here, so let's keep a wary eye on both fronts."

* * *

Eight days later, the legates of the eight legions stationed along the Rhenus assembled around a long rectangular table in the headquarters. Valerius had tactfully placed both himself and Labenius at the head of the table, reflecting a shared responsibility. When the servants cleared the last of the mid-day meal's dishes from the table, Valerius caught the eye of the centurion in charge of the guard detail, who nodded affirmatively. After ensuring only the legates were present in the room, the centurion closed the door behind him.

Valerius eyed each of the legates, all capable men, loyal to both him and the emperor. He began. "Gentlemen, thank you all for gathering here on such short notice. I know how busy you are commanding your legions and ensuring the river border is secure. However, some extraordinary developments have occurred requiring immediate discussion. No doubt you are aware I was recently summoned to Rome to meet with Tiberius. He is extremely pleased with the state of affairs in Germania. Thank you all for that. He even paraded me before the senate. Commerce is flowing and peace is at hand. As a result of our success, he wants me to see if we can achieve the same results along the Danubius with the barbarian tribes located there."

The room stirred with muted gasps as the legates processed the pronouncement. Before anyone could speak, Valerius stood, holding his hands down. "Please, before you ask any questions, let me apprise you of how this will impact you. First, General Labenius will become acting governor, although he will still report to me. You already receive your orders from him, so this will not pose a big change."

Valerius paused briefly, surveying the room. "I would like to highlight a few key points. "First, we must present a business-as-usual setting to the Germans. Our conduct should reflect that nothing has changed. Second, it is likely our resolve will be tested by this shift.

If that is to be, any hostile incursions into Roman territory should be dealt with maximum force. We will show no weakness and will not tolerate any hostilities in our provinces. And third, in the event matters escalate to a crisis stage, I will return to Germania at once. Now, any questions?

The youngest of the legates, General Florus, commander of the Thirteenth Legion on the southernmost fortress along the Rhenus, Argentorate, stood up to speak.

Valerius smiled at him. Only four years ago, the man had been a green-as-can-be tribune. He had surprised everyone, and perhaps himself, with his innovative thinking and determination to help save Rome from a German rebellion as well as a Roman coup to overthrow the government. Tiberius had personally promoted him to legate because of his decisive actions.

"Governor, I have worked with you for several years now and have been amazed at how tactfully you and your wife have managed these Germans, who can be a prickly bunch. I have great faith and admiration for General Labenius. He is my commanding officer and an outstanding leader. Please forgive my candor, but without the presence of your wife, Hereca, and you, I fear we may be significantly weakened, and some Germans may attempt to take advantage."

Some of the legates gasped at the boldness of Florus's remarks. Valerius anticipated that this subject might come up. He needed to respond and convey confidence in General Labenius. "I noted that you put Hereca's name first, so what you really mean, General Florus, is that Hereca's absence will be a true loss, and in truth, I am the man who is tasked with accompanying her to bargain with the German tribes. General Labenius made similar comments when I met with him, so it appears to be a popular, if not unanimous, sentiment."

The room shook with laughter. Valerius had turned the situation around with some not-so-subtle self-deprecating humor.

Florus flushed in embarrassment. "Putting Hereca's name first was unintentional, sir, and conveyed no hidden connotation. My brashness only extends so far. Perhaps I did speak too bluntly."

More laughter followed. Valerius raised his hands to silence the room. "Your question is valid. In fact, I anticipated someone would ask it, although in a more obtuse manner. I understand that the Germans have great trust in both Hereca and *me*. Hereca is, in no small part, responsible for our success. As I stated earlier, if our absence creates too much turmoil, we will return to Germania. But, saying all that, I have faith in General Labenius. I have high expectations for him to succeed."

Suddenly, General Pulchrus, commander of the Fifth Legion at Vetera with years of experience in Germania and the Eastern Empire, stood. A hulking figure, he towered over most legionaries. "The Germans will no doubt note your absence, and word will spread quickly. What are we to tell the German leaders when they inquire about you?"

"Another good question. The answer is simple; we tell them the truth: I am on a temporary assignment securing peace in the Danubian territories. Our message to the Germans should be clear that we have been dispatched to promote commerce with the tribes along the Danubius. The Germans will react strongly if the word gets out that we are attempting to subjugate the peoples along the Danubius. Be clear in your communications with the Germans."

General Strabinius, commander of the Twelfth Legion at Moguntiacum, rose. "Sir, like the others, I have faith in General Labenius. He is a good leader and tactician, but still, we will miss your leadership.

On behalf of all of us, we wish you well. May Jupiter and Mars guide your hand."

"Thank you, General. It has been a privilege serving with all of you. I could not ask for a better group of officers to govern the German territories. I hope to return here as soon as possible."

"When do you plan to leave here, and are you going to detach a vexillation of any of our forces?" Labenius asked.

"I want to spend some time here with my family and ensure all is well before I depart. I would say three weeks. As for the detachment of forces, as much as I would like to take some of my own troops, I will not. It would not be fair to you. I will detach a small security force to accompany me, but that is all."

CHAPTER VI
CHATTI TERRITORY

Valerius and Hereca lounged on the rectangular quilt, facing their guests, Dagobert and Ada, members of the Chatti tribe. At Hereca's suggestion, the pair periodically socialized with German couples on the opposite side of the river to solidify their relationships with their German trading partners. The Germans they mingled with could not be characterized as friends. There was a collegial tone to their conversations, yet a certain wariness pervaded both Germans and Romans due to years of hostility and suspicion. Valerius was reluctant at first to hold these gatherings, but much to his amazement, these social get-togethers proved effective, establishing trust and goodwill. Hereca had been right once again.

The two couples were having a picnic lunch on the banks of a small feeder stream that flowed into the Rhenus five hundred paces away. Earlier that morning, a small naval craft with several sailors and bodyguards had transported Valerius and his family there. The boat and crew were moored by the riverbank, giving them some privacy with their clients. Valerius could hear the excited chatter of his four children, Aulus, Julianna, Calvus, and Paulina, mingling with the laughter of the German children, Landric, Odovacar, and Gerhild. Valerius's oldest, Aulus, now sixteen, was about the same age as Landric. He could see the seven children frolicking on the banks of the small creek.

Valerius fervently hoped that the futures of these children would be better than what he and Dagobert had experienced as young men. The battles between Rome and the German tribes had been epic, beginning over thirty years ago. The two couples were chatting, about nothing in particular, in German, for the Chatti couple spoke only basic Latin. Dagobert, a handsome chieftain of the Chatti, looked up from the rim of his glass of wine. "You know, Valerius, the Romans really know how to produce wine. There are so many varieties and flavors. It's hard to pick a favorite."

"Funny you should say that," Valerius replied. "Our friends Julia and Lucius, who reside in Gaul, are exporters of wine. As much as I hate to admit this, I believe the wines from Gallia are equal to or surpass the wines from Italia. I'll have to bring some of their vintage next time."

Dagobert gave him a confounded look. "You mean there are better wines than this?"

Hereca laughed gaily. "Some would say yes."

Ada, a beautiful woman with long, braided hair, almost as tall as her husband, frowned. "Dagobert, enough with the wine. I am beginning to believe that you love wine more than me."

Dagobert feigned indignation. "Never, my love. You know that could never be the case. Besides, you enjoy the wine as much as I do."

Ada stroked her long braids in contemplation. "That I do, but I am not obsessed with it."

"Perhaps you are correct, Ada," Dagobert replied. "But the trade with the Romans has made the supply of wine plentiful. Blame Valerius and Hereca. They are the ones bringing it to our shores."

"No one is bending your arm, forcing you to drink the product of the grape," Hereca quipped.

Dagobert snorted. "I think it's time we change the subject. Tell me again about the city of Rome. I hear you just returned from there a short while ago."

"Yes, we did," Valerius replied, "and we are glad to be back here. Rome is the center of the empire, with many temples and government buildings. They are magnificent structures, built of polished stone, some of them the size of a small Chatti village. The rich elite have houses with gardens in the center and fountains with running water. The city's water supply comes from large bridge-like structures called aqueducts that transport the water from the mountains many miles away. There's a track where chariots race called the Circus Maximus, capable of seating as many people as that live in a hundred Chatti villages. There are public baths built of stone where people can bathe and clean themselves."

Ada gasped. "Hereca, your husband is a jester. Surely this is not possible."

Hereca laughed lightly. "But it is. I did not believe the descriptions of Rome until I saw it myself. Listen, Ada, for all her magnificence, Rome has her flaws. There are many poor people crammed into a small space, the streets are filthy with waste, and it's unsafe to walk the streets at night. The air is foul from cooking fires, not fresh and clean like out here in Germania. That's why we choose to live here."

"And what do the women wear?" Ada inquired.

The rich women wear long gowns of finely woven cloth in many colors called stolas. Many women wear simple tunics, and in cold weather, they wrap long cloaks around them."

Ada beamed at her husband. "I would like to visit this place someday."

"Don't get any ideas," replied Dagobert. "We have everything we need right here."

"I am definitely not getting in the middle of this," Hereca said. "But, Dagobert, let me just say this, I believe you would enjoy a visit, especially the chariot races. And, Ada, you would look stunning in a stola. I believe a darker color to contrast with your pale skin and flaxen hair would be best. The Roman women would be envious of your beauty."

"Perhaps someday," Ada said wistfully."

"And what is this Tiberius like?" Dagobert asked. "That is the name of the emperor, correct? Is he a mighty warrior?"

"Tiberius is the stepson of the previous emperor, the great Augustus," Valerius replied. "He is quite old now. He was a competent general when he commanded the legions. He campaigned here in Germania and along the Danubius many years ago."

"Now, let's talk some business," Dagobert said. "Word is that you will shortly be traveling to the territory of the Danubius. Is this not true?"

"Rumor spreads quickly," Valerius replied. "The answer is yes, Dagobert. My wife and I will be traveling along with a few others to those lands. The Emperor has commanded that I assist Rome in bringing peace and prosperity to the tribes along the Danubius. They continue to raid the Roman provinces on the other side of the river."

"And who will be in charge while you are away?"

"General Labenius, who you know, will be the temporary governor. If the need arises, Hereca and I will return to Germania. We will be journeying to a fortress named Vindobona, our designated headquarters in a province called Pannonia."

Valerius studied Dagobert. He and his wife were sociable, and he was enjoying his time with them, but he remained guarded in his dealings with them. Dagobert, being around the same age as him, was likely a young warrior who participated in the massacre of three Roman legions in the Teutoburg forest nearly twenty years ago. Valerius briefly wondered if the two men had been near while fighting on opposing sides. He involuntarily shuddered at the memory. The German uprising was mostly the Cherusci, led by Arminius, but other tribes were involved, including the Chatti. So, beneath Dagobert's pleasant exterior was the soul of a German warrior.

Dagobert nodded sagely. "I know this Labenius. He is a good choice." He then raised his goblet. "Safe travels to you and your wife. I hope you are successful in your endeavors."

"Thank you for those kind words," replied Valerius. An uncomfortable silence followed, broken as the seven children rushed up to the seated adults.

"Father," Aulus, their eldest, said, "Landric and I were talking, and we thought it would be a good idea for him to come and spend some time with us this summer. Landric's brother and sister overheard us, and they wanted to come also. Can they come, please?"

"It was nice of you to invite them," Valerius replied. "They may certainly come visit if their parents permit it, but it will have to wait until after your mother and I return from our duties along the Danubius. You will be watched by your grandmother and grandfather while we are away, and I cannot have them responsible for the other children as well. But the answer is yes, as long as Dagobert and Ada give their permission."

Aulus frowned in disappointment. "They cannot visit while you are away? We want them to come. Please."

"Listen, I think it's wonderful that you are getting along so well, but you'll have to wait until we get back. I promise that as soon as we return from our temporary assignment, you can get together, assuming Dagobert and Ada agree. We will even plan some special activities, like sailing on some of the smaller naval craft up and down the river. Until then, you will have to wait."

* * *

The next day, Marcellus, Hereca, and Valerius gathered around a small table with General Labenius to discuss their travel arrangements. A large map was the focus of their attention as Labenius traced their intended route with his finger.

"Here we are in Oppidum Ubiorum," Labenius explained. "You will travel south upriver on the Rhenus into Germania Superior past Argentorate, home of the Thirteenth under General Florus. Once the river becomes too shallow for ships to navigate, you will need to disembark from your imperial naval vessel and travel for a short stint on land by foot, heading north until you reach the Danubius. We will need to coordinate with the Danubian fleet to arrange ships for you at one of the small garrisons.

"Once you rendezvous with the designated ships, you can sail downstream through Raetia, Noricum, and then to the fortress at Vindobona, in the Roman province of Upper Pannonia. I estimate the overall distance from here to be over five hundred miles. Fortunately for your feet, most of the time will be spent on ships—first on the Rhenus fleet and then the Danubian fleet. Naturally, you will need to stop every night, as the navy cannot navigate the rivers in darkness, given the shoals and potential obstructions. Since we are in mid-summer with extended periods of daylight, you should make excellent progress."

"What about security?" Marcellus inquired. "What I am asking is how safe will we be? This is the Roman governor of two territories, one of the most powerful men in the empire. It would be a huge setback for Rome if something were to happen to him on the way there."

"There is always an element of risk, and I cannot guarantee your safety if that's what you are asking," Labenius said. "My suggestion is that you have a contingent of heavily armed bodyguards. I'm certainly not suggesting an entire legion, but you need to be well protected in the event of an unexpected attack from bandits or a group of hateful barbarians."

"I was hoping to have a minimum number of legionaries as escorts," Valerius chimed in. "It makes the journey less burdensome. We will have much greater flexibility with a smaller contingent of guards—fewer ships, fewer supplies."

Marcellus grimaced. "Ordinarily, Tribune, I would agree with you. But this is different. You are a very tempting target. Some wild-arse barbarian might get a notion that he can achieve glory and fame by killing or taking hostage the governor of Germania and the Danubian provinces. That is a chance I would not like to take. There is an old legionary saying: It's better to have maximum security and not need it than not have maximum protection and need it."

Valerius gave Marcellus an exasperated glance. There he was with that *tribune* reference again. Whenever the former centurion wanted to make a point that was contrary to his, he used the *tribune* word. "Understood, Marcellus, but it is not as if we are going to publicize this trip. Very few will know of our itinerary, which is why I prefer the smaller option in terms of protection with just a few men."

There was a brief silence in the room.

"Sir," Labenius cautiously spoke up, "I have to side with Marcellus on this. You are too enticing a target, given your status in the region. It is not worth the risk to have you exposed to an ambush or assassination attempt. It's your decision, but I respectfully implore you to utilize a full contingency of bodyguards."

"My husband," Hereca intoned, "I believe you need to listen to Marcellus and General Labenius. I think we've become too complacent as of late with our travels in Germania. We only employ a small group of guards. Perhaps we have become too trusting. But we are going into an unknown situation that may—and I use the word *may*—be perilous. We just don't know. Furthermore, I believe it is likely that your itinerary will leak out, making you an inviting target."

Valerius pretended to study the map while evaluating the advice of his three closest friends and advisors. As much as he disliked having a heavy complement of guards, he saw reason in their counsel. "Very well, I see that I am outnumbered on this matter, and your suggestions have merit. So, what is the optimal number of guards? The more we have, the more cumbersome our journey. Is it a cohort or a century? What do you suggest?"

"I propose we take one century of legionaries with us," Marcellus recommended. "Eighty heavily armed men should be enough to discourage any bandits. I'm guessing this will require us to have a small flotilla of boats, but that can't be helped. General Labenius, I will defer to you regarding the number and types of ships required."

Labenius paused in thought. "Probably three boats, maybe four. The journey should not be too arduous, and our main priority is getting you there safely. I hope to see you back here before too long. May Fortuna be with you."

CHAPTER VII
VOCULUS

Roman Province of Pannonia

Voculus stood in the darkness at the edge of the Danubius, his hulking bodyguard and aide, Centurion Gordianus, beside him. It was two hours past sunset, and the only sounds to be heard were the rushing of the river and the occasional calls of the night birds. Since his arrival three weeks ago, Voculus had been a busy man, meeting with each of the provincial governors and legates, sizing them up, and judging their capabilities, as directed by Valerius. But he had an ulterior motive as well: He was seeking allies in his quest to stymie the efforts of the future governor. He had more work to do on that front, but there were some interesting possibilities. He would need to cultivate his relationships with some legates and governors who were unenthusiastic about Valerius's appointment. While meeting with the leaders, he had adhered to Sejanus's words and refrained from being openly critical of Valerius or praising him either. He also countered any complaints directed at the newly appointed governor.

Sejanus had been explicit in his orders to Voculus: He was to thwart the efforts of Valerius Maximus through any means available. If he could have him murdered and the blame attributed to a barbarian tribe, that would be ideal. But under no circumstances could anything be ascribed back to Voculus. Sejanus had stressed several times that Maximus should not be underestimated, but Voculus silently scoffed at the statement. He was not overawed by Maximus. The man had just gotten lucky and survived some dicey situations. But Voculus would ensure his demise and then reap his reward. Sejanus would be the empire's next imperator, and he would be beholden to him. Imagine that.

Voculus's plan was simple. He would recruit one of the more disreputable tribal chieftains—there were a few he knew—of the Quadi clan to ambush Maximus and his party when they entered the Danubian territories from the Rhenus. He had the perfect candidate. The chieftain's name was Ivarr, a disreputable figure, who made his living looting and pillaging anyone weaker than his band of marauders—Romans, other clans, it did not matter. He had first come to Voculus's attention five years ago when he had been posted along the Danubius with the Seventh Legion. In a lucrative scheme concocted by Voculus, he alerted Ivarr when merchant caravans arrived or departed the Roman provinces of Raetia, Noricum, Pannonia, or Moesia. In return, Voculus received twenty percent of the value of the pilfered merchandise. The fact that innocent merchants were cruelly slaughtered mattered little to him.

In the dim moonlight, Gordianus shifted uncomfortably. "Are you sure this barbarian is going to show?" the centurion asked.

Voculus beheld his aide's brutish features and replied in a laconic tone. "Ivarr may not always be on time, but if there is money involved, he will be here. Now stop fidgeting and relax."

"Sir, forgive me, but no one knows our whereabouts, and we are beyond the protection of the Roman garrison. These barbarians could leap out of the surrounding forest and slaughter us at will."

Voculus chuckled slightly. "Not to worry, Gordianus. I know this man. He loves money and cruelty—in that order. He will be here."

Before long, a slight rustle was heard in the bushes to their right. A large figure with cruel features materialized from the darkness. Two other men followed behind him, all heavily armed with swords and spears. "Voculus, my friend, I heard you were back. Are you ready to make me some money again?"

Ivarr approached closer, announcing his presence with his pronounced body odor. The legate did his best not to recoil from the stench, lest he offend his ally. He stifled a gag. *Does this man never bathe?*

"Ivarr, I have some work, if you think you and your friends are up for it. It will be a demanding task but rewarding if you are successful."

"My men and I can handle anything. Have we not performed satisfactorily in the past? Now, what is this difficult undertaking you want me to accomplish?"

In the waning moonlight, Voculus scrutinized his confederate. His face was heavier than the last time he had seen him. Several pronounced scars, which he had had for as long as Voculus had known him, streaked his face—the first vertically from his left ear lobe to his chin and the second horizontally across his right cheek. A small pointed beard adorned his chin. "Have you heard of Governor Valerius Maximus of Germania?"

Ivarr scoffed. "The name is familiar to me, but what has this to do with the Roman territories along the Danubius?"

"He is coming here to bring peace and prosperity to this region. He has been appointed procurator of this region by the emperor. But this Maximus has offended some powerful people in Rome. They do not wish for him to succeed in his mission and have asked that I discretely intervene in whatever way I can." Voculus grinned wolfishly. "Perhaps he could meet some unfortunate end at the hands of barbarian outlaws on his way here from Germania."

Ivarr snorted, stroking his chin in thought. "*Intervene*, what a kind word you use. What you really mean is that you want him killed." Ivarr paused and contemplated his assignment. "If he is traveling from Germania, the journey will be mostly by water, which means he will be on ships under the protection of the imperial navy. That will make him beyond our reach. Untouchable."

"Does that mean you are refusing the assignment?"

"I didn't say that. I was just noting that our window of opportunity is limited. He will be on land for a short distance between the Rhenus and Danubius rivers. That is far from here. I will have to march my men many miles to perform this task. How large will his contingent of bodyguards be? And when do you anticipate he will arrive at that location."

"Unknown. Those details have not been shared with me or anyone else for that matter."

"You are a wealth of knowledge," Ivarr said sarcastically. "This will prove to be a difficult task. In addition to a faraway location, the number of foes is unknown. I will need to bring many men, and I anticipate losing some of my warriors in the ambush. I'll need to compensate the widows for their losses."

Voculus smiled inwardly. Ivarr would accept this task. He was now in the negotiating phase, posturing for as much money as he could get. "The reward will be handsome," Voculus said. "How does two hundred gold coins sound? That is two hundred Roman *aurei*." He could almost hear the rogue gasp. He had him. In fact, he already knew what his response would be.

"For such a dangerous undertaking, I'll require three hundred gold coins."

Voculus pretended to consider the counteroffer. "You drive a hard bargain. All right, I agree. Three hundred gold coins, but that is the limit. Not one gold aureus more. It's settled at three hundred."

"I want half now and the other half after completing this task."

"I can arrange to get you the first half by tomorrow. Maximus and his entourage are set to leave Germania within the next fifteen days, which means you'll need to move quickly to intercept him after he disembarks from his ships on the Rhenus. I'm guessing it will take you a week if not more, to get there. There is only one main trail from the Rhenus to the Danubius. Choose your ambush spot wisely. If I hear of anything else in terms of troop dispositions or timing, I will let you know. Meet me here tomorrow night at the same time, and I will advance you half of the agreed-upon sum."

Voculus and his bodyguard turned and walked away. After some distance, Gordianus glanced behind him to ensure they were not being followed. "Not to be impertinent, sir, but how do you do business with that man? Can he be trusted?"

Voculus halted abruptly. "Trust Ivarr? Most certainly not. He is a rogue and a brigand. Men of his breed should be nailed upon a cross. But I do trust his greed. He will do anything for money. He will kill and pillage any tribe or people, including Romans, as long as there is a coin in it for him."

"But, sir, how do you know he will not abscond with half the gold you advance him?"

Voculus glared impatiently. "It is quite simple. First, I know he wants the other half of that money plus what he can loot from the dead. And second, he knows that if he cheats on me, I will come after him hard. Despite his bravado and fearless looting of lesser foes, he understands that Rome is a powerful force and that I will personally hunt his ass down and slaughter him and his people. He is not stupid. Ivarr and I make strange bedfellows, but he is our best option to rid ourselves of Maximus. Even if he fails, we can point our fingers at the barbarian tribes and blame them. Enough of your questions. Let us return to the fortress."

CHAPTER VIII
TIBERIUS'S IRE

Imperial Palace, Rome

Tiberius slammed the dispatch down onto the tabletop, causing the aide standing in the background to flinch. "What in Hades is Maximus up to? Damn that man and his impertinence. I gave him a job to do. When I give orders, I expect them to be followed expeditiously." He directed his gaze at Sejanus. "Your General Voculus reports that Maximus has not yet arrived in Vindobona nor does he have any idea when Maximus is expected. It's been what, over three months since he departed Rome?"

Sejanus grinned inwardly. This was going to be easier than he expected. He had ensured that the dispatch was at the top of the pile of messages for Tiberius to review. Perhaps the emperor would become impatient and remove Maximus from his position, and better yet, exile him to some far-off island. "Maybe Maximus has been delayed for some unexpected reason," he said smoothly. "Then again, maybe you have overvalued Maximus. He has always harbored a certain disdain for the authority of Rome."

Tiberius glared. "So what are you suggesting? That I relieve him of his command before he has even begun? Then what would I do? Who do I have to replace him?"

Sejanus recognized that Tiberius had now transferred his wrath toward him. He needed to recant his words or modify them quickly. "Not at all, sir. Like you, I am aware that Maximus has achieved some extraordinary success in Germania, but like most men, he has his flaws. I believe a strongly worded dispatch, reminding him of his new responsibilities, is in order. You need to explain that you expect results and that he needs to address the situation on the Danubius immediately. I would also humbly suggest that, as a precaution, you begin to consider a possible replacement in the event Maximus fails."

Tiberius heaved a sigh and stared off into the distance. "I am getting too old for this job. Between the revolts in our provinces, the need for new taxes, conspiracies to rid me of this position, and dealing with that damn senate, I find myself bedraggled and powerless to solve Rome's problems. I don't know how Augustus managed it."

Sejanus replied in an unctuous tone. "Yes, sire, it is a difficult task. But take heart, the empire is functioning and intact. I will always be here by your side to assist you. I will do whatever I can to support you, no matter how onerous the task. Regarding Maximus, would you like me to craft a dispatch informing him of your displeasure? I shall send it to both Germania and Vindobona. Who knows where he might be?"

Tiberius scowled. "Please do. Make it so. And don't mince words. I want him to know I am not satisfied with the speed of his movement. He has not embraced his new responsibilities"

"If I am dismissed, I will begin immediately."

"Yes, you are dismissed," Tiberius said wearily, waving his arm.

Sejanus exited, thinking of how the old fool was complaining about his position as imperator. Perhaps his death would come soon from natural causes. If not, Sejanus would find a way to end his days and then seize power. But first, he needed to deal with Maximus. With all of the legions under his control, he would prevent any unlawful transition of authority. The senate, he could handle. Most were a bunch of sheep. He had mostly eliminated the strong ones. His Praetorians would ensure the senators voted him as the imperator. He would find a way to handle Maximus and assume temporary command of the Danubius and then the whole empire. A silent smirk crept across his face as he thought of how the Julio-Claudian line would end with Tiberius.

CHAPTER IX
THE JOURNEY BEGINS

Weeks Later

The morning sky was a pale blue, and the air quickly warmed with the rising sun. Valerius stood beside Hereca along the riverine warship's rail, heaving a sigh of relief. At last, they were underway. The small fleet of three vessels maneuvered to the middle of the river, whereupon the sails were hoisted. The ships were a combination of merchant and Roman warships at seventy-five feet in length, a smaller version of the Roman trireme without a battering ram and fewer oars. For ease of navigation upon the river, the vessel had a shallow draft to prevent grounding. With a mighty *thwack*, the sail filled, and the boat knifed upriver. The ships were built for speed. The presence of the menacing crafts was a reminder of who really controlled the river.

He turned to Hereca. "I never imagined it would take us this long to finally begin our journey. The German chieftains wanted my personal assurance that their trade terms would remain in place and that the Roman legions under Labenius stationed along the Rhenus would not invade their territory in my absence. And it was not just one tribe. Almost every one of them wanted to meet, including the Chatti, Sugambrii, Usipetes, Marsi, and the Suebe."

"We must have been doing something right," Hereca said. "They appear to have a lot of trust in us, and better yet, they have a lot to lose if the status quo gets disturbed. But putting all that aside, some may plan some mischief and attempt to take advantage of the situation, namely the Cherusci and the Suebe, who are lukewarm at best to our presence."

Valerius feigned indignation. "I am shocked to think that some of your fellow German tribes would seek to turn this situation to their benefit."

"Spare me the sarcasm, my husband. You know as well as I do that Labenius will have his hands full. Did he not inform you that he's going to double the naval patrols as a show of force?"

"Yes, and it's a terrific idea. The presence of the naval patrol craft will remind the Germans, even the most hostile ones, exactly who is in charge of this river without offensive actions against their shores. I am confident Labenius will handle whatever situations arise."

"And I'm thankful for the delay. We got to spend more time with the children. I know they were sad to see us leave so soon after our extended stay in Rome. I promised them that Dagobert's children could join us as soon as we returned. Perhaps I pledged too much, as Dagobert and Ada have not yet agreed upon the visit."

Valerius smiled. "I believe Dagobert and Ada will give their permission. I don't think we have any worries on that front. Dagobert appears anxious to cultivate better relations with us. He views the past as I do—something not to be repeated. He had the same experiences as me, only on the opposite side. The carnage of the German wars was heavy on both camps. The present reflects an equilibrium devoid of hostilities."

"I would like to believe that's true," Hereca said, "but remember, Varus had the same thoughts, and then Arminius appeared on the scene. Look what happened. He was the mastermind who triggered an apocalypse. Many Germans and Romans were killed because of him. It only takes one man to create a tempest."

"Let's hope another Arminius is not forthcoming," Valerius said.

Marcellus sauntered up to the pair. "Did someone mention that arse-hole Arminius? Thankfully, he is with his gods now."

"We were just hoping another Arminius is not waiting while we are away," Valerius said. "But we have our own problems. Here, read this. I received it yesterday." Valerius reached down to his leather dispatch bag and withdrew the recent communication from Tiberius.

Marcellus opened the parchment and squinted at the writing. He took his time reading the terse missive before looking up. "Who does Tiberius think he is, the emperor?"

Valerius chuckled. "Yes, the temerity of that man. In any event, I believe I see the hands of Sejanus and Voculus in this. Voculus was probably most eager to report that I had not yet arrived on the Danubius. They are stirring the pot, hoping to discredit us."

"It looks like they are succeeding," Marcellus said. "Tiberius appears to be under the impression that you are lollygagging about and avoiding your new posting. How will you respond, Procurator?"

"Meekly. No sense in exacerbating the situation. I will grovel and apologize, stating the delay was unavoidable. The German tribes sought my assurances that our trade terms would remain the same and that Rome would not instigate hostile actions against any of the German tribes in our absence. We could not afford to risk all that we had achieved here on the Rhenus. Most importantly, I will let him know that we are on our way and that I am looking forward to my new position."

A figure in a Roman naval captain's uniform approached and spoke in a loud, clear voice. "Excuse me, sir; I thought I would properly introduce myself to you, Governor Maximus. I am Captain Decimus Mucius Flavius at your service. I am in charge of this small fleet." He offered a brief smile. "I trust your journey will be pleasant and, most of all, uneventful."

Valerius eyed the captain. His first impression was that the naval officer looked to be in his early thirties with a firm build, enhanced by his leather muscle cuirass. He appeared to be of an amiable disposition yet a man of experience who knew his trade and brooked no nonsense from those under his command.

"Nice meeting you, Captain. This is my wife Hereca and my right-hand man, Marcellus."

The captain nodded. "Your reputation precedes you. I am honored to serve as the officer in charge of this flotilla. My orders are to deliver you and your accompanying escort to the disembarkation point. Rest assured, I will get you to your destination safely."

He then fixed his gaze squarely on Valerius. "Sir, as you are aware, we have fortifications all along the river, some rather large but most of them small, used primarily for observation. They only hold ten to twenty men. We sail by day and stop at night. We should make good progress with the long summer days. Given the relative size of our fleet, we will be staying at the larger citadels for the night, ensuring decent food and comfortable accommodations. Your first scheduled stop will be the fortress of Moguntiacum. Over the coming days, we will travel as far up the river as possible. From there, you will disembark and proceed overland north to the Danubius, roughly a two-day march. There's only one road, and it's not an especially good one, but it will get you to your destination. Although there has been talk about building a canal between the two rivers, as of yet, the funds have not been allocated by Rome. Bunch of stingy bastards, if you ask me. Once you reach the Danubius, there will be boats waiting to take you downriver to Vindobona. If you have any requests or concerns, please bring them to my attention. But rest assured that I know this river both upstream and downstream. Relax and enjoy the journey."

"Thank you for the briefing, Captain Flavius. We look forward to a pleasant journey. You need not worry about pampering us. Most of my time is not spent in plush accommodations, even as governor. So please spend your time overseeing the flotilla, and do not worry about us. Pretend as if we are not here."

"Yes, sir. Please let me know if you need anything or have any questions.

After the naval officer departed, Valerius turned to Hereca and Marcellus. "Looking ahead, when we reach Vindobona, we must assemble the various legates and governors of the provinces. We will need their help to identify who the movers and shakers are among the Danubian tribes. Once that is accomplished, we can begin meeting with them to convince them that trading with Rome is a good idea, which will, hopefully, lead to peace and prosperity. I think this might be a tough sell with some leaders."

"Indeed," Marcellus remarked. "I'd like to believe that we can mirror our success in Germania, but from what I understand, the barbarians on the Danubius are a tough bunch."

"Hereca, your thoughts?" Valerius asked.

She paused, contemplating the question. "No doubt it will be a difficult process, but as I recall, the Germans were hostile to any Roman trade ventures, with perhaps a few exceptions. So I believe we can make progress. My concern is General Voculus and his close ties with Sejanus. I suspect he will work behind the scenes to undermine any success we might achieve."

"Your point is well noted," Valerius responded.

"If he becomes too big a pain in the arse," Marcellus opined, "I shall find a way to deal with him, and he will not like it."

"Voculus may try to be disruptive, but we have the smarts and the will to out-maneuver him. Others of his ilk have attempted to challenge our authority in the past, and we have prevailed. I rather like our odds."

Later that afternoon, the ships sailed to a stone quay jutting out into the river. Perhaps a hundred paces away stood the massive fortress of Moguntiacum. As Valerius, Marcellus, and Hereca disembarked, an honor guard from the fortress formed a double line, greeting the trio. Ceremonial horns blared, and the gates swung wide open.

Valerius gaped at the reception and fanfare. "This is not necessary."

Marcellus turned to Valerius. "It's not every day that the governor visits a legionary fortress. I know you prefer to be unobtrusive, but you are the appointed leader of this territory. Like it or not, they are going to prepare a proper welcome for you."

"Yes, dear," chimed Hereca. "This is your time to shine. Let the legionaries see you. You are a hero to them. Make a speech. Wish them good fortune."

As the trio advanced down the quay, the legate of the fortress and commander of the Twelfth Legion, General Aulus Strabinius, and his staff—all attired in their finest armor—approached to greet Valerius.

"Welcome, Governor Maximus. My staff and I have been antici-pating your arrival. My entire legion is assembled inside the fortress awaiting your review."

"It's good to see you again, Aulus. The Twelfth has a proud and honored tradition, but all of this fanfare was not necessary. However, I would be pleased to review your legion. Let's not keep the troops waiting. I know what it is like to stand out in the sun or rain waiting for some dignitary or esteemed senator."

'I will definitely second that," Marcellus quipped.

The legate grinned. "Yes, I remember those days as well. Nothing worse than standing in full armor under the blazing sun or in a torrid downpour waiting for some strutting peacock. But, sir, you are different. The men love what you have done in Germania. You have saved the lives of countless legionaries with your actions against certain rogues who acted in their self-interest. They also know of your valor from years ago when you survived Arminius and rebellious Germans. They are eagerly awaiting you."

With that, Valerius, with Marcellus and Hereca trailing behind him, entered through the massive gates flanked by enormous watch-towers. On entering the open parade ground, shouted commands echoed from the ten cohorts and sixty centuries. Along with Strabinius, Valerius mounted a raised dais, facing approximately five thousand troops of the Twelfth in tightly packed ranks. There was a spontaneous roar as the men shouted their acclaim to the procurator, their ultimate commander in Germania. "Maximus, Maximus, Maximus," they bellowed.

Valerius turned to Strabinius and yelled above the chants. "Better have them tone this down. I don't want Tiberius to hear that I have supplanted him. I say that in jest, but it is partly true."

"Would you say a few words, sir? Then we can review the troops together."

"Certainly." Valerius strode to the front of the platform and held his arms up, signaling quiet.

"Legionaries of the Twelfth," he exclaimed, "I am honored to be governor of Germania and commanding troops such as you. There is an enduring peace over this land, and why? I will tell you why. It's because of troops such as you. You, the legions of Germania, are a formidable deterrent to any rebellion that might arise. You are the best-trained, fiercest legionaries, led by the finest officers in all of the Roman Empire. When I look at you, my heart swells with pride. Commerce flows throughout the northern territories because of Rome's legions and naval forces." His speech was interrupted as the men cheered freely at his remarks.

Valerius raised his hands for silence once more. When the noise abated, he continued. "I was recently in Rome and met with our great imperator, Tiberius Caesar. If he were here right now, he would echo the exact words I have just spoken. He is delighted and amazed at what we have accomplished. While in Rome, I was invited to speak to the senate about our progress here. They are astounded at what has transpired in Germania. It's the talk of the city. This was once the most feared and turbulent postings in the empire. No longer, my friends, thanks to men like you."

The men cheered and bellowed some more. General Strabinius and Valerius descended the speaking platform and moved to the left to begin their inspection of the first cohort.

As they approached the first cohort, the four hundred and eighty men snapped to attention as one. The cohort commander stepped forward. "Sirs, Centurion Pontius, first cohort commander, at your service. The men have been anticipating this all day."

The review began as they walked past the ranks of legionaries. Valerius stopped randomly in front of a man, who stiffened further from his position of attention.

"Relax, Legionary. I do not bite," Valerius said.

"Yes, sir," the figure replied.

Valerius assessed the legionary in front of him, who was of medium height. His helmet was pulled down low on his forehead, and his armor gleamed, no doubt from a recent polishing. "What is your name, and what part of the empire are you from?" Valerius asked.

"Name is Beldrus, sir, from Gallia. Been with the legions going on seven years."

"I have served with men from Gallia. They make good legionaries. One of them saved my life several times. Are your officers taking care of you, and have you made good friends? I know centurions can be strict arseholes but besides that?"

The legionary proffered a grin. "Yes, sir. My officers are first-rate, and I have good mates. We stick together."

"Well, Beldrus, good fortune to you. The legions and Rome need men like you."

Accompanied by the other senior officers, Valerius spent the next hour reviewing the ranks of the Twelfth. Overall, it was a fairly impressive showing. The men appeared well-fed, their uniforms were immaculate, and their attitudes were outstanding. He fervently hoped the legions posted along the Danubius were just as good.

CHAPTER X
BETWEEN THE RHENUS
AND DANUBIUS RIVERS

Province of Raetia

Ivarr stood in the middle of his encampment, fuming. He and his posse had made the long trek from their home in the heartland of the Quadi. Upon their arrival, he had sent his scouts to reconnoiter the road between the two rivers, hoping to spy the approach of the new procurator, Maximus, and his entourage. Now, days later, and much to his frustration, there was still no sign of their quarry.

Their bivouac was set up beside a small stream about half a mile from the dirt road between the two rivers. They had selected a location around ten miles south of the Danubius. It was far enough from the Roman garrison on the river to avoid attracting attention from any patrols. While Ivarr and his three hundred men were an armed force, the encampment was hardly military style. Tents and shelters were erected haphazardly around the site, and there were no sentries. Armor and weapons were strewn about or leaning against trees. The collection of cutthroats, rapists, and thieves milled around aimlessly.

Ivarr was not a patient man. He wanted to get this ambush over and done with and collect the remainder of his generous bounty of gold coins from Voculus. Adding to his ire, they were running out of food. Their provisions back in Pannonia were already low, so he had instructed his men to only pack enough food for two weeks. But it had taken his men almost two weeks to march here. They had attempted to hunt and forage for food, but the size of his small army made such efforts impractical.

Instead of blaming himself for his lack of foresight while planning, Ivarr cursed Voculus for not furnishing him with adequate information. He and his men were starving, and there was no place they could purchase food. It was almost a wilderness with thick forests, devoid of towns and farms to raid.

His fury continued to boil when he spotted a shiftless bunch near him. "What are you doing here, lounging about when we have no food?" he bellowed. "Get off your arses and go forage." For effect, he drew his long, iron sword. "I mean right now. Get out of my sight, or I will cleave your head in two."

The men scattered away from him for, in the past, they had witnessed his outbursts, and they never knew when his vile temper would overcome reason. He had slain some of his followers in fits of rage.

* * *

Valerius and his contingent of guards disembarked from their ship. Now, it was time for the second leg of their trip. The third leg would be via ship down the Danubius. Valerius stood with Marcellus, facing the officer commanding their bodyguard, Centurion Rennatus. Valerius addressed him. "I understand General Labenius personally selected you and your century to escort us. I assume, then, that you and your men are well-trained and highly regarded."

Centurion Rennatus, a heavily muscled officer who appeared to be in his mid-thirties, beamed. "I would like to think we are, sir. We are the third century of the first cohort, Twentieth Legion stationed at Oppidum Ubiorum. My men are good, and I have trained them thoroughly. Many have combat experience. We have a few newbies, but the bulk of the century are veterans. They know what to do in the event we are attacked."

"Ever been on this road before?" Marcellus asked.

He frowned. "No, sir, and neither have any of my men, except one. He and I spoke about this trail, and I understand that it is a two-day journey through sparsely inhabited terrain. I am told the road heads north to the Danubius."

"That about sums up my knowledge," Marcellus replied. "Where the road intersects the Danubius, there is a small Roman fortress with docking facilities where ships are expected to be waiting to take us downriver to Vindobona."

"Your presence here is only a precaution against possible marauders," Valerius emphasized. "If all goes according to plan, we should not encounter hostilities. I will leave the tactical formation during the march to you. I know my former centurion, Marcellus, will be eager to advise you, but the decision is yours. I'm sure you know how to position your men. So, whenever you're ready, we can proceed."

"Yes, sir. I'd appreciate Marcellus's input," he said, giving Marcellus a knowing grin before turning back to Valerius. "Permission to form up my men?"

"By all means, yes," he replied.

As the centurion turned around smartly and departed, Valerius shared his impressions with Marcellus. "The centurion seems highly competent. The men are confident, and their kit is immaculate. It appears Labenius chose well."

"How did you know I wanted to advise Rennatus?" Marcellus asked.

"It was an easy guess. As I've mentioned on previous occasions, the centurion part of you will never die, so don't deny it. But let Centurion Rennatus do his job."

"I will. But if I was asked to deploy our legionary escort, I would have the bulk of the century in a tight wedge formation, leading the way. The porters carrying our luggage would be in the rear, while Hereca, you, and I would be in the middle."

Valerius rubbed his chin in thought. "Yes, that seems like a logical choice. Any attack would come from the front and the forest on both sides of the road. We would not get a lot of warning."

Marcellus nodded. "I know the century of bodyguards is only a precaution, but I propose we remove our bows from their satchels and wear our swords. They are of no use if we are attacked and they are inaccessible to us. We should treat this as a tactical situation in a hostile environment."

"I can remember a few occasions when you have suggested the same, and I'm glad I heeded your warning. Sometimes, your advice is uncanny. I will have my bow and sword ready."

Marcellus offered a triumphant grin. "Now, if you don't mind, please excuse me. I would like to discuss our situation further with Centurion Rennatus. We are kindred spirits. I promise not to be overbearing and to let him do his job. I will only offer suggestions if asked." He turned and strode to Rennatus.

They journeyed without incident the entire day along the lightly traveled road and established their overnight bivouac—complete with an earthen rampart and ditches. Along the way, they had witnessed a few mules loaded with farm produce and an occasional wagon burdened with freshly cut timber, plodding slowly on the deeply rutted path. Off in the distance were some random farms and small settlements that could hardly qualify as towns. Mostly, they passed dense forests and fallow fields.

Early the next morning, they departed their fortified camp. If all went according to plan, they would reach the Danubius by late afternoon. A wedge-shaped contingent of legionaries led the way, while Valerius, Marcellus, and Hereca walked in the center. Behind them marched the porters with the baggage, and a small group of men formed the rear guard. Thus far, their overland journey had been uneventful.

"I wish I knew precisely how much farther we have to journey before we arrive at the Roman garrison," Marcellus said. "I always like to know when we are expected to finish the march. In this instance, it is only a presumption that the journey will take two full days and we will finish sometime near dusk."

Valerius shrugged. "Given some of the marches we have undertaken on the campaign, this is easy stuff. Then again, we were much younger then. I am confident we will get there by this evening." He turned to Hereca. "How are you holding up, my dear?"

Hereca looked down at her mud-covered boots and sighed. "Truth be told, I would much rather be on a boat, but I'm cheered by the prospect of arriving by the end of the day. It's not too much to endure. We have, at most, twenty miles, yes?"

"I would like to believe that's a good estimate," said Marcellus. "We are all spoiled by our tranquil lifestyles and our aging bodies, especially me. There, I said it before you could hurl some age-related quip at me."

Valerius scoffed. "I was thinking no such thing. You are too sensitive, Marcellus."

"Don't give me any of that. I have been on the receiving end of many of your older-person jibes."

Valerius grinned. "Maybe a few, I'll admit. But I promise not to say a thing on this march."

The trio walked on into the morning with sparse conversation, mostly grunts. The going was hard as Centurion Rennatus set a rapid pace. Trudging onward on the dirt road, they marched through alternative swathes of shade and sunlight.

Lost in thought, Valerius pondered the list of duties and tasks he needed to perform once at his headquarters in Vindobona. First and foremost, he needed to meet with the provincial governors and the legates stationed up and down the Danubius and take measure of them. Once satisfied with the deployment of his friendly forces, he would need to engage with the various tribal leaders. He knew nothing of the clans and their chieftains, so he would need to absorb as much information as possible to identify the leaders of the tribes. He would need to rely on the governors for much of this intelligence.

His mind was preoccupied when a sudden feeling of dread trickled down his spine. While thinking of matters to be resolved in Vindobona, a part of him was also acutely aware of his surroundings. His past experiences in the German wilderness had instilled a sense of caution when plodding through similar terrain. Something had changed. A subtle change, but it was different. The normal sounds of the forest had hushed. The birds had stopped their twittering. Even the insects had silenced. He turned to Marcellus with a questioning look.

"I noticed it just a few moments ago," Marcellus said.

"What did you notice?" Hereca asked.

"The forest has become hushed, which means there is either a large predator around, such as a wolf or a bear, or there are creatures of the two-legged variety spying upon us."

Hereca listened for a few moments and gasped. "You're right. I should have picked up on it. I remember such events from when I lived with the Dolgubni."

Without a word, Marcellus hurried toward the front of the formation. Centurion Rennatus had positioned himself somewhat behind the lead elements to direct the men in the event of an attack. He turned as he heard Marcellus approaching him.

"Centurion," Marcellus hailed, "are you aware of the change? The forest has gone silent."

"Affirmative, I detected it as well as some of my men. We are on heightened alert. I'd like to believe it is just a large predator, but my gut tells me it's something more sinister. We are in the middle of nowhere, with limited visibility on either side of the road because of the woods—a perfect place for an ambush. If and when these arseholes, whoever they are, show themselves and attack, my men are ready. We have tightened our formation. I was just about ready to inform the governor and you of the situation. I should have known you were aware of the threat."

Ivarr waited for the Romans to appear. He had positioned his ambush so that the bulk of his forces would charge unimpeded down the road directly at the Roman front, and simultaneously, some of his men, concealed in the woods, would attack from the flanks. His advanced scouts had reported that his men heavily outnumbered the Romans. He had selected this location because it was close to his encampment, and the Romans would be tired from marching most of the morning. Rumors of a woman with them brought a wolfish grin to his face. He would keep her for himself and enjoy her flesh. Better yet, he would soon own a huge amount of gold.

From his concealed position, he watched the Romans approach. They were around one hundred paces away. Patience was not his virtue. He could not wait any longer. Now was the time. He stepped out of the forest and shouted the command to attack.

Marcellus was on his way back to Valerius and Hereca when he heard the war cries. Without breaking stride, he smoothly unlimbered his giant war bow and notched an arrow. Turning quickly, he moved to the front and unleashed his arrow. He knew Valerius would be doing the same.

Rennatus shouted his commands, and the century perfunctorily moved into a box formation, protecting the front, rear, and sides, with a heavier concentration of men at the front.

Measuring the enemy in front of him, Marcellus shot another arrow at the charging mob. He observed that most were armed with spears, but some had swords. Many of the warriors carried small wooden shields like those the tribes along the Rhenus used. Valerius appeared by his side.

"Aim your arrows over our men in the front ranks," Marcellus said.

Valerius released an arrow, not bothering to follow it down range since he could not miss the tightly packed mass charging at him. He retrieved another arrow and sent it streaking toward the foe.

Rennatus calmly issued his commands. "Shield wall. Prepare to throw." His men cocked their arms, each with a pilum in hand.

Ivarr scowled as some of his men fell quickly to a sudden barrage of arrows. Where had they come from? He cursed himself for not waiting longer before charging. It gave them too much time to prepare. Despite the losses, his men surged onward, howling. They were now within forty paces from the front ranks of the legionary shield wall. A volley of *pila*—deadly front-weighted Roman javelins—descended upon the leading warriors. Shrieks and cries arose from the pack as men stumbled and died, the fearsome lances protruding from their bodies. A second wave of pila hit the marauders, killing even more. The charge broke and then halted.

"Keep those ranks tight," bellowed Rennatus from the center of the squared formation. "I want those shields overlapping."

Despite their losses from the barrages of javelins, Ivarr and his men regrouped, rushing forward once more. They smashed into the impenetrable shield wall, dying on the razor-sharp points of the Roman gladii. The men in the rear ranks pushed forward, inadvertently shoving those in the front into the pointed Roman swords. Ivarr lost almost a third of his force in the first few minutes of the battle.

Valerius and Marcellus, standing behind the shield wall, had dropped their bows. It was strictly close-quarters combat now. Valerius carried a spatha, a longer version of the Roman gladius, while Marcellus was armed with a gladius, the short stabbing sword of the legions. Hereca retrieved a javelin that had been thrown over the ranks of the shield wall. She briefly examined it and then hefted it, deeming it fit for use. Though out of practice now, as a young woman, she could beat most of the men in her village in heaving their lances. The porters and slaves, all seven of them, stood behind them, cowering in fear.

Marcellus yelled above the din. "I guess we are the reserve force. Kill anyone who gets through the shield wall. He turned about and eyed the trembling porters. "Any of you know how to fight?"

A medium-sized figure with short brown hair stepped forward. "I do," he said.

"What's your name?"

"I am called Radulf. I'm a Batavian."

Marcellus appraised him quickly, noting that he appeared strong around the arms and shoulders and looked like he could fight. "Alright, Radulf, time to battle for your life. Stay here with us. If any of these rogues get through our defenses, kill them."

"I need a sword."

"I will see that you get one."

Before the man could reply, Marcellus moved to his right, where a severely wounded legionary was on his hands and knees, out of the fight. Marcellus retrieved the man's sword from the ground and handed the bloody gladius to Radulf. "Get ready."

Radulf gripped the sword tightly and nodded at Marcellus.

A few moments later, a large warrior bearing a long sword burst through the ranks to the left side of the formation. He stumbled slightly over the body of a slain legionary. Before he could regain his balance, Marcellus strode over and thrust his sword through the man's throat, killing him instantly.

The howling pack of barbarian bandits, despite their heavy losses, relentlessly pressed upon the besieged Roman century. A wiry warrior with a ragged beard howled in triumph as he stabbed the legionary in front of him. Before the ranks closed, he rushed through the gap. With one swing of his sword, Valerius nearly severed the man's arm. He fell into the dirt, howling, only to be finished by Radulf.

The shield wall continued to hold, and the men fought valiantly. The barbarian dead piled up in front of the Roman formation. Then, disaster struck. A wedge of enemies penetrated the Roman position from the right flank. Several men swarmed over Centurion Rennatus, stabbing him repeatedly with their spears, leaving him in a bloody heap. Valerius, Marcellus, Hereca, and Radulf charged at the collection of barbarians. They had to seal the penetration, or they would all be dead.

The four barbarian warriors who had breached the shield wall saw the three men and a woman and charged at them. Both sides clashed with a resounding thump. Valerius circled, eyeing his opponent, who was armed with a spear. The figure snarled and thrust a lightning jab at Valerius's mid-section, which he knocked aside with his long sword. The man thrust again. Valerius deftly stepped away and, with his long reach, chopped down on the hand holding the spear. The weapon dropped from his nerveless hands. Before the man could recover, Valerius thrust his sword hard into the man's torso. When he tugged to free his weapon, he understood it was lodged firmly in the dead warrior's spine. Looking up, he spotted another warrior bearing down on him, his spear ready to thrust. Before the figure could complete his lunge, he received a hard jab into his back and collapsed to the earth, revealing Radulf behind him, the bloodied gladius in his hand. Valerius nodded his thanks and turned back to the fray.

Marcellus, armed with a discarded Roman shield from a slain legionary, was trying to fend off two attackers. Abruptly, the man circling to his left gasped and fell to his knees, Hereca's spear sticking obscenely out of his torso. With only one opponent left, Marcellus charged, bowled the enemy over with his shield, and dispatched the man.

In the chaos, the optio, second in command to Centurion Rennatus, calmly took over the Roman century. He bellowed commands above the fray, urging his men to tighten ranks. "Push and thrust," he bellowed, rallying the legionaries to push with the shield and thrust with the gladius. The ranks stabilized under his leadership, keeping the enemy at bay.

Suddenly, a wayward spear sailed over the ranks of legionaries. As if guided by the gods, the javelin wobbled slightly and descended, striking the ill-fated optio in the throat. He fell to his knees and collapsed. The Roman century was now leaderless. In a heartbeat, Marcellus raced forward and seized the helmet of the fallen Centurion Rennatus. Placing it on his head, he stood in the middle of the formation. "Keep it up, men. They are almost beaten. Push and thrust."

But the barbarians were not finished yet; they were intent on their prize. They continued to attack, whittling down the outnumbered legionaries. After another surge slammed into the legionaries, several more barbarians broke through the Roman ranks. Valerius and Radulf, now armed with a small shield in addition to his sword, charged at them. The duo quickly cut down the two leading barbarians. However, two others warily circled Radulf and Valerius.

Valerius attacked his opponent, slashing wildly with his sword. With several long thrusts, he forced the barbarian back toward the shield wall. A legionary turned toward the movement, and quickly dispatched the man. Valerius peered behind him to see how Radulf was faring. Amidst the chaos, Valerius saw him wrapping a piece of cloth around a wound on his arm, his foe dead several feet away. *This man is definitely an asset; one worth keeping on,* thought Valerius.

A large figure, reeking of body odor, penetrated the ranks and attacked Marcellus. Seeing the older man, the barbarian figured it would be an easy victory. Out of the corner of his eye, he spotted the woman. She would soon be his.

Marcellus held up a rectangular shield just below his eyes, his short stabbing sword aimed menacingly at waist level. Glaring at his foe, he noticed the man had a long well-crafted sword, wore an armor-plated cuirass, and held a small oval shield in his left hand. This was no ordinary foe but someone of high status.

Marcellus snarled and nodded with his head as if to say 'Come and get me.'

The pungent barbarian screamed an oath and charged at Marcellus. He slammed into the shield, expecting to knock the older man over, but it was he who bounced back.

Marcellus cursed himself. He had missed his opportunity. He was so concerned with bracing for the charge that he did not react quickly enough to thrust his sword into the man's innards. The ugly warrior backed off, circled warily, and then unexpectedly thrust his sword directly at Marcellus's face. The veteran warrior barely got his shield up in time to deflect the blow.

Marcellus then backed away from his adversary to avoid another thrust. His opponent was quicker than he had thought. No matter. He would find a weakness and send this odiferous cutthroat to the underworld.

The barbarian advanced at Marcellus again, a smug grin on his face streaked with rivulets of blood. He judged his opponent's retreat as a sign of weakness. Confident, he slashed his sword horizontally, but Marcellus easily deflected the blow.

The barbarian retreated slightly, evaluating his strategy. He stepped forward with his right leg and jabbed his sword at Marcellus's torso. Marcellus blocked the blow with his large shield. but aimed a chopping blow at the man's right kneecap. This maneuver was taught to all legionaries—a knee stroke would not kill a man but would certainly disable him. Once the enemy was on the ground, he could subsequently be dispatched. The barbarian saw the blow descending and attempted to withdraw his leg. But he was late. The sword stroke missed the knee but sliced his lower leg, opening a thin gash. The man shrieked in agony.

When the ruffian retreated, limping away, Marcellus doggedly advanced. He aimed a thrust at the foe's head. But at the last moment, he changed the stroke, striking downward and opening a gash on the man's other leg near the thigh. His opponent hobbled backward, but Marcellus relentlessly pursued. In a panic, the barbarian chieftain sought reinforcements, looking around wildly, but none were near him. In a desperate maneuver, he aimed a wild swing at Marcellus, who blocked it disdainfully with his shield. Foregoing the figure's armored torso, Marcellus jabbed an upward thrust into the man's groin, penetrating deeply.

He withdrew his stabbing sword quickly, lest it got stuck in the man's flesh, twisting the razor-sharp blade on the way out. His foe collapsed to his knees, spurting blood into the air. The mortally wounded man attempted to stop the flow with his hands but in vain. Ivarr died, bleeding out in the dirt.

As if someone had turned off a flowing fountain, the enemy force melted back into the forest, leaving their dead and wounded behind. A silence enveloped the battlefield, with only the moans of the wounded and dying.

Marcellus immediately took command of the survivors. "I want everyone to remain vigilant and maintain formation. I doubt it, but they may return." He then pointed at several individuals. "You, you, you, and you, see that the wounded are brought to the middle of the formation. Leave the dead where they lie.

He moved to where Centurion Rennatus, the unit commander, was lying prone on the ground. Marcellus bent over and checked for any sign of life. He stood, shaking his head. "I rather liked that young man. He was a fine officer."

"Yes, he was," Valerius replied. "I don't mean to sound uncaring, but we need to get ourselves sorted and get underway to our destination."

"I agree," said Marcellus. He grabbed a legionary from the ranks. "Do you know how to count?"

The man nodded.

"Excellent. I want you to get me a status report—the number of men killed, seriously wounded, and walking wounded. Got it?"

"Right away, sir." The figure moved toward the front ranks to begin his grisly task.

Marcellus turned back to Valerius and Hereca. "I will get us moving as soon as possible. I don't think our foe has the stomach for any more fighting since I killed their leader, I believe." He gestured with his sword to Ivarr's figure laying crumpled on the ground.

"Forever the centurion," Valerius said.

"I can't help it. That is just me," said Marcellus with a slight grin.

Valerius's face suddenly dropped to a scowl. "This was no random ambush by a bunch of bandits. We are in the middle of nowhere. Why would anyone want to conduct their raids here? There are far more lucrative places to attack wealthy merchants with fat purses. Any ambush here would find slim pickings. This was a planned assault. Maybe we could question some of their wounded who were left behind and discover who was behind this."

"I will gladly do that. Let's go find one." They ventured to where many of the bandits had fallen in front of the shield wall. Most were dead or too far gone to question. They walked farther and found a man transfixed on the ground with a pilum deep in his torso. His face was contorted in agony, and blood seeped from the edges of the gruesome wound. No doubt it was a mortal injury. Belly wounds were usually a slow and painful death. Marcellus moved his face close to the man and stared at him. He then arose and kicked the protruding spear shaft. The man let out a tormented howl.

Marcellus turned to Hereca, who had joined them. "This is going to be an unpleasant experience for this rogue, but I need you to translate. You sure you want to stick around?"

Hereca gave him a steely glare. "Yes, I have seen dying men before. Proceed."

"Very well. Translate my words for this scoundrel." Marcellus squatted down so that he was close to the man's face. "Tell him he is dying, and we can make his death extremely unpleasant. I just need to wiggle this offending spear." For effect, he pushed the shaft sideways, back and forth. The man screamed once again. "I want to know where he lives and why they ambushed us."

Hereca translated the words, speaking to the wounded man without a trace of pity in her eyes. The figure scowled at her in silence.

Hereca smiled coldly at the man, took hold of the butt end of the spear, and without compassion ground the lance deeper. He howled in agony. "Speak if you know what's good for you," Hereca said. The man responded quickly in a guttural language.

Hereca translated. "He said that they are bandits who live several hundred miles to the east downriver. Their leader, called Ivarr, promised them gold if they ambushed an expedition of Romans between the two rivers. They have been waiting for days for us to appear."

"Ask him what their leader looks like," Marcellus said.

Hereca spoke to the barbarian, who coughed up a glob of blood before responding.

"He says he has two pronounced scars on his face, carries a long sword, and smells," said Hereca

"Just as I thought; that's the one I killed. He broke through our lines, and his body is back there. That's why they retreated so quickly. Ask him who paid their leader to ambush us."

The wounded man grimaced in pain as he responded to Hereca.

"He doesn't know," she said. "Ivarr wouldn't say. All he knows is that they were to be paid in Roman gold coins after the ambush was completed."

"I have heard enough." Marcellus drew his gladius and stabbed the wounded man in the throat, silencing him.

Just then, the legionary whom Marcellus had ordered to get a head count approached. "You have a report for me?" asked Marcellus.

"Yes, sir. We have forty able-bodied men. That count has been verified. In addition, we have seven walking wounded. I am not a *medicus*, but there are four others whom I doubt will survive. There are thirty-one dead, including the centurion and the optio. Oh, we also lost three of the porters."

"Thank you, you are dismissed."

"Jupiter's arse," exclaimed Valerius. "We've lost almost half of our bodyguard and both officers. I will have someone's head for this."

"And we all have strong suspicions as to who that is," Hereca voiced. "Voculus is the only man on the Danubius who knew we were coming."

"But we have no proof," said Valerius. "We will concern ourselves with Voculus later. For now, we need to get to the Danubius. Marcellus, I will leave it to you to get the men ready, including the wounded. I say we leave the dead here as they lie and have someone from the garrison come back and attend to that matter later."

"Agreed," said Marcellus. "Our main concern is getting you to the river and then downstream to Vindobona." With that, he strode over to where the surviving legionaries had gathered. "Listen up," he bellowed. "Get ready to move out. Gather up the weapons of the fallen and bring them with us."

CHAPTER XI
ARRIVAL

Fortress of Vindobona
Roman Province of Pannonia

It had been a five-day journey from the small fortress in Raetia to Pannonia. The three ships of the small flotilla deftly navigated their way from the middle of the river and nudged against the huge quay on the right bank. Valerius was always amazed at how captains skillfully maneuvered their boats so that the vessel's side kissed the stone pier with just a slight bump, made more difficult with the stiff breeze surging down the river that day. The ships were quickly secured with heavy ropes, and the boarding planks were lowered. Marcellus organized the guard, and the contingent marched along the wharf to the main gate of the fortress, flanked by two looming towers.

An optio stood just inside the open gates, watching as the ragged contingent of legionaries escorted three civilians into the fortress. He noted blood spatters on the armor and shields of some of the men. Others sported bloodied bandages. Strangely, their shields bore the symbol of lightning bolts, unlike his legion's symbol of a prancing bull or that of any of the other five legions stationed along the Danubius.

Trailing the formation were several wounded, supported by their comrades. *Who in Hades are these people entering my fort?*

The optio stepped into the path of the marching formation. "Halt." The legionaries stopped. He spoke in a condescending tone, "Who are you? What unit are you?"

Marcellus, at the rear of the formation with Hereca and Valerius, glowered. "Let me handle this." He strode forward, his eyes blazing.

When Marcellus reached the front of their formation, he stopped and glared at the officer, scrutinizing the man's uniform. Marcellus scowled at the dented armor and tattered ends. His marching boots were worn and looked like they had been repaired many times. "You, who are you?"

The man withered under Marcellus's stare, losing his previous bluster. "I'm the officer of the guard, Optio Segundus." Aware of Marcellus's disapproval of his uniform, he straightened his tunic to appear more presentable.

"Well, Optio, do you see that man back there?" he asked, pointing at Valerius.

"Yes, what of him?"

"His name is Valerius Maximus, and next to him is his wife, Hereca. You may have heard of him. He is the newly appointed procurator of this region. Now, I suggest you get your arse moving and find the legate of this fortress so he can properly welcome his new commander and show him to his quarters. Is that too much to ask?"

The optio spluttered. "Of course, sir. I was not informed you were coming."

"No matter," Marcellus replied. "Now, go find the legate." He watched as the figure turned about and hurried down the main avenue to the military headquarters.

Marcellus returned to Valerius and Hereca. "As you can see, your reign here is off to an inauspicious start. The gate guards were not expecting us, and what is more, the officer's uniform, as well as that of the others, looked deplorable. I have dispatched the optio to get the commanding legate."

Valerius chuckled. "Are you sure you do not want to reenlist as a centurion?"

"Sometimes, I do miss it."

"While we wait for the legate, we need to talk about Radulf," Valerius said. "We have not addressed his status yet. Given he traveled on a different ship than us on the voyage from Raetia, now would be a good time." He looked around and found the porter standing with the survivors. Catching his eye, he waved him over.

Radulf hurried over eagerly and stood at attention. "Yes, sir."

"I want to thank you again for saving my life back there in the forest. I noticed you're a skilled swordsman. Have you been trained?"

"In a matter of speaking, sir. The men I associated with were trained."

"And who might they be?" Marcellus asked skeptically.

Radulf shuffled his feet and looked at the ground. "Uh, we were an independent group," he replied reluctantly.

"And what does that mean?"

"We were raiders. Thieves, if you want to be blunt about it."

"So, you were captured, and that's how you became a slave?" Valerius demanded.

"Yes, sir, that about sums it up."

Marcellus sniggered. "At least he's honest about it."

Valerius looked sternly at Radulf. "Well, Radulf, former Batavian raider, I have a proposition for you. How would you like to be a free man? In exchange for your emancipation, you will become my personal bodyguard. How does that sound? You will receive a standard legionary's salary plus all the other benefits."

Radulf replied immediately. "I would be honored to serve as your bodyguard. Not only am I skilled with weapons, but I can also speak both Latin and German. Also, I am an excellent horseman. When do I start?"

"Right away," Valerius replied. "You will accompany us to the headquarters and begin your duties."

As Valerius spoke, he spied a figure, obviously a high-ranking officer, accompanied by Optio Segundus, rushing toward him.

The figure halted just short of Valerius, heaving from his exertions. "Sir, General Marcus Caelius, legate of the Vindobona garrison, Tenth Gemina Legion, at your service. My sincerest apologies for not greeting you at the gate. We had no idea when you would arrive. No one informed us."

Valerius studied the man. He was in his late forties, his short hair graying at the temples. He appeared fit but was obviously flustered by the huge social breach of etiquette. "My name is Valerius Maximus, appointed the territorial governor by Tiberius. I am not one to stand on ceremony. But I do need to have my military escort housed and cared for. We were ambushed by a party of bandits overland between the two rivers. There are wounded men who require medical attention."

"Right away," he replied. "I will have the officer of the guard take care of it."

"This is my wife, Hereca, and there is my advisor, Marcellus, a former centurion. Are our quarters ready?"

"Yes, sir. They are spacious, with several meeting rooms for entertaining foreign dignitaries, but I must admit they require a bit of sprucing up. We have not done much in the way of furniture and decorations. We thought we would leave that up to you."

"That would be fine. We can take care of that later. Lead the way."

The small group strode toward the center of the fortress along the main avenue. "By the way, where is General Voculus?" Valerius asked.

Not here, sir," replied the legate. "He departed four days ago to Carnuntum, around twenty miles downriver. He said he wanted to visit the garrison there and meet with Governor Portunus."

"When will he return?"

"I asked him the same, but his response was vague. Didn't really say when he would be back."

Valerius fumed. Of course he didn't say. He wanted to be as far away as possible and out of touch so he could disavow any association or connection to the ambush. The man was shrewd. Perhaps Marcellus's suggestion that the man should meet an unfortunate accident was the best alternative.

* * *

Ten days later—he had to allow for travel time—Valerius convened a meeting at his headquarters, gathering the governors of the four provinces—Raetia, Noricum, Pannonia, and Moesia—along with the legates of the six legions, including the overall legionary commander, Voculus. Valerius scheduled the meeting to expound his purpose in the Danubius territory to these powerful men and what he expected of them. He also wanted to get to know the governors and the generals of the Danubian legions.

They assembled in a large rectangular room. The governors and legates were seated at an assortment of tables, all facing Valerius. The group had mingled and chatted for perhaps half an hour, getting to know one another, before Valerius signaled it was time to begin. He nodded at two stern-faced legionaries who shut the door behind them.

Valerius stood. "Gentlemen, it's been a pleasure meeting each of you. Thank you for coming here at such short notice. Some of you are probably wondering what I am doing here, so let me get right to it. I have been appointed by Tiberius to temporarily assume command of this territory. What does that mean to you? Hopefully, nothing. It is not my intention to stick my nose into every little detail of how you govern your province. I was not appointed to this post to lord over you. So please continue your operations as usual."

He paused. "So, again, why am I here? To wage war on the tribes north of the river? Hardly. In fact, quite the opposite. Tiberius has asked me to encourage the barbarian tribes to establish commerce with Rome to make their leaders rich. More succinctly, the emperor wants me to replicate the success I attained as governor of Germania. Not to boast, but with the assistance of my wife, Hereca, and my associate, Marcellus," he gestured to both, "we have achieved extraordinary results with the German tribes along the Rhenus. To be clear, the tribes and clans across the Rhenus are not conquered. There is, however, a prevailing peace. Most of the tribes engage in trade with Rome and have established markets. It appears to be a mutually beneficial situation."

Valerius paused, letting his gaze wander over each of the powerful men in attendance. "Before this meeting was convened, I got the opportunity to greet each of you and speak to you, albeit briefly. Several of you have already pleaded to have your garrisons reinforced with additional legions. Let me just say this: I am reluctant to petition Tiberius for additional legions here on the Danubius. He would be most displeased with such a request. That is counter-intuitive to what I am supposed to be doing here. The idea is to pacify the tribes on the other side of the river so that we can manage the border with the existing forces or less. So, the only way any of you will get additional troops is if I shift troops from one province to another. And I am not ready to proceed with that initiative."

Governor Iacomus Portunus of Pannonia, a former senator and the most senior among the four governors, arose, shifting his portly frame from out of the chair. He had been among those requesting more troops. "Speaking for all of us, we hope you are successful in your quest. But you must understand that the tribes along the Danubius are not the same as the ones along the Rhenus. I would go so far as to characterize some of them as pure evil. Many are devoted to looting and killing. They only respond to force. Candidly, the sharp end of a gladius is our best option. This is not Germania but a different breed of barbarians. What we have achieved and are continuing to do is keep the barbarians at bay on the opposite side of the river. I'd like to believe we have been successful to that end," he concluded in a pretentious tone.

There was a chorus of muttering among the audience. Valerius should have anticipated that response. He quickly assessed Portunus. He was the first to speak and, if not the leader, the one with the most influence. His words, although politely and glibly delivered, reflected intransigence. He labeled Portunus as *the pompous ass*. Valerius needed a proper retort quickly to countermand Portunus's words and avoid the risk of losing his audience.

He raised his hands for quiet. "Iacomus, you are correct. The tribes along the Danubius—the Marcomanni, the Quadi, the Iazyges, the Roxolani, and the Dacians—are unlike those along the Rhenus." Valerius's voice rose in volume. "But don't tell me how ferocious these men are. I have fought the Germans on and off over the last twenty years. They damn took my head on several occasions. I was one of the few survivors of the Teutoburger disaster." He pointed to Marcellus. "My associate, Marcellus, was a centurion in Germania for over thirty years. He could tell you tales that would chill you to the bone about the savagery of the Germans along the Rhenus. But things have changed. Now, they are more inclined to trade than battle. One thing all men have in common is greed. These tribes want what we possess in the way of goods—luxurious items such as wine, silk clothing, jewelry, furniture, and iron tools. In the coming days, I intend to confer with all of you on how best to deal with these tribes and their leaders. I welcome your thoughts on how to proceed."

Another figure stood. "Sir, Aelius Avilius, Governor of Noricum. I agree with Governor Portunus. The barbarian tribes along the Danubius are different from those along the Rhenus. I am not sure you will have the same success that you achieved along the Rhenus. The circumstances are not the same."

Valerius seethed but offered a disarming smile. *How much does this horse's arse know about the German tribes? Probably nothing. He is merely supporting Portunus.* "Governor Avilius, we will never know unless we try."

Next, Governor Gnaeus Antonitus of Moesia stood. He was responsible for the largest province, which was the farthest to the east. He was a thin man with a severe appearance. "I would welcome enhanced trade with the Dacians, Iazyges, and the Roxolani, but I hope you understand that this is a vast territory, and the tribes are a fractious lot. Some might welcome your trade initiatives, others would be opposed, and many will be cautious and adopt a wait-and-see approach. I view this as a long-term venture, but as time goes by, alliances shift and change. Frankly, I am pessimistic that much can be achieved in Moesia, but I'm willing to attempt this strategy."

Valerius nodded. "Thank you for your remarks, Governor Antonitus."

Surveying his audience, Valerius noticed several of the legates fidgeting about, looking uncomfortable. No doubt Voculus had already attempted to poison their thoughts regarding the competency of Valerius and his team.

"As to the six legions posted along the river, we shall not be soft on any transgression by the tribes. The raiding and looting must cease. We will maintain a strong posture. If need be, we will cross the river on punitive raids to make our point."

One of the legates stood. "Sir, there is a standing policy that we are not to cross the river under any circumstances."

"That rule is no longer applicable," Valerius replied sharply. "We must maintain a strong posture. Otherwise, the tribes will think we are negotiating out of weakness. I'm sure the legions are up to the task."

He gazed over his audience, noting a great deal of skepticism over what he had just laid out. He gave them a severe glare. "Gentlemen, I did not ask for this assignment. I was quite content as the procurator of the German territory. However, Emperor Tiberius gave me my marching orders to bring enhanced trade and commerce to this region. I intend to prosecute his directives to the fullest of my abilities. Please enjoy your stay here in Vindobona. I will speak with each of you individually before you leave. That is all."

Valerius watched the men exit, unable to ignore the smug grin etched upon Voculus's face. After everyone had departed, Valerius gathered Hereca and Marcellus and gestured for Radulf to shut the door.

"That went well," Marcellus said. "You would have thought we were taking their first-born children. I have never witnessed such dour expressions."

"Did you notice Voculus?" exclaimed Hereca, "His haughty expression? I kept my eyes on him throughout the meeting. I wonder if he exhibited the same smug look when he learned we survived his planned ambush. My husband, it appears we are fighting on two fronts once more."

Valerius fretted. "Nobody said this would be easy, but this is worse than I anticipated. Did we survive that ambush to face this reception? It's apparent they do not want another superior to dictate any policy changes. They prefer the status quo, which, does not look that favorable to me. Judging from Portunus's and Antonitus's words, things were not going smoothly here."

"If the appearance of their guards at this fortress is any indication of their readiness, we are in a shit-load of trouble," Marcellus commented.

"I noticed that too," Valerius replied. "They look slovenly." He paused and heaved a sigh. "We have our work cut out for us. Now, Hereca, I'm going to need a woman's touch here. We must decorate our headquarters here to reflect the finer things of Roman life, just like we did in Germania. I want comfortable billets and a luxurious setting for meetings with the tribal leaders. I know we are at the ass end of the empire, but see what you can do on very short notice. There are roads from our provinces directly to the Adriatic. See what you can acquire in the way of deluxe trappings from across the empire. Marcellus, I appoint you as the master wine steward."

The former centurion beamed. "I always wanted that job. It has been a life-long ambition."

"See what you can procure. There must be some good wines being transported up and down the river. Maybe you could cozy up to some of our esteemed governors and learn how they procure their supply. Win them over with your charm. Ask for their advice.

I can't imagine any of them skimping in terms of the quality of their wines. I will personally pay for accommodations and the wine and not charge the Roman treasury."

He paused, glancing at Hereca and Marcellus. "I am counting on you both to help me sway these bastards to our thinking. Portunus will be a problem. The others, I am not sure about. We must convince them to go along with us and buy into the program. We must plead and cajole, whatever needs to be done. But let me clear, if that does not work, I will personally rip them a new arse-hole."

"Now you're talking!" Marcellus yelled, punching the air.

Hereca took her husband's arm in hers. "My husband, sometimes, you are so eloquent."

"That's because I have been associated with Marcellus for too many years."

* * *

Later that day, Valerius and Marcellus went to their new offices to review any new correspondence, while Hereca decided to begin her task of beautifying and furnishing their headquarters. The duo discovered a pile of dispatches awaiting their review, some from Rome and others from Germania. Hours later, toward late afternoon, Valerius let out an exasperated sigh. "Enough for today. I promised Hereca a stroll outside the fortress. Do you want to join us?"

"Would love to, but I'm meeting with a few centurions from this fortress to give me the lay of the land from a centurion's viewpoint. Should be interesting. You go ahead. Enjoy the tranquility. Oh, don't forget to take the bodyguards with you. Just remember what happened to us on the way here from Germania."

"I will. I need to get Hereca out of this military fortress, if only for a while. Let me know how your discussion goes."

Valerius and Hereca strolled arm and arm along the river road. Radulf and two other legionaries followed discreetly, ensuring they could not overhear their conversation.

"This reminds me of our home along the Rhenus," Hereca said. "I love the sounds and smell of the river. It has a pulse all its own. We walked along the Rhenus on many occasions. I would like to do the same here. Can we do this regularly?"

"Of course, my dear. It will be a welcome break from our duties."

"We haven't been gone for long, but we are so far away. I miss our children so much."

"Then I have good news for you. When I went back to our headquarters, there was a mountain of correspondence, including a letter from my parents. They say all is well with the children."

Hereca stared at him petulantly. "Why didn't you tell me?"

"I just did."

She glared at him, letting him know that was not an acceptable response.

"The letter is waiting for you back in our quarters. I knew you would want to read it and savor its contents. Everything is fine. Both of my parents wrote it. There are two different scripts. In summary, the children are fine and doing their lessons. My father wrote that Aulus is now taller than him. In fact, they are all growing up quickly."

"And I'm hundreds upon hundreds of miles away missing them," Hereca lamented.

"We shall be with them soon enough, so don't get glum. There is more in the letter. I will not spoil it by revealing the contents."

"From whom else did you get dispatches?"

"Labenius. He reports that all is well. Everything is peaceful, and there have been no incidents. He told me not to worry about Germania and concentrate on the Danubius."

"That's good news," Hereca replied.

"Yes. The truth is that I didn't anticipate any problems, although I say that with caution, for one never knows. We have established a firm foundation in Germania. When we departed, I was confident that everything was in place for continued peace."

"And what about here?"

Valerius strolled along in silence for a few moments. "No doubt about it, this will be a difficult process, but we are going to give it our best effort. If we don't attain the success that we achieved in Germania, so be it. Tiberius can appoint somebody else. For now, we will be working on two fronts. First, we will need to vet the governors and legates to determine who is reliable and who is not."

"Based on your first meeting, it seems you will have a few who won't be cooperative," Hereca commented.

"Maybe so. But I will give them every opportunity to distinguish themselves. Furthermore, Tiberius would frown upon wholesale replacements. I will admit that our first impressions were not all that positive, but things can change."

"So, what about the tribes to the north, bordering the Roman provinces?"

"That is the second front. We need to assess who we're facing across the river. Naturally, I will heavily rely on you to help me with this."

"I feel confident that we will achieve success. I just don't know to what extent. It took us a long time to earn the trust of the German tribes. Now, we are thrust into a new situation, and we don't even know who the leaders are."

"We shall soon find out," said Valerius. "Let's talk of something else. I feel like we are living, eating, and breathing our new workplace. Let's talk of our children and their futures."

Hereca beamed. "Gladly. Where do you see our children ten years from now?"

"Believe it or not, I have contemplated their future. I hope to see them settled in Gallia or Germania. I don't want them in Rome, but I will give them that option. We have more than enough money to get them established. I hope their future is more peaceful than what we experienced."

"I wish for that as well," she said, looking at the evening sky. "Before we talk more of our children, we must turn around. It will be dark before we get back."

While Valerius strolled with Hereca, Marcellus was doing some fact-finding. Seated at a small table in a recessed corner of The Happy Goat—one of the better taverns, he was told—he made conversation with three centurions from the Tenth Legion posted at Vindobona. He had picked the men at random earlier that afternoon, overhearing their conversation next to the main barracks. They were discussing their choice of taverns for the night. Marcellus had approached them, introduced himself, and told them he would pay for the wine if they would indulge him in a brief discussion about life in the legions along the Danubius. Actually, his motive was a bit more circumspect, and he intended to probe these officers about their shabby appearance and uniforms. None of them were up to legion standards. It didn't make sense, and he was going to find out why.

Marcellus ordered another round of wine from the serving girl. Thus far, the conversation had been guarded, perhaps better described as stilted. His questions were mainly about their past assignments and current duties, and their responses had been clipped, wary. He was not getting anywhere with his subtle approach.

The wine arrived, and all the men took a deep draught. Marcellus heaved a sigh. "Listen, let me be more direct. I'm a former centurion, and I managed my men well. I was dismayed when I entered the fortress and observed the condition of the men's uniforms, even the optio of the guards. I am not a stickler for appearances, but it was hard not to notice. I expected better. So, what gives? Please, be honest with me. I'll keep your remarks confidential."

The three centurions exchanged glances, silently determining who would speak first. Finally, a centurion called Junius spoke up in an angry tone. "You think we don't know our uniforms look like shit?"

Marcellus held up his hands in a placating gesture. "That's why I'm asking. There must be a reason."

"It's like this. We put in requisitions for uniforms, equipment, weapons, and you know what we get? Nothing. Our quartermaster stores are empty. Except for our rations, all of our requests seem to go nowhere. The men are wearing armor and tunics that are beyond repair. All of the centurions in the Tenth have a real case of the ass about this subject. So consider yourself lucky you broached the subject with us. We are more of the mellow sort."

Marcellus surveyed the three faces. "So, what gives? I know how the legions work. You request stuff, and you get around half of it."

The one named Laurentius spoke up. "We don't get any of it. If we were to conduct a forced march tomorrow of, say, fifty miles, I believe many of the men would be barefoot by the time it ended, and that's not an exaggeration. Their marching boots are in tatters beyond repair. I can't even get replacement hobnails for my men's marching boots. What kind of shit is that? It's a disgrace."

"What does General Caelius say about all this?"

"Not much," said the third centurion, Nonus. "Don't get me wrong, I believe our legate is a fine officer. The word I'm hearing is that the officers of the Tenth go through the normal channels and request uniforms and equipment, but nothing happens."

"What are these normal channels?" Marcellus asked.

The three centurions looked around silently. Finally, Junius spoke. "You didn't hear this from me, but the word going around is that our requests go through Governor Portunus, and then, nothing happens.

Marcellus offered a tight-lipped expression. "Let me take this up with Governor Maximus. I will say that I heard this through an anonymous source. You should know that he was a tribune and served under Germanicus on the German campaign, so we understand a thing or two about how the legions operate. Consider both the new governor and me as your allies. We will get to the bottom of this mess." Marcellus waved his arm to attract the attention of the serving girl. "Let's order some more wine."

CHAPTER XII
PORTUNUS

The next day, upon General Voculus's invitation, Governor Portunus met in Voculus's office for a private discussion. Portunus adjusted his substantial bulk in the narrow, wooden chair and sipped wine from a silver goblet. He gazed at General Voculus across the rim of his glass as he thought about his long service of over ten years as the procurator of Pannonia, well past the longevity of most imperial-appointed governors. A former ally of Tiberius in the senate, Portunus had leapt at the opportunity when the imperator suggested that he consider the position of governor. Why? Because his financial fortunes had plummeted. His shipping company had experienced horrific losses from a plethora of storms that had plagued the seas that year. Needing to replenish his coffers to escape penury, he saw the governorship as a way to do it. In his ten years as governor, he had systematically looted the province of Pannonia, stealing every denarius he could. Now, he had more money than ever.

Despite his newfound wealth, a persistent source of annoyance was his wife's incessant complaints about the living conditions and lack of sophistication of Pannonia, compared to Rome. Portunus had grown tired of his wife, and now, he found pleasure in a host of concubines. He rather liked the current arrangement. If he was lucky, perhaps that bitch would return to Rome. That would be the best scenario.

Aside from his nag of a wife, an emerging problem was this new man Tiberius had appointed to oversee the territory. If his financial manipulations were ever exposed, he would be in such deep trouble that even his friendship with Tiberius would not save him. Thus, he harbored a natural antipathy toward Maximus. A bit of snobbery was also involved. He was of the senatorial class, while Maximus was of the lower equestrian rank. Why should someone of lower status lord over him? That would not do. Portunus understood right away that the man across the table from him had been appointed by Tiberius through Sejanus, and he intuitively assumed Voculus had no love for Maximus. If all went well, the two men would form a partnership against the new governor.

"So, General Voculus, what are we going to discuss today?"

"Oh, I think you know," Voculus replied. "Let's be candid with each other, shall we? I believe we are of the same mind regarding Maximus. This man thinks he has all the answers based on his achievements in Germania. Quite frankly, what this man is proposing to do is sheer folly. Just so you understand, I was nominated for this position by Sejanus to oversee the legions here. So, while Maximus is technically my superior, I hold much sway back in Rome. To be blunt, I would not shed a tear if Maximus failed in his efforts."

Portunus offered a smug smile. "Yes, I believe we should become allies. This man could disrupt everything. There are mutterings among some of the other governors as well. I do not believe they have any love lost for Maximus. How do you think we should proceed?"

"There are several things we can do," Voculus responded. "First, we should subtly impede his initiatives. Please note I said *subtly*. We cannot oppose him outright. Remember that Maximus was appointed by Tiberius, who holds him in high esteem for his past actions and service to Rome. We must not appear to be obstructionists. However, since we will control much of the narrative in the dispatches to Tiberius from you and others in positions of power, we must cast Maximus in a bad light. Another advantage we have is that the dispatches composed by Maximus will be vetted by Sejanus in Rome. Any messages critical of us can disappear.

Portunus stroked his ample chin in thought. "I see. This could be a long process. Would it not be easier for Maximus and his followers to meet an unfortunate accident?"

Voculus refrained from sharing his botched attempt at killing Maximus and his colleagues. The fewer who knew about that failed assassination, the better. He silently cursed Ivarr for his abortive attempt to kill Maximus.

Portunus noted the dour expression on Voculus's face. "Is something wrong?"

Voculus offered a thin smile. "No, I was just thinking of something that annoyed me. It is of no consequence. Getting back to your question, it would, but we must be extremely careful that nothing can be traced back to us. If Tiberius ever discovered our complicity in such an event, nothing could save us from his wrath. Furthermore, Maximus is a capable opponent. He is not easy to eliminate."

"So, how do you want to proceed? I hate to sound impatient, but this man is already a thorn in my side. What are the next steps?"

"I will get back to you. Once Maximus articulates his strategy, we can begin. Every mishap and failure will be embellished and blamed on him. If there is a raid across to our side of the river by a hostile tribe, we will trace it back to his failed policies. We must point a finger at him at every opportunity."

"I am in agreement with you, General Voculus. Let us rid ourselves of this arrogant figure as soon as possible."

* * *

Two days later, Valerius, Hereca, and Marcellus met with Titus Placidius, the governor of Raetia. To date, their meetings with the other three procurators could hardly be termed a success, more aptly described as a disappointment. The atmosphere of the meetings had been cold; their ideas received a hostile reception and were, for the most part, scorned.

At the moment, they were seated around a small round table with Placidius, the youngest of the governors, probably in his late thirties. He was a tall, lean figure dressed in a simple tunic.

Valerius dreaded another interview. He was prepared for more pushback and stubbornness. Were all these governors alike? He guessed if he were in their boots, he might feel somewhat threatened, but the obstinacy and sheer hostility he had experienced thus far were beyond his expectations.

Valerius began his usual pitch. "You know, Titus, we have had stunning success in our mercantile dealings with the Germanic tribes. Tiberius was elated with what we had achieved. As you probably know, the emperor and his late brother, Drusus, spent their earlier years fighting the Germans. He thoroughly loathed them as a people, which made our accomplishments all the more spectacular. I could use the word victorious, but that would be incorrect, implying there was a loser and a winner. In this case, both sides won. There is lasting peace, and people on both sides of the river are becoming rich."

Before Valerius could continue, Titus interjected, "Yes, I'm anxious to begin this quest with the tribes across the river from my province. We have a strong military presence with the Third Legion based in Castra Regina, which is our main fortress in Raetia. Yet, we still face sporadic raids, primarily from the Marcomanni and, to a lesser extent, from the Quadi at the far eastern end of our province. It all seems so pointless. The raiders gain very little. Oh, they do capture some booty, but many are caught and either executed or sold into slavery. I think much potential can be unlocked with more commerce over armed conflict."

Valerius exchanged sideways glances with Hereca and Marcellus, not quite believing his ears. "Titus, let me ask you something. Do you think you could identify the Marcomanni leaders so that we could have discussions with them? When I say *we*, that would include you."

"Titus pondered for a few moments. "Yes, I could, but I would need to qualify that statement. I'm sure there are chieftains whom I don't know but should be invited and some who shouldn't. I can only guess about the hierarchy of some of these peoples. We may need to consult with some Marcomanni leaders to obtain a comprehensive list of names."

"Do you speak any of the languages?" Hereca inquired.

Titus shrugged. "I'm a relative newcomer. I've been here for less than two years. I understand a few phrases and know about their gods, but that's about it."

"What about them? Do they speak any Latin, perhaps some Greek?" Hereca asked.

Titus shook his head. "Some of them speak a bit of Latin. We always bring interpreters when interacting with the various clans."

Marcellus edged forward in his chair. "Tell us about your conflicts with them. Are they pitched battles or just skirmishes?"

"The river serves as an effective barrier," Titus replied. "But they occasionally cross at fords, assuming the water is not too high, as it oftentimes gets in the spring runoffs. Sometimes, they swim across. While they have some crude boats, they are no match for our navy. When they raid, it's strictly hit-and-run. They understand that if they dally or take too long to plunder, we will be on them. The navy ensures my legionaries quickly reach where they need to be. Hence, the Marcomanni success rate is nothing to brag about."

"Tell us about their trade goods," Valerius said.

"They produce the same goods that I'm guessing the Germans do on the Rhenus—you know, timber and hides—but they also have other sources of material wealth. They have gold and silver mines, and they smelt the metal themselves."

Valerius exchanged knowing glances with Hereca and Marcellus. "Now we know why Tiberius is interested in seeking favorable trade with these people. Titus, we would like to begin our trade negotiations in your province. We want you to be part of the process, but please understand that Hereca and I will be doing the negotiation. We both speak the language and have experience in this matter."

"Fine by me. As long as we can put an end to this incessant raiding. The inhabitants of Raetia look to Rome for protection, and sometimes, we do not do a good job fulfilling their expectations. Frankly, they deserve better."

"We will be in touch, Titus. I'm looking forward to dealing with the Marcomanni. Together, we can achieve good things for Rome, the people of Raetia, and the Marcomanni."

After Titus left the room, Hereca beamed. "It's a start. Raetia is the smallest and westernmost province along the Danubius with minimal hostilities. We can set an example that the others will envy."

* * *

The next day, Valerius, Marcellus, and Hereca were scheduled to meet again with Governor Portunus. The fortress of Vindobona, their home base, was in his province of Pannonia. The governor had made his headquarters in the fortress of Carnuntum, about twenty miles downriver, which was odd because Vindobona was a much larger base with greater activity. Portunus entered the meeting room with a scowl, accompanied by the military commander of the Tenth Legion, General Caelius. Portunus sat down and held up a wax tablet for all to see. His jowls shook as he spoke, his voice shrill. "I just received this an hour ago, a message from one of my cohort commanders. Apparently, some local members of the Quadi tribe raided one of our settlements not even ten miles from here. How brazen of them! No doubt they are aware of your presence and are sending you a message. They slaughtered several villagers and rustled some of their cattle. They were seen herding the cattle across the river at a nearby ford. Your efforts to pursue trade with these filthy barbarians will never work."

Valerius looked up calmly from his seat at the table. "So, Governor Portunus, what is your response in such situations? What do you do?

Portunus glanced at his legate before responding. "Unless we catch them on our side of the river, we do nothing."

"That's right," General Caelius added. "It is standard operating procedure for us to refrain from crossing the river in pursuit of raiders."

"May I ask why not?" Marcellus inquired frostily.

"This policy was enacted for two reasons," Portunus explained. "First, we do not want to inflame the passions of the barbarians, making it appear we are invading their territory. Second, years ago, when a partial cohort crossed the river in search of bandits, they were ambushed and killed by a much superior force. The raiders were merely bait, enticing us to chase them."

Valerius silently fumed. He deliberately did not speak, letting the silence convey his displeasure.

The legate and Portunus exchanged nervous glances, wondering how to break the uncomfortable quiet.

Caelius cleared his throat. "Our naval patrol boats have caught—"

"Let me see if I understand this," Marcellus interrupted. "You do not pursue or retaliate across the river because the Quadi, or whoever they are, might believe Rome is invading their lands, which, in turn, might spawn further raids, but it's acceptable for these barbarians to set foot on Roman soil and do their dirty work. Is that what you are saying?"

Caelius fidgeted before replying. "Yes, but it has been effective. There have been no full-scale invasions by the barbarians."

"Is that so?" Marcellus replied skeptically. "Yet we let them pillage Pannonia with impunity." Turning to Valerius, he continued, "This is definitely not Germania."

Marcellus turned back to Portunus. "As I recall the other day, you stated that the only thing the Quadi understood was force and cold steel, or words to that effect. Your policy certainly does not back this up."

Valerius ignored Portunus and looked directly at Caelius. "General, do we have any idea who might have raided the village on our territory and stolen the cattle?"

"No, not really, but I would venture to guess that the raiders do not live far from the river."

"I see," said Valerius icily. "If we were to bring some villagers who had their cattle pilfered on a punitive raid across the river, could they identify the culprits? I assume they would know their cattle if they saw them."

"Yes, I believe they would."

"Good," replied Valerius. "Because two days from now, one of your cohorts—no, make that two of your cohorts—are going to cross the river along with some of the villagers and seek out these raiders to retrieve their cattle. I will also be joining. This will be a retaliatory expedition. We are going to bring the cattle back and let the Quadi know that this behavior will not be tolerated in the future."

Portunus stood. "I must protest. You cannot do this. Only I can authorize military force. This is my province."

"You are mistaken, Governor. I believe Tiberius apprised you and the others of my authority. It extends above all the provinces, including yours. Furthermore, this is not your province; it is Rome's. And I just permitted General Caelius to gather his forces for a punitive raid across the river."

"You are going to get us all killed and incite a major uprising," Portunus retorted. "I strongly object."

"Your objection is noted," Valerius replied dismissively. "I cannot negotiate trade with these barbarians from a position of weakness." He stared directly into General Caelius's eyes. "General, you have your orders. I will leave it to you to assign the required cohorts and arrange the necessary naval forces to transport us across the river. Please inform my headquarters when and where we will cross the river."

"Yes, sir," he replied.

"Fine. You are all dismissed."

* * *

Portunus stormed out of the room, heading toward the military headquarters of Voculus, who had conspicuously not been invited to the meeting. He barged into Voculus's office without so much as a hello, his face enflamed in anger.

Voculus looked up from a dispatch he was reading. "Governor Portunus, you look a bit ruffled."

"How dare that man. Damn him to Hades! Do you know what he's going to do?" Portunus ranted without awaiting an answer. "He has authorized a military operation across the river without my consent and against standing orders not to engage the barbarians on their side of the river. He is upsetting the status quo and risking a catastrophe. I know I report to him, but I also answer to Tiberius. He is the one who appointed me to this position. I'm going to inform the emperor of his risky and irrational behavior.

Voculus grinned inwardly. His mission of upending Maximus was looking easier by the moment. People in power were approaching him, and he had hardly begun his quest. "So, why has Maximus sanctioned military action across the river? Do tell."

"Because I mentioned that the barbarians had raided one of our settlements, killed some of the inhabitants, and rustled their cattle. He chose to unilaterally conduct a reprisal raid using my troops. The Tenth Legion billeted here are my troops. I decide how to deploy them. I won't take orders from a man of his inferior birth. In hindsight, I never should have mentioned about the bloody raid to him. It was a mistake."

"The unmitigated gall of that man!" exclaimed Voculus. "I agree. Why don't you craft a dispatch to Tiberius? If you don't mind, I would like to review it before you send it. Perhaps I can add some observations that may strengthen your points. It's up to you; just a suggestion. I would write my own dispatch, but the message will carry more importance coming from you."

"I would gladly accept your additions, General Voculus. I cannot wait to craft this communication. Tiberius must understand what problems he has created by appointing Maximus.

136

"Good. Let me know when you are finished."

He watched Portunus exit. He preferred complaints or negative comments about Maximus coming from others than himself. That way, he could not be viewed as obstructing Maximus's efforts. Let someone else do that.

CHAPTER XIII
RETALIATION

Two days later, Valerius, Hereca, and Marcellus strode down the broad main avenue of the fortress to General Caelius's military headquarters. They passed formations of legionaries going about their duties, guard details patrolling, and work crews improving and repairing the fortress. Huge storage granaries towered over them on the left side of the avenue. Both Marcellus and Valerius wore their armor and swords and had their bows strapped across their back. Upon entering the *principia* of the legate, they were ushered into his office by an aide.

Caelius, in the process of strapping on his armor, had a slave behind him buckling his armored cuirass. He motioned for the slave to leave and his aide to shut the door. When they were alone, he began, "I just wanted to let you know that I am not opposed to this action. I wholeheartedly agree and endorse its purpose. I do not get to set policy around here and must obey what the governor orders. Please don't get the idea that I will undermine this military endeavor. Quite the opposite. I have selected two of my best cohorts, the first and the fourth, to partake in this effort. I believe you will be pleased with my men's state of readiness. The ships are ready at the quay. I had to do a bit of pleading and cajoling to persuade the navy to provide these vessels on such short notice, but when I said the orders came from you, they snapped right to it. For your information, we will be sailing about ten miles upriver to the crossing the Quadi used to raid our shores. I have also summoned several village leaders whose cattle were stolen. They are waiting at the dock."

"Were they reluctant to come? Did you have to force them? "Valerius asked.

"By Hades, no. They want retribution and their cattle back. The village chieftain believes he knows which tribe did the raiding and where they are located. He thinks it's not too far from the river, an easy march."

"So this operation can be accomplished in one day?" Marcellus asked.

"If all goes according to plan," the legate replied.

"Good," Marcellus remarked. "In my experience, the simpler and shorter a military operation is, the better. Time to teach these arse-holes—what's their name—the Quadi, a lesson.

Valerius added, "By the way, General, why does Portunus have his headquarters downriver at Carnuntum? It's about twenty miles away. This is by far the largest fortress for Pannonia, and your legion is based here. It seems a bit odd."

Caelius shrugged. "I'm not really sure. He chose Carnuntum before I arrived. The man is highly guarded in his dealings. He does not want others to know about his business affairs. I have heard rumors that he sometimes furtively conducts commerce in the dead of night. It all seems rather strange, so I would prefer not to speculate."

Marcellus snorted. "Possibly not all of the emperor's taxes collected from Pannonia find their way to Rome. It is not unheard of that some governors enrich themselves at Rome's expense."

"Interesting," Valerius remarked. "We will need to examine the finances of Pannonia when the opportunity arises. I suspect that our friend Portunus is funneling large amounts of cash into his personal accounts."

"Then we can get rid of the lout," Hereca opined.

"Again, I have no first-hand knowledge," Caelius said, "but it wouldn't surprise me. There's a lot of unrest in Pannonia concerning the tax levies. "

Valerius smiled. "We can tuck this tidbit away for future use. For now, we need to concentrate on the task at hand—foraying into the barbarian lands. Let's get going."

* * *

The centurions quickly organized their troops, around a thousand legionaries, to begin the boarding process. Transport ships were lined up along the quay, while others were anchored in the river, awaiting their turn to dock and pick up their men. Valerius and Hereca walked toward a small group gathered to the side and away from the centuries. On observing several indigenous civilians surrounding a centurion and General Caelius, Valerius and Hereca approached the group.

Caelius looked up and gestured toward the three men. "This is Detlef, Merten, and Theodor. They are members of the village that was attacked. I've been attempting to discuss with them the exact location of the settlement of the Quadi invaders but without much success. We are facing some communication issues, which is a raging understatement. They do not speak Latin very well and neither I nor my aides have much expertise in their language. Also, our usual interpreter is missing. But I've heard that you and your wife speak their language."

Hereca stepped forward. "Why don't you let me have a go at this." Without waiting for a reply, Hereca began conversing with the three men. Smiles immediately lit up the faces of the villagers as they chatted back and forth. The dialogue continued for a while.

When they were finished, Hereca addressed the legate. "This is a summary of our conversation and what you need to know. They say the leader of the raiders is a chieftain named Urs, whom they recognized during the attack. He and his men have crossed the river on other occasions. Some of his warriors raped their women and killed a few men who resisted. They have stolen about fifty head of cattle. They think this Quadi village is no more than three miles from the river and situated along a small brook. When I asked them about the size of the settlement, they said they weren't sure, but they guessed it's no more than a thousand warriors. I asked how they knew this, and they said other people from this side of the river occasionally cross over to trade, and this is what they reported."

Caelius adopted a look of awe. "Amazing. Thank you for that. It might have taken us hours to garner that information. If this village has only a thousand warriors, my cohorts should be able to subdue them in short order. We can raze the village and kill or capture the inhabitants and be back before nightfall."

"Hold that thought for a moment," Valerius said. "I don't want to destroy the village and annihilate the residents."

"Then what do you have in mind? I thought this was a punitive expedition," Caelius remarked.

"It is, but not exactly. I would like to surround the village and herd them into the center using your two cohorts. Defend yourselves if needed. Any resistance is to be met with force. Once they are gathered with Roman steel poised at their throats, I will give them two alternatives: Either they promise to cease their raiding on this side of the river and adopt trade with the people of Pannonia or, if they continue their previous ways, I will return and cross the river once more and crucify every single man, woman, and child in the village. It is a rather strong message. Do you think that might get their attention?"

Caelius grinned. "I believe it would."

"So, General Caelius, can your cohorts surround this village with minimal bloodshed so I can deliver my message?"

"I will discuss it with my two cohort commanders, but I believe they will agree this is achievable. As mentioned earlier, our men are well-trained. I will send cavalry scouts to reconnoiter the area and determine the exact location of these thieves. By the time we board the ships, sail to our destination, and unload, my cavalry should have them located."

"Excellent. Let us know when you want us to board the ships."

* * *

The flotilla journeyed upriver without incident. Upon arrival at the designated location, the men prepared to disembark their ships. Valerius stood alongside General Caelius on the command ship—anchored in the middle of the river—and watched as the transport ships methodically began unloading their human cargo. Five ships at a time nestled close to the shoreline, and the armored troops leaped into the shallows, charging toward the sandy beach. The centuries quickly formed up, securing the area and ensuring no barbarians were waiting to ambush them.

A bit later and now ashore, Marcellus approached Caelius. "Nicely done, General. The coordination with the naval fleet was impressive."

"Thank you. You know, given the short distance we had to travel upriver, my men could have just as easily marched. But between the legions and the imperial navy, we have a combined responsibility, so I thought it best to keep them involved."

"Understood, General. Your legionaries appear to be fit and proficient. You know, I had some reservations about them when I first arrived at Vindobona. The uniforms of the guard detail were not up to my legionary standards."

"What you mean, Marcellus, is that their appearance is slovenly," replied Caelius.

"I was attempting to be diplomatic in my language, which, as Governor Maximus will tell you, is not my strong suit."

"Not to worry, I have some pretty thick skin. My legion is a bit unkempt, but don't let that fool you. My men are capable. As to their appearance, their kits are worn and in need of replacement or repair. Not to whine, but I have requested funds from Portunus to replace their uniforms and weapons but without success. He promises to do something about it but never delivers. My legionaries are frustrated by the lack of an adequate supply chain."

Valerius, who had been listening from the side, spoke up. "General Caelius, Marcellus has relayed to me a conversation he had with a number of your centurions regarding your supply situation. They told him the quartermaster's warehouse is all but empty despite their frequent requests for uniforms and equipment. Quite frankly, I find this appalling. Once again, the finger points at Portunus. So here's what I'm going to do. Until this gets sorted out with Portunus, I'm going to place a temporary levy on legions from the other provinces to provide some relief from your shortages. The legates will grouse about it, but those will be my orders, like it or not. Furthermore, I will ensure that they are made whole with whatever stores they ship to you. Will this suffice as a temporary fix to your supply issues?"

"Yes, it would be most welcome. My centurions will be doing handstands. Well, maybe not, but you get the picture. Many thanks."

"My colleague, Marcellus," Valerius said, "is still a centurion at heart. He took over command when the officers of my guard detail were killed in the ambush on our journey here. He noted the shabby uniforms of the guard detail at Vindobona as soon as we entered the fortress. Frankly, I also noticed them and shared similar concerns about your legion, but, I must say, this landing is impressive. I hope the remainder of our foray into the interior goes as smoothly."

"Thank you for that," Caelius said. He then pointed upriver. "You see those riffles in the water directly ahead? That is the crossing the Quadi used on their raid. Although we will most likely be marching on a dirt path, it will not take us long to reach the village and complete our mission."

Marcellus glanced at the sky. "Appears to be a tad cloudy and cool with the threat of a rain shower. The weather should not be a factor in the movement of the two cohorts."

Caelius nodded in acknowledgment. Then, eying the bows strapped across Valerius and Marcellus's backs, he remarked. "I don't know where you got those bows and their quivers of arrows, but they are huge. Unusual weapons. I would not want to be on the receiving end of those things."

"Marcellus introduced me to these weapons many years ago," Valerius said. "They are of Egyptian origin. These weapons have saved our asses on several occasions. We don't anticipate using these today, but we always keep them ready as a precaution. One never knows."

Caelius was about to respond when a decurion approached, leading his horse by its bridle, and stood at attention. "Ah, Decurion Segundus, what do you have to report?"

"Sir, on your orders, we advanced upriver a bit earlier. My men and I followed the dirt trail inland led by one of the men from the pillaged settlement in Raetia. The village is right where it was reported to be—around three miles inland from here. We observed the village from afar. It is of modest size. My guess is less than a thousand warriors, probably more like seven hundred."

"Were you spotted by the enemy?"

"Don't think so, sir. As far as we can tell, there are no guards or lookouts. The village appears complacent. They are not expecting trouble."

"Excellent, Decurion. You may return to your men."

Caelius turned to Valerius. "So they are exactly where they were expected to be, and it appears we are undetected. I say we begin to move out right away. The last boats are discharging their men as we speak. I will briefly confer with my cohort commanders before we proceed."

Before long, the two centurions, cohort commanders, both middle-aged burly individuals, stood in front of Caelius. "This is what we are going to do," Caelius explained, "Centurion Manilius, you are going to take the lead with your first cohort. The cavalry scouts will show you the way. It is no more than three miles inland. Before you reach the village, advance to the right in the tree line so you will not be observed. Circle your men to halfway around. Centurion Faustus, your cohort will swing to the left and circle them. We must do this quickly so that we are not detected. The objective is not to destroy the village and its inhabitants but surround the village and force them toward the center."

"And what if we are attacked?" Manilius asked.

"Then defend yourselves with maximum force. But we want the village's inhabitants pushed to the center of the village. Governor Maximus will deal with them there. When you surround the village, have your men spread out, but not too far that your lines might be breached. I know this is a delicate maneuver and not one we have trained for, but I believe you can handle it. Any questions?"

Both centurions shook their heads.

"Excellent. Let's get moving.

Valerius, from his position in the middle of the Roman formation, walked next to Marcellus, while the ever-present Radulf moved alongside Hereca. Valerius warily eyed the surrounding forests on either side of the road and shuddered involuntarily. As he knew from experience, one had to be extremely wary in such situations. The column of men moved rapidly, unencumbered by marching yokes. The men carried only their shields and weapons, as this was to be a one-day excursion.

It began to rain lightly, and the drops trickled off the leaves. Marcellus sniffed the wind and then looked at the swirling gray skies. By his reckoning, it would not be a severe storm and would not threaten their plans. Even better, the sound of the pattering rain would mask the sounds of their movements. The two cohorts surged ahead, quickly closing the distance to Ur's village.

After a short period, they arrived at a point where the cavalry scouts were waiting, just a short distance from the settlement but out of sight. The thick forest gave way to cleared pastures up ahead. The men of the first cohort under Centurion Manilius began to file his troops quickly to the right side into the tree line. Caelius stood in the middle of the road, signaling the fourth cohort and its six centuries to move to the left to complete the encirclement.

Valerius anxiously strained to hear shouts of alarm, but all remained quiet. Caelius turned to face him. "We will remain here. Messengers will alert us when the encirclement is complete."

After what seemed like hours but was only about thirty minutes, they received word that the legionaries were in place. "Have your commanders begin their advance through the village," Caelius instructed the two messengers. "Have them move quickly but deliberately."

Valerius waited some more. A protective contingent of half of a century accompanied Caelius and Valerius as part of the command group. They were not part of the maneuver elements but would move directly down the road to the center of the village.

Caelius nodded to the commanding centurion of the bodyguards, and they began their advance down the dirt path entering the settlement. There was still no outcry. They continued to advance. Valerius craned his neck to see ahead, but the road curved, obscuring his sightlines.

Shrill screams pierced the air to the left and then to the right. Some of the Roman encircling force must have been spotted. As of yet, there was no clash of steel. The gods were looking favorably on the Romans that day. The frightened villagers, upon spying the menacing legionaries advancing toward the village from the rear and flanks, fled toward the center of the settlement, just as Valerius had hoped.

The village chieftain, Urs, bolted out of his crude hut. Not exactly understanding the tactical situation and the numbers he was up against, he began waving his spear and organizing his men into a defensive line near the center of the settlement, unwittingly aiding the Roman strategy of having everyone clustered in one area.

Valerius and the command group rounded a slight bend in the road and observed the first clustered huts and the now panicked inhabitants up ahead. The legionaries, almost a thousand in number, emerged from the surrounding forests and fields, cordoning off the village. The men of the twelve centuries moved forward, tightening their ranks into an impenetrable wall, herding the villagers toward the center. Caelius shouted for his men to halt. The impenetrable ranks of the legionaries presented a barrier of shields with razor-sharp swords protruding menacingly.

Valerius and Caelius, together with their bodyguards, entered the village front entrance and past the outer ring of dwellings, directly toward the heart of the settlement.

Not waiting for orders from their chieftain, a group of warriors, perhaps thirty in number, rashly charged at the legionary shield wall of the first cohort. Their efforts were futile. A handful was summarily slaughtered by the short Roman stabbing swords. The remainder of the Quadi quickly retreated to their village chieftain, while the legionaries held their ground and did not pursue their attackers.

Valerius turned to Caelius. "Let me take it from here." He stepped forward and shouted, "I want the chieftain and his advisors in front of me now. No harm will come to you if you do as I say. If you attack, we will kill each and every one of you."

At first, no one stirred. Urs scowled, and then he and a few of his lieutenants moved forward toward Valerius.

"Halt," barked Valerius. "Drop your weapons before you come any closer. Do it now."

After exchanging glances, Urs motioned for his men to drop their spears and swords. They approached closer and halted, staring at Valerius with hostile gazes.

"Hereca, come forward," Valerius said. "I want you to speak to them, as your language skills are better than mine. Besides, you are a more disarming figure than me."

Hereca came and stood next to him.

"Ask which one is the chieftain, named Urs."

Hereca translated, speaking in German.

A towering individual of wide girth stepped forward. "I am Urs."

"Tell him I am Valerius Maximus, and I now have oversight of all the Danubian provinces."

Once Hereca translated, Urs began to object. "Why are you invading my lands and why—"

"Silence," Valerius sharply interrupted him. "Tell him to be quiet and maybe he will live."

Hereca barked the commands at Urs.

"I will do the speaking now," Valerius said. "It has come to my attention that you and your fellow warriors raided a village across the river in a Roman province. Do not deny it. I have brought some of the victims from the village with me," he said, gesturing to the three men from the Pannonian village. "Now, listen carefully. First, you will return the stolen cattle without protest plus an additional fifty head as a penalty for your transgression. Second, you must promise never to cross the river again for looting and pillaging. You may journey across the river to engage in trade, but that is all. Rome welcomes your commerce. You should try it. Your village will be more prosperous. Our markets are open and waiting for you.

"In exchange for your promise to never cross the river to raid, I will spare this village today. If I find out you have broken this oath in the future, I will cross the river and crucify every man, woman, and child in this village. Do you understand? This is no idle threat. I took your village with ease today, and I can do so again in the future."

Urs paled at his words, glancing around at the Romans surrounding him with their shield wall and drawn swords. He looked at Valerius and noticed the huge war bow strapped to his back and then the handful of dead warriors who had foolishly decided to battle with the legionary forces. Urs nodded resignedly. "I comprehend."

"Good," Valerius replied in their dialect. "We understand one another. As a gesture of my magnanimity, I will not even require hostages to ensure your compliance. But believe me when I say that I will personally come here and slaughter this village if I find you to be duplicitous."

"Now, round up the stolen cattle immediately, plus the additional fifty and anything else that you stole, and return it to these three men. Consider yourself lucky. You are getting off easy."

Urs looked up briefly at Valerius, who, in turn, returned a steely gaze. The chieftain then barked a command to his men to round up the cattle plus an additional fifty heads and bring them to the Romans. This was done quickly without protest or incident. All the while, the Roman legionaries remained poised with their shields and drawn swords.

Valerius turned the proceedings over to Caelius with a nod of his head. "As a suggestion, General, you might want to assign some of your legionaries to help the men from Raetia with the cattle if we hope to get back before darkness."

Caelius summoned his two cohort commanders and issued their marching orders. Before long, the Roman centuries began their withdrawal, along with the cattle, slowly but with purpose, never once turning their backs on the village.

Valerius released a breath he seemed to have been holding for the last hour.

"Nicely done, sir," Caelius said. "I never thought we could achieve such success without some major bloodletting. Your strategy worked perfectly."

"Thanks to you and your cohorts," Marcellus voiced. "A most impressive performance. I hope the other legions along the Danubius are as proficient."

Caelius grinned. "My men are good. They are experienced and well disciplined."

Hereca sidled up to her husband. "You would not crucify the entire village if Urs broke his oath, would you? That would be the height of cruelty—a terrible death."

"Both you and I know that I wouldn't do that, but what's important is that Urs believes me. Fear is an important motivator. Let's hope that the chieftain never tests our resolve. We have accomplished two things today: We have restored the faith of the people of Pannonia that we will defend them and their property, and more importantly, we have sent a message to the Quadi. Rome will no longer tolerate these across-the-river raids, and we will engage them in trade discussions, a much more peaceful alternative. Word will spread quickly among the Quadi settlements. I am giving them a chance for a more prosperous future. I believe my clemency of Urs and his warriors was a good decision and not a sign of weakness on our part."

Caelius grinned. "I am not opposed to what you did today. If needed, my men will gladly serve as your iron fist. I have no doubt that at least one group of arseholes from some village will test your resolve. When that happens, we will engage them and make them pay."

CHAPTER XIV
MORE ANGER

Imperial Palace at Capri

It was mid-afternoon, and Tiberius was seated at his desk, squinting as he perused a dispatch. Two secretaries sat nearby, awaiting further instructions. The emperor frequently dictated his replies to the correspondences funneled to him from all over the empire. Across the table from him sat Sejanus, dressed impeccably in the uniform of the Praetorian prefect. Tiberius grunted and discarded the dispatch, selecting the next one from the top of the pile marked urgent—it was from Governor Portunus.

A cool breeze wafted through the open shutters of the room, gently fluttering the drapes. Out the window and in the harbor far below, the sea sparkled in the summer sunshine. Tiberius paused to savor the comforting draught before he began reading. A look of annoyance crossed his face, quickly transforming into a cold fury. He slammed the dispatch on the tabletop. "Damn that Maximus! What in Hades is he doing on the Danubius? This correspondence is from Governor Portunus of Pannonia. He states that Maximus has usurped one of his legions, crossed to the north side of the river, and invaded the lands of the Quadi. Who does he think he is, the next Julius Caesar? I sent him there to establish commerce with the barbarian tribes, not lead a military excursion. It is against our policy to cross that river unless absolutely necessary."

Sejanus remained silent, allowing Tiberius's anger to build. He smiled inwardly. His plan was unfolding just as he desired. Soon, it would be complete.

Tiberius continued. "Portunus further states that Maximus's wife, Hereca, has indulged in a spending splurge to lavishly decorate the praetorium. She has purchased some statuary and ordered fine wines, furniture, and tapestries from across the empire. I would not have suspected her of such behavior. The pair of them have disappointed me."

"I'm sorry to hear of these developments, sir," Sejanus replied glibly. "If you so desire, you can recall Maximus to Rome, and I can have General Voculus take over for them."

Tiberius fumed. "No, not yet. But I am going to send an urgent dispatch to Maximus demanding to know what in Hades he thinks he is doing there and let him know of my profound displeasure. He better have some good answers. First, he took his sweet time getting there, and now, this debacle."

"Certainly, sir," Sejanus replied in a neutral tone. He was disappointed that Tiberius did not recall Maximus, but he remained patient, at least for now. He had time. He knew he would eventually prevail.

Tiberius turned to one of the scribes. "Write this down. It is an urgent dispatch to be delivered to Maximus. It is as follows: I have been informed that you crossed the river on a military invasion using the Tenth Legion, which, I remind you, is against standard operating procedures. I sent you to the Danubius to encourage commerce, not start a war. I have also been informed that your wife has been busy procuring lavish furnishings for your praetorium. I am most displeased with these reported actions. Please explain yourself."

Tiberius turned to Sejanus. "I believe that conveys my dissatisfaction. It's blunt and to the point. He better have a good justification for all of this. I want this dispatch delivered quickly. If the messengers have to ride day and night, so be it."

Sejanus offered a thin smile. "Sir, I believe your dispatch will get his attention." He paused. Now, for the next part of his strategy, which he had been planning for weeks. "Sir, I know you are in an ill mood, but I have one other item requiring your urgent consideration. It cannot wait."

Tiberius sighed. "What now?"

"My informers have uncovered a nefarious plot against you. Even I was shocked when I saw the names of those involved. High-placed senators have made treasonous statements against you."

Tiberius's curiosity was piqued. "Who is it this time?"

"None other than a member of your inner council, Senator Marcus Hordeonius Flaccus. Also implicated are two of his confidants, Senators Magnus Decebalus and Cornelius Egnatius." He walked over to where Tiberius was seated and dropped several scrolls, documenting through sworn statements of others the treasonous declarations of the senators.

"It's all here, sir. I cannot believe that these men are plotting sedition. What's also concerning is that these men were seen conversing with Maximus before he departed for Germania. I hope there is no link. What would you like me to do, sir?"

"I will not tolerate any interference with this realm," Tiberius said testily. "Have those three senators arrested and thrown in the dungeon. I will decide their fate later. As to Maximus, let us wait to see his reply to my dispatch."

CHAPTER XV
A STRATEGY

Twilight settled upon the praetorium in the fortress of Vindobona as Valerius, Marcellus, and Hereca huddled around a polished table in the deepening shadows. Valerius shifted the oil lamp, illuminating the map of the vast area entrusted to them. They were discussing their strategy—the next steps in fostering trade with the tribes across the Danubius.

Valerius began. "We have put the word out to the Quadi that we are open for trade. Furthermore, our intrusion against Chieftain Urs and his followers several weeks ago set an example and conveyed our determination to those on the opposite side of the river. Thus far, we have witnessed no other raids on Roman provinces, so either we have made our point or they are plotting their next move. I would like to think it's the former. We have sown the seeds of progress."

Marcellus concurred, "I agree with what you said. I believe that our conquest of the village has set an example. Our incursion across the river let them know this is not business as usual, and we are not taking their shit anymore. It was a definitive statement of purpose. Your leniency towards the raiders was a master stroke, emphasizing that we are not waging war but will not tolerate future acts of marauding. It's their choice now."

"So, what are our next steps?" Valerius asked rhetorically. "This is what I believe we should do." He stabbed his finger on the map. "I strongly suggest we travel northwest back upriver to Raetia and begin there. Why Raetia? Several reasons. It's the beginning of our territory along the Danubius. So, we can start at the beginning and work our way downriver. There are other reasons as well. We have a governor, Titus Placidius, who, on the surface, appears enthusiastic about our project, much more so than the others. Also, it is the smallest province and thus more manageable. Next, across the river from Raetia are the Marcomanni. We have some familiarity with them from our experiences in Germania. Their lands are vast and border the Rhenus and the Danubius. What say you, Hereca? You know the Marcomanni better than anyone."

Hereca tilted her head in thought. "Yes, we have had dealings with the Marcomanni, and yes, that is a positive. The nation—and it is a large one—has experienced the benefits of trade with Rome. The issue, as I see it, is that the Marcomanni lands are vast. I fear there might be two factions, one on the Rhenus, the other here. The fact that we have dealt with the Marcomanni before may not be as great an advantage as you believe. But still, I think your plan has merit. As you noted, Raetia is the smallest province, it has a governor eager to enhance trade, and again, we have a perceived advantage in that we have done business with the Marcomanni. I see the other provinces as having greater challenges—they are geographically larger and have more hostile tribes and less friendly governors." She smiled. "So, yes, I like your plan."

Valerius turned to Marcellus. "What say you?"

"I agree with both of you, but I have one caveat. I don't like the thought of leaving here and losing any momentum we may have achieved in Pannonia, especially with that horse's arse, Portunus, in charge. We will have to put our trust in General Caelius. I have a high opinion of him and believe he is well qualified. But, putting that aside, I agree with your plan. When do we leave?"

"As soon as possible. We will need to arrange for ships to take us and our bodyguard upriver to Raetia. This is how I wish to proceed. First, I want to begin our negotiations with the Marcomanni. Assuming we have a modicum of success, we turn it over to Titus Placidius. After that, we will move eastward, downriver, to the next province, Noricum, and then after that, farther downriver back here to Pannonia. Then, it's onward to Moesia to deal with the Iazyges and, finally, the Dacians, who are considered by far the most bellicose. A simple plan—we move in a linear fashion from west to east. As to your point regarding losing momentum in Pannonia, I agree that is a risk. I'll have a long talk with Caelius before we leave. He has my permission—no, make that my mandate—to counter any hostile movements across the river by the barbarians. He is to retaliate by tracking down the offenders and dispensing Roman justice."

"What about the possibility of ambush?" Marcellus inquired. "He and his forces could be lured across the river and trapped. They might be vulnerable."

"He is to use his discretion. He is a capable commander and will need to exercise caution if circumstances warrant it."

"Are you not putting him in a quandary? Hereca asked. "Portunus will likely want him to stay on this side of the river."

"As I stated, I intend to discuss with Caelius before we depart. I will give him a direct standing order that he is to pursue any Quadi if they cross the river. I am the supreme commander of this territory. Portunus cannot countermand my orders."

"What about Voculus?" Marcellus asked. "Are we bringing him with us to Raetia?"

"Why should we? What purpose would he serve? No, we will keep him here, and he can stew over the fact that we did not invite him to come along. If he is offended, good. Time to put that man in his place."

"I really like that part," Marcellus said. "You know, if you ever decide to live in Rome again, there is a place in the senate for you. You are getting quite good at navigating your way around some very two-faced people. You have both ruthlessness and finesse."

"Thank you for that, but I will not be returning to Rome any day soon, especially the senate. We have enough of these cunning and deceitful types out here. Back in Rome, they are all gathered in one building."

* * *

The next day, Valerius, Hereca, and Marcellus assembled in their headquarters, finalizing plans to sail upriver to Raetia. Suddenly, an aide knocked on the door. "Sir, General Voculus is outside. He's wondering if he could have a few words with you."

"Certainly, send him in."

Voculus entered with his aide. "Thank you for seeing me on such short notice. I've brought with me my aide de camp, Centurion Gordianus. I hope you don't mind. I wanted to introduce him to you."

Valerius offered an insincere smile. "So, what do we need to speak about besides introducing your aide?"

"Sir, I heard you are heading west upriver to Raetia."

"Yes, that is true. It's no secret."

"I was wondering if I was to go also."

"I thought about that, General Voculus," said Valerius, "but decided you would not be needed there. This is not a military matter. We are attempting to encourage the tribes to establish markets for Rome's goods. I do not believe the presence of the commanding general of the Danubian legions will be of any value in establishing any rapport. Don't you agree?"

"Yes, but what if there is resistance and armed conflict ensues."

"Then I will have the legate commanding the Third Legion in Raetia handle that problem. If it is too much for him, I will send for you."

Voculus frowned in disappointment. "I see. But due to the possibility of an armed conflict, I thought it might be prudent for me to be there."

"You may have a point there, but the answer is still no. I want as small a retinue as possible. Consider the subject closed."

"Very well. I must confess I am dissatisfied with your response."

"Thank you for your time, General."

Throughout the conversation, Marcellus had been glaring at Gordianus. He had an instant visceral dislike for the man. Gordianus maintained a vacuous expression, with eyes like cinders, devoid of emotion or humanity. Marcellus had occasionally encountered such men. They were reprobates and to be avoided at all costs. These were the kind of men who tortured for pleasure and killed without mercy. Compassion for their fellow men was absent.

Gordianus caught his hostile gaze and returned it with a smirk, daring Marcellus to do or say something.

A cold fury welled up in Marcellus. He had dealt with such foul creatures on previous occasions. He knew that at some point, his sword would terminate this evil from the world, and the empire would be a better place.

159

CHAPTER XVI
PLACIDIUS

Raetia
Several Weeks Later

The ship, propelled by its oars, moved slowly, swinging sideways before gently touching the wooden pier. A small breeze blew across the water under an azure sky. A large welcoming committee stood on the wharf, awaiting the arrival of their honored guests.

Valerius observed the tall gangly figure of Titus Placidius at the head of the group. Behind him was a cluster of assorted military and civilian figures. The boarding plank was lowered to the dock, and as per custom, Valerius, the most important and powerful figure aboard the ship, was the first to depart the ship, striding across the plank.

Placidius stepped forward with a warm smile. "Sir, welcome to the province of Raetia and Castra Regina, home of the Third Legion. It's good to see you again." He then introduced his retinue of perhaps a dozen officials.

Valerius nodded and smiled and then introduced Hereca and Marcellus. He turned toward Placidius. "It has been a long journey. Would you please show us to our quarters? We all need a bath and a change of clothes. My escorting century from Germania, what is remaining of them, will be staying here with me at Castra Regina, so could you have someone point them to where they will be billeted? After we have refreshed ourselves, I would like to meet with you."

"Yes, sir. Your accommodations are waiting. I hope you find them comfortable. Your security detail will be billeted next to my legionary barracks. We will treat them as if they are part of our legion."

"Thank you for that."

* * *

Later that afternoon, Valerius, Hereca, and Marcellus gathered in a small meeting room richly appointed with fine draperies and polished furniture. They sat at a small rectangular table with Placidius.

"Let me elaborate on our strategy, "Valerius said. "There are several reasons we chose Raetia to begin our quest to establish commerce in the Danubian territories. Your province is the farthest west and closest to the Rhenus, and we have some relationship and familiarity with the Marcomanni across the river from Raetia. But, more importantly, you are the only governor who appears receptive to our efforts."

Placidius chuckled slightly. "You have no idea. The governors and their staff all met in Vindobona before you arrived in the country. The discussions were strident surrounding your appointment, and I am being kind by using the word *strident*. The dialogue was much worse. One would have thought you'd been sent to confiscate their wealth and violate their wives. The cries of ire and gnashing of teeth that accompanied the discussion were epic. I tried to introduce a modicum of reason into the conversation, but my efforts were quickly rebuffed. I am the junior-most governor, and my reasoning was rejected. I was told to keep quiet. Frankly, I do not believe Rome selected wisely while selecting this bunch."

"I expected a chilly reception, but even I was surprised at the level of acrimony," Valerius said. "But putting that aside, we are beginning our mission here. I hope you are agreeable to it."

"I am looking forward to it," Placidius said. "These governors are all from the senatorial class and were appointed by Tiberius, so they believe they have some kind of elevated status. Snobby bunch, if you ask me."

"That's rich," Marcellus opined. "Do these peacocks not realize that Tiberius appointed Valerius to this post and that he has overall jurisdiction? If they continue this self-indulgent behavior, they might find themselves without a province to govern."

"Have you had much interaction with General Voculus?" Valerius inquired.

Placidius frowned. He paused, searching for the right words.

"It's alright. You can be candid with us," Valerius reassured.

"I don't know what it is with him," Placidius began. "I can't put my finger on it, but I don't trust that man. I've had a brief discussion with him along with my legate of the Third Legion, General Petillius Severus. I trust my legate implicitly and rely on him to help administer this province. He agrees with me that there is something sinister about Voculus. Oh, he says all the right things, but he lacks sincerity. We have misgivings. For now, we are steering clear of him. He did not have much to say in the way of flattery directed at you. And although he was not openly critical of you, he made it a point to say that since Tiberius appointed you, we should cooperate whether we liked it or not. He spoke not a single word of praise about you or your accomplishments. Essentially, he implied that you were being forced upon us."

"As you are probably aware, the politics of Rome are quite complex," Valerius explained. "Voculus was appointed on the recommendation of the prefect of the guard, Sejanus. In reality, Voculus's primary role is to ensure that the legions on the Danubius remain loyal to Tiberius. I don't have a problem with that, but since the appointment was made by Sejanus, it has other implications. Putting it mildly, the prefect and I have a strained relationship. I believe he would like nothing better than for me to fail in this undertaking. My escort and I were ambushed on the road connecting the Rhenus and the Danubius. I believe this was the work of Voculus, who gets his marching orders from Sejanus. Of course, I cannot prove any of it, but I have no doubts as to who was responsible."

"I heard about that ambush, but I did not want to bring it up. Thought it might be a sensitive subject." Placidius said. "So, what are the next steps? What do you want me to do?"

"I will let Hereca answer that," Valerius said.

Hereca spoke up. "As you will remember, when we discussed strategy back in Vindobona, the first thing we decided to do was convene a meeting of the Marcomanni tribal leaders here at the fort. Invite as many chieftains as you can. If you miss some names, we can meet with them on a separate occasion. Word will spread quickly. Have plentiful food and your best wines. Offer a small sack of coins, a donative, for their attendance. We will discuss what we intend to do here and tell them Rome has an interest in their cattle, timber, their gold and silver mining. We are prepared to offer favorable trade terms with them. This is what we do. It has worked well in Germania."

"I have already compiled a list based on your instructions in Vindobona," Placidius said proudly. "Perhaps not a complete one, but it's a starting point."

"Good," said Hereca. "The important thing is to get as many bodies in the room as possible. If we've excluded someone inadvertently, we can soothe injured feelings later."

* * *

Several days later, Valerius sat with Hereca and Marcellus. Leaning back in his chair, he heaved a weary sigh. "So, this is where we are. The meeting with the Marcomanni leaders is set for two days from now. Placidius has extended the invitation to many of the settlements on the opposite side of the river. He used some of his auxiliary forces who were Marcomanni to spread the word. We will have to wait and see how many show up. Then, there is this." He tapped a scroll on the tabletop.

"This dispatch is from Tiberius. He writes that he was informed that upon my order, we invaded—that's the exact word he used, *invaded*—the opposite side of the river, contrary to standard operating policy. He demands to know what we are doing. He states that he did not appoint me here to start a border war with the barbarian tribes. There is more. Hereca, believe it or not, you also have incurred his wrath."

"Me! What have I done?"

"He's been informed that you are purchasing luxurious furnishing for our quarters in Vindobona at great expense."

"I wonder who could have communicated that information to him," Marcellus mused.

"Have no doubt that Voculus and Portunus have joined forces," said Valerius.

"How are you going to respond?" Hereca inquired.

"I will get to that. There is yet another problem. I just received a new dispatch equally as troubling." He picked up the post. "This is from my friend, Senator Quintus Salvius back in Rome. He informs me that Senator Flaccus of Tiberius's advisory council and his two colleagues, Senators Magnus Decebalus and Cornelius Egnatius have been arrested and charged with treason. These were my allies who pledged to help me against Sejanus. The prefect is trying to isolate me, and he is doing an excellent job. I'm told he has informers and spies everywhere, even out here on the frontier. Word must have gotten back to him that I met with Flaccus and the other two senators. Of course, these are all trumped-up charges. But this shows that no one is safe from Sejanus, no matter their position. Flaccus was well-liked by Tiberius and on the advisory council. That's pretty high up."

Valerius put down the dispatch. "Getting back to my response to Tiberius, I want to think about it a bit more, and then, we can all review it together."

"Fine by me," Hereca said.

"Have at it, my friend. You are much better at crafting the written word than me," Marcellus said.

* * *

The gathering of the Marcomanni chieftains was held in the praetorium of Castra Regina. The mid-day sun filled the room with bright sunshine, and a comforting breeze wafted through the window, ruffling the colorful drapes framing the window. Around twenty chieftains had opted to attend, most from villages within fifty miles of the fortress. A murmur of conversation filled the room. Several pitchers of wine, as well as silver goblets, had been placed on the table, along with assorted honeyed pastries, fruits, and cheeses.

As a whole, the chieftains harbored a deep-seated distrust of the Romans. They had been informed that the meeting's subject was the Romans' desire to increase trade with the Marcomanni. As a show of good faith, each man present had been promised a payment of twenty silver denarii. They had grumbled when they were required to leave their weapons and their retainers who had traveled with them outside the Praetorium. Only the chieftains could enter.

After waiting a bit for the chieftains to enjoy the wine—a good vintage, mellow in flavor—Valerius strode into the room, accompanied by Hereca, Marcellus, and Titus Placidius, followed by the ever-present Radulf. They had decided not to invite the legate of the Third Legion, General Petillius Severus, whose presence representing legions might arouse antagonistic feelings. Similarly, Valerius, Marcellus, and Titus eschewed wearing any armor or other military trappings. They were in strictly civilian garb.

The atmosphere suddenly hushed at the presence of the Romans. As they had rehearsed, Valerius moved to the front of the room, while his small entourage stood respectfully to the side. Valerius began, speaking fluently in their language. "Good afternoon, chieftains of the Marcomanni. My name is Valerius Maximus, newly appointed procurator of the Danubian territory."

Some of the chieftains perked up and glanced around in astonishment, not expecting a Roman governor to speak German. Others remained steadfast, glaring at Valerius, their arms folded defiantly across their chests.

Valerius continued, "Please continue enjoying the refreshments. When we have finished, each of you will be handed a small sack with the promised twenty silver denarii. Let me introduce my associates." He motioned with his arm. "This is my wife, Hereca, a native of the Dolgubni tribe in Germania, my long-time friend, Marcellus, and Titus Placidius, the governor of the province of Raetia. Some of you may have heard of me, or perhaps not. I have functioned as the procurator of the German territory for several years. In that time, commerce with the various German tribes has flourished, including the Marcomanni living along the Rhenus."

A large, middle-aged figure with an extremely broad chest and powerful arms stood. "So, what does that have to do with us, Roman? the figure sneered. "The Marcomanni along the Rhenus have their own lives to live, and we have ours." The other chieftains nodded in agreement.

"I'm sorry, I did not catch your name. Please introduce yourself. I would like to know to whom I am speaking," Valerius said.

"My name is Theudhar. Theudhar of the Marcomanni," he said proudly.

"Theudhar, it is a pleasure making your acquaintance. Do you not have a single king in charge of the Marcomanni?" Valerius asked. "I believe his name is Landebert. Is that not so?"

Theudhar scoffed. "Yes, he is the king, but he pays us no mind. I do not believe he has ever visited any of our villages."

Valerius smiled back politely. He was beginning to lose his audience. *Best to move directly to the purpose of the meeting.* "Regardless of who your king is, I am proposing a plan to enhance Roman trade with the Marcomanni and any other tribes along the river. Rome will grant you favorable trading status. In exchange for your gold, silver, and copper, plus timber and hides, Rome will supply wine, grain, and luxury items such as glass and fine clothing."

Another chieftain stood, an older man with thinning gray hair. His eyes blazed with intensity. "My name is Meinhard. There has to be more to this than the exchange of goods. What do you require from us?"

Valerius nodded to Titus, who moved beside Valerius. "It is quite simple. You must promise to cease your raiding and looting across the river. Not that all of you have participated in this, but some have. Rome desires peace in her provinces. I do not believe that is demanding too much."

The chieftains stirred amid muttered conversation, but the elderly man remained standing. "You must understand that what you call Raetia was once our land. Why should we stop our raiding?"

Hereca stepped forward. "Because there is a better way. In the end, it's all about the prosperity of your people. What we have proposed worked well in Germania. Why? Because many of the tribes have become rich and enjoyed many of the finer things in life in the way of wine, food, and clothing. Let me pose a question for you to ponder. What do you really gain from your raids? You lose some of your men in the forays, making widows grieve, and the amount of booty obtained is minimal. You could garner much more through honest trade."

A burly figure, heavily muscled with broad shoulders, stood. "My name is Gerbold. My village is not too far from the river. I have listened to what you have said. Perhaps your plan has merit. In our trade, would you consider iron ingots and weapons?"

Hereca frowned. "No. That would be one of the stipulations of our agreement."

"I understand," Gerbold said before turning around and addressing his fellow chieftains. "Although I'm disappointed that we cannot trade in iron to defend ourselves, I think this proposal is something we might consider on a trial basis."

Valerius observed the actions of the other chieftains. They appeared to defer to Gerbold. Was this the real leader of this group? He looked the part. Should he attempt to curry favor with this man?

"Rome desires to enhance trade and commerce with the Marcomanni as we have done on the Rhenus," Valerius replied. "I believe many of you will be pleased with the benefits of this trade. If you decide not to, that is your choice. But let me stress one important point. Some of you in this room have raided across the river with impunity. That will no longer be the case. I am not making threats to the Marcomanni, for that is not my intention. Quite the contrary. I am offering wealth and riches for your people. But do not test my resolve. Any future raids will be met with severe consequences. Hereca, would you please explain to these gentlemen about our trade with the German tribes?"

Hereca began. "There are many ships that travel the river that divides the German people and the Roman provinces. We have built docks, bridges, and roads on the German side of the river to facilitate trade." She was interrupted when the chieftain named Theudhar stood.

"Speaking for everyone here, this is exactly what concerns us. You will be building in our lands."

Hereca offered a disarming smile. "Yes, we did build on German lands, and our legionaries helped construct the roads."

There were gasps from the audience and angry mutters.

Hereca ignored the rumblings. "Everything we constructed was at the behest of the German tribes. They now own the roads and bridges. I want to calm your fears. Let me make this clear. There are no military fortifications on the other side of the river in Germania. There are no legionaries stationed on the German side of the river unless requested to help build something. What is more, all the German tribes are self-governed. They have their own rulers and gods to worship. If you do not believe me, go to the Rhenus yourselves and observe. The German peoples are not Roman lackeys and remain fiercely independent."

Gerbold interjected, "I think we will need to discuss your proposal among ourselves. This may be a good thing for the Marcomanni residing close to the Danubius, but we will have to evaluate it from all sides. One of my concerns is that we will be corrupted by the luxuries of the Roman Empire. We are the Marcomanni, and we—"

"We welcome all of your thoughts and overtures," Hereca said smoothly, interrupting Gerbold and preventing further invective.

Hereca involuntarily shuddered. This man was not to Hereca's liking. There was something in his eyes that troubled her. Though Gerbold spoke in an even timbre, he appeared to be masking a cold fury. Most people would not have picked up on this deception, but she had years of experience dealing with German chieftains, and she could sense duplicity. This man was dangerous. She needed to keep this chieftain, who appeared to have a hold sway with the others, from taking over the meeting. The sooner he exited this room, the better.

"Gerbold, thank you for considering this," Hereca continued. "I know the German tribes enjoy Roman goods, and it has not affected their culture and way of life. I think it might be best if we talk individually or in small groups to better answer any questions you might have. My husband and I will gladly discuss any aspect of our plan. Speaking for myself, I could use a goblet of that wine. Please feel free to enjoy the refreshments. For those of you who wish to leave, we will present you with your sack of coins on your way out. Thank you for your time."

Gerbold sat down, steaming in fury. He had not finished his remarks and was hoping to cast the Romans in an unfavorable light. He scowled, feeling outfoxed by a woman no less. He would show the Romans what he thought of their scheme, for that's what it was—a scheme to subjugate the Marcomanni.

* * *

Hours after the meeting concluded and all the Marcomanni had departed, the Roman contingent gathered in the same room. The doors were shut tightly so that no one might overhear their discussions.

"I believe that went fairly well," remarked Valerius. "When I spoke with the chieftains individually or in small groups, they appeared more receptive. That was exactly what I was hoping for. On the other hand, there was some resistance at the group level, particularly from this Gerbold. I don't know what to make of him. Some, but not all, seem to value his opinion. What do you think?"

"You've hit the nail right on the head, my husband," Hereca said. "Gerbold is a dangerous man. I have seen his type before. They suppress their anger when they speak, but underneath is a cauldron of fury. He is duplicitous. His eyes gave him away. He is against whatever you are proposing and will do everything in his power, including armed conflict. He is not to be trusted.

"If you ask me," blurted Marcellus, "Gerbold is a lying sack of shit. His eyes wandered as he spoke. People with shifting eyes are liars. I agree with you, Hereca."

"Thank you for your habitual eloquence," said Valerius.

"I believe my words are more descriptive than Hereca's. She said *duplicitous*. I said lying sack of shit. Which is more expressive?"

"Your term is certainly more graphic."

"Well, you asked for our opinions, and I just gave you mine," said Marcellus. "Governor Placidius, I believe the next time we see Gerbold, he will have a sword in his hand. The Third Legion will have to deal with him at some point."

"Titus, what did you think of our little summit?" Valerius asked.

"Believe it or not, I was pleasantly surprised. My interactions with the Marcomanni during my short stint here as procurator have not been especially agreeable. More succinctly, my naval and legionary forces have been chasing these raiders all over the province and on the river. We have peace but a tenuous one. Men such as Gerbold make life miserable. I have no proof, but I strongly believe he is among the clans who raid Roman settlements. But, putting that aside, I picked up on some of the conversations with the other chieftains and was amazed at their level of interest. So, I'd conclude by saying that I'm encouraged by our discussions here today."

"Sir, permission to speak?" Radulf asked. All eyes turned toward the newly appointed bodyguard.

"Definitely, Radulf. Please speak your mind," Valerius said.

"Since I'm only a bodyguard, I kind of blend into the background, and nobody notices me. So I heard some things that, perhaps, I was not supposed to hear." He hesitated, looking for permission to continue.

"Radulf, tell us what you heard," Marcellus said. "Speak up. Valerius is not the fucking emperor."

Radulf proffered a tremulous smile. "Only this. I positioned myself to be near this Gerbold. Like the rest of you, I distrusted this man immediately. He and two other chieftains huddled in that far corner after the meeting," he said, pointing. "I could not hear all his words, as I was discretely some distance away, but the gist of the discussion was about teaching this Roman garrison and the people of Raetia a lesson they would not forget."

There was a brief silence as everyone absorbed this latest bit of information. "Fucking Hades," Marcellus exclaimed. "There's always one arsehole to disturb our plan."

"The next question is what do we do about it?" Valerius asked and then turned toward Titus. "What indigenous assets are at your beck and call?"

"You mean spies? Informers?"

"I was trying to be a little more subtle, but yes, what assets do you have to keep us informed of what's happening in the lands of the Marcomanni?"

Titus gazed off for a moment. "We don't have any real spies who inform on their neighbors, but we do have a few men who are Marcomanni and serve as auxiliary forces for the legions. They often act as a go-between and translator when we trade, minimal as it is. So I can ask them to keep me apprised of what is happening across the river in exchange for additional silver. Does that answer your question?"

Valerius frowned slightly. "I was hoping for a more robust network of spies, but that will have to do."

"My forces will need to be on high alert given this potential threat," Titus stated. "Perhaps we can demonstrate the errors of their ways using Gerbold as an object lesson. My men know how to fight. If we can catch Gerbold in a raid, we can teach his sorry ass a lesson."

"My thoughts exactly," Marcellus said.

"All right, next on the agenda, how do we communicate to Tiberius what has transpired thus far, and how do we answer the questions he raised about us crossing the river on a reprisal raid and Hereca's furnishings? We cannot go through normal channels. Sejanus screens all correspondence, so we will have to go around him. So I plan to draft a reply to Tiberius of a mundane nature and send that through the official military couriers. Then, I will send my real response to Tiberius clandestinely using non-official couriers. Sejanus will think my dispatch through the military courier system is my official response, not knowing I am using an alternative source."

"I have men in the Third Legion under my command who act as couriers upon occasion," Placidius said. "They have made the trip to Rome, so they are no strangers to this task. My father always told me that if one uses the imperial couriers, one must assume that people other than the addressee will read it. Also, one should be extremely prudent as to what is written in a dispatch in the event it gets into the wrong hands. My couriers will get your dispatch to where you desire."

"Excellent, Placidius. Your father sounds like a wise man," Valerius said. "This is just what we need. I had planned on using Senator Flaccus as a go-between to deliver my clandestine replies to the emperor, as he was on the advisory council to Tiberius. It would have been easy for him to bring my dispatches to Tiberius's attention despite Sejanus's efforts. But that is all lost to us now with their arrests. They've probably been executed by now. That leaves me with my friend, Senator Quintus Salvius, who came to visit while I was in Rome and pledged to help me against Sejanus."

"I have no idea about his connections," Marcellus commented, "but won't it be difficult, especially with Tiberius on the island of Capri for the remainder of the summer?"

"Unknown," Valerius remarked. "But Quintus assured us of his assistance, so we will have to trust in his abilities. What I would like to do now is sit down and craft my response to Tiberius and then have you review it. Governor Placidius, would you please round up your men and get them prepared for the journey? Thankfully, we are much closer to Rome from here than in Germania, so the time taken to get to Rome will be shorter."

Later that day, Valerius sat with Marcellus and Hereca. "For your information, I have already sent a dispatch by military courier to Tiberius, noting our arrival in Vindobona and our journey here. I wrote about meeting the governors and the military leadership, plus other routine observations, such as troop strength and the status of the riverine fleet. It's a rather boring piece of correspondence. I shall label it the decoy."

Valerius then picked up a tightly wrapped scroll. "Now, here is the real message, which will be delivered to Senator Quintus Salvius in Rome. I will skip the introduction and get to the heart of the document. It reads as follows: *You inquired about incursion across the river into the lands of the Quadi. First, I would hardly characterize this operation as a military invasion. I requisitioned two cohorts—well trained, I must add—to cross the river to seek out a group of Quadi who had looted cattle from a settlement in Pannonia. The people of Rome's client states deserve our protection. This was not a punitive raid but one to set a precedent for future actions. So, why did we do this, you might ask? The answer is simple. I cannot negotiate from a position of weakness. The Quadi and all other tribes must understand they will not be allowed to raid and loot with impunity. Now, for the best part. The cohorts surrounded the offending Quadi settlement. There was a minor loss of life among the Quadi for those who foolishly challenged our legionaries. I informed the village chieftain that I was charging him fifty head of cattle for his transgression. I spared the inhabitants of the village when we could have easily slaughtered them all, but I warned them that if they raided our territory again, I would cross the river and crucify every man, woman, and child in the village and raze it to the ground. I then offered terms of trade, which, I stated, would be a more preferable course of action for his village. I hope the word spreads. I believe Governor Portunus was upset that I usurped his authority and led two of his cohorts of the Tenth Legion. I took no pleasure in this, but something had to be done to serve as an object lesson to the Quadi. I would also add, sir, that there was no tolerance back in Germania for across-the-river raids by the German tribes. They knew a price would have to be paid for any transgression. I firmly believe it should be the same here. I am now in Raetia with Governor Placidius, dealing with the Marcomanni. I will send you a separate dispatch as the events unfold here.*

Finally, regarding the lavish spending by Hereca on furnishings and luxury items, my apologies for not informing you of this. We are doing this to impress the barbarians. But, more importantly, I am using my own funds to do this, not the resources of the imperial treasury. Overall, I believe we have made progress, although it is too early to determine how substantial it is.

Valerius looked up from the scroll. "What do you think?"

"Masterful," Marcellus said. "You objectively stated the reasons behind your actions without being too defensive, and you did not put any blame on that arsehole, Portunus. I would send that out this evening and hope Tiberius gets it."

"Hereca?"

She pursed her lips in thought. "I agree with Marcellus. Without being directly critical of the leadership here, you have cast them in a bad light. They seem like a bunch of whiners and backstabbers, intent upon maintaining the status quo."

"It's settled then," Valerius said. "The dispatch goes out this evening using Placidius's couriers."

CHAPTER XVII
GERBOLD

It was mid-afternoon, and Gerbold huddled with three other chieftains from nearby villages. Over the last four days, he had hoped to recruit more to his cause, but for the most part, he was politely rebuffed. He had argued and cajoled with other tribal leaders but with little success. Some had outright rejected his entreaties while others, wary of Gerbold's power and prestige, had tactfully promised to consider his plan and get back to him. They never did. Today, he had chosen his hamlet's central hall to discuss his plan to attack several villages across the river in the Roman territory. The four chieftains gathered in the cavernous structure, the feast hall, ensuring privacy with guards posted outside.

Gerbold began. "You all attended the Romans' invitation to their fortress several days ago. They served us fine wine and gave us some coins. In my view, it's a show of weakness. They are afraid of us and are attempting to bribe us with favorable trade terms. Look at our Marcomanni brethren on the Rhenus. They are but a shadow of their former selves. Once, they were proud and fierce warriors. Now, they are a bunch of merchants, docile to their Roman master, eating out of their hands. Is that to be our fate?"

One of the chieftains nodded sagely. "What you say is true Gerbold, but the Romans have established a strong defensive barrier along the river to keep us on this side. It's a risky proposition"

Gerbold scowled. "This new Roman leader, Maximus, dangles the possibility of riches from trade. All they are trying to do is buy us off. I propose we conduct a massive raid across the river. We loot not one but several settlements to show our contempt for the Romans. This will send a clear message. Once the other Marcomanni leaders see what we have done, they will flock to our cause. This Maximus will have his answer—one he will not like."

"Gerbold, what exactly is your plan?" one of the other chieftains asked. "How many villages?"

Gerbold's mouth twisted into a vulpine smile. "This is what I propose: In three days, we bivouac at the ford near the village ruled by Chieftain Adobert. You all know the crossing and have used it before. It's about twenty miles from here. Adobert has opted not to partake in our undertaking, damn his craven heart, but no matter. If he objects to us gathering on his lands, he can kiss my arse."

The others sniggered at the remark, which heartened Gerbold even more. "So this is my plan," he continued. "We gather at the crossing, and between the four of us, we should be able to muster over two thousand warriors. That may be too many for this undertaking, but no matter. What I want to do is simple. We will cross the river in the early morning when the mist is rising off the river, obscuring our presence. Besides, the Roman ships will not be on patrol at that hour. Three villages are situated on the opposite side of the river near the ford. We divide our forces and attack all three villages simultaneously.

We take anything of value and then retreat across the river. I am not that interested in what we loot, although we will enjoy the spoils. What is important is that we send a powerful message to the Romans that we are not interested in their decadent proposals of trade."

"What about the presence of legionaries and Roman patrol ships upon the river?"

Gerbold scoffed. "The villages are not guarded by the Romans, and by the time word spreads to the Roman navy, we will be back on our side of the river. This is strictly a hit-and-run operation. I don't expect much resistance from the villages. They are ripe for our plundering."

"Might the Romans learn of our plans and be prepared to meet us?" A burly chieftain asked.

"Look around you," Gerbold said, beaming. "Do you see anyone else present? I am not announcing our intentions for all to hear, nor am I boasting about this plan. We can stick our chests out after this is over. You should take the same precautions in your own villages. Furthermore, I have set a tight time frame. We attack in three days. Even if word filters back to the Romans, it will be too late for them to do anything."

* * *

Valerius sat alone in his quarters, reviewing various reports concerning the deployment of the legions and the naval forces. A pile of scrolls on his table required his attention on various administrative matters, mostly associated with mercantile taxes. He briefly stared out the window, pondering how he had gotten here and what his next steps should be. He was optimistic that he would achieve success in Raetia. Just how much was the question? Earlier this morning, he had met with three other Marcomanni chieftains who had not attended the

179

initial gathering held a few days ago. The meeting was fairly benign, with polite exchanges between the two parties, but the good news was that this was proof of word spreading across the Marcomanni lands that Rome was open for business.

His musings were interrupted as Titus Placidius barged into his office unannounced. "Sorry for the disruption, sir, but I have urgent news requiring your immediate attention. One of my informants just delivered some disturbing information to me about a half hour ago. He said that our friend Gerbold and some of his associates are planning to raid three of our settlements tomorrow!"

Valerius sat straight up in his chair. "Is your source credible?"

"I would like to believe so."

"Radulf," Valerius called, and his bodyguard appeared at the doorway. "Yes, sir."

"Would you please fetch Marcellus and Hereca right now? We have a matter of some urgency."

After Radulf departed, Valerius addressed Placidius. "Is your legate, General Severus, nearby? He should be here for this discussion. I remember meeting him back in Vindobona."

"As a matter of fact, he's waiting outside."

"Excellent. You are way ahead of me. Bring him in."

Severus entered, his breastplate gleaming and his helmet held in the crook of his right arm. He nodded politely to Valerius. In a matter of moments, Marcellus arrived, followed by Hereca. Both looked at him inquisitively, curious to know what was going on.

Valerius spoke. "We have a situation requiring a rapid response. Placidius, tell everyone what you know."

"One of my informants came to see me this afternoon. He reported hearing that Gerbold—you remember him from our meeting days ago—met with three other leaders a few days ago, and these men plan to raid settlements in Raetia. He said that the men would cross the shallows at Adobert's village."

"And where is that?" Marcellus inquired.

"Not far from here," the legate Petillius Severus replied. "It's only fifteen miles upriver."

"What else do we know?" Valerius asked.

Placidius shrugged. "That's about it. My snitch stressed that he got this information secondhand from another source, but he believed it was credible."

"So we don't know how many warriors are involved or when they might cross?"

"Dawn," Hereca interjected. "That's when the Germans along the Rhenus would attack. It makes sense when you consider that our naval patrol boats become more active as the day progresses."

Legate Severus nodded. "That would be my best guess as well."

Valerius eyed the assembled group. "Alright, so they attack at dawn. Let me be clear about this. I don't want to just stop this raid; I want to capture or kill every one of these marauders. I sense that this Gerbold wants to make a statement of defiance against Rome, and in particular, me. Well, I want to make a statement too—that a steep price will have to be paid by those who defy Rome. We have offered our hand in friendship, and they have chosen to spit in our faces. It is time they face the consequences of their actions."

Placidius looked toward General Severus. "Given Governor Maximus's stated objectives, what would you suggest?"

Severus briefly contemplated the matter. "These are my preliminary thoughts. I propose making this a joint operation with our naval forces. The centuries will ambush Gerbold and his raiders at or near the villages they are attacking, catching them in the act. The naval forces will seal the border, preventing them from returning across the river. We should bag most of them if we time this right.

"How many men will you require?" Marcellus asked.

"Still contemplating that. Too many men and it will be difficult to keep our presence hidden. We want to surprise them. Taking that into consideration, I figure two cohorts, around a thousand men, should be the maximum. I will consult with my naval counterpart and see what he thinks is necessary in the way of ships and crew."

"And where will you position yourself to command this operation?" Valerius asked.

"Probably with the first village, nearest to the ford. That way, I can coordinate sealing off their escape route. That's where they will flee once they realize that they are the ones in peril."

"Fine," Valerius replied. "That's where I will be as well."

Marcellus grunted. "Esteemed Governor, not to be impertinent, but don't you think you should leave this military operation to the legate? You are the appointed imperial governor of two territories, the largest in the empire, I might add, and here, you want to become a participant in a perilous military action. You are not a young tribune anymore. You will be at risk. We don't how many men we will be facing." Marcellus looked toward Hereca for reinforcement.

"Marcellus does have a point, my dear," Hereca said. "You need not be there."

"I do need to be there," Valerius countered. "I have my reasons."

"Which are?" Hereca asked cynically.

"I intend to nail this bastard Gerbold's hide upon the wall. General Severus, you will be in charge of your troops, not me. I will only be an observer. But when all is said and done, I want the Marcomanni to know that it was me who laid a giant hurt on Gerbold and his followers. This is not my ego talking. Gerbold is challenging my authority and leadership of the province, and I am going to personally return that challenge."

"I guess that means I will also be there, along with Radulf," Marcellus said.

"Oh, stop with that. You and I both know you want to be there, so admit it." Valerius then turned toward Severus. "General, I will leave you and your staff to plan this endeavor. Please keep me apprised."

Hereca threw an icy stare at both Marcellus and Valerius and stormed out of the room.

Marcellus chuckled slightly, knowing Hereca was no longer there. "It appears you have a problem on the home front."

Valerius frowned. "Sometimes, that woman confounds me."

CHAPTER XVIII
BATTLE LINES

Gerbold waded farther out into the river, the water reaching near his waist. He raised his arms, holding his sword above his head. Although the water was chilly, he paid it no mind. Glancing behind him, he observed the mass of men following him. Just as he had anticipated, mist rose from the rushing water, shrouding the river valley and swallowing him and his men. He strode forward confidently, knowing the Roman patrol craft were not yet out and about. These Romans were so predictable. He could feel a slight incline in the river bottom as the water became shallower as he neared the opposite side. He trudged to the shore, entering Roman territory.

His plan was simple. Each of the three chieftains was assigned a village. The first group to cross would be assigned the farthest village so that they would be in position to attack upriver while the remainder of the small army waded across. The second group would follow the first and attack the middle settlement. Gerbold and his men would devote their attention to the nearest village, which was, by far, the largest. The second and third hamlets were dwarfed by the one closest to the crossing. If they were to meet any serious resistance, it would be here.

Gerbold and a small retinue of his followers were the first to reach the opposite shore. As the warriors of the first tribe reached him, he waved his arms, indicating the dirt path bypassing the first village and leading to the other two. Other than the gurgling sounds of the river, all was silent. Gerbold looked behind him. A horde of warriors were entering the river and quietly wading across it. He grinned wolfishly. This was going to be an easy victory. His name would be exalted among the Marcomanni for years to come.

On the Roman side of the river, Valerius stood beside Marcellus and Placidius in the deep woods, trying not to fidget. They had arrived there the previous day, late in the afternoon of the previous day. The three men were in the middle of the command group under General Severus. The legate had distributed his force of twelve centuries as follows: villages two and three had one century each hidden within the village dwellings and two centuries hidden in the woods around five hundred paces outside the settlement. Village one, the largest, had two centuries concealed in the huts and four centuries around five hundred paces away.

At the first sounds of armed conflict, the centuries outside the villages would close in, trapping the marauding forces between the legionaries in the village and those outside. In addition, a contingent of cavalry, with around one hundred horses, would wreak havoc among the raiders. For those who escaped the carnage, naval vessels were poised to seal the river, capturing or killing those entering the water and attempting to escape. They would get their boats in position after Gerbold and his men had crossed.

Valerius worried. He was positioned with General Severus outside the first village. The battle strategy was complicated with many moving parts. What if any of the centuries outside the villages were discovered? Would the naval forces arrive too soon, alerting the crossing Marcomanni warriors of their presence? Were there enough men hidden within the villages to protect the inhabitants and ward off the initial attack? He wondered where Gerbold and his followers were at this moment. He took a deep breath, realizing he needed to have faith in General Severus and his legionaries.

Marcellus edged over and whispered in his ear. "Please stop with the fiddling about. You are not the legate here. Let General Severus do his job. These are his troops, and his men are well-trained and disciplined."

Valerius offered a weak grin. "Force of habit, you know. Can't be helped. And speak for yourself. I saw you eyeing the formation of centuries, ensuring they were positioned for battle."

"As you said, it can't be helped. I do hate standing about, waiting for the fight to begin. I have never been a patient man."

They waited some more. The morning was silent without any signs of the enemy. Off to their left, a horse nickered, and then another. Severus shot them an annoyed glance. Quiet descended once again, but not for long. The stillness of the morning was pierced by the sounds of battle erupting in front of them. Men screamed and weapons clashed.

"Advance," roared Severus. The centurions echoed his command. The four centuries and the leadership group moved at a rapid trot through the brush and trees toward the main village. On the left, the cavalry surged ahead, lances poised.

The Roman force moved rapidly toward the village till some of the outermost dwellings were in sight. "Form lines," Severus bellowed. The centurions repeated the order, and the legionaries formed lines three men deep. Shields at the ready and swords drawn, the legionaries surged forward and burst into the clearing.

Concealed within the village, the two centuries had each formed a square, besieged by a large number of Marcomanni warriors. Judging by the piles of dead marauders in front of the Roman lines, the barbarians had made little progress. With a shout, the main Roman force charged into the Marcomanni rear ranks, slaughtering many of them from behind.

Gerbold looked around in shock. Moments earlier, his men had charged into the village, fully expecting to find the villagers in a complete panic. Instead, his men were met by a mass of legionaries. Somehow, his enemy had discovered his intentions. Since his men outnumbered the Romans, he had screamed for his men to attack. The pillaging of the village would have to wait until he had defeated the legionaries. His men had engaged the Roman soldiers, but only for a short time since a fresh wave of legionaries had poured from the fields and forests to his rear. Caught in the trap, his men were being slaughtered.

Gerbold was no stranger to combat, and while no coward, he intuitively realized that they were doomed unless they escaped this vicious ambush. He would deal with the failure later, but at the moment, his men needed to flee this killing zone. Looking around, he saw that the Romans had not yet fully encircled his men. He observed a gap in the lines where the road bisected the village. He yelled and pointed his sword in the direction of the main road. Wading into the midst of his men, he began grabbing them, gesturing urgently to retreat down the road parallel to the river.

General Severus watched on with satisfaction as his attacking legionaries smashed into the Marcomanni warriors. This was going just as he had envisioned, except that the Roman lines had not completely surrounded and collapsed the enemy ranks. Some of the warriors were escaping, leaking through the gaps in the Roman lines. He shouted above the fray for the century on the far right to seal off the retreat. The centurion quickly marshaled his men to close the escape route, and they immediately found themselves engaged with a huge force of panicked Marcomanni.

Severus waved with his long sword to the retinue of men in his command group. "We must reinforce the right flank before they push through our men. They are escaping." About thirty men, including Valerius and Marcellus, trotted with the others to assist the beleaguered century.

Holding out his long cavalry sword before him, Valerius realized he was about to enter combat once again. He briefly thought of Hereca and how furious she would be at him if he was killed.

The Marcomanni, desperate to flee the killing zone, forged a small gap in the Roman lines and, through sheer weight of numbers, began surging through.

Marcellus, Valerius, and Radulf charged into the fleeing men. Valerius swung his sword, inflicting a serious leg wound, incapacitating one of the barbarians. Radulf and Marcellus stepped forward, stabbing several more. Several warriors fell from their wounds, temporarily blocking the escape, but more of the Marcomanni emerged. Fortunately, a group of six bulky legionaries, much more capable of halting the breakthrough with their large shields, appeared and immediately relieved the trio.

Seeing their only flight option to escape the ensnarement blocked, the terrified barbarians bunched up and pushed at the slight breach in the Roman lines. Even the legionary reinforcements could not hold their place. They were shoved backward by the human wave. More legionaries arrived from other centuries to reinforce the ranks and close the breach in the Roman lines.

Suddenly, a large warrior broke through and rushed directly at Valerius, who nimbly parried the figure's spear thrust and ducked as the man swung his small oval shield at him. But Valerius was not quick enough. The wicker shield struck him a glancing blow to the head, sending him reeling. The ever-present Radulf stabbed the attacking warrior in the torso with his gladius, incapacitating him and removing him from the fight.

Valerius knew from experience that staying on the ground meant certain death, so he hurriedly pushed himself off the ground and onto his knees. As he slowly wobbled to his feet, he wiped a trickle of blood running down the side of his face and stood poised to take on the next man. Marcellus arrived, his sword dripping with blood, and gently ushered Valerius away from the melee, knowing their presence was not going to stem the tide of fleeing invaders and, more importantly, keeping the dazed Valerius away from the fight. The legions had easily won the battle. The only drawback was that some, not many, had escaped the Roman trap. But if all went according to plan, the Navy would take care of them.

The battle that had engulfed the village gradually subsided. The ground was littered with the Marcomanni dead, while a few were captured. Satisfied with the outcome, General Severus coolly observed the scene before him. He pointed with his sword down the dirt path and commanded one of the centurions and his men to pursue and kill any warriors fleeing down the road. He then dispatched riders to check how his other forces were doing in the smaller settlements upriver.

The village dwellers took their revenge on the wounded warriors and looted the bodies. Centurions began barking orders, informing their men to secure the prisoners and care for any Roman wounded.

Gerbold ran like he had never run before. Somewhere in his flight, he had shamefully lost his sword. All vestiges of command and control had been lost. He had no idea of the fate of the men attacking the two smaller villages. His men ran like rabbits, occasionally looking over their shoulders, fearing pursuit. The chieftain reached the ford in the river where they had crossed earlier that morning. But on glancing out into the river, he spied several Roman naval craft waiting for them.

Gerbold stopped and stared at the Roman patrol boats, bile rising to his throat. "Run downstream," he screamed. "We will swim across."

He bolted down the road, not bothering to see if any were following him. Now, it was all about self-preservation. His legs churned, and he gasped for air. But his spirits soared when he noticed no Roman ships were blocking his escape farther down the river. He could still get out of this. He ran some more, his legs weakening. Suddenly, he heard screams behind him. Turning around, he saw a formation of Roman legionaries in the distance, trotting down the road after them. Those of his men who were too slow or hindered by their wounds were dispatched.

He needed to get across now.

Gerbold ran into the river, his legs churning in the water. Some of his men followed. As the water deepened, he began swimming. He did not notice the Roman patrol boat rapidly descending upon the hapless swimmers. Gerbold sensed a shadowy presence and a disturbance in the water near him. Looking up from his thrashing strokes, he heard several javelins whistle past his head.

The Roman pilum, a devastating six-foot weapon with an iron pyramidal head and a weighted iron shaft in the front to enhance its penetrating force, could wreak havoc upon contact. It can inflict a grievous wound, piercing deeply into the flesh.

One of the lances found its mark, plunging through the water and into Gerbold's torso. Gerbold opened his mouth to scream as the iron head penetrated deeply. As blood gushed from his wound, he inhaled a bucketful of water, muffling his anguished shriek. He sank to the bottom, never to be seen again.

Later, the naval fleet triumphantly transported the two victorious cohorts back to Castra Regina. Valerius and Marcellus stood with the command group in the lead ship.

"Well done, General Severus," Valerius said. "I must admit I had a few doubts whether we would be able to pull this off. The timing had to be perfect, and it was. You achieved total tactical surprise. Some of the Marcomanni made it across the river, but not many. I heard from one of the captives that Gerbold was slain while crossing the river."

"Serves the arsehole right," Marcellus voiced. "He learned a rather painful lesson. Do not fuck with the legions."

Severus beamed. "It could not have gone any better."

"Today, we triumphed and sent a clear message to those of the Marcomanni who tried to sabotage our planned trade strategy," responded Valerius. "I trust your losses were minor."

Severus grimaced. "Yes, it couldn't be helped, but we lost some good legionaries today. According to the last tally, we lost eight men, and twenty were wounded. Most of the casualties occurred in the third village. The Marcomanni heard the battle sounds from the first and second settlements, so we lost the element of surprise. While my losses may be deemed acceptable considering what we were up against, it still hurts. Those were my men."

"General, you probably routed a force of over two thousand men," Marcellus declared. "That's quite an accomplishment. I know how much it hurts when you lose legionaries from your units, but your men performed extraordinarily well today."

"Thank you for those words, Marcellus. I am proud of the officers and men under my command. I take some comfort in knowing that we achieved a worthwhile mission today. Those men did not perish in vain. In the long run, we are all going to be better off with less bloodshed."

Severus turned toward Valerius. "Sir, speaking of wounded, you should have one of our physicians examine your face."

"It is but a minor wound," Valerius replied. He touched his left eyebrow and winced. "However, it is a bit tender."

"You're going to have some explaining to do with Hereca," Marcellus said. "The left side of your jawline is turning a lovely shade of purple. I do not want to be there when she sees your face. If I recall, she was opposed to you going on this little adventure."

Placidius smirked. "I believe the legate and I have some business to attend to when we dock. Good luck with your wife."

"This could be worse than facing the Marcomanni," Valerius said dolefully.

CHAPTER XIX
NEXT STEPS

Over the next five days, more chieftains and village elders arrived at Castra Regina to discuss the potential for increased trade. News of the fate of Gerbold and his rebellious raiders had spread far and wide. The Marcomanni leaders who sought discussions at the headquarters made it a point to condemn the actions of Gerbold and his followers. While their business in Raetia was far from settled, it was off to a rousing start.

Early one morning about a week after the triumph over the Marcomanni invaders, Valerius decided to meet with his inner circle and flesh out future plans. Valerius, along with Placidius, Hereca, and Marcellus, convened in a meeting room at the headquarters. "I could not be more pleased with the progress we have achieved," Valerius began. "So, what are the next steps? I have already sent a dispatch to Tiberius, noting our progress with the Marcomanni. As much as it pains me, I was thinking of leaving Hereca behind with you, Placidius, to facilitate trade negotiations. Meanwhile, Marcellus and I will venture downstream to the fortress at Lauriacum in the province of Noricum and get the lay of the land. What do you think?"

"I believe we can manage that," Hereca said, looking at Placidius. "Things are going smoothly now, but what if that changes? I would like to believe there will be continued progress, but one never knows."

"Then we will return here if needed. We will be less than a hundred miles downriver. We could return in two days. Placidius, what say you? This is your province."

"Like you, I am amazed at the headway we have made in such a short time. Am I ready to declare victory? Hardly. But I have a good feeling about the direction we are headed in. I'm glad Hereca will be staying here. She has a lot of trading savvy that, I admit, I do not possess. So I agree with your proposed action plan."

"Excellent," Valerius said. "Now, what I need from you, Placidius is your assessment of the province of Noricum and your Roman counterparts there. The governor is Aelius Avilius. You already told me that he's not overly enthusiastic about my presence on the Danubius. I have met him only once and was not overly impressed."

Placidius paused in deliberation. "Be careful. His father is a rich senator who toadies up to Tiberius. As expected, Aelius followed his father's footsteps into the senate. His father, who goes by the name of Plinius, is extremely smart. I can't say the same for his son. He has never had an original thought in his life. Definitely inexperienced. He was easily swayed by the pompous utterances of Portunus."

"Is he corrupt?" Marcellus asked.

"Corrupt," scoffed Placidius. "He is too feckless to be corrupt."

"Thank you for that flattering portrait of the procurator," Valerius jested. "Tell us about the legate. Seventh Legion, right?"

Placidius shrugged. "General Severus would be a better person to ask on that front. However, my impression is that the legate, Lucius Fabianus, merely follows what he is ordered to do by Avilius. He does not show much initiative. I have not interacted with the man, so he may indeed be a qualified commander. We really should consult with General Severus."

"Moving on, what can you tell me about the tribes on the opposite side of the river in Noricum?"

"Not much, I'm afraid," Placidius replied. "As you can understand, I'm preoccupied with my problems here with the Marcomanni. But, from what I have heard, the barbarian tribes are primarily the Quadi. Anecdotally, the Quadi villages are fiercely independent. Here in Raetia, the Marcomanni are more like a loose confederation. I don't know if that's good news or bad. On one hand, in Noricum, you may have two neighboring villages opposed in their views on Rome. On the other, a coalition of forces that might wage war is less likely."

"You are a fountain of good news," said Marcellus with a chuckle. "To recapitulate, you're telling us that it might be considerably tougher than we thought."

"I wish I had better news," Placidius said with a sigh. "But I must stress that my observations are from afar and what I have gleaned from other sources. It could be that the Quadi people will be more receptive to trade than we imagined and Aelius is more competent."

"And it could be that I will sprout wings out of my arse and fly away," Marcellus quipped.

Hereca giggled. "Thank you for that imagery."

"On that note," Valerius said, "let's adjourn for the day. Oh, and Placidius, one more thing, I have a favor to ask of you. Since I've loaned Hereca to you, do you think you could reciprocate and spare General Severus for a short while? Consider it a trade, a *quid pro quo*. All is peaceful here at the moment, so I do not see the swap as putting your province at risk. I would like to have him assess the military situation in Noricum—both the readiness of the Seventh Legion and the opposing forces. I could tell Fabianus and Avilius that, based on his success here with the Marcomanni, I want him to observe the situation in Noricum. I think he could do that without ruffling any feathers. What do you say?"

"Noricum's stability does impact my province. I believe Severus would be an asset in an advisory capacity. Just make sure you return him to me. He's a valuable resource."

* * *

Hundreds of miles downriver at the fortress of Carnuntum in Pannonia, General Voculus sat with Governor Portunus in his plush headquarters. The man had spared no expense in adorning his residence with luxury. The colonnaded building was furnished with the finest tapestries, rugs, and statuaries, while brightly colored frescoes and mosaics decorated the rooms. His wine cellar was well stocked with the finest vintages from across the empire.

Voculus, placing his wine glass down, began sharing critical information. "I have received word from Raetia that Maximus has the Marcomanni eating out of his hand. They are flocking to him to expand their trade with Rome. There was a minor foray by some of the dissidents into Raetia to loot some villages, but the raid was crushed by the forces of the Third Legion. Now, the Marcomanni either want to trade with him or are scared to death of him."

"Damn that man!" Portunus thundered. "What are we going to do?"

Voculus contemplated the question. "Our friend Sejanus warned me that this Maximus was a skilled and resourceful man. Now I understand why. He appears to be winning the hearts and minds of the barbarians. He had a modicum of success with defeating Chieftain Urs here in Pannonia, and he has taken Raetia by storm. I've received word that he plans to travel downriver to Noricum. Remember that whatever we do to impede him must not be traced back to us. We must be discrete."

"So what do you suggest?" Portunus whined. "His status here is growing stronger, and our reports to Rome deprecating his efforts have not borne fruit—that is, as far as I know."

"I will think of something," Voculus assured. "He will spend some time in Noricum and then return here. We must come up with a plan for when he returns."

"Maximus must not look at my financial affairs and trade agreements. It would be extremely detrimental to me. I cannot have my monetary dealings exposed. Do you understand?"

"Yes, Governor, I understand. But we must be judicious in our approach. I assume you have contacts among the Quadi and the Iazyges who share in your illicit gains and whom you can count upon as allies?"

"I do. They are hard men, and they appreciate wealth."

"Fine. Think about who you might want to contact to help us with our problem. We will meet again in ten days. Meanwhile, I'm going upriver to Noricum—uninvited, I might add. I have been advised that Maximus is supposed to meet with Governor Avilius next, and I want to be there."

* * *

Eight days later, Valerius, Marcellus, and General Severus gathered in a conference room at the headquarters of the Noricum province in Lauriacum. Valerius was positioned directly opposite Aelius Avilius, the appointed governor. Also present were General Fabianus, and General Voculus, who had boldly invited himself to the meeting. He had arrived late the previous afternoon. An awkward silence filled the room.

Valerius cut through the small talk. "I bring good tidings from your sister province, Raetia. As you may have heard, trade discussions are underway with many of the Marcomanni villages. My wife remains there to facilitate discussions. That's what she does best. I admit there were some rough patches. Several of the chieftains decided to test my resolve and conducted a raid on some villages across the river. Fortunately, I got wind of the intended attack and acted accordingly. Thanks to General Severus, we killed or captured almost all of them. That's precisely why I brought General Severus with me today, on loan from Governor Placidius. I think he would be an excellent source of advice on dealing with any unruly barbarians."

Valerius paused briefly. "I believe our military victory sent a strong message to the uncommitted Marcomanni. For days afterward, the Marcomanni leaders flocked to discuss possible trade discussions. I would wager that word has spread downriver to the Quadi peoples across the river from your province."

Avilius shrugged noncommittally. "I congratulate you on your success, Governor Maximus, and you as well, General Severus. However, I remain cautious. You and your wife have had some experience with the Marcomanni. The Quadi opposite our shores are a different breed altogether. They may not be as easy to sway. I hope you can be as successful here."

"We," Valerius said.

Avilius gave him a puzzled look, not picking up on Valerius's diction.

"I said *we*, Governor Avilius. This is not just my undertaking; it is ours. I am here to facilitate things. You and your staff will be doing the bulk of the lifting. Let me make this clear, Governor," Valerius continued, his tone icy. "If you do not wish to willingly participate in this process, I will send a dispatch to Tiberius, telling him you are not up for the job and suggesting your replacement."

"You would not dare," Avilius retorted, puffing out his chest. "I am the son of Senator Plinius Avilius and from a powerful noble Roman family. I was appointed to this position by Tiberius four years ago."

Marcellus snorted in derision. "Obviously a mistake."

Valerius shot his former centurion a stern look, signaling disapproval of his scorn. "As I told you when we met weeks ago, Tiberius was succinct in his orders to me. I am to develop trade on the Danubius like I had done on the Rhenus. He told me without equivocation that I should inform him if anyone proves uncooperative, and that includes you, Governor." He pointed his finger at Avilius's chest for effect.

Avilius appeared to withdraw into himself, his earlier bravado now gone. "I was not opposing your efforts. I was only saying that taming the Quadi might be more difficult. Isn't that right, General Fabianus?"

The legate was taken aback by the sudden question. All eyes in the room turned to him. The man stuttered, unsure of what to say. "Yes, yes, the Quadi can be a prickly bunch. I would welcome General Severus's advice."

Voculus, who had been silent the entire time, intervened, speaking in a smooth tone. "Governor Maximus, I believe it would be a bit hasty to report anything negative to Tiberius at this time. After all, Governor Avilius is only concerned about the peace and prosperity of his province. If something were to go askew, he would be blamed. When taking such bold steps as you are proposing, it's only natural that individuals are reticent to embrace them. You see that, don't you?"

Valerius glared at Voculus and then Avilius. He was having none of Voculus's conciliatory words. "No, I don't see it that way. I'm not asking a lot. I want the full support of the governor, his staff, and his legion, and now would be a good time to begin acceptance of my doctrine."

The room fell silent once again. "Marcellus, why don't you tell the governor what our next steps are going to be and what is expected from him and his staff."

"Certainly. We intend to meet with as many Quadi leaders as possible to explain our proposal and how successful we have been thus far. On your part, you need to send your messengers and interpreters into the Quadi territory and invite them here, where we can wine and dine with them. I'd suggest you arrange a cash donative as an inducement for each leader who attends. Is that something you can manage, Governor?"

"Yes. We have some liaison people who interact with the Quadi," Avilius replied. "I will consult with them and have them get the word out. How much of a cash donative should we offer?"

"We paid twenty silver denarii to the chieftains who gathered in Raetia. I think that should be sufficient."

* * *

Voculus walked away from the gathering, attempting to maintain his composure. Despite his title, he had just been spoken to like a schoolboy. Furthermore, Valerius had excluded him from all of the military operations, disregarding his role as the overall military commander of the six legions. It had been a deliberate snub. Somehow, he would find a way to defeat Maximus and his cronies. He would find a weakness and ruthlessly exploit it. He had attempted the blunt approach of having Maximus killed, but that had failed. What a disappointment Ivarr had been. Then, he had tried to subtly discredit him through complaints directed to Tiberius. That did not appear to be successful either since Maximus was still in good standing with the emperor.

He pondered some more what he could do. Maximus was too well-guarded and insulated for an attempted assassination. Then, it struck him like a lightning bolt. Maximus was guarded, but what about his wife? She was back in Raetia helping Placidius. She could be killed or kidnapped for the right price. Voculus walked out of the headquarters building, his mind churning. He would find a way.

CHAPTER XX
REVELATION

Rome

Senator Quintus Salvius smiled as he read the dispatch from Valerius to Tiberius. He looked up from the scroll and stared off at the far wall of his study. Maximus had chosen wisely to send this post to him. The contents would have never made it past Sejanus's scrutiny. It was masterfully worded, explaining his actions and only indirectly placing blame on those in power in the Danubius. Now, he thought, he must do his part.

The imperial palace on Capri was closely guarded, and all the visitors were screened—or almost all of them were. Salvius had a close ally who worked for the courier service. Official couriers were granted access to the palace since dispatches were always coming and going. Sejanus and his minions could not keep track of everyone, which was their weakness. Salvius's secret ally was a courier who had delivered many communications to the imperial palace and would ensure Tiberius received the dispatch. His ally would surreptitiously leave the document where Sejanus's men would not detect it. A sly grin crossed his face at the thought of outmaneuvering Sejanus. Better yet, someday he would rid Rome of that ambitious prick.

* * *

Tiberius glared at Sejanus, tapping a scroll against the edge of the tabletop." I received this message from Maximus. It explains a lot."

Sejanus looked puzzled. "I'm unaware of any dispatch. When did it arrive?"

"I don't know. Isn't that your job? It was on my desk to read. Right on top," he said tersely

"What does it say, sir?"

"Maximus explained that he engaged some barbarian tribes because they raided villages in our provinces. He stated that he had taken similar actions as governor of Germania. He further explained that he was merciful but taught them a lesson. He warned them that if they did not cease their aggressive posture and look toward more peaceful solutions, there would be consequences. I judged him unfairly. I should just let him do his job. Also, he noted that the furnishing of his headquarters with luxurious items was at his expense, not Rome's. The purpose of these trappings was to impress the barbarian leaders, subtly showing them the benefits of enhanced trade. So, based on these other dispatches I have received from a few of my governors, I'm inclined to believe that they are nothing but a bunch of whiny do-nothings, afraid of progress and changing the status quo. I have judged Maximus unfairly."

Sejanus smiled smoothly. "I'm glad to hear Maximus is making some headway. Is there anything you want me to do?"

"No, not for now. I will craft a response to Maximus, informing him of my satisfaction with his message. It's important that he succeed."

Sejanus strode away from the emperor's chambers, a scowl etched upon his face. How in Hades did Maximus get his dispatch through to the imperial chambers? Who was aiding him? Was it someone in his employ? One of his Praetorians, perhaps a visitor to Tiberius? He would find out. He prided himself in having many sources of information and absolute control of the palace.

CHAPTER XXI
MOVING ON

Fortress of Lauriacum, Noricum

Valerius sat back and massaged his temples, attempting to rid himself of a nagging headache. They had just finished meeting with a large number of Quadi leaders. Overall, it had gone well. Although the Quadi looked and dressed like the Marcomanni and spoke the same tongue, they were quite different. They were a guarded lot, not committing to anything but not opposing what was put forth. As they departed, their body language and mannerisms appeared to indicate a favorable inclination to the idea of expanded trade.

Other leaders had stayed behind and asked him questions, discreetly seeking insights into what goods the Romans were seeking in trade and what the best way was to facilitate discussions. Again, a good sign. He wished Hereca were around. She was generally more intuitive about how the room had reacted to various proposals.

He turned to Marcellus and General Severus. "What do you think?"

"I sensed it was positive. But what do I know; I'm just an old centurion. You need Hereca here. She could give you a better answer."

"I was just thinking the same thing."

"What about you, General Severus? Your thoughts?"

"Impressive. I kept scanning the audience for any adverse expressions indicating opposition. I also lingered around afterward, attempting to overhear any murmurs of dissatisfaction. Although my understanding of their language is basic at best, I couldn't detect any invective directed at you. I also observed that there does not appear to be any one leader who holds sway with the others."

"Perceptive, General," Valerius acknowledged. "I came up with the same conclusions. I know that Raetia and Noricum are probably the least troublesome provinces to facilitate change, but by Jove, I believe we are making real headway. Of course, there is much more to be done here, but it's a good beginning."

"Next steps?" Marcellus asked.

Valerius frowned. "Not sure. I do not have enough trust to leave this process up to the illustrious governor here. Aelius Avilius, even his name sounds like he's an arse-hole."

Marcellus snorted. "You are beginning to sound like me."

"I have been spending too much time in your company," Valerius replied. "But seriously, it is beyond me how that man was appointed to his position. Governors are supposed to be the best and the brightest. I don't trust him. I think he kowtows to Portunus, who is definitely from the opposition camp. In turn, Portunus is allied with that snake, Voculus. I shall send for Hereca to come to Noricum, assuming she has made sufficient progress with the Marcomanni and her presence is no longer needed there. General Severus, I need to borrow you for some additional time. I will inform Placidius. I don't believe the military commander here, Fabianus, is up to the task. If something went awry and a military response became necessary, he would likely fail."

"Undoubtedly, sir. I agree with your assessment. I would not entrust Fabianus to command a military operation, not even a century."

Valerius pondered the matter for a moment. "Not to diminish the importance of Noricum, but it is a small province with little unrest. Our thorniest problems will be downriver with the provinces of Pannonia and Moesia. Let me summarize my thoughts. Once we get things rolling in Noricum, we need to move on and return to Vindobona in Pannonia. Our challenges lie there, both with the barbarian tribes and Portunus. Last month, I believe we set an example with Chieftain Urs and his followers, but in our absence, Portunus has probably undermined our efforts. Marcellus and I will sail to Vindobona in a few days. Meanwhile, I will send a dispatch to Hereca, asking her to come to Noricum and oversee the trading negotiations. As I mentioned, General Severus will remain here in Noricum for as long as he deems prudent, and then, he can return to Raetia."

"What actions do we take in Pannonia once we get there?" Marcellus asked.

"We have a lot of work to do. We made some initial progress, but the province is much larger than Raetia and Noricum. We will need to travel downriver to Carnuntum and Aquincum to deal with the Quadi and the Iazyges. I expect to have Hereca back with us by that time, once she finalizes her discussions here in Noricum. I say we leave for Vindobona within the next several days."

* * *

The Roman naval vessel smoothly navigated downriver toward Vindobona. Valerius leaned on the ship's rail, staring off into the distance, lost in thought as the main sail filled with the breeze, and the river sparkled like a thousand jewels.

Marcellus sauntered up next to him. "A copper coin for your thoughts."

"Oh, I was just pondering our progress to date. Overall, our trade discussions have proceeded swimmingly with the tribes on the opposite side of the river."

"Swimmingly?" Marcellus asked.

"For lack of a better word, yes, *swimmingly.* I would venture to say that our talks with the Marcomanni and Quadi have gone better than I anticipated. I expected a tougher sell. But, on the other hand, I am concerned about our problems with our putative Roman friends, Voculus and Portunus. We have not seen the last of them, and they are by no means finished in their opposition to us. There is no limit to how far they will go to discredit us or eliminate us altogether. That ambush on our journey from the Rhenus to the Danubius was most likely plotted by Voculus and shows to what extent they will go. This is not your typical Roman squabble. My concern is what they might attempt next."

Marcellus gazed out at the glistening river for a short time. "As you know, my approach to problems is not often subtle."

"No, you don't say," Valerius jested. "I never would have guessed that."

"My point is this," explained Marcellus. "Sooner or later, you will have to confront this evil—and make no mistake about it, this is evil. And when you do, you may have to venture outside the laws of Rome. Adopt the centurion approach. More bluntly, kill the fuckers. Naturally, I would be pleased to assist you in this endeavor."

"Voculus and Portunus are clever men who are leveraging their favor back in Rome. But I have, in the past, flouted the rules and intricacies of Roman law on occasion. When the time comes, I may be forced to use the iron fist approach, consequences be damned. Stand ready, Centurion Marcellus, for this battle has hardly begun. I will not let those despicable, poor excuses for men get the better of me."

"Now you're talking, Tribune! Can't wait until we get to Vindobona."

CHAPTER XXII
DAMNING PROOF

Fortress of Vindobona, Pannonia

The room was filled with Quadi chieftains, their expressions earnest but noncommittal. Valerius had just finished his speech, welcoming the Quadi leaders and then explaining his proposed expanded trade agreement. Like the other groups in the provinces of Raetia and Noricum, they were promised a small purse of twenty silver denarii. He had smoothly made the presentation, but he wished Hereca were there, for she explained it much better. Marcellus and Radulf stood in the back of the room, observing the attendees.

Valerius gazed at his audience. "I'm sure you must have some questions, so please ask."

A tall bearded chieftain arose. "My name is Siward. I live not far from here. Why should we believe any of your words when, a few weeks ago, you invaded the lands of Chieftain Urs? We must defend ourselves against Roman aggression. Is it Rome's intention to invade our lands?"

There was a murmur of agreement among the assembled men.

"I'm glad you asked that question. I was going to bring the matter up. Yes, I did cross the river and venture inland with two cohorts of legionaries. Many of you are probably thinking, here come the Romans with their new leader, poised to invade our lands. Why would I do such a thing? I will tell you why. Urs attacked a village across the river, stole their cattle, and murdered some of their inhabitants. In response to their aggression, we surrounded their village. Several of Urs's men who resisted were killed. I gave Urs and his village an ultimatum: they could accept the new conditions of peaceful trade, but if I discovered that they raided across the river again, I would retaliate and slaughter everyone in his settlement. For the moment, I spared everyone except those unfortunate few who were killed in the brief skirmish. Oh, and I levied Urs and his village fifty head of cattle for their transgression. In my opinion, a small price to pay. The choice was his. Does that sound like an invasion?"

Valerius paused, assessing the assembled Quadi. "Gentlemen, this is no idle threat. If I find Urs has returned to his old ways, I will do exactly as I promised. It is not my intention to threaten you, but I shall not tolerate any more of this looting and killing. Those are the only circumstances where I will implement military action across the river. I hope my words about my intentions are clear. Again, I have no desire to wage war on the Quadi people, but Rome will retaliate if need be. I adopted the same policy in Germania. It seems to be working rather well there. I have not received one complaint that Rome has invaded the lands of the German tribes. I must emphasize that there is no Roman military presence on the far side of the Rhenus, and likewise, there will be none here."

The discussions continued on a more cordial note into the afternoon. Overall, the situation was looking favorable.

Later that day, Valerius settled down in his headquarters, catching up on his correspondence and reading various dispatches. It was nearing dusk, and he was getting hungry since he had skipped the mid-day meal due to his lengthy meeting with the Quadi leaders.

Just then, Marcellus, who had been reading reports on the far side of the room, stood. "Are you finished yet? I'm famished."

Valerius was about to reply when one of the scribes positioned in the vestibule knocked politely and entered. "Sorry to bother you, sir, but there's a merchant waiting to see you. Won't give his name. I told him he needed to make an appointment like everyone else, but he said it was an urgent matter. Says it's important. He seems agitated. What do you want me to tell him?"

"He will not give you his name, but says he has something important to say?"

"Yes, sir. I tried to dissuade him, but he says he has information you should know."

"Do you want me to send this rogue on his way?" Marcellus asked. "Needs some lessons in manners."

Valerius contemplated the matter. "Maybe he does have something important to tell us. Send him in here. He better make his point quickly, or he'll be out the door."

A few moments later, the scribe ushered in a grizzled figure, probably in his fifties, dressed in a tunic and wool trousers. He carried a battered felt hat in his left hand. "Thank you for seeing me on such short notice."

"More like no notice," Marcellus chided.

"What is your name and what do you want to talk to us about?" Valerius demanded.

"Name is Rufinus. I captain a merchant vessel that navigates these waters. Been doing it for a good number of years. Bring all sorts of cargo in and out of these river waters. I have heard good things about you, Governor Maximus. Someone who will listen if there are issues. I also knew Captain Sabinus, who you were once partners with."

"So, Rufinus, we have established that you're a merchant captain and you trade in these waters, and like a few thousand other people, you knew Captain Sabinus," Valerius said. "So, why have you come here unannounced? Your time is running out. Speak."

The man shuffled his feet. "'Tis a delicate subject."

Marcellus advanced rapidly toward Rufinus with long strides. "And it's going to remain a delicate subject unless you talk. Otherwise, you'll be out on your arse."

Seeing Marcellus's menacing form approach, the captain backed up. "All right, I will speak. He shuffled his feet, his lips still pursed.

"Enough is enough. Out with you. Governor Maximus does not suffer fools." Marcellus grabbed the figure by the collar and began dragging him across the room.

"It's about rampant corruption here," Rufinus blurted.

Valerius held up his hand, signaling Marcellus to stop. "What corruption?"

Rufinus, now released by Marcellus, smoothed his wool tunic and spoke hesitantly. "As you may be aware, there's a tax on merchandise for all vessels transporting goods downriver. Each ship sailing downriver must stop in Carnuntum for a tax assessment."

"Rome has many ways to tax cargo and goods. The tax collectors are very proficient at their jobs," Valerius said.

Rufinus looked down at his feet. "Not all ships stop at Carnuntum. Some are given a tax stamp for their goods. In exchange, a payment is made to certain officials at an amount less than the actual tax. This benefits the merchant ship, and the money paid to certain officials never reaches the provinces' coffers."

"Captain Rufinus, are you admitting complicity in this unscrupulous scheme?" Valerius asked.

Rufinus nodded. "Aye, I am, reluctantly. But I don't have much of a choice."

"Please explain."

"If we do not go along with this arrangement, it has been hinted that our assessed cargo in Carnuntum would be taxed much higher, exorbitantly so, putting us out of business."

Marcellus raised an eyebrow. "Do you have any proof that the levies you pay don't get into the coffers of the province?"

"No, but it should be easy enough to verify."

"And who is behind these financial trickeries?" Valerius asked.

"Who else but Portunus? He has his fingers in everything. He will return to Rome a wealthy man. His cupidity knows no bounds."

"Let me ask you something, Captain Rufinus. Are there others who will attest to what you have told me?" Valerius questioned.

Rufinus nodded. "Aye, they may be a bit hesitant to come forward, but they could be persuaded. Nobody likes the current arrangement, but they don't want to be complicit in the fraud. Governor Maximus, as you probably know, ship captains are not necessarily the most scrupulous of individuals. They may bend the rules a tad, but what we are being forced to do goes far beyond that."

"All right, Captain Rufinus. For the moment, we are going to keep silent on this matter. If Portunus finds out you were here spilling your guts out, I fear you may encounter an unfortunate accident. He is not above that. When the moment is right, with your help, I will require the various captains to testify, and I will grant them immunity. Leave your contact information with the clerk on your way out. Also, please provide a written summary of what you've just described to the secretary

214

and sign it. You are excused, but not a word about this discussion to anyone. We will find a way to purge ourselves of this sorry-ass excuse for a governor."

"Yes, sir. Thank you for being so understanding." Rufinus backed out of the room.

After he had departed, Marcellus smacked the tabletop. "Now we have cause to get rid of this arse-hole. Throw him in chains."

"Agreed, but we need to pick the right moment."

* * *

The next day, Portunus huddled with Voculus on the first floor of his headquarters at Vindobona. At Voculus's request, Portunus had made the twenty-mile journey from his base in Carnuntum. Standing in the background was Gordianus, Voculus's henchman and designated thug. It was a warm day with bright sunshine, and the wooden shutters were thrown wide open to allow the slight breeze of the river to enter. Portunus was agitated, an angry scowl etched upon his face. Maximus was winning. He had usurped his authority, rendering him a useless puppet. Portunus's commands had been overridden, leaving him humiliated. He briefly considered returning to Carnuntum downriver and staying out of Maximus's way, but that would be admitting defeat. He had too much pride to be eclipsed by Maximus and his cronies. His forfeiture of the Tenth Legion under General Caelius was the unkindest cut. Caelius had changed loyalties, embracing Maximus's doctrine. Even more galling, the discussions of enhanced trade with the barbarian tribes appeared to be gaining support. Once this debacle was over and Maximus had moved on, General Caelius would pay a steep price for his disloyalty and find himself in some obscure post commanding a bunch of misfits. His military career would be over. He would teach that arrogant general a strong lesson, one he would never forget.

"Why the long face, Portunus?" Voculus asked. "We must remain calm and rational if we are to defeat this threat."

"Easy for you to say. I have been demeaned by Maximus and shoved aside. I am the appointed governor of one of the largest provinces in the empire. But here I am, groveling at the feet of this arrogant pup. I tell you, Voculus, it makes me sick to my stomach."

Voculus pounded his fist on the table. "You think you're the only one who has a grudge? He has snubbed me from the beginning. At the meeting in Noricum, he chastened me like a schoolboy. But we must not let our anger get the better of us. Now, I have an idea on how to defeat Maximus—a plan I have already begun to hatch."

"What do you intend? I'm eager to undertake anything to rid ourselves of this vexation."

Voculus wore a smug expression. "Let me ask you, what have we learned so far in our attempts to discredit Maximus?"

"Several things. We know that Tiberius thinks highly of him. We tried to cast him in an unfavorable light through dispatches to Tiberius. Perhaps it worked a little, but Tiberius now supports Maximus. So, for now, that is a dead end. The indirect approach got us nowhere. The possibility of physically attacking Maximus presents difficulties. He is always well-guarded. Those with him are loyal. So, what is his weakness? What we can do?"

"I will go back to the point you made. You said that Maximus is always well-protected. That may be true, but what of his followers? What if something were to happen to his wife, Hereca?"

Portunus's face lit up. "I like this idea. I hear she is off doing trade discussions. I'm sure she is under protection, but how much? What do you have in mind?"

I have contacts with a few of the Quadi chieftains who are less than enthusiastic about these overtures. They are bound to the traditional Quadi warrior code. I would describe them as opportunists, perhaps a bit unscrupulous. They believe it is their right to raid the provinces across the river. Hereca will soon journey back here to Vindobona. I don't know of her security arrangements, but when she sailed from Raetia to Noricum, there was only one small patrol boat as her escort. While the Quadi do not have much in the way of riverboats, they have some, which should be enough to kidnap Hereca. As part of the ransom, in addition to substantial coin, we could demand that Maximus leave the territory. Best of all, I have already set the plan in motion."

"I like this. But what happens when Hereca is returned after the ransom? Maximus will be back with a vengeance."

"Who says she will ever be returned? We will break this man, and he will wish he never set foot in these lands. This plan has to work. My patron in Rome—you know who that is—is becoming impatient. In his last dispatch to me, he said all is nearly ready for him to appropriate leadership. He is waiting for me to neutralize Maximus. We must succeed. It's important to remain on the good side of my patron, as he's an extremely powerful man with a long reach."

"Quite agree. Much better to have him as a friend."

* * *

Legionary Castor Longinus, a veteran of the legions for over five years, paced restlessly in front of General Voculus's headquarters, as he had been assigned guard detail for the afternoon. He loathed this duty. It was boring. Even though the shift was only three hours, it seemed to drag on endlessly. Thank the gods the weather was decent.

Even better, he had been assigned the afternoon shift and not the dreaded night duty. That totally fucked up your sleep, and you were expected to partake in the following day's activities. When he was finished with his guard stint, he would join his mates in town for a few glasses of wine, assuming he could avoid his centurion, who was always lurking about, seeking volunteers for work details.

As he patrolled, he could hear loud voices, sometimes strident, coming from the open shutters right in front of his post. He tried not to listen, but the words were easily discernible. What he heard was alarming. Were these words true or just his imagination? The men inside, General Voculus and Governor Portunus, their voices easily recognizable, were discussing kidnapping Valerius Maximus's wife. This was high treason.

While Voculus and Portunus were engrossed in their discussion, Gordianus abruptly moved across the room toward the open window. He stuck his head outside the open window and observed the legionary guard. "You there! What's your name, and what unit are you assigned?"

Longinus was startled by the sudden appearance of a figure, whom he recognized as Voculus's aide. "Sir, my name is Legionary Longinus, third cohort, second century."

"Have you been listening to the conversation in this room?"

Longinus answered quickly, lest he appeared guilty of the accusation. "No, sir. I've been marching back and forth. I heard voices, but that's all. Just going about this mundane guard duty."

Gordianus glared at him menacingly. "Very well. Carry on with your duties, Legionary Longinus."

Gordianus firmly shut the heavy wooden shutters and turned to the two men seated at the table. "Sirs, best to keep your voices down given the sensitive nature of this conversation."

"Do you think he heard anything?" Voculus asked.

"Hard to say," replied Gordianus, "but no matter. I have his name and unit. I will take of the problem and ensure his silence."

"See that you do. We can't have this conversation leaking out."

Longinus was finally relieved of his post. It could not have come soon enough. As walked back to his barracks, his thoughts were troubled. What was he to do? Those men were plotting to kidnap the newly appointed governor's wife because of some animus that existed between the men. He pondered his options. Following the chain of command, he could relay the information to his commanding centurion. But there were several problems with that choice. His centurion might not believe him and would be reluctant to push it up the ladder. And if he did, Voculus and Portunus could deny it. It would be their word against his. He would be ridiculed and cast out of the legions or worse.

He could ask some of his mates what to do, but then they would be ensnared in this mess. He ruled out that choice. No need to get his friends in trouble as well.

Alternatively, he could attempt to get an appointment with Governor Maximus to alert him of the danger, but the chances of that happening were slim to nonexistent. A common legionary requesting an audience with the appointed governor—fat chance. He pondered his options some more since his conscience would not let this matter slide. He must do something.

He recalled hearing that Governor Maximus had an associate who was a former centurion named Marcellus. He might be more approachable than Governor Maximus. Longinus decided he would seek an audience with this Marcellus and report what he had heard. He was supposed to be off duty the next day, a rare occurrence in the legions, so he would find a way to speak with Marcellus.

Early the next morning, Longinus headed toward the governor's headquarters. He reached the quadrangle surrounded by porticoed buildings. It was crowded, filled with people moving with urgency, ignoring him completely. He nervously glanced about, wondering what his next steps should be. He gazed at the structure. No, he would not enter. He was just a lowly legionary. He would be tossed out on his arse. Furthermore, Voculus might hear reports that he was seen near Maximus's headquarters. So he waited. Before long, the clouds rolled in, obscuring the sun, and it began to rain. Longinus sought shelter under the eaves of the headquarters building. But before long, the centurion of the guard spied him.

"You there! What are you doing lounging about? This is not a common shelter unless you have business here, which I doubt. Be on your way. Go back to your barracks. I'm sure your centurion can find something for you to do."

Chastised, Longinus slunk away, but not too far. He continued to surreptitiously hover around, out of sight of the centurion. He walked about aimlessly but always within sight of the headquarters. He cursed his luck, knowing his armor would need to be scoured to remove the rust as a result of the rain. He knew that, sooner or later, this Marcellus would need to leave the building, but he hoped he would not have to wait all day. No matter. The information he possessed was too important to worry about corroded armor or standing in the rain.

After several more miserable hours of constant showers, Longinus spotted the former centurion—at least, he thought it was the centurion based on the description he had been given—scurrying across the courtyard through the rain toward another structure. Longinus hurried after the figure, not letting him out of his sight. He had to intercept Marcellus before he reached the other building.

Marcellus had been engaged in meetings all morning and did not even realize it had been in raining. He had left his cloak back in one of the offices. "Shit," he exclaimed. He briefly considered returning for his cloak but decided to continue on. He was starved, and the officer's mess was down the street.

He hurried across the quadrangle, dodging raindrops. Out of the corner of his eye, he noticed a legionary following him. He continued onward, but the figure moved quickly after him. Finally, Marcellus stopped abruptly, confronting the hurrying young man approaching him. "Why are you following me? Have you taken a fancy to me?"

"You are Marcellus, a former centurion and confidant of Governor Maximus. Correct?"

Marcellus glared sternly at Longinus. "I am. So what is that to you?"

"I have important information to convey to you."

Marcellus assessed the legionary. He was very young, and judging from the appearance of his uniform, he had been out in the rain a considerable time. His tunic and cloak were soaked. "What's your name, and what unit are you assigned?" Marcellus demanded in a stern tone.

The man snapped to attention. "Sir, Legionary Longinus, third century, second cohort."

"I see, Legionary Longinus, third century, second cohort," he parroted back. "Now, what in Hades would you possibly know about that I need to hear? Answer quickly. My patience is running thin, and I am standing in the rain, wet and hungry."

"Sir, I had guard duty yesterday, and I overheard things I was not supposed to."

"And what might that be?"

"It was a conversation between General Voculus and Governor Portunus."

His hunger forgotten, Marcellus grabbed the legionary's shoulder and guided him back to the headquarters. They ducked inside, safe from the rain, and into a small alcove. "Please tell me exactly what you heard."

"As I was saying, I had guard duty at General Voculus's headquarters. The window was open, and I could hear most of what they said." He hesitated, unsure how to continue. "I… I…"

Marcellus grabbed his shoulder reassuringly. "It's all right. Speak plainly and repeat exactly what you heard. It could be really important."

"They–they said…," he stammered, "that they planned to kidnap the governor's wife, Hereca, using some Quadi outlaws."

"You're sure about this?"

"Yes, they repeated it several times."

"What else did they say? Please try to remember."

Longinus paused. "Oh, yes, now I remember. I believe it was Voculus who said that his patron in Rome was getting impatient and that he was nearly ready to appr… appr…. I can't remember the word."

Marcellus glared. "Appropriate."

"Yes, that was it. He was ready to appropriate the leadership."

"Have you told anyone else about this?

"No. I thought you would be my best option."

"Good, you made the right decision. Tell no one. No one! You possess dangerous information."

"Voculus's aide came to the window and asked me if I had overheard the conversation. I said that I had not."

"That would be Centurion Gordianus. Keep clear of that man. His mind is full of wormholes, and he's not worth a bucket of goat piss. Come with me. You're going to tell Governor Maximus exactly what you told me."

Marcellus burst into Valerius's office with Longinus in tow. "Sorry to bother you, but this young man has just told me some disturbing information. This is Legionary Longinus, third century, second cohort."

Valerius nodded at the figure and leaned back in his chair. "All right, Legionary Longinus, speak."

Longinus repeated what he had told Marcellus. When he was finished, Valerius arose. "Thank you, Legionary Longinus. You have done Rome a great service. If Centurion Marcellus has not already told you, speak to no one about this. It could be perilous if others find out what you know. Understand?"

"Yes, sir. Glad to be of service."

"Now, before you leave, I am going to write down exactly what you told me on some parchment. You are going to sign your name on it. Understood?"

"Yes. You want me to swear to this, like an oath."

"Exactly." Valerius then wrote down what the legionary had told him. Ordinarily, he would have a scribe do it, but this information was too sensitive. In a short while, Valerius held up the finished copy. "I forgot to ask. You can read, can't you?"

"Yes."

"Good. Now, read this and sign your name at the bottom."

After Longinus had read the document and signed his name, he handed it over to Valerius

"Excellent. We will be in touch, but for now, you are dismissed. Remember, not a word."

After the legionary had departed, Valerius addressed Marcellus. "We need to get word to Hereca right away that she is in danger." Valerius summoned Radulf from the vestibule. "Go to the headquarters of the Tenth Legion, and ask for General Caelius. Tell him to report to me immediately on a matter of great urgency."

Radulf nodded and ran out of the room to complete his mission.

Valerius began pacing back and forth. "We must get there as soon as possible. I do not know when Hereca is scheduled to return here and what her travel accommodations will be, but she is in imminent danger. We must get word to her and increase her security in Noricum. Voculus and Portunus have stooped to new lows. I should have anticipated this. I will deal with those two debauched rogues later. But, for now, there's no time to waste."

"Agreed," said Marcellus. "I suggest we sail at dawn. I'm sure General Caelius can arrange a ship for us. As I recall, we provided four men as bodyguards for Hereca. They never let her out of their sight during daylight hours."

"What are four men? You saw the force that Voculus sent against us when we marched between the two rivers. We must warn Hereca and her guard detail. I hope General Severus is there. He can ensure her protection."

Just then, General Caelius rushed into the room along with Radulf. "Is there a problem?" Caelius inquired.

"Yes, thank you for coming here so quickly, General Caelius. We have received information from a credible source that Hereca is in danger back in Noricum. One of your men, Legionary Longinus, third century, second cohort, overheard a conversation between Portunus and Voculus while on guard duty at Voculus's headquarters. Please keep that name confidential. Some group of unknown villains plan to kidnap her to get to me. We must get word upriver to Noricum."

Caelius considered the situation before replying calmly, "There are two things we can do. "First, I suggest we immediately send a rider upriver to alert her and the legionary commanders there. Next, at first light, we could send a couple of naval patrol craft upriver. It will take at least two days to get there."

"How soon can the rider get to Noricum?" Valerius asked. "One day?"

Caelius frowned. "Probably sometime tomorrow. It's late afternoon, so if he leaves now, the messenger will be traveling by horse in darkness over broken roads. Unfortunately the river flooded last month washing away portions of the main thoroughfare."

"Marcellus and I will be on the boat tomorrow morning. Someone must warn her that she is in danger."

"Then, if you'll excuse me, I will see to getting the rider on his way and upriver. There's no time to spare. I will also arrange for several naval patrol craft to be ready at first light tomorrow. Is there anything else I can do?"

"No, that will be all for now," Valerius responded. "Thank you for your assistance, General.

Caelius departed.

"Why don't you rest for now," Marcellus advised. "We have an early start tomorrow. I will handle any issues that arise for the rest of the day."

"I'm going to pack. I'm taking my bow. When this nasty business is finished, I'm going to personally gut Voculus and Portunus."

"Can I help you do that, sir?" Radulf asked.

Marcellus laughed lightly. "It appears you have helpers in that particular endeavor. Count me in too."

* * *

Later that evening, Valerius stood alone on the small balcony extending from his bedroom. The full moon was rising, blood-red.

225

He shivered involuntarily. He hoped this peculiar hue of the moon was not a bad omen. He did not believe much in the gods or portents and thought using priests to read the auguries was a waste of time. Still, this unusual color unsettled him. He wondered if Hereca was observing the same moon and hoped she was safe.

* * *

Legionary Castor Longinus brayed in laughter at a joke by his friend and fellow legionary, Tullius. He may have heard it before, but he was about five glasses of wine deep into the night, and at that point, everything sounded funny. He sat at a table in Sword and Shield, a dingy inn outside the fortress, with his usual four mates, relieving the boredom of life in the legions. Longinus was especially animated since he had relieved himself of the burden of information he possessed. It was like a huge weight had been lifted off his shoulders.

Heeding Marcellus and Governor Maximus's warnings, he had not disclosed this information to anyone, not even his four friends with whom he had shared every aspect of his life under the eagles. Life, death, snow, rain, ice, bad food, and exhausting marches—they had persevered through it all together.

Sextus, one of his other friends, rose and waved his glass at the serving girl for another round of drinks. Longinus rubbed his face, which was starting to become numb from all the wine he had consumed. He rose unsteadily from his seat. "My back teeth are floating. I've got to go out back a take a piss."

"Hurry back," Sextus yelled, "or we'll drink your wine."

Longinus unsteadily wove through the other occupied tables to the back door and stepped outside to the trench that served as a latrine. He undid his tunic and hummed a merry tune about a legionary and a buxom barmaid. When he was finished, he fastened his tunic and turned around to find himself face-to-face with a figure in a black cloak. Longinus gasped. He felt a terrible pain in his gut—a gladius was savagely thrust into his midsection all the way to the hilt. The figure then ripped the sword upwards through his internal organs, slicing them. Longinus's vision darkened, but before he fell, he vaguely recognized the man as the one who had caught him listening outside Voculus's office. Those were his last thoughts as he rapidly bled out on the grimy floor.

CHAPTER XXIII
HERECA

Early at dawn, Hereca found herself smiling and humming a merry tune. After leaving Raetia and having spent two weeks in Noricum, she was returning home to her husband. She had coordinated her boat transportation the previous day. She would be boarding a small cutter with a crew of six and her four bodyguards at first light. She looked forward to surprising Valerius with her sudden appearance in Pannonia. She grinned in anticipation of the two-day journey. Her work at Noricum was finished for now. She had met with various tribal leaders, and they appeared willing to expand their trade with Rome. Although not a unanimous sentiment, the majority seemed willing.

Exiting her quarters with her small valise, she found her four bodyguards waiting to escort her down to her transportation. The four legionaries formed up around her and began walking toward the dock not far down the fort's main avenue. Glancing up at the sky, she spotted the sun rising, a pure yellow orb resembling a molten flame. She shaded her eyes against the early morning glare over the water and placed a wide-brimmed bonnet on her head, tugging it down securely to ensure it wouldn't blow off into the river. The day promised to be idyllic, and it was time to board the small craft.

Meanwhile, a Quadi lookout groggily awoke from the shelter of a beached vessel. He heard people talking, their voices resonating in the still morning air. He peeked his head up from his prone position, scanning the area, and saw the woman, the one he was supposed to be watching. She had to be the one. He saw the sailors and bodyguards mingling about. They were already at the wharf, getting ready to leave. It was his responsibility to alert the others when the governor's wife departed. He badly wanted to piss but quickly arose and sprinted down the path along the river. He had better alert his chieftain in time to ambush the boat. Thinking about the consequences if he failed, he ran even harder.

The leader of the band of Quadi thugs and outlaws, Gundahar, was a formidable man that most other chieftains avoided if at all possible. He led a group of Quadi who were nomadic and made their living herding cattle and stealing from the settlements in the Roman provinces of Noricum and Pannonia and even their fellow Quadi—they were not too particular.

Gundahar had been approached by a Roman general named Voculus, whom he had done business with years ago, stealing cattle and horses from villages and selling them to his fellow Quadi. Voculus wanted Gundahar to kidnap a woman, the wife of the new governor, and await instructions as to her ultimate fate. In exchange, he had been promised an insane amount of gold coin—three hundred gold aurei.

His encampment included around sixty men, his best warriors, whom he had chosen for this foray. Perhaps they were way too many for the task at hand, but he wanted to ensure the abduction was successful. There would be no second chances. They had departed their main bivouac around fifty miles downriver several days ago and settled around a mile downstream from the wharf at Lauriacum.

Surveying his campsite, Gundahar observed several cooking fires that had been started as the men arose to greet the day. Suddenly, one of his men, whom he had placed near the wharf of Lauriacum, burst into his encampment. "She's coming!" he shouted. "They are getting ready to sail."

"What is her escort?" Gundahar asked eagerly.

The messenger panted in exhaustion. "One boat, a small one. Maybe four armed guards and a handful of sailors."

"Get ready to move out," Gundahar commanded his men. He savagely kicked one man who was lounging against a tree. "Get off your lounging arses now, and grab your weapons."

The men quickly obeyed and trotted down to the river bank, weapons in hand. Hidden along the shoreline in the dense brush were a dozen skiffs of different sizes, a motley assortment of craft. Some were barely able to float, but he had enough to get the job done against a single, small Roman transport.

Gundahar's boats were strategically situated in a bend in the river so that by the time he and his men were spotted, it would be too late for the approaching Roman craft to turn around. He grinned. This would be easy pickings. The gold would be his. What's more, Voculus had informed him that their intended prey was quite attractive. His wife was back at their main encampment. Maybe he could have some sport with this Roman woman.

The Roman sailors stoically stroked their oars, maneuvering the boat to midstream, and then hoisted the square sail. The river was empty at that hour with no other vessels out yet. They needed to start this early to complete the journey to Vindobona in two days.

Hereca looked around over the placid flowing river. A fish jumped, gobbling an early morning breakfast. She loved the early hours when everything was so still and calm. There was little talking as the sailors and bodyguards went about their duties. Hereca, from her seated position, leaned back, enjoying the tranquility.

One of her guards was the first to spot the assailants. He pointed ahead as they rounded a bend in the river. "Turn around," he yelled. "Hostiles on the water."

"Too late," replied the young skipper in charge of the boat. "We cannot turn about in time. We must go through them." He yelled at four men stationed at the oars, "Row for your life!"

Turning, he screamed at the sailor manning the rudder, "Steer toward the right bank, away from the attackers."

Hereca gasped at the assortment of boats approaching from the left bank, closing in on them. Their intentions were far from friendly. Armed men stood on the boats, hefting spears and bows. She gauged the angle of the attacking boats to the track of their craft. Her stomach churned at the impending onslaught. The situation did not look good, and they had no options.

Her four bodyguards drew their swords and picked up their javelins. It was four against a mob. Hereca instinctively ducked as arrows whistled through the air. The first volley was fired too soon, badly missing the crew and her bodyguards. But the second volley was more accurate. Two of the oarsmen bunched over in pain. One of her bodyguards—an arrow protruding from his neck—gurgled and toppled overboard. Two of the attacking boats rammed the Roman vessel but with little effect. Several attempted to board but were impaled with spears by her bodyguards. Another boat, with full momentum, rammed the Roman cutter, creating a jagged hole in the wooden hull. More boats slammed into the Roman vessel, propelling the boat to the opposite shoreline. Spears whistled in the air again. Another of her bodyguards was down. Three raiders successfully leaped onto the boat, slaying the captain.

Recovering from her initial shock, Hereca grabbed a discarded sword from a slain bodyguard. When an arm reached out and grasped her roughly, she chopped at the offending limb, sending the man howling in pain. She stabbed another man in the leg. He collapsed on the deck. With a crash, Hereca's ship, driven by three other enemy vessels, plowed into the opposite bank. Thrown off balance by the sudden stop, she was hurled to the deck. Rising to her knees, she looked up just in time to see a shadow cross her vision. Then, a giant fist crashed into the side of her face. Everything went black.

In a short time, the raiders were back on the other side of the river with their captives. The wreckage of the Roman transport lay on the opposite shore, the bodies of the sailors and bodyguards strewn about.

CHAPTER XXIV
WORST OF FEARS

Valerius stood on the prow of the boat, heading upstream toward the fortress of Lauriacum in Noricum. Anxious, he scanned the water up ahead. They had made excellent progress owing to favorable winds. It was near dusk, and the river was clear of traffic; he reckoned they would shortly arrive at their destination. The boat, a large cutter with a squared sail, rounded a bend in the river. In the deepening gloom, Valerius spotted the wreckage of a small Roman transport beached on the left shoreline. A gaping hole indicated the vessel had been rammed. Valerius's heart was in his throat, a feeling of dread pervading him. *No, this is not possible.*

Marcellus stepped to his side, placing a reassuring hand on Valerius's shoulder. "Best not to leap to conclusions. Hereca is most likely having her evening meal in the fortress headquarters."

"I would like to think so, but this is hard to explain," he said, gesturing at the wreckage.

"We shall be there shortly," Marcellus responded as the boat continued to make headway and the wharf of Lauriacum came into view.

As the boat edged closer, Valerius spotted a group of people waiting to meet him. One of them was General Severus of the Third Legion, who, thankfully, had not yet returned to his home base in Raetia. When the boat nudged against the dock, Valerius leaped out and hurried toward Severus.

The legate wore a grim expression. "Not good news, I'm afraid. She has been taken. Early yesterday morning, a group of Quadi attacked her transport, slaughtering her bodyguards and the sailors manning the boat. One of the crew was still alive when we arrived. He said an assortment of vessels, around ten of them, attacked their boat at the bend in the river. They were quickly overwhelmed by the large number of brigands. He said that they took Hereca alive and fled back across the river. The sailor later succumbed to his wounds."

Valerius let out an anguished sigh, struggling compose himself. "Have we received any word of demands? Any communication whatsoever?"

"No, not yet," Severus replied. "May I ask how you learned of the threat? It might provide some indications as to who was responsible."

Valerius glanced at the assembled men. "I will tell you later in private. We need to plan out our next steps. There's no time to waste."

"Affirmative, sir. Why don't we adjourn to the headquarters? We can further discuss our options there."

Valerius, Marcellus, Radulf, and Severus sat in a small room, the outside door firmly shut. Valerius began, "A legionary guard in Vindobona overheard a conversation between none other than Voculus and Portunus. The legionary, who shall remain nameless for now, got a hold of Marcellus and relayed the information to him. They planned to kidnap Hereca employing forces unknown. By abducting her, they would force me to abdicate my position here on the Danubius. Voculus and Portunus may be acting on orders from someone in Rome. I heard this three days ago. It was too late to depart by boat, so we dispatched a messenger, but apparently, he didn't get here in time to warn her."

"Yes, I spoke to the messenger. He arrived just a tad too late," Severus responded with a tingle of sadness.

Valerius's expression resembled a storm cloud. "We must find her and rescue her. They will never release her. She could identify her abductors, plus I doubt these men would have the rectitude and integrity to honor any agreement. General Severus, we need your leadership here. You have men with agents and informers on your payroll. You must have them scour the countryside for word of Hereca's captors."

"I have already put out word seeking information on her where-abouts. Most of my agents are based in Raetia, but they know Noricum as well. What of Governor Avilius and his legate, Fabianus? Surely they have sources."

"Jupiter's teeth, no! That man is not to be trusted. For all I know, he is in league with Voculus and Portunus."

Severus nodded. "I guess I agree with your assessment. What do we do about Voculus and Portunus?

Valerius scowled. "I will deal with them in due time, and they will regret what they have done. For now, I must concentrate on Hereca." He smacked his fist on the tabletop. "We must find her!"

Marcellus stepped in front of Valerius. "But first, we must peel you off the ceiling. For the moment, there is nothing you or I can do. We must let General Severus's posse of informers venture out into the hinterlands. It is a vast area."

"General Severus, any idea who these people might be? Where they are heading?" Valerius asked.

"I am sure they are Quadi, and they retreated somewhere into the interior on the opposite side of the river. My guess is they have moved to the east. That's what I would do if I were them. This is how I plan to find her. I will send word to my network of agents and informers throughout the region to ask the following questions. First, who among the Quadi would do such a thing? If we know that, the next query would be where they live. Lastly, if anyone has seen anything. Chances are someone must have witnessed Hereca's captivity."

"You almost sound heartening," Valerius said. "I request that tomorrow, first thing in the morning, spread the news that I will offer two hundred gold aurei to anyone who has information on her where-abouts. That should light a fire under anyone who might want to help locate my wife. I assume they'll begin their search here in Noricum and expand out from there. Next, send for those two cohorts who helped us take care of Gerbold and his raiders. I know good troops when I see them. I want them here to help search for Hereca."

"You're not going to use any of the legionary units stationed here?" Severus inquired.

'No. They have not proven themselves. I have no faith in anyone from this garrison. It's a sad statement, but I cannot entrust Hereca's life to anyone here."

"We must get the word out about the reward and that you are here," Marcellus said. "If the kidnappers are going to make demands, they must know where we are. And if we do receive some sort of an ultimatum, perhaps we can trace it back to the source."

"That makes sense," Valerius replied. "General Severus, this is about more than just my wife. Not to put any undue pressure on you, but the fate of the empire may be at stake. This could have repercussions all the way to the imperial throne. You have your orders."

CHAPTER XXV
CAPTIVITY

When Hereca awoke, she found herself curled into a fetal position with a raging thirst. The right side of her face ached like her flesh was on fire. Looking about, she groggily surveyed her surroundings. She was in a mud daub hut, much like the one she, as a member of the Dolgubni tribe, had lived in during her youth. The interior was shrouded in shadows, the only source of light coming from the gap between the hide that hung over the entrance and the edge of the doorway. She groaned and rolled onto her side—a difficult maneuver since her hands and feet were tied securely. *Where am I?* Then, it all came flooding back to her: the sudden attack on her boat by hostile barbarians, the ensuing fight, and then, blackness.

She had been spared. But why? She realized that she must have been the object of the attack. Was she a hostage? Who were these brigands? Who hired them?

Her thoughts were interrupted as an older man, sweeping aside the flap covering the doorway, entered the dwelling. He brought a pot for Hereca to relieve herself, a container of water, and a stale crust of bread. Without a word, the figure freed the ropes fastening her arms and legs. Once done, he headed toward the doorway.

"Who are you? Where am I?" Hereca asked.

The man hesitated briefly, then thought better of it and exited the hut.

Hereca scurried over and greedily drank the water before devouring the bread. She then relieved herself and leaned against the wall, exhausted. She poured some water into her cupped hand and splashed it on her face, hoping it would ease the pounding in her head. It didn't help.

Later that morning, a totally repulsive man with long greasy hair and a thick, powerful body entered the dwelling. He had a bulbous nose and eyes that were black, vacant. He stared at her, undressing her with his eyes.

Hereca backed away from the stranger, her skin crawling at the thought of this man possessing her. "Who are you? What do you want with me? Why have you abducted me?"

The man smirked. "So many questions." He stepped forward, roughly grabbing her right breast. "I heard you were a beautiful woman. They were correct. Perhaps later, when you have recovered, we will have some sport together."

Hereca remained rigid as the chieftain fondled her breast, touching her nipple through her garment. Noting her lack of resistance and mistaking it for willingness, he edged closer, feeling more confident, letting his guard down. "My name is Gundahar."

Before he could continue, Hereca struck. She savagely kneed the man in the groin.

The man paled, letting out an agonized shriek and collapsing to his knees. "Guards," he croaked. Two hefty men entered, looking expectantly at their leader. "Tie her back up. It's time she learned some manners."

Her captors roughly grabbed her and tied her up, securing the knots snugly. She yelped at the tightness of her bonds. One of the men forced her to her knees and dispassionately kicked her over. The two men departed without a backward glance, sniggering at the captive.

Hereca struggled with her bonds, but it was of no use. Tears of frustration rolled down her cheeks. She chided herself for her weakness. Assessing her situation, she realized she was in extreme danger. Her prospects did not look good, but she would never give up. It was not in her nature. She was a princess of the Dolgubni tribe, the daughter of a chieftain and wife to the governor of the Danubian territory.

Please come for me, my husband.

CHAPTER XXVI
THE QUEST

Hereca had lost track of time. She guessed she had been captive for four days. Her abductors were on the move again. Evidently, the previous encampment was only a temporary stop at an abandoned village. Judging from the position of the sun over her right shoulder, she deduced they were moving east. Throughout the day, she had struggled down a muddy road full of puddles, her hands tied together and the other end of the rope fastened to a horse's pommel. She was deprived of water and half dragged along by the plodding steed. Chieftain Gundahar rode up beside her. "Not so full of pluck today, are we? I will break you. Then, you will beg me to mate with you." He laughed scornfully and rode away.

The caravan of brigands, around sixty in number, labored on into the late afternoon. Occasionally, they passed others heading in the opposite direction. Some of the travelers stared in pity at the unfortunate woman with the swollen and discolored face, hauled along by a rope tethered to a horse, ridden by a brutish man. But they knew better than to say anything since the members of the troupe looked to be an unsavory lot. All of them were armed, their appearances grubby and their clothes filthy.

As dusk approached, Hereca was ready to collapse, her knees quaking from weakness. They arrived at a small village, the huts scattered randomly about. One of her captors untied her, grabbed her by the shoulder, and half pushed, half dragged her through the center of the settlement. The woman and children of the village stared at her with expressions devoid of pity.

They arrived at a daub hut, and the guard shoved her roughly through the doorway onto the floor. "Enjoy your stay," he said mirthlessly. "This will be the last place you see before you greet your gods."

Hereca sprawled upon the dirt floor of her prison. She was too weak to even attempt to rise. She wished she had a spear or a knife, any kind of weapon, so she could at least die fighting. As twilight settled over the village, a woman brought in a container of water and a bowl of barley stew and departed without a word. Hereca quickly drank the water and wolfed her food down. She had no sooner done that than a guard entered and tied her feet and hands again.

"Sweet dreams," the guard sneered before exiting the dwelling.

Anger surged through Hereca's body. She vowed not to give up. She would see her children once again. She would not succumb to this barbarian filth. They were nothing better than pond scum. She thought of Valerius and Marcellus. They would find a way to rescue her. She knew they would. Men far superior to this lot of uncouth renegades had attempted to stymie them in the past, and all had failed. She needed to survive long enough for them to locate her.

* * *

In the past five days, nothing had changed at Lauriacum. They had received no ransom demands, and there was no word from informers north of the river where Hereca might be held captive. Valerius had dark circles under his eyes and generally looked like Hades, while Marcellus did not appear much better, both suffering from lack of sleep and anxiety. The waiting was excruciatingly painful. They could do nothing and remained powerless until they had a proximate location of where Hereca was being held captive.

Valerius sat with Marcellus and Radulf, waiting and hoping for some new information. Before long, Severus entered. "I'm afraid there's no word yet on her whereabouts. I know it's asking a lot, but you must be patient. Some of my messengers, agents, and informants just began their search yesterday, while others have been looking for her for days. I'm confident they will turn up with something. In the meantime, my legionaries, who will arrive here shortly, will be primed and ready to go. We have around three hundred men, including a few cavalry scouts.

"Only four centuries?" Valerius queried. "That's less than a cohort. I thought we were bringing two cohorts."

"I took the liberty of requesting only four centuries. The more I thought about the proposed number of two cohorts, almost a thousand legionaries, the less I liked it. Four centuries, around three hundred men, should be enough. It may be a risk if we face a far superior number, but I don't think so. I believe the group responsible for this abduction is of a smaller tribe, most likely renegades. Next, once we discern where she might be, speed is of the essence. Four centuries can move faster and make less noise. Three hundred men may not be inconspicuous but a bit stealthier than two cohorts. Not to be grim, but we don't know how long she will be kept alive. The sooner we get there, the better our chances."

"Makes sense. Thank you, General Severus. I have faith in you and your men," said Valerius. "Your strategy makes perfect sense. Not to tell you your business, but I have been thinking about our tactical situation as well. Should we discover her location, as you stated, we will need to move rapidly. So no baggage or packs. Just weapons and rations."

Marcellus chuckled slightly. "You are thinking like a centurion. I was about to mention the same, but I believe General Severus is a step ahead of us."

Severus grinned. "As I said, my men will be ready at a moment's notice. We will carry weapons, a few days' rations, and our canteens. But, sir, again, you must be patient. My agents are fanning out far and wide. Someone out there somewhere must have seen something. We will get word and soon. My spies are aware of the urgency of the matter, and then, there is the reward. I will come back to you as soon as I hear anything.

Late that afternoon, Severus returned. Valerius and Marcellus looked on anxiously. "Two things. We have received a ransom demand—here." He thrust the message in Valerius's direction. "Next, my four centuries should be here today or tomorrow morning at the latest."

Valerius read the note aloud. "Governor Valerius Maximus, you will pay a sum of one thousand gold coins at a location to be determined and immediately vacate the territory. Once the coin is received and you have left, your wife will be released." He looked up from the note. "That's it. How did you come into possession of this?"

Severus grimaced. "Not much help there. A merchant traveling along the river road had this thrust into his hands. He was told to deliver it to you, and then, the man who handed him the message disappeared into the forest. When he reached the fortress and asked to see you, my men intervened and reviewed the dispatch. It offers no clues in the search for your wife. Her captors are cagey. I need not tell you that even if you comply with these demands, it is doubtful you will save your wife. I know it's asking a lot, but please be calm and wait. As I stated before, we will find a way." The general turned about and departed.

* * *

Pepin was born in Raetia, and being a loyal servant of the Romans for many years, he enjoyed working for them. His trade ventures took him all over, up and down the river, mostly in Raetia and Noricum but also Pannonia. A merchant by occupation, he often crossed the river to barter with the tribes. Recently, he had shifted his market to wine and olive oil, trading with the barbarian tribes along the Danubius. Commerce was favorable, and if this new governor had his way, Pepin would make a fortune. During his trade discussions, he would pick up all kinds of useful information and relay it to the Romans. Crop harvests, tribal feuds, rebellious groups, migrating peoples—the Romans listened to everything, and he was rewarded handsomely with silver coins. Hence, he had been urgently sought out in Noricum to assist in the search for the abducted governess. He could not refuse this proposal. Better yet, there was a huge bounty in gold coins if he was successful. He could not believe how much was being offered—two hundred gold coins from the Roman treasury. Regardless of the generous recompense, he would have gladly assisted his benefactors. He liked working with the Romans, and they had always been fair to him in the past.

It was nearly dusk, and he resignedly led his horse to a small stable opposite the long hall that served as an eatery and billet for weary travelers—and he was weary. His body reminded him that he was no longer a young man. He had been on his horse all day in the barbarian lands opposite the river from Noricum, seeking information on the new governor's wife. Usually, he gathered intelligence as a sideline to his trading ventures, but not today. The sole purpose of his trip was to find the location of this captured woman. But his search had been fruitless.

He entered the dim inn and plopped himself down in a chair, exhausted. A plump waitress approached him. "We have barley stew, fresh bread, and ale."

"That would be fine." In a matter of moments, his dinner was served along with a tankard of brew. He quickly gulped down his food and then leaned back in his chair, his eyes heavy. All he wanted to do was sleep. He had covered many miles in his fruitless search for the kidnapped woman. It was not quite dusk yet, so he decided to stay awake a while longer. Besides, there was too much noise in the main dining room, which would surely carry upstairs to the sleeping loft.

He peered around the gathering as shadows crossed the room, noting an assortment of men and women. His mercantile senses had been honed from years of experience, so he was always searching for new trading partners. Though these folks looked plebian and not wealthy, appearances could be deceptive. Wandering over to two men seated at a small table, he introduced himself and talked of his trading business. "We are not interested," one of the men said gruffly. "Be on your way."

Pepin was about to offer a sharp reply but thought better of it. It would be futile. He drifted away, and on looking around, he spotted an elderly couple finishing their meal. "Mind if I join you? Name's Pepin. I trade up and down the river, mostly in oil and wine, but I have traded in other goods as well."

They introduced themselves as Bardolf and Adela. "We are merchants too," Bardolf said. "We make and sell leather shoes and sandals. We've been doing it for years. Normally, we do business from our shop in Noricum, just east of Lauriacum, but we occasionally visit across the river to expand our markets."

"I think I know where your shop is located. In fact, I have purchased sandals there on previous occasions. You make a quality product."

"Thank you. So, what brings you to this section of the land?" Adela asked. "It would be difficult to transport wine or oil this far from the river."

"You are very perceptive," he replied. "The Roman authorities back in Lauriacum have asked me to assist them on a search for a missing woman, an important one, the wife of the new territorial procurator. She has been kidnapped."

"What does this woman look like?" Adela asked.

"Never seen her. But I am told she's very beautiful, maybe in her early forties. They said she's tall with auburn hair."

Adela gasped. "We saw a woman matching that description yesterday. Her hands were bound, and she was tethered to a horse. Her face was swollen like she had been struck, abused."

Pepin rose, not quite believing what he was hearing. "Where did you see her? What distance from here? This is important. The procurator will be extremely grateful."

Adela turned to her husband. "How far from here?"

"Not far," he replied. "I'm guessing ten miles—no, more like fifteen."

"Do you know who has her?"

Bardolf rubbed his chin in thought. "The name is familiar to me. We know better than to do business with him. He's a disreputable figure, a rogue. Gottfried? No. But it begins with a *g*. Let me see… Gunther? No. That's not it."

"Gundahar," Adela chimed in.

"Yes! That's it, Gundahar!" Bardolf exclaimed.

246

"Any idea where these people are located?" Pepin asked eagerly.

"Not exactly sure. They move around quite a bit. But, generally, they are camped northeast of here."

"Thank you so much. If this information leads to her release, you will be handsomely rewarded. I'm sorry to have to leave you, but I must be on my way back to Lauriacum."

"It's almost night. It's unsafe to travel at this time," Adela cautioned.

"Does not matter. This is urgent. An important woman's life is at stake I must be on my way. Thank you again!" With that, Pepin dashed out of the inn toward the stable.

CHAPTER XXVII
A GLIMMER OF HOPE

Lauriacum

Valerius glumly stared at the four walls of his headquarters. He tried not to be dismayed, but he knew that with each passing moment, the odds they would recover Hereca alive grew slimmer. Surely someone must have heard or seen something by now.

Marcellus sat in the opposite corner, attempting to put on a brave face, but his glum disposition betrayed him. Looking up, he asked, "Should we alert Tiberius of what has transpired?"

"I've been thinking about that. I see no purpose in informing him of the developments here on the Danubius. What is he going to do? We must solve this challenge on our own. Besides, knowing Sejanus, he will somehow twist this to gain an advantage over us."

"I guess I agree with you…" Marcellus began, but before he could continue, General Severus barged into the room followed by a short, middle-aged figure dressed in mud-spattered garb.

"I believe we may have a sighting," Severus exclaimed.

Valerius bolted from his chair. "Where?"

"Let me introduce you to Pepin. He's a trader dealing in oil and wine, mostly in our provinces of Raetia and Noricum but across the river as well. He also feeds us information from what he sees and hears. Pepin, tell Governor Maximus what you heard."

"Pardon my appearance, sir. I've been riding for three days. I had stopped at an inn two nights ago. That day, I had scoured the roads, fields, and villages searching for any word on your wife, inquiring if anyone had seen her. I heard nothing. That evening, I had dinner at an inn and chatted with an older couple. They peddle shoes and sandals to the tribes across the river. When I mentioned to them that I was searching for the governor's missing wife and described her, they told me they had spotted a captive woman matching your wife's depiction. They were unaware she had been kidnapped. They said she looked like she had been mistreated, her face bruised and swollen."

Marcellus walked over, holding a crude map of the area. "Can you show us?"

"I will do my best." He studied the map and then stabbed the document with his finger. "I ventured forth from Lauriacum, here. I crossed the river and then proceeded east for a time along the river road. I then went and turned north, away from the river, and then headed east again." He traced his journey to a spot on the map and stabbed it again with his finger. "I'm only guessing, but I believe it was somewhere in this general vicinity. The couple I spoke with believes the chieftain's name is Gundahar. They implied he is a nasty bloke."

Valerius turned to Severus. "I don't mean to be impolite, and I'm sorry to have to ask you, Severus, but given what's at stake, do you believe Pepin to be a credible source?"

Severus answered promptly. "Yes, Pepin has proved to be a valuable informant. I have used his services in the past."

Valerius then faced Pepin. "I didn't mean to offend you, but I had to ask."

"Sir," Pepin replied, "given what's at stake, no offense taken. If I may speak freely, I staunchly believe the couple's story. They have a firm reputation, and they were not drunk. I, uh, promised them some reward money if this leads to the rescue of your wife."

Valerius laughed lightly. "Pepin, if your information is correct, both you and the shoemakers are going to be highly rewarded."

CHAPTER XXVIII
PURSUIT

General Severus gazed at Valerius and Marcellus, who were discussing their next steps. "Gentlemen," the general interrupted, "we have several hours of daylight remaining. I say why waste this precious time? My legionaries are ready, and the naval ships are waiting at the wharf to take us downstream. I plan to sail until dark and then find a spot along the river to bivouac for the night. Are you ready?"

Valerius picked up his bow and quiver of arrows, as did Marcellus. "Let's get going," Valerius said.

Severus turned to Pepin. "I know you must be exhausted, but would you mind coming with us? We could really use your help."

"I'm dog-tired," Pepin replied, "but the demonic hounds of Hades could not prevent me from joining you. Lead the way."

Marcellus chuckled. "The hounds of Hades indeed. I believe that is an affirmative. Thank you for agreeing to accompany us."

Down at the dock, the centuries were quickly split into quarters, twenty men to a boat. Despite the reduced forces, the armada was still unwieldy with eighteen boats, including those for the cavalry horses and riders. But they loaded quickly and soon set sail downriver.

To Valerius's disappointment, they did not get that far. Shadows were soon cast over the river, as the days were getting shorter with the waning summer. Severus approached him. "The commander of the flotilla just informed me that it's time to stop for the night. I have to defer to his judgment on these matters. We sail at first light. The men can eat their morning rations on the boat."

"Then that's what we will do," Valerius replied. "As anxious as I am to keep going, I know it could be foolhardy to sail the river in darkness."

* * *

The next day, the men were awakened before dawn. True to the captain's words from the previous night, the ships were underway as dawn crept upon the river. Valerius stood next to Pepin and Severus along the ship's rail. "How far are we going to sail downriver?"

Severus turned to Pepin with an inquiring look.

"I am familiar with this territory," Pepin said. "My best guess is that we will sail into the afternoon. When we disembark, we march north into the interior of the country. I sense that we will not reach our destination tonight but at some time tomorrow or the next day. Then, we should be near the village of Gundahar, although the precise location is unknown. Once there, I pray Jupiter and Mars guide us to his village."

"Once we reach the area where Hereca might be held, I will send out my cavalry scouts and search the countryside," Severus added. "We will also question anyone we come across. Don't worry, we will find her."

Before long, the river traffic increased as the morning progressed. Besides the ubiquitous Roman naval craft, there were boats of all shapes and sizes plying the waters. They steered clear of the armada, which hogged most of the river. The ships were at full sail, speeding toward their destination.

They navigated their way downriver most of the day, passing villages and docks. People stared at the small convoy of ships with its cargo of heavily armed men. Late in the afternoon, Pepin approached Severus. "General, I believe this is the place to turn to shore. Once we disembark, I believe we should head due north with the daylight remaining."

You're sure this is the spot?"

"I think so," answered Pepin. "If my reckoning is correct, we should pick up a well-used trail heading north that passes by many villages."

The four centuries disembarked quickly and formed up, ready to go. Pepin took the lead, walking along a mud path perhaps three persons wide, surrounded by hanging branches and pitted with muddy craters. Up ahead, the trail split into two branches. Pepin paused, contemplating his options.

Severus approached. "Are you lost?"

Pepin shook his head. "Don't think so. I just want to be sure I pick the correct one. Bear to the left."

"I hope this trail becomes a bit wider," Severus said.

"If my memory serves me correctly, we will soon find the road you desire."

After several more miles on the rustic path, just as Pepin predicted, they intercepted a major road, wide enough for the centuries to march six abreast. Onward they advanced, the clinking of their armor and weapons resonating through the forests and fields. Before long, they neared a settlement.

A column of marching legionaries is an awe-inspiring sight, an intimidating force. The men moved along the road, their shields attached to their left shoulders with a baldric, a single pilum on their right shoulder, and their sheathed swords hanging from their right hip. The usual marching yoke, burdened with possession and other assorted gear, was absent. The formation of legionaries approached a small village located in a large clearing. Mud huts and a single feasting hall were visible.

Women shrieked at the appearance of the heavily armed intruders and frantically ushered their children to the safety of their dwellings. The men of the village scurried toward their weapons.

Severus turned to his centurions and bellowed, "Do not move, and above all, do not draw your weapons." Severus ordered his two scouts and Pepin to approach the village entrance with him. They halted about thirty paces from the village. Severus directed Pepin to speak for them since, as a civilian and unarmed, he was the least threatening among the group. "Tell the villagers to stay back. We are only passing through and are not here to attack them."

Valerius watched as Severus and the three men reached the hamlet entrance and halted. The village chieftain approached them, scowling. Behind him was a large posse of warriors, brandishing spears and swords.

"What are you doing here?" the chieftain asked. "We have no quarrel with you."

Severus turned toward Pepin. "Tell him to remain in the village if he knows what's good for him. We are pursuing a group of bandits and thieves and have no interest in his settlement. We will be on our way if they do not interfere with us."

As Pepin translated, the chieftain observed the heavily armed troop of legionaries, noting their sheathed swords, and then turned back to Pepin. He nodded, turned about, and yelled to his followers, "Go back. The Romans are not here to attack us." The warriors, who had been edging forward, cautiously returned to their settlement while keeping a wary eye on the Romans.

Severus returned to the command group, while Valerius heaved a sigh of relief. "General Severus, not to tell you your business, but I suggest we should have the scouts alert us when we approach any other villages up ahead. That almost turned into a melee back there. Can you send your cavalry scout ahead to warn us and the village?"

Severus grinned embarrassedly. "My mistake. I wanted to keep our riders close, as we will soon be stopping for the evening. You are correct. They should have been scouting well ahead of the column. That was almost a disaster. As we speak, the shadows are lengthening. I say we put another mile behind us and stop for the night. I will defy standard operating procedure and not build a fortified camp. Besides, we did not bring our shovels, and I'm not going to have the men hack out ditches with their swords. I want the men fresh and rested for tomorrow."

"Fine by me, General Severus. Lead the way."

It had been an exhausting day, and it was near dark. Leaning against a tree in the night encampment, Valerius munched on his stale loaf of bread and then guzzled water from his canteen, while Marcellus did the same next to him. "Tomorrow or the next day," Valerius said, wiping his mouth on his arm, "if we locate Gundahar, and Hereca is not alive, I am going to do several things. First, slaughter every male warrior in Gundahar's village, and then, when we return to Vindobona, I will personally ram my sword through both Voculus and Portunus. After that, I will request Tiberius that I be relieved of my duties."

Marcellus was silent for a spell. "I think you're putting the cart before the horse. Let's not contemplate that scenario just yet. Is Hereca in extreme peril? Yes. But my gut tells me she is alive. We will find her tomorrow and rescue her. For now, Tribune, let's cut the doom-and-gloom shit. Stop thinking like that and instead plan how we are going to take Gundahar's village and keep Hereca alive."

* * *

They were on the move shortly after dawn. After several miles, they came across another hamlet, a large one, given the number of huts visible from the road. A wide stream flowed off to their left. Unlike the encounter from the previous day, the settlement had been given advance notice of the approaching Romans and the purpose of their intrusion. Many of the villagers lined the side of the road, guardedly watching the legionaries march past. The Romans were not challenged.

The four centuries marched into the afternoon, passing by villages of various sizes before taking a break at a small spring. The legionaries greedily replenished their water supply, as they were almost out. Off in the distance, cattle and horses grazed in nearby fields. Severus and Valerius approached Pepin, who was sitting against a tree, wiping his face with a cloth, as the day had turned warm.

"Pepin, any idea how close we are?" Severus inquired.

"Remember that we don't have his exact location, but I believe we are close enough to begin asking about the whereabouts of this Gundahar and his followers. I noticed you did not ask anyone about him in the settlements we passed. I assume there was a reason for this."

Severus nodded. "Now that we are, hopefully, closer to this scoundrel, we can ask for information on his whereabouts. He will not get much of an advance notice of our presence, if any, as we will be moving rapidly."

"I sense that he is a bit farther north," Pepin said. "Do you think the locals will inform us about Gundahar?"

"I think they will for a lot of reasons," Valerius said, holding up a pouch of coins. "This should prove a strong motivator. Also, we have been told that Gundahar is not held in high esteem by his fellow Quadi. I intend to inform any villages we stop at of the crime committed by this rogue. We should eschew any kind of force. We want cooperation, not coercion. I want these people on our side."

"I believe that's a good assessment. No need to threaten anyone," Severus said. "Now, let's go and find this bastard and rescue Hereca."

The centuries were on the move once again. Before long, they halted outside another settlement about two miles farther up the road.

Valerius, Pepin, Marcellus, and Severus stood respectfully outside the entrance of the village, while the chieftain and his associates stood by stoically. Valerius inquired about Gundahar's location, but they all shook their heads.

Valerius raised the sack of coins. "Are you sure? Gundahar is a criminal who has committed a horrific act of kidnapping. He has abducted the governor's wife; I am the governor."

The chieftain gaped, not quite believing that the new governor was actually here in his remote village, far from his headquarters on the river. "I have heard of this Gundahar and his followers. He is not a good neighbor. He lies, cheats, and steals from others. But, to answer your question, no, he is not around here. I believe he moves around frequently."

Valerius walked away, disappointed. He approached Marcellus. "What do you think? Was he lying or telling the truth? You're good at judging these sorts of things"

"I think he is speaking fact. I saw him eye that sack of coins you produced in front of him—an enticing offer. I say we move onward. Maybe we have not advanced far enough north."

The Roman formation trekked on through the late morning and into the afternoon. At every village they stopped, the answer was the same. They had not seen Gundahar and did not know where his village was located. Even worse, the villages became less frequent, the countryside more rustic.

That night, Valerius sat with Severus, Marcellus, and Pepin around a small cooking fire. All were silent, contemplating the distinct possibility of failure. Valerius stared bleakly off into the night. A breeze rustled through the forest, the leaves ticking with the wind. He returned his gaze to his companions. "What are our next steps? What should we do differently?"

Pepin spoke cautiously, "I must confess, I have not been this far north before." He paused, looking around, expecting some rebuke.

"Alright," Valerius said. "So what are you suggesting? Should we change direction?"

"A practical alternative given our rations," Severus said.

"No!" Pepin exclaimed. "I sense that we did not travel far enough east down the river before turning north. I did not travel this route on my quest days ago, so it's only a reckoning on my part. Remember, this is a vast territory."

Valerius looked at Severus. "Are your men up to it? You mentioned we are short of rations."

Severus straightened up. "My men will march until I tell them to stop. Yes, they are tired. To be a legionary is to be exhausted and hungry half of the time. Men of the legions have endured far worse. You know that, sir."

Valerius nodded. "Understood."

Marcellus snorted. "Yes, I could not agree more. This is but a short stroll in the woods. A picnic. I have been through far worse—wet and freezing my arse off."

"So it's settled," Valerius said. "We proceed onward tomorrow, venturing farther east, hoping to find the elusive Gundahar."

"Yes. I propose that we head east on the first trail we find going that way," Pepin said. "We should make inquiries from any village we come across."

"Tomorrow is the day!" Marcellus exclaimed. "We will find Hereca and rescue her. I can feel it in my bones."

CHAPTER XXIX
GUNDAHAR

Gundahar strolled through his village, a haphazard collection of scattered huts. It was a dingy place, strewn with animal bones and other refuse. They would need to move again in the spring. This location was a poor choice on his part. The land had sparse vegetation for the grazing animals, most of them stolen. Also, they were too far north of the river. Much of the wealth of his clan came from raiding across the river. He needed to move closer to the river border since it took too long to get there. On the other hand, this spot offered better security, as it was in the hinterlands, and if the Romans did venture across the Danubius in search of him, which was doubtful, he was fairly secure there. So, for the moment, his remote location served him well.

He contemplated his current circumstances. He had sent his messengers days ago to meet with the Roman, Voculus, and pick up the other half of the gold that had been promised to him. In addition, he was waiting for orders on the final disposition of the woman. He could not kill her until he had permission. His men should be back soon. They had been gone for over a week now. He briefly pondered how to collect the ransom he had demanded from the Romans. Pursuing this course of action was risky, but the amount of coin involved, one thousand gold pieces, could not be passed up. He decided to wait. First, he needed to hear back from Voculus.

His loins stirring, Gundahar thought of his captive. But he had a problem, his wife. She was suspicious of him. She had observed the captured woman and her exceptional beauty, and she knew Gundahar all too well. He would need to find the right time to ravage her. Perhaps tonight after his wife consumed too much ale, as she was wont to do. He could help her reach her state of stupor and then visit the governor's wife.

* * *

Hereca lay curled up. She could feel her strength waning from the ordeal over the past few days. Her captors barely fed her. Her wrists were bound tightly, but she managed to reach up and probe her face with her fingers, wincing from the pain. Her jawline was tender, the flesh swollen. She could only imagine what she must look like. Would she ever be rescued? She would not give up hope, for it was not in her nature. She silently raged at her circumstances.

Glancing downward, she observed her feet securely bound and tied to a staunch wooden post driven deep into the earth. She had tugged and twisted her bonds until she was screaming from the pain, but there was no give, and even if she freed herself, a guard was always posted at the entrance of her dwelling. Every so often they poked their heads in to check on her. Glancing at her wrists and ankles, she noted the chaffed and bloody flesh. Then, there was that pig, Gundahar. He would try to ravage her again—of this, she was certain. She had seen the way he leered at her. Hereca looked around for some sort of weapon but found nothing. She would die before she spread her legs for that swine.

Later that afternoon, Gundahar entered into her dwelling, eyeing her up and down with a lascivious grin. "I will see you later tonight, my pretty. You might as well resign yourself."

Hereca threw him a scornful look. "What's the matter, you can't satisfy your wife, so you look for other pastures? You're pathetic."

"You leave my wife out of this. I will make you scream tonight. Just wait!" With that, he ducked back out, closing the flap that served as a door behind him.

Hereca anxiously looked around again. She needed something, anything, to defend herself. The floor of the dwelling was packed earth, devoid of rocks. She had no eating utensils and was forced to use her hands. The only items in the hut were a pot to relieve herself and her clay-fired porridge bowl. She picked up the eating vessel and turned around in her bound hands. The rope tether securing her to the post was at about an arm's length. Taking up the slack, she tapped the pot against the thick, wooden shaft. If she smashed it hard enough against the wooden post, it would break, leaving a jagged shard. It was not much, but it would have to do. She would wait until later in the day after her dinner was brought to her before carrying out her plan.

Toward evening, she could hear the villagers feasting and celebrating. There was shouting and loud talk outside her dwelling. A woman entered and ladled out some barley stew in her bowl from a larger pot and threw a piece of stale bread over the steaming stew. She checked the waste pot, and seeing nothing in it, she departed.

Hereca gobbled the food down. It was awful, but she needed to maintain her strength. As the merriment outside seemed to increase, she grabbed the eating bowl with both hands, extended her arms along the tether, and dashed it against the wooden stake. Nothing happened.

The bowl remained intact, but she did observe a small crack on the side. She lifted the bowl again, and using the force of her body to enhance the impact, she struck the post. The clay container shattered into multiple pieces, most too small to use as a weapon. However, one was large enough to suit her purposes. She eagerly grasped it, her hands now bleeding from the fragments. She tested the jagged edge with her finger. It was sharp enough to do some damage. She hurriedly cleaned up the fragments and scattered them around. The large fragment, she concealed behind her.

As darkness settled on the village, Gundahar entered her hut. He wobbled slightly, reeking of ale. "It is time, governess," he exclaimed with a laugh. "I have been waiting for this all day." He slid his dirty tunic off his shoulders and then down his legs, exposing his privates. He got down on his knees and began to crawl toward her. "I will untie your feet so you can open your pretty legs wide." He began fumbling with the tight knots on the hemp.

Hereca gripped the clay shard tightly. She would only get one opportunity to strike, so her thrust must be a good one. Gundahar's face, now that he was on his hands and knees, was at the same level as hers. She ruthlessly thrust the sharp shard, extending her arm as far as the rope would allow her and tearing it down his jawline upon contact

Gundahar howled in pain, rapidly crabbing backward, holding his injured face. When he moved his hands away to check for bleeding, Hereca saw the injury she had inflicted. It was not what she had hoped. The wound was bleeding but hardly incapacitating.

"You haughty bitch!" he cried, delivering a backhand to her already bruised face. It sent her flying across the floor of the hut. She lay sprawled in the dirt, stunned by the blow.

Gundahar retrieved the bloody shard and angrily stalked out, holding his hands to his bleeding face. "I am not finished with you yet."

Hereca heard Gundahar speak to the guard outside. "Tie her feet back up, and make it tight."

CHAPTER XXX
THE RESCUE

The Roman column resumed its march at dawn without eating their morning rations since they were out of food. Before long, they arrived at a small hamlet near the junction of the main avenue and a much smaller road. Pepin entered the village and conferred briefly with the leaders. Hurrying back to Valerius and Severus, he reported, "The right fork of this lesser trail leads to the east. They said it intersects with a much larger road less than a half's day march from here. I asked about Gundahar, but they know nothing of him."

The Roman force pivoted and bore to the right on the smaller road. It was a walking path at best. There was no way a cart could navigate on the pitted and uneven surface. Onward they marched to the east through forests and fields, occasionally crossing small streams with no bridging. Overgrown branches, vines, and thorn bushes impeded their movements. Towering forests of larch, beech, and oak swallowed the Roman legionaries. There was little in the way of habitation other than a few scattered settlements. The men swatted away buzzing insects that tormented them as they pressed on.

By late morning, they arrived at a road junction, just as the villagers had stated. The intersecting road was much wider in a north-south direction.

"Hold here for a break," Severus commanded to his centurion commanders. The men all but collapsed. The lack of food and constant forced marches were beginning to take a toll. Severus observed his men with a worried frown. Gathering with Valerius, Marcellus, and Pepin, he expressed his concern, "Gentlemen, we are at a tipping point. I'm sure that if I ask the centurions, they will say the men can continue the search. But I don't like what I'm seeing."

"Aye," Marcellus agreed. "But from my experience, they will continue onward because they can. These are good legionaries, well trained. They still have a lot of fight in them."

Severus nodded. "Thank you. Yes, they are good men." He turned to Pepin. "We need to make a decision. Do we go north or do you believe we have already journeyed too far north and exceeded our quest in that direction? Do we head south from here?"

"I have been contemplating your question the entire time we were on that piss-poor road. I believe we need to turn south."

"Are you sure?" Valerius asked.

Pepin answered without hesitation. "Yes. That is my best judgment. We must have ventured too far north and not far enough east. If your wife is held captive by a group of Quadi along this road, they are south of us."

"That's good enough for me," Severus said. "Any objection to us heading south from here?" No one spoke. "Then let's get moving. We have a lot of daylight ahead of us. I will send my riders down this trail. We will follow the same protocol in any village.

The Roman column resumed its march once more. There were some muttered curses from the men, but icy glances from their centurions quickly silenced them. After several hours, they had encountered three small hamlets of perhaps a few hundred souls. They all said the same thing: they had not heard of Gundahar's whereabouts. They marched another hour till they reached a large settlement on the banks of a wide stream slowly meandering through a broad meadow.

Valerius, Severus, and Pepin approached the village leaders at the entrance to the hamlet. Valerius observed many dwellings and two long houses. There were crops, barley, oats, and herds of cattle in the distant fields. An older man with a long white beard stepped forward, glowering at them. "Roman legionaries. You are far from your home base, are you not? Are you lost?"

Valerius stepped forward, speaking in their tongue. "Yes, we are far from home but not lost. What is your name, please?"

"I am called Berthhold, and these are my people."

"I am Valerius Maximus, governor of the Danubian provinces."

Berthhold's face became animated. "I know that name."

"Listen, we are sorry for the incursion into your lands, and we bear you no ill will. We are on a quest to find my wife, who has been abducted by a group of Quadi led by a man named Gundahar. Would you happen to know the location of his village?" Valerius held up his sack of coins, jingling the contents. "We will reward you if you can furnish us any information on his location."

A dark look crossed Berthhold's face. Valerius assumed the chieftain was going to tell them to get off his land or face the consequences.

"I know that piece of offal. He and his men established a village on our lands. They steal our cattle in the middle of the night. He's around five of your Roman miles down the road. You would be doing us all a favor if you rid the world of him and his followers."

Valerius, Marcellus, Severus, and Pepin looked at each other in astonishment. Valerius thrust the sack of coins at Berthhold. "We will grant you your wish. Gundahar will be with his gods by the end of the day. Please take this coin as our thanks."

Berthhold's eyes gleamed as he accepted the coin.

Severus stepped away and bellowed for his centurions and scouts to meet with him. The lounging legionaries suddenly became energized, checking their weapons and adjusting their armor. They knew it was time for battle.

Severus looked at his four centurions and the decurion in charge of his scouts. "We have received news. The village chieftain reports that Gundahar and his followers are about five miles down this road. We can easily be there before dusk. We intend to attack today. I want you to get your men moving. We will confer again once we get away from this village. I don't want to discuss our strategy this close to the settlement. For all we know, Gundahar may have allies here. It is best to be prudent. Understood?"

The men nodded and returned to their units. The lead century quickly advanced out of the area, the other units following closely behind. Like a hunting hound that caught the scent of its prey, they moved with purpose.

Several miles from the village, Severus halted the centuries. He gathered the leadership group around him. "I know the men are tired. So am I. It's imperative that we move fast for two reasons: We must get there before dusk so we can attack in the daylight, and second, if our foe is somehow alerted, we must arrive before they harm Hereca. This brings me to my final point. We will move stealthily so as not to forewarn the Quadi." He addressed his cavalry commander, Decurion Silvus. "When you get close to the village, you must be cautious. Stay back from the settlement. It would be helpful to reconnoiter the size of this hamlet and the strength of their numbers, but that is a luxury we cannot afford. If we move quickly and conceal our presence, we will catch them with their tunics down. It will make our attack that much more successful. I say this with full confidence. We are to maintain complete silence from here to the village. Any questions?"

"Sir," the decurion spoke up, "when do you want us to ride ahead of the centuries and determine its location."

"Now would be a good time. They said five miles, and that was a while back. So, in about three miles, you should be there. Once you have spotted the village, return to the marching column. Are my orders clear?"

"Yes, sir."

The small detachment of cavalry thundered off down the road. Severus briefly watched the horses leave the clearing. As the echo of the horses' hooves faded away, Severus issued his orders. "Form up." The centuries quickly moved into formations. Seeing the men in place, Severus commanded, "At the double-time, advance."

The weary centuries trotted down the road amid grunts and the jingling of armor. They exited a forested area and entered a wide field. Off in the distance, a solitary herd of cattle grazed in the late afternoon. Onward they hurried, chewing up the distance to their destination. The men were huffing but stoically continued. Though the weather was warm, a cooling breeze offered a bit of relief to the exhausted legionaries.

* * *

Decurion Silvus eased his horse into a slow walk. The horse huffed, welcoming the leisurely pace. Silvus led his small troop of men silently down the road, surrounded on both sides by trees and shrubs. Ignoring the presence of the intruders, songbirds twittered gaily. The decurion could almost sense a village up ahead. Peering ahead, the officer observed a small cleared field, but no dwellings. Off to the right in the distance, he spotted a figure in a meadow. He nudged his mount forward to get a better look. It was a young woman in a long tunic, her long hair tied back. She was picking berries.

Silvus held up his hand for the men to stop. He glanced around, noting his men were hidden in the shadows of the trees. His directive was to remain unnoticed. He reviewed his options. It would be difficult to advance any further without being detected by the woman. So he decided to take her captive and then interrogate her. She would tell him what he needed to know. Gesturing at the man to his left to join him, Silvus dug his heels into the horse's flanks and charged ahead.

The woman looked up, startled by the two horsemen charging out of the tree line at her. She let out a frantic yelp and turned to run, but she was trapped. The two mounted men closed in swiftly.

The woman tried zigging and zagging but to no avail. The decurion leaped from his horse, tackling his quarry. The woman shrieked, her basket of berries scattered on the ground. He hefted up the woman and threw her across the pommel of his horse, her legs and neck dangling from either side of Silvus's mount. The two men quickly galloped away from the site of the abduction to join their comrades.

One of Silvus's men spoke the language. He dismounted and roughly pulled the woman off Silvus's mount. "Where is the village? How far up ahead?"

Ignoring the question, the woman screeched hysterically. Silvus dismounted and slapped her hard across the face. "Tell her to shut up and answer our questions, and no harm will come to her."

The interpreter repeated Silvus's words. The woman became silent, then shrieked again.

Worried that someone might hear her, Silvus clamped his hand over her mouth. But she bit down, drawing blood. "Shit!" he exclaimed. He backhanded her, knocking her to the earth. "Repeat your questions."

The woman lie stunned, tears streaming down her face. When the questions were repeated once again, she pointed with a shaking hand down the road. "It's not far down the road."

"Ask her if this is Gundahar's village," Silvus commanded.

The interpreter asked the question. She nodded, not speaking.

"Let's get moving," Silvus said. "We need to report back to General Severus."

"What about her?" his interpreter asked.

"We bring her with us. She can ride on the back of one of our horses or we can sling her over the pommel. The choice is hers."

Her options were explained to her. She quickly mounted one of the horses and clung to the torso of the rider.

The cavalry detachment rode vigorously to catch up with the marching column. Silvus then quickly dismounted and approached Severus. "Sir, the village is not too far ahead." He gestured toward the woman. "We found her picking berries. She confirmed the location and that it's Gundahar's village."

"Were you observed?" Severus queried.

"Don't think so, sir, but we never got to view the settlement."

Valerius walked over to the captive. "You have a captive woman held in your village? A new arrival?"

The woman beheld Valerius with frightened eyes. She nodded timidly.

"She is alive?"

"I think so. She was the last time I saw her yesterday."

Valerius gave Severus a knowing look.

"Centurions, on me," Severus commanded.

Once more, the men gathered around the legate. "The village is not too far ahead. How far would you say, Decurion Silvus?"

"Two miles at the most. Probably closer to one."

"This is what we're going to do. Leave the javelins here. We will bind the woman and leave her here as well. This is nothing fancy. It will be close-quarters fighting. We will approach the settlement from the main road and charge through the main entrance down the middle. Kill anyone who opposes you. Maintain the ranks in your century so you fight as a unit. We may be outnumbered, but nothing we can't handle. Governor Valerius and I plus a small group will search for Hereca. Any questions?"

The centurions shook their heads. It was time to fight.

The Roman column moved at an easy trot down the road. They advanced speedily but not so fast that they would be exhausted when they arrived at the village. It was late in the afternoon, and the sun was dipping in the west, casting shadows. The Roman centuries approached the village entrance undetected. No cries of alarm had yet been sounded. The four centuries thundered into the settlement, catching the renegade Quadi completely by surprise.

Because of the breadth of the village with its scattered dwellings, the four centuries fought autonomously, each in a squared formation rather than the typical double or triple line extending throughout the hamlet. They did not have enough men to stretch the width of the village in a line formation.

Women and children screamed, fleeing the area, which was exactly what the Romans desired. The warriors quickly came to their senses and rushed to get their weapons from their huts. A few of the women joined them.

Valerius, Marcellus, and Severus were surrounded by a cadre of bodyguards. They trailed the four centuries. The Quadi warriors hurled themselves at the Roman shield wall and died upon the thrusting blades. Additional men joined the fray, attacking the centuries from all directions.

The centuries halted their advance, absorbing the charges of the barbarian warriors. More men surged against the shield wall but to no avail. It was an uneven contest with the odds stacked heavily in favor of the Romans, with their steel blades and armor from head to groin. When a Quadi spear thrust did manage to breach the almost impenetrable shield wall, it often glanced off the plated armor or broke against the armored cuirass of the legionaries.

A group of Quadi assaulted Valerius and the command element protected by thirty legionaries. A warrior broke through the formation and ran at Marcellus. Instead of backing up, Marcellus advanced at him, engaging his foe in close quarters and dispatching him with a thrust to the neck.

The battle raged as the Quadi attacked in a frenzy, defending their home. The four centuries held their ground, repulsing the waves of attackers. From his vantage point inside the hollow square, Valerius searched for a dwelling that might be holding Hereca. He knew he should concentrate on what was taking place in his immediate vicinity. Any kind of distraction could have fatal consequences, but he could not help himself. He needed to find Hereca before it was too late.

Severus anxiously scanned the battlefield, ensuring his centuries maintained their unit integrity. None of the formations had been breached. The village was larger than he had anticipated, but the ranks were holding fine. The enemy continued to attack his men without success. His legionaries had not retreated one step and were slaughtering their attackers.

Marcellus, standing close by Valerius along with Radulf, yelled above the fray. "Here we are again, Tribune, engaged in close combat. Even as governor, trouble seems to find you. Over twenty years and nothing has changed."

Valerius was about to reply when another warrior surged through the shield wall, stumbling slightly. Before the warrior could react, Radulf jumped in front of him and dispatched the man.

Severus glanced in all directions, studying the conflict. He saw the pressure lessening. Some of the Quadi broke away from the attack and fled. Now was the time.

"Advance," roared Severus.

The four centuries edged forward, methodically progressing down the length of the village, shields interlocked and swords at the ready. More Quadi died from the stabbing swords.

Valerius craned his neck, frantically searching for Hereca. All the dwellings looked the same. He feared they had come this far only to lose her at the end.

Gundahar swiveled his head in panic. Two of his bodyguards stood by his side, swords drawn. How had the Romans found his village out here in the hinterlands? His warriors were being systematically slaughtered, proving no match for the disciplined and heavily armored adversaries. He gazed at his wounded arm, blood streaming down his appendage courtesy of a Roman sword thrust. Realizing defeat was inevitable, he dashed toward his captive's hut, his two men following. She would be his leverage. All he had to do was escape with her. He could bargain with the Romans later.

Hereca sat with her legs and hands tightly bound. She perked up when she heard screaming, yelling, and the clash of arms. Soon, above the shrieks and battle cries, she heard bellowed commands. They were in Latin, not Quadi. They were here. She tugged at her bonds, but there was no slack. She was stuck there and could not see what was happening outside. The battle sounds approached nearer. *Come save me, Valerius. I'm here.*

Just then, a shadow darkened her doorway. Dread overcame her as Gundahar entered the hut, wielding a long sword. *Is he going to kill me now?* The chieftain raised the sword, and Hereca flinched, waiting for the killing blow.

Instead, he sliced the hemp bonds on her feet. "You are coming with me. I'm not finished with you just yet." He yanked her up off the ground and, grabbing her roughly, propelled her forward toward the entrance. Peering out the doorway, he ensured that the legionaries had not yet advanced that far into the village. They were still around fifty paces away. He shoved Hereca outside, knowing he needed to move quickly.

Hereca gasped at the sudden onslaught of sunlight. Weakened and dazed, she stumbled to her hands and knees. She blinked, attempting to rise to her feet, but fell back down again.

Valerius glanced around, his head swiveling. Suddenly, he spied movement forward of his position in one of the huts to his left. His heart leaped as he recognized Hereca, surrounded by three Quadi. He shouted to Marcellus, pointing with his sword. "There she is!" Valerius bolted from the protection of the Roman formation, followed by Marcellus and Radulf.

Gundahar's escape was slowed down by the faltering Hereca. He cursed at her for impeding his flight and yanked hard at her bound hands, jerking her upright. Looking up, he saw three men charging at him in full sprint.

Gundahar released Hereca, and she collapsed like a sack of barley. He quickly realized he could not get away from these men. He would have to stand and fight off these Romans. He barked orders at his two henchmen, who turned to face their quickly approaching foes, their swords poised.

Valerius slowed his advance, eyeing his opponents. He noted his wife's battered figure on the ground. She was alive. Out of the corner of his eye, he saw that Marcellus and Radulf had joined him. In a matter of moments, the six men paired off against each other. The one who had dragged Hereca, a figure of large girth and power, made the first move. He made a quick thrust, belying his size. Valerius was almost taken by surprise. He backpedaled and deftly blocked the thrust. On either side, he spotted Marcellus and Radulf engaged with their adversaries. Satisfied that his flanks were secure, he advanced at his foe.

Gundahar scowled, disappointed that his stab had not ended the fight. He glanced at the Roman opposite him. He looked to be a wealthy man with the sword of an officer. For certain, he was no average legionary. Undeterred, Gundahar attacked with a number of furious slashes and thrusts. Again, the Roman nimbly blocked the manic assault, almost with ease. The two men circled to the left. This time, Valerius was the aggressor, advancing with a series of jabs.

Gundahar retreated, putting space between himself and the Roman officer. He pretended to stumble slightly and then snatched a fistful of dirt with his left hand. He charged at the Roman and deftly hurled the soil in an underhanded motion at Valerius's eyes.

Valerius saw the ruse at the last moment, turning his head to the side and backing off. Still, some of the grit found its mark. He wiped his eyes with his free hand, chiding himself for not seeing the ploy he had trained against and encountered before. He blocked another thrust from the Quadi and then countered it with a series of stabs of his own, advancing on the offensive.

Hereca groggily attempted to crawl away, but the fight seemed to circle and follow her movements. She saw Gundahar backpedaling away from Valerius, not looking behind him.

Hereca decided she would have her revenge. She scuttled unseen behind the retreating Gundahar. Fate can often be unkind to men in battle. In an unexpected twist, the back of Gundahar's legs hit Hereca's hunched form, sending him sprawling in the dirt.

Seizing the opportunity, Valerius leaped forward and delivered a savage downward thrust. His stab was so hard that it went through Gundahar's torso, pinning him to the ground. The Quadi leader screamed in agony. Valerius ruthlessly ripped the blade upward and out, inflicting even more damage. The barbarian convulsed on the ground in a growing puddle of crimson and then fell still. With the loss of their leader, the men engaged with Marcellus and Radulf fled for their lives.

Valerius sunk to his knees, embracing his wife. She was safe. Safe at last.

CHAPTER XXXI
AFTERMATH

Lauriacum, Province of Noricum

Days later, Valerius and Marcellus gathered in their quarters. Things were slowly returning to normal. Pepin had been handsomely rewarded for his services. General Severus had been ordered by Valerius to return to his home base in Raetia. Before his departure, Valerius had taken him aside to tell him he was one of the best legates in the empire. It was no idle praise. He truly was an extraordinary leader. If Valerius had his druthers, Severus would be the corps commander for the Danubius region. That would be impossible at the moment given the current politics and Sejanus, but in the future, when the timing was right, he would suggest this to Tiberius.

Rain pattered outside, casting a chill in the air. The battered and bruised Hereca entered. Though she showed some improvement, her face remained swollen and discolored. Her wrists and ankles were raw where her bonds had been cruelly fastened. Upon return, she had soaked in a bath several times a day. She still appeared ragged, but a little less so. Despite her condition, she insisted on being present with Valerius and Marcellus to discuss the next steps and their future strategy.

"How are you feeling, my dear?" Valerius asked.

Hereca adopted a frosty look. "I know you mean well, but please stop asking about me. I suffered some physical injuries, but they are not life-threatening, and they will heal in time. I am more concerned about our actions going forward. That's what is important at the moment."

"Sorry. Can't help it. All I thought about the last several weeks was getting you back safely."

"I understand. I knew you would come to the rescue. But that is now in the past, and we must confront the urgent problems facing us."

"Agreed. I have been contemplating our next steps. Voculus and Portunus continue their efforts to discredit and destroy us. I would like nothing better than to throw them in chains, but that carries its own risks. Both men are politically well-connected, either through Sejanus or Tiberius. Taking such drastic action on our own initiative would invite serious consequences."

"Maybe so," Marcellus voiced, "but we have sworn testimony from legionary Longinus, who was an eyewitness to their treachery. Isn't that enough to warrant their arrests?"

"Yes, it is, but you might want to hold that thought," Valerius said. "I received a dispatch hours ago from General Caelius at Vindobona. Apparently, Longinus was murdered outside the fort."

"Pluto's cock!" Marcellus roared. "And I bet I know who did the deed. It was that pig fucker, Gordianus."

"It is unfortunate," Valerius replied calmly. "All we now have is a written testimony of a common legionary who is now dead. I should have brought him with us to Lauriacum. This is my fault, and the young man's death falls on my shoulders. He was a brave legionary for coming forward. Once this mess is over, I will see to it that his family, wherever they may be, is well compensated for his courageous efforts. Somehow, Voculus and Portunus uncovered his involvement with us."

"Where does that leave us?" Hereca inquired. "You know those two will come at us again. From what you've told me, this Longinus heard Voculus state that Sejanus was getting impatient with their efforts to eliminate or neutralize you. What will they do next? They have such a long reach that even our children back in Germania could be a target. We cannot afford to sit on our hands. We must do something."

"What about the proof of Portunus's corruption based on your discussion with the merchant captain?" Marcellus asked. "What was his name? Rufinus, yes, that was it. We have something concrete to pin on him."

"That is true," Valerius replied. "But that would involve a trial, which could take many months. We don't have that luxury."

"So what do you suggest?" Hereca asked.

"I propose a bold move, not without significant danger. We must personally travel to Rome, all three of us. It would put us out of reach of Portunus and Voculus. But this course of action has its own risks. Word may reach Sejanus of our intentions, and he will hunt us down. Then, there is the problem of getting an audience with Tiberius in his palace on Capri or in Rome or wherever in Hades he is these days. Assuming we get to Tiberius, we must persuade him that his realm is in danger and that Sejanus, Portunus, and Voculus are conspiring against him. I have commented in the past about the impracticality of arresting Portunus and Voculus. Think about it. How do you think Tiberius would react if he were to learn through my dispatch that I had arrested Portunus, a good friend of his, and Voculus, Sejanus's handpicked legate to oversee the legions? Wouldn't

Tiberius be just a tad suspicious of our actions? Furthermore, Sejanus would be whispering in his ear about treason, and we would not be there to defend ourselves. Our word has much more weight if we do this in person rather than by courier. To me, the choice is obvious—we must go to Rome."

Marcellus chuckled lightly. "Is that all? How in Hades did we ever reach this point?"

"We will return to Vindobona and depart from there to Rome as our destination. Though we can attempt to be clandestine about this, I believe word will get out before long. If we do not intervene with Tiberius and alert him to the danger he faces, Sejanus will likely seize power. Once he does, we and our families are as good as dead."

"Once we return to Vindobona, do you think they will attempt some other nefarious scheme to end our existence?" Marcellus asked.

"Yes. No doubt about it. They are desperate. Portunus and Voculus have contacts, informants, and agents both inside and outside the walls of Vindobona. They could attempt to poison our food or drink, hire an assassin as Sejanus attempted in Rome, or use some form of brute force as they did with the ambush. As sure as the sun rises, they will make another attempt on our lives.

"I agree with you," said Hereca. "We can't risk to wait around to see what they might do next. Their wickedness knows no bounds. They will stoop to any level to accomplish their aims. Then, we have the tenuous situation in Rome with Sejanus. You are correct, my husband; we cannot inform Tiberius of the dangers on the Danubius and in Rome through a dispatch. It lacks legitimacy. He will doubt the veracity of our message. We must do this in person. The fact that we traveled hundreds upon hundreds of miles to see him should help sway him."

"So it is settled," Valerius proclaimed. "We will journey to Rome, or perhaps to Capri, which is where he might be. For now, let's make arrangements to return to Vindobona."

CHAPTER XXXII
PLANNING MURDER

Fortress of Carnuntum, Pannonia

Voculus and Portunus occupied the governor's lavish headquarters, discussing their future. "I'm telling you, General Voculus, this Maximus will return home with his tail between his legs once he learns his precious wife has perished. From what I've heard, he did not want to come here in the first place, and his family is back in Germania. We will be rid of his arrogant ways and return to normalcy."

"It will be a good thing. He has far too much power. That's why Sejanus had Tiberius appoint me, to curb his authority. Think of it, without my presence to curb his ambitions, Maximus controls nearly half of Rome's legions. I am looking forward to a new governor. I'm sure Sejanus will suggest someone suitable to replace Maximus."

"Maybe he will suggest you, General Voculus, as you are already on station."

Voculus offered a wry smile. "I would not hesitate to accept. My first act would be to rid ourselves of Titus Placidius, Governor of Raetia, who toadied up to Maximus. Then, there are those two legates, Severus of Raetia and Caelius, the commander of the Tenth Legion at Vindobona. Their careers are going to be in the latrine.

"That prick Caelius is also on my shit list. Imagine, my own legate sided against me. I will be glad to get rid of him."

A sudden knock on the door interrupted them. Gordianus, Voculus's aide burst into the room. "Sorry to disturb you, sirs, but I have news. Governor Maximus and a small force from the Third Legion out of Raetia have rescued the governor's wife and slaughtered the warriors under Gundahar. Rumor has it that they will soon be journeying back to Vindobona."

Voculus waved his aide away, who promptly exited the room.

"Damn that Gundahar!" thundered Voculus. "Can he not do anything right? I had sent word he was to execute that bitch and paid his men the additional coin. Now, we're back to square one. Gordianus, explain to me exactly what you have heard."

"Only this, a small force of legionaries under General Severus, along with Maximus, tracked the location of Gundahar's clan into the interior of the Quadi lands. They attacked the village, killing many of the warriors including Gundahar, and rescued Hereca.

"You know they are going to suspect us of fomenting this plot, don't you," Portunus remarked.

"They have no proof. Besides, with Gundahar dead, they have no witnesses."

"So, what do we do now?" Portunus asked.

Voculus turned to Gordianus. "We must make another attempt on their lives. We cannot afford to wait. There must be times when they are vulnerable. I know they don't stay locked in their headquarters all day. What say you, Gordianus? You are at the fortress more than I. What are they up to all day?"

The centurion shrugged. "I have only seen them on occasion when they venture out of their headquarters. Sometimes, they stroll along the river in the evening."

"Go on," Voculus said.

"They have a few bodyguards with them, but not a lot."

"Do you think that if we recruited enough men, we could successfully attack them? The force could escape along the river or across it."

"It can be done if we have good people. I should have thought of this before. It presents a good chance of success," Gordianus said.

Voculus struggled to contain his fury and keep a benign expression. *Of course you should have thought of it, but you didn't because you're a dolt. You're only useful for maiming and killing others.*

"Let me understand this," Portunus said. 'You're telling me that Maximus and his wife saunter outside the walls of the fortress in the evening with a small contingent of bodyguards?"

"Yes. That's what I and some of my men have observed. We could attack quickly and then disappear down the river road."

"I like this idea," Portunus said. "Centurion Gordianus, do you think you could recruit a band of men to execute this mission? You would be the appointed leader."

"It can be done. Given the stakes here, they would need to be well compensated. This goes beyond a simple assassination."

"How much?" Portunus asked.

Gordianus shrugged. "Given the risk, I would venture ten gold pieces per man."

Voculus stewed. Here was an opportunity to eliminate Maximus with a simple plan, and that fat arsehole, Portunus, was worried about the cost. Well, he was not going to pay for this one. He had financed the other two botched attempts. It was time for Portunus to fund something since his ass was hanging out with his tax skimming. Besides, he probably embezzled more in a single day than this endeavor was going to cost.

"I think it's time you bore some of the financial burden, Portunus. I funded the other attempts at considerable expense. My patron does not have unlimited funds."

"How many men would you need?" Portunus inquired anxiously.

"I would say twenty should do."

"Two hundred gold pieces!" he shrieked.

"Well worth the cost," Voculus stated. "Think about it. You will be free of Maximus and his inquisitive ways."

Portunus looked like he swallowed a turd. "Two hundred gold pieces…. All right, but you better succeed."

Voculus turned to Gordianus. "How soon can you assemble your men? We need to do this quickly before word leaks out from your recruited assassins. They cannot be trusted to keep this secret."

"Give me a day or two."

"See that you do this expeditiously," Voculus said. "We cannot have any survivors. Everyone with Maximus must die, including his escort. Understood?"

"It will be done."

"Oh, Gordianus, one more thing. Since you are participating in this endeavor, make sure you wear a hooded cowl so no one will recognize you. Nothing must be traced back to Governor Portunus or me, but then again, I don't expect any survivors."

CHAPTER XXXIII
GORDIANUS

Three days later, they were back at their home base in Vindobona. Valerius and Hereca were preparing to take their evening stroll along the river. Valerius was strapping on his sword when Marcellus approached.

"If you don't mind, I will tag along. Too much has happened lately. It seems every time we are outside the headquarters, something nasty ensues." Marcellus grabbed his gladius and belt from a peg on the wall. "I would also suggest we double the guards... no, make that triple the guards. One cannot be too careful. Our adversaries are bold and desperate. I believe they have thrown caution to the wind."

"For once, I will not object to your suggestion on our security," Valerius replied. "You have amazing clairvoyance on these matters. I agree. I believe our antagonists are getting frantic."

The trio exited the fortress gates, trailed by six armed legionaries plus Radulf. They sauntered past the docks and wharves, now quiet at this time of day. They followed the river road and nonchalantly strolled along the flowing watercourse. The river burbled and splashed, creating a pleasant melody. Most of the road traffic had dwindled to a few stragglers as the sun sank lower. The trio walked in silence, enjoying the tranquility, with river birds flying overhead, and heading to their nests.

Marcellus was the first to break the silence. "Have you decided when we leave for Rome?"

"As a matter of fact, yes. We will finalize our plans tomorrow and leave the following day. This is what we are going to do. I will send dispatches to the governors of Raetia, Noricum, and Moesia, informing them of our journey. I will simply say that we have been summoned to meet with Tiberius to discuss our progress. Here in Pannonia, I will inform General Caelius that we will be traveling, but I will not inform Portunus or Voculus. That should send them a strong message. It is a deliberate snub on my part, and I'm letting them know that I have full knowledge of what they have been up to."

Marcellus nodded. "Have you selected a route for our journey?"

"I have a general idea, but I want to review it with you and others. We will be traveling by land and sea, an arduous journey. I hope to reach Rome before Sejanus discovers we are on our way there. If he is uninformed of our intentions, he will not have time to ambush us on our journey. That leaves Rome. We will have to take our chances there."

"How many men will accompany us?" Hereca inquired.

"Good question," Valerius replied. "We will need to move quickly. The smaller the party, the faster we advance. Our journey will be through Roman-controlled lands. Security should not be an issue. I'm thinking the three of us plus Radulf and two experienced couriers who serve under Caelius's command should suffice. They will know the lay of the land, the best places to stop, and so forth. Tomorrow, we will sit down with Caelius and two of his men to map out our journey."

"Assuming we get to Tiberius in Rome, what are you going to tell him, and what if he does not believe us?" Hereca asked.

"I will inform him of everything that has transpired here on the Danubius: the plots to kill us, the masterminds behind these plots, Longinus's signed confession about the conversation between Voculus and Portunus, and Portunus's suspected corruption involving the legion's supplies and tax revenues. If he chooses not to believe us, that will not portend well for us, but at this point, we have few options. The status quo is untenable for us. Eventually, Voculus and Portunus will get lucky and eliminate us. Alternatively, if Sejanus seizes power, that would also be a death sentence for us."

Marcellus slowed his pace. "I think this would be a good place to turn around. We are out of sight of the fort, and darkness is approaching. Let's not push our luck."

* * *

Gordianus crouched in a patch of trees with fifteen recruited cutthroats. Even he had to admit they were a vile lot. The men were a collection of deserters, thieves, and murderers. He wanted more men, but they were all he could gather on such short notice. His superiors desired Valerius and his associates dead and quickly. He had hoped to assemble a force of twenty men, but still, this group should be enough. Even better, he could pocket the coin for twenty men and only pay fifteen. Portunus would never know.

He and his band of miscreants had watched their quarry walk by to the east, downriver, but Gordianus wanted to wait for their return to the fortress before he struck. He required no witnesses to the ambush. Road traffic diminished significantly as darkness approached. He had selected a position far enough from the civilian town outside the fortress so that no one would hear any sounds of the clash. His prey would pass their hidden location on their return journey. He was dismayed that the number of bodyguards had increased, but his men should still prevail. They had the element of surprise and should be able to overwhelm the bodyguards. He placed the cowl over his head and drew his gladius. It wouldn't be long now.

Marcellus turned around and motioned for the guard contingent to move abreast of Valerius and Hereca. They had finished discussing their affairs for the evening, so there was nothing of importance to be overheard. As the couple ambled onward, enjoying the evening serenity, Marcellus turned his attention to their front and slowed his pace. Something was off. He smelled something. It was the scent of unwashed bodies. It was an odor incongruous with their surroundings. He glanced at his six legionary guards. It wasn't them. He would have smelled them before now. Besides, legionaries used the baths at the fortress almost religiously.

"Halt. Draw your swords," Marcellus bellowed. The legionaries hesitated slightly but then obediently drew their swords and brought their shields into a defensive posture.

From the landward side of the road, a rabble burst forth, emerging from a thicket, screaming and wildly waving their swords and daggers. The pack hurled themselves at the legionaries, but due to Marcellus's warning, the advantage of surprise was lost. The leading assassins died quickly on the thrusting blades. A scrofulous-looking figure leaped at Valerius. He had just cleared his blade from its scabbard when the scoundrel attacked. The man snarled, his face contorted in fury, and stabbed. Valerius easily parried the thrust. He smashed the pommel of his sword into his assailant's mouth, scattering his teeth. Before the man could recover, Valerius chopped down on his neck, killing him. Another figure charged to take the place of his slain comrade. He carried a long-handled axe, a fearsome weapon if utilized correctly, but the man was an amateur. He swung clumsily, missing and throwing himself off balance. Valerius thrust his blade through the man's torso and quickly withdrew it. The ruffian collapsed in a heap, his tunic stained a bright scarlet.

Marcellus sidestepped a sword thrust by one of the brigands and chopped down on the figure's right arm, nearly severing it. The man screamed and ran back into the woods. Out of the corner of his vision, he noticed that three of their bodyguards were out of the fight. The bodies of their assailants lie scattered on the ground, but the surviving assassins renewed their efforts to overwhelm the Roman contingent. Two men rushed at Marcellus, one a tall, lanky figure wielding a long-bladed dagger. The man thrust savagely at Marcellus's mid-section. But the former centurion knew a thing or two about close-quarters fighting. He blocked the stab with his short sword. With the assailant now within arms' reach, Marcellus delivered a powerful, crushing blow with his left fist, crushing the man's face and sending him sprawling into the dirt. He did not rise, so Marcellus pounced upon the remaining figure and quickly disposed of him.

Gordianus scowled from the cover of the brush along the road. His hired men had not yet overcome Valerius and his entourage. Most of the bodyguards were down, but the job was far from finished. He decided to go all in. To Hades with his anonymity. He leaped out of his concealed position and attacked.

Marcellus looked up just in time to see a hooded figure rapidly closing the distance, sword held menacingly at waist level. Marcellus deftly avoided the thrust and quickly backpedaled to allow more room to maneuver. Something was familiar about the size and build of the man attacking him. Although the face was hidden in the shadow,

Marcellus caught a quick glimpse. It was Gordianus. No longer a man who fought from the shadows, he had become bold, sure of his success.

Marcellus had to be careful. This was no ordinary assassin but a trained and experienced Roman legionary. Regardless, Marcellus was confident he would prevail. Better yet, he was going to enjoy killing this worthless prick. "I see you, Gordianus. Come and get me if you're brave enough to do so."

With a snarl, he leaped at Marcellus, his blade slashing wildly. The cut missed Marcellus's chest by a hair's breadth. He could feel the passing wind of the stroke. Marcellus countered with a series of thrusts and slashes, forcing him back.

Gordianus expertly parried the sword blows. Gordianus eyed his opponent, who was a much older man he could easily prevail over. It was just a matter of time. He would wear him down and then take pleasure in ending Marcellus's life. This time, Gordianus advanced, compelling Marcellus to retreat.

Marcellus heaved in exertion. He was facing an accomplished opponent, but he had done so before and always prevailed. Marcellus exaggerated his heavy breathing, hoping to make his opponent overconfident. Despite the battles going on around him, Marcellus narrowed his vision, shutting out all other distractions. He quickly glanced behind Gordianus and instantly knew what he had to do—something he had done on previous occasions.

Marcellus advanced with a series of slashes and thrusts, forcing Gordianus backward, directly into the path of several bodies. As Marcellus had anticipated, Gordianus slipped slightly on one of the puddles of blood. With his opponent off-balanced, Marcellus struck hard, stabbing his gladius into the lower abdomen. His sword penetrated deeply, incapacitating his opponent. Marcellus quickly withdrew the blade and slashed Gordianus in the neck. A spray of blood smacked Marcellus in the face.

His body spurting blood from two different wounds, Gordianus collapsed in a heap. Struggling to rise, he propped up to his hands and knees before sprawling on the ground, still.

Seeing the fall of their leader, the few surviving ruffians ran into the forest, leaving their dead behind. Marcellus glanced around and saw Hereca and Valerius standing tall, seemingly unharmed. Relieved, he looked toward the bodyguards. Radulf was still standing with his sword poised, the blade dripping with blood. Four legionaries were down but moving. The other two were still poised for combat, their shields held at the ready and their swords at waist level.

Hereca hurried toward Marcellus. "You are hurt. Your face is covered in blood."

"Not mine," Marcellus said, spitting some of the offending substance from his lips. He pointed with his sword. "It's from that spawn of Hades, lying there in the dirt."

Valerius hurried over. "Is that Gordianus?"

"It is. Are you surprised?"

"No, I guess not. It's one more piece of evidence we have to present in Rome."

Marcellus nodded. "Let's bind their wounds and get our four wounded men back to the fortress. They fought bravely."

The two unscathed legionaries provided some quick first aid and helped support their two comrades. One had a nasty shoulder wound, and the other two had stab wounds to the head and neck. Two others managed to walk despite their wounds. The contingent hobbled back to the fortress in the dwindling light.

CHAPTER XXXIV
PLANNING THE JOURNEY

Headquarters at Vindobona

It was mid-morning on an early fall day when Valerius invited General Caelius to discuss urgent matters. He had also requested that he bring two of his men who could guide them to Rome.

Valerius motioned for one of his aides to invite General Caelius into his office, where Marcellus and Hereca stood beside Valerius. Radulf positioned himself inconspicuously in the corner.

Caelius, his helmet positioned in the crook of his right arm, entered the room, quickly noting who else was there. "I heard about your troubles last evening. That is intolerable and a stain upon the Tenth. I take this extremely personally. We shall turn over every stone to find out who is responsible."

Before he could continue, Valerius raised his hand. "General Caelius, no need to apologize. It was not your fault. There's nothing you could have done. The men assigned to my bodyguard fought valiantly. I hope the wounded recover.

Caelius grimaced. "One of our men has succumbed to his wounds. The medicus says the other three should recover and return to duty."

"My condolences on the loss of your legionary. As for who is responsible, we know that already. One of the men slain was none other than Centurion Gordianus, aide and right-hand man to Voculus. That should tell you something. The others were brigands of no account."

"I can have my men arrest General Voculus if you so desire. Just say the word."

"While you're at it, arrest Portunus as well," Marcellus voiced.

"No doubt they are in league together," Valerius said. "But that can wait. It would not be prudent to do so at this time. They have powerful connections in Rome, so the order for their arrest must come from Tiberius. We intend to travel to Rome tomorrow as fast as possible. We are floating the story that we have been summoned to Rome to discuss our progress. We will seek an audience with Tiberius and present the preponderance of evidence concerning the rampant interference with our duties on the Danubius. I want to keep our journey quiet for as long as possible. Word will leak eventually, but by that time, Voculus and Portunus will not have an opportunity to interfere with our travel. No doubt they will send word to Sejanus in Rome. We will deal with him there. Can I count on you?"

Absolutely, sir. I have no love for those two. What can I do here while you are gone?"

"That's simple," Hereca chimed in. "Please oversee the continuing trade discussions with the Quadi. If any of the chieftains ask for us, tell them we are temporarily unavailable but should be back soon."

"Understood."

"Good," Valerius said. "Now you probably understand why I asked you to bring us your best guides."

"My men are waiting in the vestibule. Would you like me to summon them now?"

"Yes, bring them in. We have much to discuss."

Caelius exited the room and returned with two legionaries, lean and grizzled in appearance. "Let me introduce to you my couriers. This is Terentius," he said, gesturing to the taller one, "and this is Domitius. They have made the journey before. They used to be part of the courier service when they were younger but now serve me in various capacities that are less physically challenging. Gentlemen, this is your boss, the ruling governor of the territory, Valerius Maximus, his wife Hereca, and the large one there is Marcellus, a former centurion in the legions."

Marcellus observed the pair. They would do. They looked to be tough, resourceful men—just what they required for the journey.

Both men bowed stiffly in deference to Valerius.

"Terentius and Domitius, we urgently need to get to Rome," Valerius explained. "As to why, you need not be concerned about the particulars, but I will say this—it's a matter of national security. The journey could be extremely hazardous. Just so you know, several attempts have already been made on our lives. So, not only must we be fast but we must travel surreptitiously. Are you up for it?"

Terentius spoke up. "Begging your pardon, sir, but Domitius and I were born for this. Of course, we will accept this mission."

"Excellent. Let us move to the map table over there, and you can show us how we will be journeying to Rome. I think I have a pretty good idea, but I need both of your expertise.

Terentius studied the map, tracing their route with his finger. "We will move almost due south from here. The roads are passable, especially this time of year. We will journey to the port of Aquileia, the northernmost port on the Adriaticus. From there, we get a ship and sail south to the port of Ancona on Italia's east coast. It's a good time of year. The winds will be favorable, and there should be no storms. From Ancona, we travel by road southwest to Rome. So the journey will be in three phases, two by land and one by sea."

He looked up from the map. "It will be an arduous passage. May I inquire how many people you are bringing?"

"Just what you see here," Valerius replied. "Besides me, there's Marcellus, Hereca, and my bodyguard, Radulf," he said, pointing to the corner of the room."

"This is good. The smaller the party, the quicker we can move. I assume you are familiar with horses?"

"Well enough for this journey," Valerius replied.

"How long do you think it will take to get there?" Marcellus queried.

"Depends," Domitius said. "Not to be vague, but it is contingent upon several factors. While the weather, which can be a significant factor, should be favorable, there may be other reasons for interruptions. We will need to change mounts often; the pace will be rapid. However, sometimes fresh mounts are not always available. A more pressing issue might be the availability of a ship once we reach the Adriaticus. On some days, numerous vessels are available to transport us south; on other days, there are none. One never knows."

"I have the seal ring as governor of these provinces. That should be able to get us anything we need," Valerius replied. "I will also bring an ample amount of coin from the coffers.

"What about bandits?" Marcellus asked.

"I would have my weapons ready to use, but the problem of brigands is not commonplace, at least not anymore," Terentius said.

"Terentius and Domitius are good," Caelius assured. "If anyone can get you there quickly, it's these two men. I will have sturdy mounts waiting for you in the morning. I wish you good fortune in Rome."

CHAPTER XXXV
VOCULUS AND PORTUNUS

Several days later, Voculus and Portunus met downriver in Portunus's office. Both men were ill-tempered due to another failed attempt to eliminate Maximus. The previous day, one of Portunus's informers had reported about the botched ambush back in Vindobona. "Your centurion," Portunus snapped, "has linked us to the failed ambush. Everyone knows he reports to you, and his body lies with those rogues who perished with him. What are we to do?"

"Damn, his worthless carcass!" Voculus spat. "I should have known better than to entrust him with the ambush. We must deny any involvement in this undertaking and claim that Gordianus went rogue and joined a gang of outlaws. He is dead, so they have no proof he was under our direction. It's all circumstantial."

Portunus continued to fret, not placated by Voculus's vindications. "So now what, Voculus? We are under heavy suspicion, and Maximus is still with us despite everything we have attempted. What is your patron in Rome going to think when he hears about this? Didn't he say we must not do anything that is connected to us? Maximus could issue warrants for our arrest."

Voculus grimaced. "He might, but we are too powerful. Without direct evidence linking us to the attempted assassination, he will not get convicted. Tiberius and Sejanus would frown upon our arrest without proof."

"So, again, what are we to do?"

"I need to think about our next steps. I will inform Sejanus of our failure. He will not be pleased. We must find a way to salvage the situation."

There was a heavy knock on the door. Portunus, his face masked in fury, went and opened it. One of his aides stood there.

"I said no interruption. Is that so difficult to understand?" He was about to slam the door shut when the figure spoke in a tremulous voice. "Sir, there is a messenger with urgent news. He said you would want to be notified right away."

Portunus scowled, angrily waving for the haggard rider to enter. He then shut the door. "What is so urgent that you must interrupt my meeting with General Voculus?"

The man bowed in deference to the powerful figure. "Only this, sir. There is a strong rumor that Governor Maximus, his wife, and his former centurion have departed for Rome. It is said that Tiberius summoned them to report on their progress to date."

Portunus gave him an incredulous look. "What? Are you sure of this?"

"I cannot guarantee the veracity of this information with total certainty, but I have several sources in Vindobona, and they are all reporting the same."

"You were correct to bring this to my attention. Thank you. You may return to Vindobona. Let me know if you hear anything else."

After the messenger departed, Portunus glared at Voculus. "What does this mean?"

"I find this hard to believe," Voculus said. "Maximus just got here a few months ago. Why would Tiberius request his presence all the way back in Rome? It makes no sense."

"I agree, but if we are to believe the report of one of my informers. that is the story they are putting forth."

"I am not exactly sure what's happening. Maybe Maximus is going to Rome to inform Tiberius of our disloyalty? That would make more sense. I will craft a message to Sejanus and have it on the road before the close of the day. Sejanus must be informed. He can defend our actions to Tiberius and stop them on their way to Rome. I will inform the imperial couriers that this message is extremely urgent and must be delivered quickly. If all goes well, the message will get there before Maximus."

CHAPTER XXXVI
ON THE ROAD

They had been riding for five days, not at the pace of couriers with urgent dispatches but still a demanding one, sometimes extending into the evening hours. The small band of riders halted their mounts as twilight approached; they had been at it since dawn. Terentius turned in his saddle. "Good news. There's a way station just ahead. As I remember, it's one of the better ones. Good food and comfortable beds."

"I'm ready to stop," Marcellus voiced. "My ass is flatter than a crushed biscuit, and I'm starved."

"You will not be disappointed," Domitius said. "The inn is at the intersection of this north-south road and a major east-west road. It's just around the bend."

Later that evening, the group of six sat around a rectangular table. The dishes had been cleared, and the oil lamps had been lit, casting shadows across the spacious dining room. Several other travelers were present, but most others had retired for the evening.

"Terentius and Domitius," Valerius said, "I agree this is one of the better places we have stopped at. The thick stew was both tasty and filling, and the wine was passable with a decent flavor. So, what can we expect tomorrow?"

"More hard riding, I'm afraid," Terentius replied. "But take heart. I believe we will reach the seaport town of Aquileia by tomorrow evening. We will have completed the first leg of our journey, and probably the most arduous."

"What ships might be available to us when we arrive?" Valerius inquired. "As you can tell, I'm anxious to get to Rome."

Domitius shrugged. "As I said before, it's hit or miss. Sometimes, there are multiple ships to choose from—merchants, imperial navy, exporters, you name it. Other times, there's nothing going south, our way."

"Looking ahead, sir," Terentius said, "what do you expect from us when we reach Rome?"

"That depends," Valerius replied. "How handy are you with those swords you have strapped to your belt?"

"We are first and foremost trained legionaries, sir," Domitius replied. "We would gladly serve you in whatever capacity you desire."

"Then let me blunt. We may face considerable opposition. Perhaps *opposition* is not a strong enough word. Sinister forces would be more like it. There's a chance we all will be vanquished. There are powerful men aligned against us. We could use your swords."

"Then it is settled," Terentius said. "We will see this to the finish."

"Excellent. Your help is most appreciated."

They were off early the next morning, but they were unable to switch to fresh horses during the day, slowing their progress. However, as a whole, their spirits were buoyed since they would soon be off their horses and on the deck of a ship. Valerius glanced over at Hereca. Her face still bore the bruises of her beating and mistreatment by

Gundahar. The deep purple and blue had faded to an unpleasant pale yellow. She had not complained once about the hard pace they had set, even though he knew she was dog-tired, yet to recover from her ordeal in captivity. Despite her best efforts, the corners of her face drooped in exhaustion. There was no disguising her weariness.

He wondered, as he often had on many occasions, what he did to deserve such a woman. She was warm and generous, yet she was fierce and had the heart of the toughest legionary.

Hereca caught him gazing at her and offered a wry smile, conveying that she would endure another tough day no matter what obstacles they might encounter.

"You wanted to tell me something?" she asked.

"Only that you are an amazing woman. I feel like I'm ready to collapse, but here you are, enduring the same tribulations as the rest of us. I know you are tired, so don't pretend that you're not. Soon, we will end this part of our journey. Despite my disdain for traveling at sea and the misfortune that it brings to my gut, I'm looking forward to it."

"Remember when we first met and were fleeing for our lives from Germania toward the Rhenus? We were in the thick of the German territory. If we were discovered, any of the tribes would have gladly taken your head. I'm amazed we made it to the Roman garrison on the Rhenus."

Valerius smiled in reminiscence. "That was some adventure. Perilous. We were a lot younger then."

Marcellus brought his horse abreast of theirs. "I remember those days. I never gave up hope that you would return to the legions. If anyone could do it, Hereca, it was your husband. There were several occasions when he stepped in horseshit and managed to come up smelling like honey. I recall the time when he was ostracized and humiliated by General Varus in front of the entire cadre of senior officers, but he persevered. In fact, he even upstaged Varus, earning accolades from a legionary commander. Quite a feat for a young tribune. Even I was amazed. I knew then he was going to be an outstanding officer, someone special. We survived the Teutoburg disaster together. Rode all the way to Rome to inform Augustus, survived his wrath, and became a favorite of Germanicus. The retaliatory campaign against Arminius was successful, and in no small way, because of your husband."

"Those were heady days," Valerius replied. "It's hard to believe we are alive after some of the troubles we faced."

As the group rounded a bend in the road, Marcellus was just about to reply when Terentius bellowed out, "Hostiles on the road!"

Perhaps a hundred paces ahead, a group of nearly a dozen men blocked the road ahead. Even from this distance, one could tell there were not of the military but rogues intent on robbing anyone who traveled in the locality. They lacked any armor or shields. Some were armed with spears, others daggers. There was no doubt of their intentions.

The horses slowed almost to a stop. Marcellus glared ahead at the motley collection. "These fools must think we're a bunch of fat merchants and easy prey. I say we draw our swords and charge the fuckers. They will probably wet themselves and scatter. If they don't, we run them over and take their heads. Hereca, you stay in the middle."

"I agree. Let's run them over," Valerius said.

Marcellus grunted. "I'm going to enjoy doing this."

"Let's do it," Terentius yelled.

As one, the six figures drew their swords. "Now charge," bellowed Marcellus. They surged forward, the morning sun glinting off their blades. Onward they advanced, the horses' hooves thundering on the paved road. At a distance of about fifty paces, the men blocking the road scattered, panicked, and shrieked in fright. They ran into the forest on either side of the road and disappeared.

They continued at a gallop for another half mile before slowing to a trot. "I don't think we will have to worry about that lot of scoundrels for the rest of our journey," Marcellus commented. "I almost wish they had stood and fought. I would have taken pleasure in ending their existence."

"I second that," Terentius said. "Hopefully there will be no more incidents on our journey."

The riders continued their passage, the number of settlements they passed increasing the closer they drew to the sea. About an hour before twilight, the riders perked up, the scent of the sea filled their nostrils. They were getting close. Before long, they crested a small ridge. As dusk approached, the flame of oil lamps winked from the houses and shops below them in the distance.

"That's the town of Aquileia, our destination," Domitius said, pointing at the town beneath them.

Valerius happened to glance at Terentius and noticed a widening scowl. "Is something displeasing you?"

"Yes," he replied. "The harbor does not look favorable. I see no packet boats or ships of the Adriatic fleet. For the most part, the harbor is empty except for a few merchant ships. Jupiter's arse, of all the times not to have a packet ship at our disposal!"

"Is this often the case?" Hereca asked.

"No, it is not. I have experienced this problem before, but only rarely."

"I know you are not a clairvoyant, but might one of those ships arrive in the harbor tomorrow?" Valerius asked.

Terentius shook his head. "A vessel might appear tomorrow or the next day, but who knows? By Mithras's fat ass, why now?"

Marcellus spoke up. "Let me invoke the legionary code. I'm starved and tired. We need to eat and find a place to sleep, in that order. We can worry about our transportation tomorrow."

"No argument from me," Valerius said, giving Hereca a reassuring smile. "Let us not tarry. We will resolve our dilemma tomorrow. I'm sure of it."

Later that evening, the group gathered around a rough wooden table at the Harbor Inn. The last scraps of food had been devoured, and the dishes cleared. All agreed that the food was passable at best. The inn was mostly empty. The proprietor, a small wiry figure, appeared, offering an ingratiating smile, wiping his hands on a greasy apron. "The name is Felix, retired imperial navy. Bought this place last year with my retirement pay."

"We are looking for a ship to transport us to Ancona," Terentius said. "It's rather urgent. Matters of state. As we approached the town, I saw the harbor was mostly empty."

Felix shrugged. "It happens. Don't know why. Last week, the harbor was full of boats—imperial naval ships, packet boats, merchants. They have all sailed, a mass exodus. Bad for business. Last week, it was standing room only. Now, we are vacant with a few exceptions."

"From your experience, can we expect new ships to arrive any time soon?" Valerius asked.

Felix shrugged. "Hard to say for certain. If I were you, I would check out the merchant ships and see if any are going your way. With the right amount of cash, you might persuade one of the ship captains to alter their route. You said Ancona, correct?"

Terentius nodded. "I don't mean to be finicky, but the merchant ships I saw looked like they were barely able to float."

"True," Felix said. "Also, many of the merchants sail from here to Greece, not south toward Ancona. I would suggest you find the fittest ship available and offer them sufficient coins to take you to Ancona. That's the best advice I can give you."

"Oh, by the way," Marcellus interjected, "you could do better with a new cook. Your inn appears to be clean enough and quite spacious, but that dinner was just a tad better than legionary fare if you get my gist?"

Felix snorted. "You think I don't know that? I have to eat the same food, and by the way, I would trade you legionary rations for naval grub any day. Ever seen a portly sailor?" Without waiting for a reply, he continued. "This is my fifth cook. Can't seem to find a decent one. The port gets so crowded at times that it does not matter much. I get the business anyway. But I do have some pride. Your complaint is duly noted. If you ever come this way again, stop here. I guarantee better food."

CHAPTER XXXVII
FINDING A SHIP

The group strolled along the wharf, looking around, but the moorings near them were empty. Moving down the quay, they came to a small merchant ship, tattered in appearance with worm-eaten sides. Even from the vessel's moored perch, it seemed ready to sink. So they did not bother stopping to inquire if the boat was available. Advancing farther down the pier, they came across another ship, a merchant vessel fully loaded with a large amphora, probably containing oil or wine.

A stocky figure, seemingly in charge, watched them approach. Noting their inquiring looks, rich clothing, and weapons, he gazed boldly at them. "Can I help you with something?"

"Is this your ship?" Valerius asked.

"It is, he replied.

"Is your ship for hire?"

The captain shook his head. "Not now. We are fully loaded and ready to sail in about another hour."

"Would you happen to be going toward Ancona? We would pay you well," Valerius said.

"Afraid not. We are headed east toward Greece. I need to get this load there soon—as in, even today is not soon enough—or my boss will have my head. I was delayed for over a week because of stormy seas. Unusual for this time of year."

"Thank you anyway," Valerius said. The group moved onward, passing several other vacant moorings. The next ship, no more than a skiff, was obviously too small to accommodate them, so they did not bother stopping.

Valerius peered ahead and noticed a bulky vessel with ugly lines, ungainly in appearance. Approaching, Valerius witnessed the crew scrubbing the vessel down, while two men were mending a thick canvas sail. Valerius hailed one of the men, shouting above the shrill cries of sea birds. "Is your captain around?"

The crewman gestured with his thumb toward the stern. A tall man with a short beard stood on the aft deck, coiling a thick rope.

Valerius yelled across at him. "You have time to speak?"

The figure gestured toward the boarding plank connecting the ship to the wharf.

Walking across the plank, Valerius stopped about four paces from the captain. The man had a weathered appearance; his face was browned and wrinkled, offset by his piercing blue eyes.

"I was wondering if your ship's available for hire" Valerius asked. The man gave Valerius a hard stare before shaking his head. "We just pulled into port last night and unloaded our cargo. It was a rough voyage. Neptune was fucking with us again. Stormy seas and howling winds. Waves were breaking over the stern. We need to repair the ship, and my crew is exhausted."

Valerius was not about to give up. "Is your good ship seaworthy enough to reach Ancona? I will pay well."

"We need to caulk some seams that sprung a leak and repair the sail. Sorry, maybe next time."

Since her husband's entreaty was going nowhere, Hereca strode up beside him. "Captain, this is an urgent matter of state business. Perhaps you might want to reconsider. Maybe you could work through the night and get your vessel repaired."

Before the captain could object, Hereca hurriedly continued. "Let me introduce myself. My name is Hereca, and that man there," she said, pointing at Valerius, "is my husband. His name is Valerius Maximus, a hero of Rome who is currently governor of the Rhenus and Danubian territories. You may have heard of him."

Valerius offered a wide smile. He then held up his arm and flashed his pretentious signet ring, the gold glimmering in the sunlight.

The captain was taken aback by his guest's name. "Aye, I have heard of you. Everyone has. I even knew your old trading partner, Sabinus."

Valerius beamed. "Everyone knew Sabinus. He was not only my trading partner but also a confidant and friend. A truly good man, especially when things got out of sorts. Listen, I understand your crew is sapped and your ship took a battering, but if you could find a way to get your vessel repaired by tomorrow and transport my group to Ancona, I will make it worth your while for you and your crew. We urgently need to get to Rome. I will pay each of your crew members five gold aurei and reimburse you with thirty gold coins."

"The name is Captain Marius. Nice to make your acquaintance. Given your generous terms, I accept your offer. It's a bit of a risk, given the ship's condition, but we will find a way to get you there. I know my men will gladly consent to your offer of coins. They are a good lot, hardworking and loyal. Knowing who you are, I cannot refuse your request. At dawn tomorrow, we sail for Ancona."

* * *

The next morning, Valerius and Hereca stood at the ship's rail, gazing at the distant shoreline, now probably about a mile away. Captain Marius planned to parallel the coast, sailing in a southerly direction. Each evening, they would stop in a protected harbor.

As the ship slowly plied through the waters, Valerius frowned at their progress. She sailed like she looked—ploddingly slow, almost wallowing against a stiff headwind. He fretted that word would get to Sejanus before they arrived in Rome. That could be disastrous. Valerius wondered if Sejanus realized by now that he was exposed concerning Voculus and Portunus's skullduggery and plotting. His minions had failed to eliminate Valerius, and he was now implicated. He would be a desperate man and throw caution to the wind.

Marcellus sidled up to the rail and spoke softly, lest they be overheard. "Can we possibly move any slower?"

"No, and it is worrisome. Every hour that we delay heightens the chance that Sejanus will get word that we are traveling to Rome. If he discovers we are coming, he will make an all-out effort to prevent us from reaching our destination. But we don't have a lot of options."

"True," Marcellus replied. "When we get close to Rome, we will need to employ stealth, assuming that he is aware of our approach. It's the prudent thing to do. As a start, we will need to change into more common clothing—a rough woolen tunic with a hooded cowl would be fitting. With the onset of autumn, the attire won't be out of place. And your signet ring will need to be hidden."

"How will we gain entrance to the palace?" Hereca inquired. "You know that the Praetorians scrutinize and vet as many people as possible."

"My initial thought is to contact my friend, Senator Quintus Salvius. He will find a way. He managed to get our dispatches through right under Sejanus's nose. He will be our main resource, possibly our only one."

Terentius sauntered over. "I could not help but overhear your conversation. Domitius and I have brought our old dispatch cases with us, which we will wear around our shoulders. This will provide us with some degree of immunity. Once we get inside the city, I know some places for lodging. They would not be my first choices under normal circumstances—dirty, dingy, and certainly unfit for a governor and his wife—but they are out of the way and the last place anyone would search for someone of your station."

"I believe I will need to take you up on that offer," Valerius said. "That's just the sort of place I've been thinking about. Sejanus has an extensive network of spies and informers, but Rome is a big city, and he can't be everywhere."

Later that afternoon, the ship entered a small harbor for the night and anchored at a quay jutting out into the protected cove. Valerius and his entourage prepared to exit the vessel and get back on terra firma. He turned to Captain Marius. "Any recommendations for a decent meal and lodgings?"

The captain spluttered with laughter, and the crew sniggering as well. "I'm sorry, sir. I did not mean to mock you. It's just that the word *decent* is an incompatible word to use for this sorry-ass excuse for a port. In case you are interested, it's called Taracum, and it's a cesspit. So the answer is no. There are no places worth mentioning. There are two choices, both despicable, and I'm not even one of discerning taste. I suggest holding your nose while you swallow your food and wine."

"It can't be that bad," voiced Marcellus.

"It can be, and it is," the captain replied. "Under most circumstances, I try to avoid this port, if at all possible, but I wanted to stay as long as possible out at sea to get you to Ancona quickly. Unfortunately, there are no redeeming qualities to this town. But take heart; other ports on our journey have much better accommodations."

Early the next morning, Valerius and his group returned to the vessel. As he boarded, Captain Marius gave him an inquiring look, his eyebrows raised.

Valerius shook his head. "No need to tell me, 'I told you so.' What a vile place. I feel like I need to bathe for a week to rid myself of the stench. The sooner we can depart, the better."

Marius chuckled lightly.

Later that morning, the ship picked up a following wind and moved with a bit more alacrity than the previous day, which seemed to lift everyone's spirits. Valerius stood near the prow, savoring the breeze.

The captain sauntered up next to him. "Governor Maximus, not to worry, I will get you there. Not to probe into your matters, but judging by your fretful state and pacing, this must be urgent."

Valerius offered a tight-lipped expression. "You have no idea. Sorry, I cannot divulge any of it to you because of the sensitivity of the subject, but I will just say this: When it comes to matters of state within the Roman Empire, things can get quite convoluted. What I need to convey is for Tiberius's ears only."

Captain Marius proffered an expansive grin. "Then I will ensure your safe journey continues on the sea leg part of it."

"I appreciate that, Captain Marius. When all is said and done, and if we ever cross paths again, I will gladly buy you a glass of wine and explain what in Hades this was all about. Until then, we need to keep our presence on this ship a tightly held secret. Can I depend on you for that?"

"You most certainly can, Governor Maximus and that goes for my crew as well. They are a good lot who have been with me for many years. When I tell them to do something, they listen well." He then turned around and went back to his post near the ship's steering tiller.

* * *

After two more days, the ship rounded a promontory jutting out into the sea. Off to the starboard side, Captain Marius gestured with his arm. "Behold, Ancona. Your destination."

Valerius gazed at the sheltered harbor and the town rising above it. There were ships of all sizes bobbing in the gentle swell of the sea. The houses along the hillside were constructed of white plaster with red tile roofs. From his vantage point, it appeared to be a prosperous port. "It's a far better sight than that other dump we stopped. What was it called? Oh, yes, Taracum."

"This is one of my favorite ports," the captain said. "There are many good places to dine and stay."

"Unfortunately, we will not have time to stop and sample its fine dining and inns."

"Perhaps on the way back," Captain Marius said. "Governor Maximus, once you leave the outskirts of town, you will be on the Via Flaminia. Can't miss it. It's the main road heading southwest toward Rome. I believe the distance is around one hundred and seventy miles. When you get to the city walls, you will be at the Porta Fortinalis. As you probably know, the Vicus Longus will take you to the heart of the city."

"Thank you for that information and my gratitude for getting us here safely," said Valerius, who personally paid the gold coins to the captain and crew. When he was finished, he turned to Marius. "Once again, many thanks for getting us here safely. I wish you calm seas and safe travels."

"I hope things go well for you in Rome, Governor Maximus. And I remember what we talked about. My crew and I have forgotten that you were ever a passenger."

After a short while, the ship reached its mooring. Valerius planted his feet on the dock and gave the captain and crew a final wave. Had he directed his gaze a bit farther out to sea, he would have observed a sleek packet ship rounding the promontory. The passengers on board included two couriers dispatched by Voculus and Portunus. They had urgent messages to be conveyed to Sejanus.

CHAPTER XXXVIII
VIA FLAMINIA

Three hard days after departing from the seaport of Ancona, Valerius and his group stopped at a way station along the Via Flaminia for the night. Everyone agreed that they had made good progress. The weather had a slight chill, keeping the horses fresh and spry, and they had advanced at a trot for most of the day. The inn they had stopped at was large, with fresh mounts available for the next day.

As dusk settled over the land, the oil lamps inside the tavern were lit, casting an eerie glow over the inn's customers. The group of six sat at a corner table away from the others so that no one could eavesdrop on their conversation. The dinner dishes had been cleared away with the onset of darkness, and most of the guests had departed to their quarters for the night.

Looking around to ensure they were alone, Valerius spoke in a hushed tone. "If all goes well, we will be at the city gates before long. It's time we start planning our entrance. As a matter of caution, we must assume that Sejanus has word of our coming. He may not, but we cannot afford to think otherwise. I sense that he will stop at nothing, including murder, to prevent us from gaining an audience with Tiberius. So, before we enter the city gates, we need to rid ourselves of the horses and disguise ourselves. Also, we should separate from one another to be less conspicuous. Terentius and Domitius, what is your take on this?"

"Both of us have entered the city many times," Terentius said. "The crowds are often massive, especially at the city gates. I assume the Praetorians will be out in force, but there are not enough of them to inspect everyone who enters. It would be impractical. So, if we are well-masqueraded, our chances are good. As I mentioned previously, once we are within the city walls, I know places where the Praetorians will not search."

"That gives me some level of comfort," Valerius said. "So, I am surmising the point of danger will be our initial entry into the city."

Terentius nodded. "Yes, but if we blend into the crowd, I'm confident we can escape the Praetorians' scrutiny."

* * *

Late in the evening, Sejanus, his face blooming in anger, sat in his headquarters, rereading the recently received dispatch from Voculus. He wondered how the man managed to fuck things up on such a grand scale. He had always judged him to be competent, but clearly, he had overvalued the man's intellect. As he scanned the words, he noted how deftly Voculus attempted to deflect much of the blame to Portunus, but Sejanus was not buying any of it. After all, it was Voculus's centurion who had been killed in the failed ambush. Furthermore, all of the other attempts by Voculus against Maximus had failed. Portunus was just a greedy buffoon who had gotten caught up in the plot to rid Maximus of his post. The blame was squarely on Voculus.

The shadows deepened, and the oil lamps flickered in the encroaching darkness. What was he to do? Maximus was on his way to Rome. Was he in the city already? Doubtful. Voculus's couriers had departed two days after Maximus, and they reported that they had ridden almost without stopping through Raetia and Italia. Maximus most likely could not maintain that kind of pace. When he had asked the couriers if they had seen anyone matching the description of Maximus and his friends, both men exchanged glances and then shrugged. One of the men admitted that he had no idea what Maximus looked like and that the Via Flaminia was jammed with travelers heading toward Rome.

Sejanus pounded his fist into his palm. He was so close to taking over from Tiberius, but he was not ready just yet. He needed full support from the legions and additional backing from the senate, but that did not appear to be much of an obstacle. Damn that Maximus. He was a thorn in his side that needed to be eliminated at all costs.

Sejanus shouted for his second-in-command, Centurion Cestius. "Centurion, come in here. I have urgent orders." The man appeared a moment later.

"Yes, sir. What would you have me do?"

"We have a problem. Do you remember Governor Maximus, his wife Hereca, and his associate, Marcellus? They were in Rome in the early spring."

"Yes, sir. I do."

"Most likely, they are on their way to Rome to see Tiberius. We must not let that happen. They are planning sedition and will speak falsehoods to Tiberius about me and the Praetorians. They must be arrested and imprisoned in the Praetorian compound. Have all the gates to the city under heavy watch, especially those to the north and west."

Cestius frowned. "Sir, I know what they look like and so do some of my men, but most of the Praetorians do not."

"Understood, Cestius. The Praetorians are to arrest anyone who might fit the description of the governor and his wife."

"Yes, sir," he responded, turning to leave.

"No, not yet. One more thing. I want a list of everyone Valerius meets with while in Rome. We will have the houses watched. Finally, double the guards at the imperial palace. No one enters unless I approve. That includes all couriers and messengers. Understood?"

"Yes, sir."

"Good. Now you are dismissed."

* * *

A few days later, the group approached the Fortinalis entrance, its gates wide open. The looming stone walls of the city stretched far on both sides of the portal. The five men and one woman were heavily disguised. They had stored their clothes and swords in a small town ten miles away, opting for humble peasant garb, something a poor merchant or farmer would be wearing. They sported drab tunics of a rough weave and a light robe with a hooded cowl. To further mask their appearances, they rubbed dirt into their clothes and smeared mud on their faces. The men had not shaved or bathed in over a week. From all appearances, they looked like members of the plebian class. It was decided that both Terentius and Domitius would keep their dispatch cases, giving them some immunity from potential searches and seizures.

The morning was overcast with threatening skies. There was a huge backup at the gate, and the crowd milled about impatiently. Valerius had no idea if this was a normal occurrence. He slowly trudged forward, not knowing where the others were in the mass of people. He absently scratched the stubble on his cheek and quickly studied the crowds plodding to enter the city. He was relieved that he looked just like them. Included in the multitude were several wagons, hauling their fall produce to the markets. Just then, it began to drizzle. *Outstanding*, thought Valerius. *Our hooded cowls are perfect for the weather.*

Valerius slowly shuffled forward, attempting to look like he belonged with the rabble. Before long, he was in the shadow of the walled gate. The line halted once more. He heard muffled, gruff commands followed by plaintive wails. They must be searching, folks. Their decision to leave their swords at the inn now seemed wise. If he was caught with his long sword, that would be the end for him. Wearing a sword was forbidden in the city, and it would invite other questions, like what he was doing with an officer's sword.

Valerius moved out of the shadow of the gate and through the stone portal. Glancing around, he spotted them—a swarm of intimidating Praetorians easily recognizable with the distinctive scorpion painted on their shields—and scrutinized the multitude. He looked down at the ground and slowly trundled forward.

"You. You there, halt."

Valerius continued moving forward into the city.

"What are you, deaf? I said halt."

Valerius gazed up, startled to realize that a stern-faced Praetorian was speaking to him. A feeling of dread trickled down his spine. If these Praetorians had ever seen him before, the deception would not have saved him. The disguise could only help so much. He fervently hoped the man who had singled him out had not seen him at the palace in the spring.

The figure roughly grabbed his arm and guided him out of the crowd. Another Praetorian joined them.

"Deaf one, what is your purpose in entering this city? Did you hear me?"

Valerius nodded. He replied with his rehearsed line in rough Latin. They had all fabricated a story about their background and purpose in the city. "I am here to assist my brother-in-law. He is a butcher working in the Forum Borium."

"A butcher, huh?" the guard replied.

"Let me see your hands," the other one demanded, grabbing Valerius's hands before he could react.

Valerius had thick calluses on the fingers of his right hand from constantly practicing with his huge war bow with Marcellus. They did not have many opportunities over the last month, but the calluses were still present.

"Strange-looking skin. I have not seen calluses like that before," said the Praetorian, letting the statement hang.

Thinking quickly, Valerius responded. "I specialize in deboning meat. I use a small knife for my work."

Then, the Praetorian who had dragged him aside spoke. "Lower your hood so we can see your face."

Valerius meekly complied, not looking the guard in the eyes.

He patted Valerius down and felt the dagger strapped to his tunic. Withdrawing it, he asked, "What's this?"

"My knife. I don't use this for work. It's for my protection. I have been almost attacked several times, both on my way into the city and outside the walls. I travel through some rough neighborhoods, you know. Everyone has a knife. What's the problem?"

"Don't get sassy with me. You are under suspicion." The Praetorian observed his unshaven face and the embedded grime on it. "What do you think, Brutus? I'm not sure, but something is not quite right about this guy. The peculiar calluses, the knife.... His clothes look as if they were deliberately soiled…like he's trying to conceal his identity. He looks vaguely familiar too."

Brutus snorted in derision. "He doesn't look like a procurator to me. He's wearing a hood because it's raining. The man is dirty and unkempt. He needs a good bath as well. I don't want our officer to chew us a new arsehole because this is the best we could do to find the governor. You want to bring him. Go right ahead."

Valerius sputtered in laughter. "Me, a procurator? Wait until I tell the wife about this."

The suspicious Praetorian threw him one final contemptuous glance. "I can do without your humor. Be on your way, butcher."

Heaving a silent sigh of relief, he slogged onward, trying not to hurry away from the Praetorians in case they changed their minds. The group had agreed to gather around two hundred paces from the gate. Looking ahead, he could see them scattered around, not coalescing but within sight of each other. More good news. It appeared that he was the only one who had been stopped.

Marcellus gazed down the Vicus Longus toward the city gate from which he had come and spotted Valerius exiting the crowd. Relieved, he edged his hand away from his dagger. He had been close to rallying the group to attack the Praetorians if Valerius was detained. It would have been a desperate action at best—four men armed with daggers against a slew of Praetorians with swords and shields. He glanced around, noting the others in his group. He frowned and sauntered over toward Radulf, speaking in a low tone, "Radulf, quit fucking gaping about. You make yourself stand out."

"Sorry, sir. Just that I have never been to Rome before. Never been to a big city."

"You have not seen anything yet. Wait till we get to the forum area. Listen, I was the same way when I first visited the city, but you have to pull it together. You are drawing attention to yourself and us. Right now, you need to fit in like the rest of us. Got it?"

Radulf nodded and moved on.

The group began advancing farther down the avenue, not together but in sight of one another, always blending in with the other people trudging along the way.

They advanced several more blocks when a Praetorian patrol of eight men swaggered down the center of the street, pushing people out of the way. Their eyes roamed back and forth over the crowd, seeking something or someone suspicious. Valerius held his breath, trying to appear like a man walking innocuously toward his destination.

Valerius briefly met the gaze of one of the guards. The figure narrowed his vision slightly and then dismissed him as no one of importance. Valerius kept walking at the measured pace, neither slowing down nor speeding up.

The cluster continued their journey down the Vicus Longus through the Viminal section of the city. Before advancing far, they encountered another roving patrol of Praetorians. This time, Terentius was the center of their attention.

"You there," barked the centurion commanding the guard, "stop where you are."

Terentius halted in his tracks.

The centurion approached, observing the dispatch satchel slung around his shoulder. "What dispatches do you carry?"

Valerius slowly continued to walk, his heart pounding. Besides other testimonies, the satchel contained the sworn damning account of the unfortunate Legionary Longinus on the conversation between

Voculus and Portunus. It also included Valerius's written observations of the treason of Voculus and Portunus as well as Captain Rufinus's written testimony of the tax scheme.

Terentius glared at the centurion, not speaking.

"I said, what is in your dispatch bag? Now speak!"

Terentius gave the officer a look of disdain. "Since when is it any of your business what is in my satchel? You know these are privileged communications for the emperor's eyes only. You should know better, Centurion."

The centurion hardened his gaze. "I am on the Emperor's business," he said in a blustery tone.

Terentius scoffed. "So am I. Let me see if I understand this. The emperor permitted you to examine his documents. I think not. I have never been accosted before by a Praetorian to examine my documents. This is unheard of."

Somewhat taken aback by the terse reply, the centurion continued, "From what province or part of the empire have you ridden, and where is your mount?"

"Again, Centurion, that is not your right to ask. As for my horse, he pulled up lame just before the city gates. You are interfering in the emperor's business and delaying my arrival at the palace. I suppose you are next going to ask me who gave me the dispatches and what they are about."

"As a matter of fact, I was."

"Centurion, I have no idea what is contained in the dispatches, and I don't know who authored them. For your information, I have never once read any of the dispatches given to me. They have seals on them, which I am not going to disturb. My centurion handed these documents to me and commanded me to deliver them to the palace.

If you know what's good for you, you will cease interfering with my duties. As I'm sure you are aware, the penalties for obstructing an imperial courier are severe. Now, let me be on my way, and I will forget this entire engagement."

The chastised officer waved his arm down the avenue. "You may proceed," he said gruffly. "Be on your way."

CHAPTER XXXIX
THE EMPTY CUP

The streets were teeming with Praetorians. Valerius had seen enough and decided they needed to vacate the streets of Rome with haste. They might not be so fortunate the next time they are stopped and inspected by the Praetorians. Valerius walked briskly so that he was almost abreast of Terentius and Domitius and spoke out of the corner of his mouth. "We need to get off the streets as soon as possible and find shelter, or sooner or later, we will be discovered."

Domitius's face brightened. "I know just the place. We will turn left up ahead. It's called the "Empty Cup." The tavern is a dirty, disgusting place. Perfect for us. I doubt the Praetorians will search such an establishment, seeking an imperial governor."

Valerius nodded imperceptibly while keeping pace with the two couriers. "We will follow the two of you. I will inform the others." Valerius then slowed down, letting the two messengers take the lead.

Venturing into the Esquiline district, the loose group turned left, each person around twenty paces away from the other. They weaved their way through several smaller streets. The farther they ventured, the more battered the neighborhood. Finally, they arrived at a small crossroad.

Valerius beheld The Empty Cup. The sign hung crookedly on the front of the building, and the walls had not seen a coat of paint in many years. A patron was sprawled, insensible, on the sidewalk. Valerius wondered what was holding the building up. He hoped the roof did not leak, but he was being optimistic.

Valerius lingered out front, waiting for the others, except for Hereca, to procure their rooms. After waiting a while, he entered the threshold. His nostrils were immediately assailed by the odor of stale wine and vomit. "Charming," he muttered.

A short while later, the group gathered in Valerius and Hereca's room—a ramshackle affair with two moldy cots and a wash basin in the corner on a nightstand. The wooden walls were warped from years of neglect. It was a tight fit, but they all managed to squeeze in.

Valerius spoke in a hushed tone. "The city is in lockdown. It's crawling with Praetorians. Being on the streets is far too risky. This is what I suggest. Tomorrow morning, when Senator Salvius meets with his patrons, one of us must pass him or one of his servants a note, informing him that I am in the city and need to speak to him about gaining an audience with Tiberius. I will request to meet him at the sixth hour, which will only be a few hours from when he gets the message. I will join him at the entrance of the Theater of Pompey since I sense that Sejanus may be watching the senator's house. In any event, we cannot be observed. So, if all goes according to plan, I shall meet Salvius at the noon hour."

"I volunteer," Domitius said. "I will deliver the message. Just let me know where he lives."

"Thank you," Valerius replied. "This could be dangerous. Terentius barely avoided arrest earlier today. Are you sure you want to do this?"

"I believe it is my duty. I have faced danger many times in the legions and as a courier. I'm not scared, and I promise to be vigilant."

"Would it be better if we both went?" Terentius queried.

Valerius paused in thought. "One messenger delivering a dispatch is less conspicuous, don't you agree?"

"I guess I kind of agree with you," Terentius said. "The less we are noticed, the better."

"Excellent," said Valerius. "Domitius, as soon as you have delivered your message, report back here. Until then, we can all enjoy the hospitality of this wonderful establishment."

* * *

Sejanus sat in his headquarters, while his three subordinate officers stood stiffly before him. He gave them a hard glare. "Have you discovered anything?"

The trio exchanged questioning looks and then shook their heads. The tallest among them spoke. "Sir, is it possible he is not yet in the city? We have our men everywhere on double shifts and have combed the city streets."

Sejanus slammed his fist on the tabletop. "Maximus is in Rome. I can feel his presence. You must find him. One hundred gold coins to the person who discovers and arrests him. Are you telling me there were no unusual occurrences while surveying the city streets?"

"Sir," said a heavyset figure, "it may be nothing…"

"Go ahead, what is it? Speak," Sejanus demanded.

"One of my centurions reported that he had confronted a dispatch rider without a horse. He challenged him and requested he examine his dispatch pouch. But the rider defied my centurion, informing him he had privileged status and asking him how he dared request to see the contents of his dispatch. I understand that these riders do have certain rights, but most would not stand up to a Praetorian officer."

"Where was this?" Sejanus asked.

"On the Vicus Longus."

"That's the direction Maximus would approach from. Tomorrow, I want all dispatch riders to be searched and their correspondence opened and read. Don't worry about the consequences. I write the laws in this city now. Understood?"

The three men nodded.

"Excellent. You are dismissed."

* * *

The next day, Domitius exited the inn and began his journey toward Senator Salvius's house. He was vaguely familiar with the locality, situated on the southern edge of Quirinal Hill, close to the Forum. The large crowds in the streets at this early hour surprised him. He pushed his way forward, moving slowly through the throngs of people. After a time, he realized his journey was going to take longer than expected.

Spotting an alley to his right, he remembered it would take him in the same direction. He trotted down the filthy side street for a few blocks and was soon back on the main avenue he was following. He was about to congratulate himself on his navigation triumph when, suddenly, his progress was halted by a thick crowd. Frustrated, he hopped up on the steps of a small inn so that he could peer ahead. All he could see was a mass of people at a standstill. He briefly contemplated returning to The Empty Cup but decided to wait before making that decision.

"Jupiter's fat arse," he mumbled to himself, "why today?" He had seen foot traffic like this on previous occasions but not often. He waited some more, staring at the backs of others' heads. *If this does not clear in another few minutes, I will return to the inn.*

As if by divine intervention, the crowd slowly began to move forward. His pace increased as the throng lessened. Relieved, he advanced. Up ahead, he saw his next turn. If his reckoning was correct, he would soon be turning left, reaching the senator's house shortly.

He strode rapidly along the avenue, like a courier, noting the ever-present patrols of the Praetorians. They were everywhere. He gave them a cautious glance and a wide berth, telling himself not to worry. He was an official dispatcher, beyond their purview. He smiled to himself, remembering how Terentius had humbled the Praetorian officer the previous day. Now confident, he moved forward. After a bit, he saw his next turn. It would be to the right toward the Quirinal. He moved along the avenue, the crowd thickening once more. Frowning, he realized the senator's dwelling was not where he had thought it was. He gazed around for a street sign, but they were few and far between. He made a quick left turn and then another sharp left and circled back. If he was correct, he had proceeded too far, and the senator's house was on a street paralleling the one where he thought it was.

Craning his neck, he saw a house that matched Valerius's description, with a marble façade and huge wooden doors painted black. Up ahead, he saw a street sign that read, "Via Pincus." Yes, that had to be it. Relieved at reaching his destination, he failed to notice the Praetorian patrol to his right. His steps were abruptly halted, as he was surrounded by three Praetorians, one of whom was a centurion.

He glared at the officer. "Let me pass," he said gruffly. "I am on official business."

The centurion smirked. "Not today, you're not. Give me the dispatch case."

Domitius protectively clutched his satchel. "This is privileged correspondence." He was about to continue voicing his outrage when one of the guards stepped forward and ripped the case from his shoulder, forcefully shoving him to the street.

The officer untied the straps holding the satchel closed and found a single sealed message within. He read it aloud: "Urgent that I meet you at the sixth hour at the Theater of Pompey. Signed VM."

He threw Domitius a contemptuous look. "Who is VM?"

Domitius remained silent. No amount of bluster could save him now. He looked around desperately for an avenue of escape but was closely surrounded.

"Not speaking today? We will change that. Arrest this man. We will take him to Sejanus immediately."

* * *

The bevy of Praetorians escorted Domitius to Sejanus's headquarters, only a short distance away, not far from the Palatine. The centurion had dispatched one of his men ahead to alert Sejanus of the recent arrest of a messenger with correspondence from Valerius Maximus.

The unfortunate Domitius was prodded and half-dragged up the steps into an imposing fortress surrounded by a ten-foot-high brick wall. Once inside, he was shoved to the floor in front of the awaiting Sejanus.

"Here is the message, sir," the centurion said.

Sejanus glanced at the document and then at the hapless Domitius. "So, you bear a message to Senator Salvius from Valerius Maximus? Who is with him?"

Domitius shot Sejanus a spiteful gaze and remained silent.

"Looks like we have a defiant one here. It will be of no use. Everyone talks eventually once my torturers get at them. They all do." He then motioned to a pair of guards standing nearby. "Take him to the cells. We will deal with him shortly."

Sejanus turned to the Praetorian who had made the arrest. "You have done well, Centurion. I'm impressed with your diligence. But we are not through just yet.... Cestius!" he shouted over his shoulder.

His second in command hurriedly appeared. "Yes, sir."

"Get me every available man in this headquarters. We are going to surround the Theater of Pompey and trap Maximus when he goes to his rendezvous with Senator Salvius. I want the men present right here in no more than fifteen minutes. Is that clear?"

"Yes, sir."

A little while later, a group of around thirty Praetorians had gathered in the room. Sejanus eyed the men. "As you are aware, I have been hunting a man named Valerius Maximus, who is considered to be engaged in treasonous activity. We believe we know where he will be at the sixth hour today—the Theater of Pompey. This is what we are going to do. We will encircle the area of the theater but keep our distance until the appointed hour. Then, we will descend upon and capture Maximus. Who knows what Maximus looks like?"

Five men raised their hands.

"Good," Sejanus said. "Maximus will most likely be in a disguise of some sort. He may have his face hidden with a hat or cowl. He will not be easily recognizable, so be on the alert. I am going with you and will position you in groups around the area. We must not alert Maximus that we know he will be coming. Now, let's move. Time is short."

CHAPTER XXXX
THE THEATER OF POMPEY

"I am departing early for my liaison with Salvius," Valerius announced to the group. "I want to reconnoiter the area as a precaution, and I don't want to be late. Who knows how congested the city is today."

"I feel uncomfortable about you going by yourself," Marcellus opined.

"I understand your concern, but the presence of one or two men is not going to make much difference if my identity is discovered. Furthermore, your company, or anyone else's for that matter, will make my charade that much more difficult. I firmly believe the best option is for me to go alone."

Hereca stood with her arms folded across her chest. "I don't like you going alone, but I agree with your logic. Please be careful."

"I shall, my dear. I will return as soon as Salvius and I finish developing a plan to get word to Tiberius of Sejanus's treachery."

Valerius exited the inn and peered around to get a sense of direction. Then, he headed east toward the Tiber at a measured pace to avoid attracting any attention. He advanced several blocks and then pretended to stop at a shop selling pastries. They looked delicious, but his purpose was to surreptitiously check to see if he was being followed.

He risked a glance down the crowded avenue he had just traveled. Not seeing anything suspicious, he continued his journey. The theater was around two to three miles away; it would take a while to get there.

Back at the inn, Terentius paced about anxiously. "I am worried. It has been too long. Domitius should have been back here by now. He is not one to dally."

"Maybe he stopped for something to eat," Hereca said.

"Not likely. He knows better and that we are waiting for his return. I don't like this one bit. He may have been captured by the Praetorians. I say we move out of here as a precaution. I will attempt to track down Valerius and warn him of the potential danger. I know the city better than anyone else here."

"Could there be some other explanation?" Hereca asked with a quiver in her voice.

"Yes, there could be all sorts of reasons, but we cannot afford to take any chances. Marcellus, why don't you take charge of the group and find another inn in case Domitius has been captured and is forced to reveal our whereabouts.."

"Gladly, but which one? Rome is a big city, and we need to find each other when you return."

"Let's do this. Head east down this avenue and stop at the third inn from here. There are plenty of lodgings along this avenue, and it's not too far from here. That way, Valerius and I will find you."

"Understood. I trust it will be better than this dive."

"Probably not, just more of the same," Terentius said. "Don't worry, Hereca, I will find Valerius and get him back here. Alright then, I'm off."

Valerius approached the Theater of Pompey from the left on the Via Tecta. The crowds were thick, which was good for him. He swiveled his head around, searching for any signs of danger. He had seen several Praetorian patrols, but nothing out of the ordinary. They had ignored him. Up ahead, he saw the gates of the theater. The crowd was of moderate size, people hurrying to get somewhere. He searched around for the senator's familiar face but did not see him, so he moved closer to the gates. Perhaps the senator was off in the distance, waiting for him to appear. It was now past the noon hour. *Had he received the message? Did he decide not to attend because of the danger it posed?*

Reluctantly, Valerius lowered his cowl, hoping the senator would recognize his face from afar. Suddenly, he heard running feet behind him. He turned to leave, but too late. Several Praetorians grabbed him by the arms. Guards materialized to his left and right, surrounding him. Before he could fully grasp the situation, he saw someone casually stroll up to him.

Sejanus smirked. "I must say, good disguise. You eluded my men for a while, but the game is up now. Take him away."

One man produced a set of chains and bound his wrists. Then, two Praetorians roughly grabbed his arms and half-dragged him away. The people in the plaza gave them a wide berth, thanking the gods they were not in his position.

Once they entered the Praetorian headquarters, Valerius was thrown into a small, empty cell with rough stone walls and a small window in the door so that the prisoner could be observed. He looked around his new domicile. The room was bare—no cot, no chair, no bowls for food, nothing. He was surprised to be in the cell. He thought Sejanus would interrogate him right away.

He attempted to organize his thoughts to tell Sejanus bits of the truth regarding why he was in Rome. He must not, under any circumstances, admit that Hereca and Marcellus were with him in Rome. That would be their death warrant. As to why he was in Rome, Valerius would say that he wanted to give Tiberius a report on his progress on the Danubius. Sejanus would not accept that explanation, but it was the best he could do.

His deliberations were interrupted by some muffled blows followed by shrieks of pain. He heard voices, but the words were indistinguishable. More groans and screams of pain pierced the air. He could hear men laughing, mocking the unfortunate victim. Cries of extreme agony echoed down the corridor of cells. And then, silence.

Valerius's cell door was flung open with a crash. Two burly guards hoisted him to his feet and dragged him down the hallway. They descended a set of stairs to a dank-smelling room. Turning his head to the right, Valerius witnessed a man hanging, lifeless, from chains fastened to the ceiling, his face and body bloody and bruised. The man's jaw was crooked, and several of his fingers were gory stubs. In a wave of horror, he realized the figure was Domitius.

Sejanus strutted in, followed by two heavy-set men with small piggish eyes and two Praetorians. They had on leather aprons smeared with blood. Sejanus cast a callous glance at Domitius. "Your man was tough. He didn't admit too much except his name and that he accompanied you and your bodyguard here. Also, he did mention where you are staying, The Empty Cup. I must say, I'm impressed. Didn't think couriers had that kind of fortitude. My men got a little too enthusiastic with their questioning… which brings us to you. First, why are you here? I know Tiberius did not summon you. I would have known of this. Perhaps you came to convince Tiberius of my deceit, my treasonous activities?" he scoffed. "Not a chance. Tiberius trusts me implicitly. Next, did Marcellus and your wife accompany you here to Rome? You might as well admit it. We have the city locked down. If they are here, we will find them. And finally, were you staying at the Empty Cup, as your courier confessed?"

Valerius quickly assessed the situation. There was no way he could convince Sejanus that he was in Rome for reasons other than what he already suspected. He could try, but Sejanus knew better. Valerius would concede that point, hoping it gained him some credibility. As to Hereca and Marcellus, since Sejanus admitted to not knowing that Hereca and Marcellus were in Rome, he might save them by not confessing to their presence. If Domitius had been as staunch and resistant as Sejanus suggested, he just might have accepted that. Furthermore, it was plausible that he journeyed to Rome without them.

Sejanus glowered at him. "Speak before I set my men upon you. Believe me, it will not be pleasant. They are experts at inflicting pain."

Valerius glared back at Sejanus. "I freely admit I journeyed to Rome to inform the emperor of the duplicity and treasonous activity of your minion. General Voculus was rather clumsy and inept in his attempts to topple my standing on the Danubius. I had no choice but to come to Rome. If I did not do something, sooner or later, Voculus and his accomplice, Portunus would have succeeded. So, yes, I am here to see Tiberius and inform him of the situation." Before Sejanus could interrupt Valerius, he quickly continued. "As to Hereca and Marcellus, they are still back on the Danubius. I briefly considered bringing them along, but I discarded that option. They would serve no useful purpose."

Sejanus glared at Valerius. "I'm not sure I believe you." He nodded to one of the tormentors, who slammed his right fist into Valerius's ribs. His legs lost their power to stand up, but he was kept upright by two Praetorians.

Valerius sagged his ribs a nexus of pain. He gasped for air, unable to speak.

Sejanus nodded again. The torturer slammed his giant fist into Valerius's left shoulder joint. "Speak up. What is the truth? Confirm you were at the Empty Cup before I order a search."

Valerius briefly panicked. He would have to tell him something. By now, Hereca, Marcellus, and the others would have probably recognized that something was amiss. First, Domitius had not returned, and now, he had not. As a precaution, they would have probably moved on to another place, or they should have. He needed to appear as if he were cooperating. Regardless, the Empty Cup would be searched, so he might as well admit it was where they were staying.

"It's the place on the Esquiline. The Empty Cup."

"Sounds charming," Sejanus sneered.

Valerius wheezed in pain. "I'm telling you the truth."

"We shall see," said Sejanus. He turned to the two guards. "Take him back to his cell. Oh, and Maximus, don't even consider the possibility of escape. No one has even come close to it."

CHAPTER XXXXI
INTRIGUE

Hereca, Marcellus, and Radulf gathered at the Thirsty Bird, the third inn down the avenue from their previous lodgings. The hours passed by with no sign of Domitius, Valerius, or Terentius. The trio waited in silence, knowing that with each passing minute, the odds of the men returning diminished. Radulf retreated to a corner of the small room in the inn's loft, anxiously fingering the handle of his dagger. Hereca gazed out the window to the streets below, while Marcellus stared morosely at the opposite wall, his dark eyes glimmering with fury.

Hours later, Hereca gasped as she observed Terentius hurrying down the paved street and then ducking into the entranceway. Radulf and Marcellus instantly became alert. Hereca opened the door to the room as Terentius took the stairs two at a time. He entered the room and shut the door.

"Not good. I searched everywhere, near the Theater of Pompey and then over by the senator's house. On the way back here, I stopped at the Empty Cup. No sign of either of them. The proprietor said that the Praetorians had searched his place and made a mess of things, breaking furniture and disturbing his guests. When he protested, one of the guards punched him in the face. He was still bleeding when I arrived. He said they asked about us, but he told them nothing. He wouldn't give those pricks the satisfaction of telling them anything. I believe Domitius and Valerius have been taken."

"We must do something quickly," exclaimed Hereca. "Sejanus will kill them before long. We must get word to Quintus Salvius."

"But how?" Marcellus asked. "The Praetorians probably have the senator's residence under surveillance."

"I think I might know a way," Hereca said. "They are guarding against access to the senator, but perhaps not his wife, Claudia. I have met her. We first spoke at the party sponsored by the late Senator Flaccus. We kind of hit it off and convened again at her house. We promised to stay in touch. I exchanged several letters with her while on the Rhenus and the Danubius. I will just walk up to the door and announce that I have an appointment with the senator's wife. It might work. Anyone observing the house will not be expecting a woman."

"And it might not work," Marcellus ventured.

"We have nothing to lose," Hereca said. "If Sejanus prevails, we are all as good as dead."

"I have an idea that might help you," Marcellus offered. "When you approach the residence, Radulf and I will stage a diversion, a fight, not too far from the doorway. The distraction will hopefully give Hereca the time to get to the entrance and announce herself."

"For the lack of better alternatives, I think it is a clever ruse that might work," ventured Terentius. "These Praetorians are always drawn to violence, so make sure it's a good fight. It is getting late in the afternoon. Hereca, when do you want to do this?

"Now would be good. We have no time to lose. Every moment that goes by lessens the chance of my husband's survival."

The foursome departed the inn. It wasn't the greatest of plans, but it was better than nothing.

They walked rapidly toward their destination. The crowds were still thick, but the farther they ventured, the lesser the foot traffic. There were a few Praetorian patrols, but they ignored the foursome.

They stood about one hundred paces away from Salvius's dwelling, blending in with the crowd. "Hereca," Marcellus instructed, "do not approach until you hear the two of us fighting. That will be your signal."

Hereca waited, gazing straight ahead at the imposing doorway of Salvius's villa. Before long, she heard screams and angry shouts. Several Praetorians stopped and began to close in on the combatants. That was her cue. She moved quickly and inconspicuously toward the massive doors. Hurriedly walking up the stone steps of the residence, she found herself facing a massive slave with his arms folded across his chest, guarding the entrance. He wielded a club tucked into the belt of his tunic.

She gazed up at him. "Lady Hereca to see the Lady Claudia. It is a rather urgent matter." The figure snorted in derision, taking in Hereca's shabby clothes and dirty face. "If you are a lady, then I am a senator's son.

Hereca spoke in a laconic tone, her eyes ablaze. "You listen to me, you oaf, and listen well. You will announce my presence right away. If you do not, I will see that you are sold to the salt mines in Numidia. It will cost you nothing to inform her of my presence. Think about it and choose wisely. Your future is at stake."

The slave gave her a curious glance, unsure of what to do. "Wait here," he grumbled and then turned to enter the house.

Hereca glanced around anxiously, waiting for someone of authority to meet her at the door. Turning around, she noticed Radulf and Marcellus continuing to tussle in the street, now surrounded by a group of gawking Praetorians. In a matter of minutes, Claudia appeared, an inquiring expression on her face. "Hereca, it is you." She rushed over, giving Hereca a quick hug. "What are you doing here? I thought you were on the Danubius. And your clothes...."

Before she could continue, Hereca brushed past her into the dwelling, throwing the doorman a haughty glance. "We must talk. It is a matter of great importance. I need to speak to you and your husband at once."

Claudia led Hereca to a small office to the side of the atrium, away from the inquisitive eyes and ears of the staff. "I will fetch Quintus," she said before leaving the room.

Claudia returned in a couple of minutes. "He is finishing up a meeting and will be here shortly."

Before she could ask any questions, Hereca began. "We are all in great danger. We believe Sejanus may be on the cusp of seizing power. There were numerous attempts on our lives on the Danubius, and they all trace back to Sejanus. In desperation, my husband and I journeyed to Rome. It was a risky move, but we had no other alternatives."

Quintus arrived at the doorway of the room and stopped, taking in Hereca's shabby appearance, not quite believing what he was seeing. "By all the gods that are sacred, what is going on?"

Hereca relayed her story and all the events that had transpired since they departed Rome. When she had finished, she gazed at both Quintus and Claudia. "You must realize that we are all in grave danger. If Sejanus is successful in seizing the purple, none of us are safe. I believe he has reason to suspect that you are an ally of my husband and me."

Quintus frowned. "I knew this day might come, just not so suddenly."

"We must get an audience with Tiberius," Hereca said.

"That might not be so easy," said Quintus. "Tiberius returned to Rome from Capri about ten days ago. The palace is locked down. No one gets in or out but the Praetorians. My source within the palace, a dispatcher, cannot get access. The only exceptions are Tiberius's concubines. They still have admission privileges, according to my sources."

Hereca cocked her head to one side, which she was wont to do when contemplating something serious. "What if I posed as one of the concubines? I know it's a desperate ploy at best, but what alternatives do we have?"

Quintus and Claudia gaped in shock.

"Surely you are not serious about this gambit," Claudia said.

"It's something I must do. My husband's life is at stake. Quintus, what time do these courtesans show up at the palace?"

"I believe they usually appear in the early evening but before dark. Most of the palace business is completed by then."

"Then it is settled. I will arrive early and attempt to bluff my way into Tiberius's lair. Claudia, I will need to bathe and make heavy use of your cosmetics and perfume."

"We have no time to lose," Claudia said. "It is already late in the afternoon."

A while later, Hereca sat next to Claudia in front of the mirror in her bedroom. Hereca looked at the assortment of paints and powders on display before her. "I hardly wear any makeup back home. There is no need for such cosmetics on the frontier. I have no idea what to use. I see you have a black powder. I believe the women of the night make heavy use of that around their eyes."

"Yes, it is called kohl," Claudia replied. "The women of the east have been wearing it for many years. It gives them a certain captivating appeal. We will need to utilize it heavily to have you looking like a true concubine. Let me help you with that."

About an hour later, Hereca turned her head and examined her face in the mirror from different angles. She hardly recognized herself. Her lips were a rich ruby color, and her eyes were heavily shaded with kohl, giving her a haunting look. Her cheeks were touched with rouge for a glowing appearance.

Claudia appeared from the doorway, holding a peach-colored gown of fine weave with a hooded cowl. "This should complete the sexy veneer. It should fit you perfectly. Please stand."

Hereca stood and shifted away from the makeup table, while Claudia held the gown up to her form.

"Yes, this should do rather nicely. Maybe a bit short but no matter. Let's get you into this right away so that you can reach the palace early."

As Hereca donned the garment, Quintus anxiously waited outside. He gaped as the heavily made-up Hereca exited the room in her revealing gown. "By the gods, I don't even recognize you. I hope this ruse works."

"If we are to survive, it must work. I'm ready."

Quintus nodded. "I will have two of my bodyguards escort you to the palace. I hope we are not too early and the guards grant you access. Good luck, Hereca. Oh, and assuming you are successful, let Tiberius know that I stand ready to assist him against Sejanus."

Claudia came over and embraced her. "May the gods be with you, my friend."

CHAPTER XXXXII
THE LIAISON

Hereca walked in silence with the two bodyguards furnished by Claudia and Salvius, her face hidden by the cowl. The streets were clearing as evening approached. Hereca's stomach fluttered as she contemplated the task in front of her. She must remain resolute. She could do this. Her life and that of many others depended on her performance. When they approached the rear entrance of the palace, they noticed two beefy Praetorians guarding it. The pair stiffened as she moved toward them.

Hereca waved off the two bodyguards and boldly advanced to the Praetorians, her face partially hidden by the cowl.

The guard on the right spoke first. "You are early tonight. He has not had his supper yet."

The other guard peered at her face. "You are not Fulvia."

"No, I'm not. My name is Marcia. Fulvia cannot make it tonight. It is her time on the moon. I'm new. That's why I'm early. No one told me the best time to arrive." She removed the cowl so the guards could see her heavily made-up face. "How does this work? Do one of you escort me to his chambers?"

She stooped slightly to adjust her gown and expose her cleavage, letting the guards get a good look. She straightened up and offered a sly smile to the Praetorians.

"We will have to search you, Marcia. Standing orders. All entrants must be searched for weapons."

"Well then, let's get this done."

The two guards expertly patted her down, letting their hands linger in certain places. Hereca stared straight ahead, pretending to enjoy their attention.

Hereca grinned lasciviously. "Maybe we can do this some more when I have finished tonight."

Both guards were all smiles. "That would be nice," one said wistfully.

"I will escort you into the palace," said the other. "Follow me. It is but a short walk."

Hereca walked slightly behind the hulking guard, passing down a columned corridor with flowering gardens on either side. They arrived at an intersecting hallway where a guard was stationed.

The escorting guard spoke. "This is Marcia. She is new. She said Fulvia could not make it tonight. It is her time of the moon."

The other guard nodded, motioning for her to enter a small bedroom across the hall. "You are early. Wait here. I don't know how long he is going to be."

Hereca decided to be bold. She could not afford to find out what would happen when Fulvia showed up. "Tell the imperator I have a special pleasure in mind for him tonight, guaranteed to give him ecstasy."

The guard hesitated before leaving, giving her a curious glance. "I will be sure to inform him." He shut the door firmly on his way out.

Hereca glanced around the room. It had a wide-framed bed and two small tables on either side. The walls were decorated with erotic frescoes depicting mating couples—men with huge phalluses and women with large breasts and shapely hips. She paced about, knowing that with every passing moment, the danger of being caught increased. She then sighed and sat down. There was a little more she could do. She hoped her comment to the guard would tantalize Tiberius to arrive before Fulvia showed up outside the palace.

Just then, a faint noise echoed from the hallway. Was it her doom or salvation? The door opened, revealing Tiberius's craggy face. "What is this I hear about a special pleasure tonight?"

"It is me, Hereca, wife of Valerius Maximus."

Tiberius's face registered shock at the unexpected encounter. "What are you doing here? Why are you dressed like that? What is happening?"

She rushed over to him and patted his arm. "Please, sit down. I have much to tell you. Your life is at risk, as are many others. Let me explain why I'm here and what is going on."

Tiberius sat in one of the chairs, while Hereca remained standing. She had rehearsed her story many times. "I came dressed as one of your courtesans because it was the only way I could gain access to you. The palace has been locked down by Sejanus. No one gets to see you. Valerius and I rode from the Danubius to warn you of Sejanus's plot against you and his bid to seize power. Valerius has been captured by Sejanus's Praetorians. If he is still alive, he is in one of their prisons."

She proceeded to relate the various assassination attempts on their lives by Voculus and Portunus, including the death of Voculus's centurion, and the written statement from Legionary Longinus on Sejanus's words about taking control. Hereca continued with evidence of rampant corruption attributed to Portunus. Once finished, she awaited a response.

Tiberius sat there, incredulous. At last, he spoke. "You rode all the way from the Danubius to warn me?"

"We had to, sire. Sejanus vets all your correspondence. Our dispatch might not have reached you. Besides, Valerius believed that what I just spoke of could not be effectively communicated in a dispatch. I implore you to please heed my warning."

Tiberius stared at the far wall in silence. At last, he rose and patted Hereca on the shoulder. "You did the right thing. Now, what to do about it."

Hereca silently heaved a sigh of relief. Tiberius believed her. They had a chance to survive. She looked anxiously at Tiberius for his next pronouncement.

Tiberius stood and opened the door and called out, "Guard.". A figure quickly appeared from the hallway. "Summon my nephew Claudius and my great nephew Caligula immediately. They are probably somewhere here in the palace. Find them now and bring them here." As the guard prepared to leave, Tiberius raised his arm, signaling him to halt. "If Fulvia shows up, tell her she is not needed tonight, give her payment, and then tell her to be on her way."

An awkward silence filled the small bedroom room as the two were left alone. Tiberius turned to address Hereca. "You know, you displayed great courage in coming here to the palace, and even more impressive is the fact that you succeeded. No wonder Maximus keeps you close by his side in his governance of the territories. When Claudius and Caligula arrive here, we will formulate our next steps."

"I sincerely hope we do something quickly. I fear my husband will not be kept alive for long if he is not already dead."

"And that is exactly what we are going to address once they get here."

Before long, there was a brief knock on the door, and the two men entered. Hereca gazed at the pair. Her first impressions were not flattering. Claudius looked to be around forty, disheveled and limping slightly. Caligula was just a young man, not even twenty, she judged. He threw her a lewd glance and then looked away.

"We are facing a crisis that we need to resolve tonight, or we could all be dead by tomorrow. This is Lady Hereca, the wife of Valerius Maximus, the governor of the German and Danubius territories. I'm sure you have heard of him. Please excuse her appearance. She has cleverly disguised herself as one of my concubines to get word to me of the danger we are facing. Hereca, please explain what is happening."

Once again, Hereca proceeded to recount the events on the Danube that led her and Valerius to journey to Rome. Once she was finished, she observed the two men to gauge their reaction. Strangely, both possessed a certain calm.

"Uncle," Claudius said, "I have long suspected Sejanus of having ambitious motives beyond his station of Praetorian prefect. It appears, for the moment, that we are prisoners in our own palace."

"Well, 'I told you so' is not much help to us now," grunted Tiberius. "We must find a way to defeat Sejanus."

Caligula gazed at the two men. "I recognize that I am young and inexperienced, but I think I know a few men we can trust. I have a permanent set of guards who I have become friendly with over the years. Also, I believe my guard commander, Macro, could be persuaded to serve our cause."

"But they are only a few among many," Tiberius interjected. "Most are loyal to Sejanus. We have to get Sejanus to a place where his guards are not with him." Suddenly, Tiberius's face brightened. "Of course!

Praetorians are not allowed in the senate. If we could lure Sejanus into the senate for some purpose, the charges could be presented, and he could be arrested by guards loyal to us. We can do it tomorrow. We can put it first on the docket and inform Sejanus that he will be presented with an award by the senate for his civic duty. We will appeal to his ego and his vanity. He will be none the wiser. In the meantime, Caligula, get this Macro fellow to our chambers immediately. We have work to do. Word of this must not leak out, or we are all dead men."

Caligula grinned. "I will summon him here at once. I know you will like him. He would be a perfect replacement for Sejanus."

"By Jove, I think this could work," Claudius remarked. "Uncle, you could recall Sejanus's loyal guards to the palace for some pretense or other while Macro's men take their place."

"Exactly," Tiberius agreed. He turned to Hereca and patted her arm reassuringly. "Don't worry. We will rescue your husband by tomorrow morning. The empire needs men like him."

"Quintus Silvius and his wife Claudia helped me disguise myself to get in here," Hereca added. "He said to let you know that he will do whatever it takes to assist you in eliminating Sejanus. Apparently, he has always distrusted Sejanus and his motives."

"Quintus is a leader in the senate," Tiberius noted. "He can expeditiously arrange our little ceremony for Sejanus."

A short while later, a stocky figure with broad shoulders and dark features, adorned in the uniform of a Praetorian centurion, appeared. He bowed to Tiberius. "Sire, you summoned me. How may I be of service to you tonight?"

Tiberius narrowed his gaze. "You are Macro? Caligula tells me you are a loyal guard and wish to serve the imperial family and the empire. Is that true?"

"Sir, I am flattered Caligula has a high opinion of me. In answer to your question, yes, I am loyal to the imperial family. How may I help?"

Tiberius studied the man, and the centurion returned his gaze without flinching. Having made up his mind, Tiberius continued. "Let me be blunt, Macro. How would you like to be the next Praetorian prefect to serve my family? We have become aware of some extreme disloyalty on the part of Sejanus and his followers."

Macro's eyes glinted with satisfaction. "What would you have me do?"

We need to arrest Sejanus. The preliminary plan is to invite Sejanus to the senate tomorrow. Once he enters, you will order Sejanus's guards stationed outside the chambers to report to the Praetorian compound on some fabricated matter and replace them with your men. We can then seize him on the senate floor, where the charges will be listed against him. You have my permission to enter the senate with your guards."

Macro answered without hesitation. "I can have my men available to arrest Sejanus. Once he is in custody, what do you want me to do with him?"

"I want him executed, along with his family and any loyal followers you consider a risk to the imperial family."

Macro nodded. "Sire, with your permission, I will withdraw and begin assembling the guards needed for tomorrow's task."

"Please do, and keep this conversation confidential. Sejanus must not be alerted. You have my sincere gratitude."

After Macro had departed, Tiberius turned to Hereca. "I will arrange for two of my guards to escort you to Quintus Silvius's residence. Once there, you can inform Quintus and his wife of our plan. He can work with his senate colleagues to arrange for Sejanus to appear there tomorrow morning."

CHAPTER XXXXIII
THE SENATE

Hereca arrived at the senator's residence to find Quintus and Claudia anxiously waiting for her. Claudia rushed over and hugged her. "I assume you were successful since you are back here with us. What's the plan?"

Hereca offered a relieved smile. "Yes, I met with Tiberius. We have a lot of work to do if we are to triumph over Sejanus." She gave them a quick summary of the discussion and explained the next steps. "Quintus, I informed Tiberius of your support against Sejanus. He wants you to arrange for the senate to present him with a civic award for his devotion and service to Rome tomorrow morning. While he is in the senate, Sejanus's loyal Praetorians will be informed that they are to report back to their barracks on some pretext or another. They will be replaced by guards loyal to Macro, the new prefect. Sejanus will then be arrested and charged with treason."

Claudia gasped. "This is such short notice. Can this plan possibly succeed?"

"It is a clever strategy," ventured Quintus. "Sejanus is prohibited by law from bringing his guards into the senate. He will be vulnerable.

This scheme just might work because of the short notice. If this was planned, say, two weeks in advance, Sejanus would surely find out about it. Because of the short window, his spies and informers will not be able to uncover any information about this arrangement."

"Will you be able to lure him to the senate?" Hereca asked.

"I think we will," he replied. "Sejanus has a huge ego. He will not pass up an award presented by the senate. The fact that it is being given on such short notice might ordinarily make him suspicious, but his ego will prevail."

"Tiberius said the same about Sejanus's ego," Hereca noted.

"So, what are the next steps?" Claudia asked.

"The next step," Quintus began, "is for you two ladies to retire and get some rest. I will send messengers to some of my colleagues in the senate. We need to get this on the docket tomorrow morning. I will have Senator Strabo, who is the head of the senate and in charge of the proceedings, schedule the award presentation. I will read the charges against Sejanus myself and take great pleasure in the man's arrest.

* * *

The next day dawned cold and windy. Sejanus was up early in his office when one of his aides entered with a dispatch. "Sorry to disturb you. From the senate, sir. It seems to be an urgent request."

Sejanus took the scroll and read the invitation. It was from Senator Strabo, who coordinated the business in the senate. The document requested his presence in the senate to present him with a civic award for his service to Rome. It further stated that though the request was last minute, they wanted it to coincide with the festival of Cerelia, honoring the fall harvest.

Sejanus pondered the dispatch. *A bit unusual,* he thought. But then again, the Senate had never given him an award before. This would just add to his credentials and solidify his support when he seized power.

He wrote a brief response, informing Strabo that he would appear at the senate at the fourth hour that morning. Rising from his desk, he handed the reply over to his messenger and then headed to the prison cells. He reached an alcove occupied by the jailer and motioned for him to get up. "I want to visit Maximus again." He walked down the corridor, past the other twenty cells, and paused while the jailer used a large iron key to open the cell door.

Valerius lay huddled in a corner of his small cell, his arms and legs in heavy shackles. He looked up at the sound of footsteps to find Sejanus's smirking face.

"I have an appointment in the senate this morning. They are giving me an award. Imagine that! When I return, we will have another discussion with my jailers about the whereabouts of your wife and Marcellus. Then, I think I will have you executed. I will enjoy watching that. You have caused me a lot of distress, but no more. Enjoy what time you have left.

Valerius silently glared at Sejanus.

"No clever retort? I guess not. You know that all hope is lost." Sejanus turned sharply and departed.

* * *

Later that morning, Sejanus arrived at the senate at the appointed hour, ensuring his uniform was immaculate. He wore his finest chest armor, the decorative set, polished to a fine hue. Upon arrival at the senate doors with his ten-guard escort, he motioned for them to remain outside. Taking a deep breath, he entered the venerable institution and stood just inside the entrance. A minor debate was taking place about securing funding for the dredging of the harbor at Ostia. He sighed. How long have these fools been talking about this project? At least a year, if his reckoning was correct. Once he seized power, he would get this matter settled quickly. He gazed toward the rostrum and caught the eye of Strabo, the senior senator and leader who had sent the dispatch requesting his presence to receive an award. Strabo nodded slightly at Sejanus, acknowledging his presence.

As the debate continued for a few more minutes, Sejanus observed a messenger approach Strabo and whisper in his ear. Little did he know that the senator had just been informed that all was set and Sejanus's guards had been replaced. The senate leader nodded and returned his gaze to the front. A few minutes later, Strabo approached the rostrum and faced his colleagues. "It appears we are no closer to resolving the funding issue for the harbor dredging. There continue to be vast disparities in the amount of funding needed to complete the project. We will revisit the discussion tomorrow. A new item has been added to today's agenda. The senate will recognize Lucius Aelius Sejanus, the Praetorian prefect, for his service to Rome. Quintus Salvius will read the proclamation." With that, Strabo motioned for Sejanus to come forward.

Sejanus frowned. What was this? Salvius was from the opposition camp. He was also in league with Maximus. Sejanus was planning to rid Rome of Salvius sometime soon. Sejanus shrugged slightly and began proceeding across the senate floor, the iron hobnails of his military boots clicking on the polished stone floor. Tall and erect, he continued forward, stopping just short of the rostrum.

Salvius approached the rostrum and unrolled a scroll. "This is a decree from our imperator, Tiberius Caesar. It reads as follows: It has become known to me that my Praetorian prefect, Lucius Aelius Sejanus, has engaged in seditious behavior, making false accusations of senators and other officials of Rome and conspiring to overthrow my realm. This is treason against the senate and people of Rome."

Salvius was interrupted by a large number of Praetorians led by Centurion Macro, who burst through the front doors and quickly surrounded Sejanus.

Salvius continued. "There is only one penalty for such behavior, and that is death. Therefore, Prefect Sejanus and all of his loyal followers are hereby condemned to death."

There was an audible gasp from the senators. While Sejanus was encircled and roughly grabbed, hisses and catcalls resonated from the gallery. He was roughly hauled out of the building, leaving the senate in a state of shock, mingled with a sense of euphoria.

* * *

Valerius heard footsteps approaching his cell. Was this the end? He hoped Hereca and Marcellus had escaped. A jangle of keys was heard as the lock on his door was turned. He looked up disconsolately, expecting to see Sejanus's leering face and his two sadistic jailers. Instead, there stood a sturdy Praetorian officer he did not recognize. Then, much to his amazement, a jubilant Hereca followed closely behind. She rushed over and hugged him.

"Sejanus is no more. You are safe," she said into his ears, unwilling to let go. "Oh, by the way, this is Macro, the new Praetorian prefect."

The officer nodded at the dumbfounded Valerius. "Pleased to meet you, Governor. The emperor would like to meet with you if you are up to it."

"Yes, I think I can manage that." He faced Hereca. "How did you manage this?"

"It's a long story I will tell you later. Tiberius wants to meet with us. There is some turmoil in the streets with the arrest of Sejanus and his followers, but Macro will escort us.

Valerius nodded numbly, still unsure all of this was happening. "Let us proceed. I could use better clothes and a bath, but if the emperor calls, one best advance quickly."

"Is Domitius in one of the cells?" Hereca inquired. "We should take him with us."

Valerius grimaced. "No. He died under torture by Sejanus's thugs. He died bravely, divulging little. He was a good man."

"I'm sorry to hear that," Hereca said with a sigh. "He was a good man. Come, let us be on our way."

CHAPTER XXXXIV
TIBERIUS

Hereca and Valerius, with an escort of Praetorians, walked toward the palace from the Praetorian compound. Mayhem ensued in the streets. Bodies, bloodied and beaten, were strewn about—the victims were allies and relatives of Sejanus. Along the way, Hereca recounted how they all had guessed that Valerius and Domitius had been captured and how she got into the palace to meet Tiberius and warn him of Sejanus.

Once they reached their destination, the pair was ushered into Tiberius's audience hall, and the emperor rose to greet him. "We meet once again. Praise to the gods; you are safe, thanks to your wife. You know, it's too bad I can't appoint women to official positions. I would make her a governor. She is a remarkable woman."

"I know," Valerius replied. "Now you understand why I have been so successful in Germania. Even my own staff compliments her and attributes much of our progress to her efforts. They are not shy about letting me know how much she contributes."

Tiberius beamed. "She is truly a gem. Now, I suggest we put this entire sorry episode behind us. My own family, Claudius and

Caligula, helped solve this problem. Perhaps I should listen to them more often."

Valerius tried to formulate a tactful reply since the emperor was admitting to a mistake, something emperors were not inclined to do. "Sire, it is good to have a family to lean upon. I know I often ask my father for advice when I have difficult decisions to make, and your decisions are much more challenging than mine."

Tiberius contemplated the response for a few moments. "Yes, they certainly can be. Now, let's change the subject. I am most pleased with the progress you have achieved along the Danubius. I knew you could do it, even with the interference from Voculus and Portunus. I will get to them shortly. For now, this is what I want you to do. Return to the Danubius and stay the winter. Continue your trade initiatives, including in the province of Moesia. You stated in your dispatches that Moesia would be the last province to be addressed. See what progress you can make there. I will appoint someone to take over for you as governor in the spring. In fact, I am going to provide a short list of names for you to consider. I want your opinion on who might be a good fit."

"I would be honored to review the names you put forth, although I'm sure there are others who would be a better judge of character than me."

"Maybe so, but you know the territory and the demands of the position."

Valerius brightened. "In that case, if I may be so bold, I have a name for you to consider."

Tiberius raised his eyebrows. "Please speak the name."

"It is Titus Placidius, the governor of Raetia. He is young but extremely capable. He has demonstrated that he is quick on his feet in times of crisis, and he firmly supports our trade initiatives. Hereca can vouch for his character as well. She worked alongside him to establish trade negotiations with the Marcomanni."

"Yes, sire. He is a competent young man," Hereca added. "Rome needs individuals like him."

"I vividly remember the appointment of Placidius a few years ago. Your recommendation carries a lot of weight. I will put him on the list for consideration."

"Also, sire, I would recommend the legate of the Third Legion, General Severus, as the overall command of the six legions along the Danubius. He has proven to be an outstanding leader."

"Thank you. I will consider this as well," Tiberius replied.

There was a brief pause in the conversation. "To conclude our discussion, tomorrow, I will issue arrest warrants for Voculus and Portunus. They will face charges of attempted murder, treason, theft, and embezzlement. They are to be brought back to Rome for trial. Before you return to the Danubian provinces, you will need to complete a deposition regarding their crimes. With Sejanus gone, they have no one to back them. If they are smart, they will open their veins and end their own lives."

"Sire, I would recommend that the commander of the Tenth legion based in Pannonia, General Caelius, serve the arrest warrant. He and Portunus do not see eye to eye, and he proves to be a capable commander when dealing with some rebellious Quadi. I believe Caelius would take great personal pleasure in arresting those two scoundrels."

Tiberius chuckled lightly. "Then it shall be so."

EPILOGUE

Sejanus huddled in his dank and dingy cell within the Mamertine prison on the northeast slope of Capitoline Hill, facing the Curia. It had been decided to incarcerate Sejanus here rather than in the Praetorian compound, where some of his followers, those who had survived, might attempt to free him.

His head perked up when he heard the sound of approaching footsteps. He shakily arose, his feet and arms bound in chains. The door to his cell swung open, and two jailers loomed over him, motioning for him to exit his cell. His eyes blinked rapidly as he entered the hallway, dimly illuminated by several oil lamps. Supported by the two guards, he staggered down the corridor and then down a second one. Sejanus did not see his executioner hidden in the deep shadows of the other hallway.

The burly figure approached Sejanus from behind and slipped the garrote over his head. The man pulled the rope tight, twisting it with all his strength. Then, Sejanus was lifted off his feet and his throat cruelly constricted. The former prefect attempted to struggle, but he had no leverage, and his life was quickly snuffed out.

* * *

There was a festive gathering at Quintus Salvius's house that night. Valerius, having managed to find time for a soothing bath and get a change of clothes from Quintus, stood sipping a goblet of wine beside Hereca. He almost felt back to normal again—almost. His body still ached from the heavy beating of Sejanus's henchmen.

Out of the crowd appeared Marcellus, Radulf, and Terentius. Marcellus beamed. "We have survived once again. The gods must be watching over us."

"Marcellus," Valerius replied, "you have told me on numerous occasions that you don't believe in the gods. Your odious sentiments are well known."

"True, I don't believe in the gods, but then again, how else do you explain this? Time and again, we have been so close to death, but each time we manage to survive. This chain of events started over twenty years ago in the Teutoburg, and on each occasion, we managed to endure despite the improbability. There is no rational explanation for it. From fierce German barbarians to rogue Roman generals, from cutthroat pirates and rebellious chieftains to ambitious Praetorians, we succeeded in cheating death every time. Either we are extremely lucky or very powerful gods watch over us."

"Maybe it is none of those," Hereca replied with a smirk, "but rather the love and partnership of a good woman."

"Forgive me, Hereca, for not acknowledging your part in our good fortune," Marcellus replied. "But the fact that you even met Valerius was the strangest of fates. I mean, the odds of that happening were beyond all probability. Think of it—a match between a Roman officer, a sworn enemy of the German tribes, and a fierce Dolgubni princess. It only validates my point. The gods have intervened generously on our behalf."

"Don't forget that others have intervened to save our lives, including Radulf and Terentius," Valerius added. "We always surround ourselves with good people."

Quintus and Claudia wandered over, catching the last few words of the discussion. "Rome is now a better place thanks to you folks," Quintus said. "Sejanus's terror campaigns are now a thing of the past. I must admit things looked a bit dicey there for a while, but once again, Valerius, you and your friends have saved the empire. I don't know how you do it, but keep up the good work. I'm curious to know what adventures await you now."

"When we finish up here, it's back to the Danubius, but only for a short while," Valerius said. "We will continue our trade initiatives through the winter. Tiberius has promised that he will appoint a successor for me, and then, I will be free to return to Germania to my family."

"A happy ending for sure," Quintus replied. "Let me propose a toast." He lifted his goblet high. "To Valerius Maximus and friends. Heroes of Rome. Safe travels and sweet reunions. Rome is fortunate to have you."

THE END

AUTHOR'S NOTES

1. Along the boundaries of the Roman Empire, the Romans established *limes*, a system of border fortifications. The physical elements comprised roads, watchtowers, and fortifications. These structural components enhanced their surveillance capabilities and reduced their manpower requirements while preventing large-scale invasions. A vast network of Roman roads plus a mobile naval fleet ensured a rapid response to any trouble spot. Besides the physical aspects, the limes were also involved in patrolling, trafficking, and diplomacy, serving as an effective deterrent to intrusions on the boundaries of the Roman frontier. Most of this novel takes place on the Danube Limes. The Danube River flows southeast from central Germany for hundreds of miles to the Black Sea, whereas the Rhine River flows in the opposite direction, northeast to the northwest. The modern-day countries along the Danube include Switzerland, Germany, Austria, Hungary, Slovenia, Croatia, Serbia, Slovenia, Bosnia, and Herzegovina. The limes were an extremely effective system that secured the Roman borders of the empire for several hundred years before eventually crumbling.

2. As with my other books, this is a work of fiction. However, some historical figures are featured in this novel. Of particular note is

Lucius Aelius Sejanus. He was the Praetorian prefect and confidant of Tiberius, who unleashed a reign of terror in Rome. He was arrested and executed in AD 31 amidst suspicions of conspiracy. My account of his arrest is fictional, though the original arrest was made in the senate. His successor was Naevius Sutorius Macro, who later served under Caligula when he succeeded as emperor in AD 37.

3. Legionary fortresses along the Danube are referenced. Their Roman names and modern names are as follows: Castra Regina (Regensburg), Lauriacum (Enns), Vindobona (Vienna), and Carnuntum (Petronell-Carnuntum).

4. Ancient Rome had no universal postal service. However, the Roman emperor and his administration had a dedicated courier service, the *Cursus Publicus,* which carried imperial mail to the four corners of the empire. The couriers had dedicated ships and waystations to ensure communications were carried quickly to their destinations.

ABOUT THE AUTHOR

Mark L. Richards is a graduate of Pennsylvania Military College, (now Widener University) and served in the US Army as an infantry officer before entering the healthcare field. A CPA, he was a chief financial officer at a large academic health center. Now retired, he resides in Downingtown, Pennsylvania. He is married with two daughters and five grandchildren.

A lifelong historian of Roman antiquity, Richards was inspired by his favorite subject to write the Tribune Valerius – Centurion Marcellus series, featuring *Legions of the Forest, Return of the Eagles, Revolt against Rome,* and *Insurrection in the Legions.* He also authored *A Barbarian in Rome's Legions* and *On Campaign with the Legions* Mark may be contacted at legions9ad@aol.com.

Made in the USA
Monee, IL
09 May 2024

58235445R00218